BOOK THREE IN THE CHARLOTTE'S WAR TRILOGY

THE
WASP TRAP

HUGO WOOLLEY

SilverWood

Published in 2024 by SilverWood Books

SilverWood Books Ltd

14 Small Street, Bristol, BS1 1DE, United Kingdom
www.silverwoodbooks.co.uk

ISBN 978-1-80042-281-0 (paperback)

British Library Cataloguing in Publication Data
A CIP catalogue record for this book is
available from the British Library

Page design and typesetting by SilverWood Books

HUGO WOOLLEY was born in West Sussex. He is married with two grown-up children. His mother was an eccentric picture restorer. His father a farmer and lawyer. As a dyslexic, he went to a myriad of schools, mainly because, in those days, dyslexia had hardly been invented, let alone treated. It was known as 'word-blindness' and dyslectics were thought to be 'simple' and below intelligence. How wrong they were!

Hugo is a caterer by training, ran various bars and restaurants in London before starting his own sandwich shops in the City of London in 1984 with his youngest brother, Oliver. In 1993 he opened designer sausage shops in Kent and Sussex, well before sausages became a fad. Unfortunately, after just over a year of trading, he was badly injured in a car accident and was airlifted to hospital, where Hugo remained for eight months being glued back together. Whilst in hospital he started writing, mainly about his experience during 'my crippledom' – as he called it.

In 2002, when Hugo was mainly recovered, he moved to Cornwall. After over twenty years running a boutique small hotel just outside of Padstow, with his wife, Hugo has retired and has moved to a quiet village on the edges of Bodmin Moor, where he continues writing.

Also by Hugo Woolley

Girl on a Golden Pillow
Book One in the Charlotte's War Trilogy

Charlotte's War
Book Two in the Charlotte's War Trilogy

To Emily, Giles, Kathryn and Joy

Part One

1

Spring 1945, Surrey

Just before the war ended, Alec Ballentine was invited by a friend, Captain Dan James, for drinks at his hotel – a hotel that had been made into an officers' convalescent home. It was very civilised. There was a mess, a bar that had a terrace overlooking the surrounding countryside, a gym and a swimming pool. It was an early spring afternoon, quite warm, with a hum of bees in the alliums.

Captain James had an injured right arm. A stray bullet shattered his elbow whilst he was on a raid on D-Day. He was captured and managed to escape six months later. As far as Alec knew, he was in the Special Boat Service, and highly decorated.

Alec and Captain James were sitting at a table on the terrace, beers in hand, talking about their war, when a stout gentleman, florid, with a full white naval beard, strode up to Captain James, a broad smile on his face.

"Sir Sussex Tremayne." James welcomed him, and both men stood. "Thank you for popping by."

"You look splendid, James. Does the elbow work?"

"No, locked at a right angle. Can just about get a pint to my mouth." He lifted his right elbow, still in a sling, to show some movement. Dan James turned to Alec. "This is Alec Ballentine, sir, the war correspondent and journalist I was talking about." Alec flashed a look of alarm at his friend. "Ballentine, may I present Commodore Sir Sussex Tremayne, head of the SIS and War Intelligence in MI6." Alec gulped.

"How do you do, sir. Why … what …?"

"Mr Ballentine, I have heard quite a lot about you," Sir Sussex said warmly. "Your Dunkirk experiences, your insights on the way the war was being conducted – in your view." Sir Sussex plainly did not agree with Alec's views.

"Thank you, sir. I hope you enjoyed—"

"I was especially interested in your articles on the poorly judged pre-war visits to Nazi Germany by the Duke and Duchess of Windsor and Sir Henry Channing MP. And your report on the demise of Admiral Canaris was most insightful."

"I met him. He turned up at the Vickers factory in 1936 and he kindly gave me an interview. I was but a boy reporter. He was an impressive—"

"Well, he is dead now, poor bugger. Killed by Himmler on trumped-up charges. He was a good man, for a Nazi. My German counterpart, you know." Alec was quite surprised by Sir Sussex's admiration. "Canaris, believe it or not, helped us a lot, trying to end this bloody war." Sir Sussex scrutinised Alec for a minute and then said to him, quietly, "Well, not to beat about the …" He stroked his beard. "Ballentine, I wonder if you would be prepared to research … investigate something for us, my boy?"

"Us, sir?" Alec asked.

"Well … me, really, as head of War Intelligence. But *not* for the Ministry. I would like this to be between ourselves." Sir Sussex indicated the three of them.

He gestured for Dan and Alec to sit and ordered a gin and water from the steward, then lit a cigarette whilst looking about the virtually deserted bar to ensure their privacy. "There is – for want of a better word – a faction, a pretty secretive bunch, possibly operating out of England. An international espionage group called WASP – War Against Socialist Parties. Heard of them?"

"No, I don't think so, sir," Alec said.

"This group specialises in selling national secrets for action against the Soviet Union. The membership consists of many eminent people, some German, some Americans – we believe all dedicated anti-communists – and it appears to be well funded."

"By whom, Sir Sussex?" Dan James asked.

"Don't know."

"Do we know any of these eminent people, Sir Sussex?" Alec asked.

"I regret none I can confirm. This has all come to light in the last day or so."

"Where are they based?"

"Don't know. The last message intercept came from London – we think – and was received in Washington in the United States. We believe it was sent via Spain."

"Who runs them, these people?"

"Don't quite know that either, except a name – Boris Quint – has come up as a part of the movement." Alec raised an eyebrow at Dan James.

"Boris Quint?" Alec asked.

"Thought to be one of our agents. Liaises with the Germans via Gibraltar."

"Thought to be?"

"Not one of my agents … run by my department."

There was a long pause as Sir Sussex was served his gin. He sat back, eyeing the younger men as he lit another cigarette.

"Do we know anything about them?" Alec asked.

"Other than the group's name, WASP, no. We know they are working with, or for, the enemy – the Nazis. They are communicating with America, via Spain, encrypting their messages through an enemy encryption machine."

"I see," said Alec. "How have you heard about this organisation, and why do you think they are a worry?"

Sir Sussex took a sip of his drink and stroked down his white beard, looking thoughtfully at the view of the Surrey Downs. "I have a contact, who has a contact, who has brought this to our attention. The contact believes they – WASP – assisted the Germans to invade northern Europe, supplying strategies and logistics to Admiral Canaris and the Abwehr. The Nazis seemed to know where all the Allied defences lay, when the Nazis rolled into the Low Countries and France, in double-quick time. And now James here got some information on his way back from Spain. He'll fill you in."

"I see," said Alec again. "So, you think Canaris was part of this organisation?"

"This chap, Quint, in Gibraltar, was in regular contact with Admiral Canaris. We think Quint was part of WASP, whilst Canaris knew him to be our operative." Sir Sussex looked uncomfortable. "It seems Quint may be double-dealing. I have only just heard about him. Hence this meeting."

"Do we know where Quint is now?" Dan asked.

"He was in the clink in Scotland but escaped – pretty easily – whilst awaiting charges. He may have been helped. Bloody Scots. Sorry, James," Sir Sussex mumbled under his breath, clearly having forgotten Captain James was also a Scot.

Alec could see the old man was angry about Boris Quint's simple exit from jail.

Alec was not quite sure how he could help find out more about this mysterious group. "Sir Sussex, what sort of role will you need me to take in researching this ... group? And may I meet this contact?"

"Ballentine, this is an initial sounding out – forgive the modern phrase. My contact is still being debriefed, and the double agent has buggered off somewhere. For now, with your connections, could you keep your ear to the ground? If you hear anything about WASP or this Boris Quint fellow, get back to me or James here. My card." Sir Sussex proffered a calling card. "That is all." Sir Sussex rose from his chair, took Alec's card that lay on the table, and finished his gin and water. "Look after yourself, Captain James. What happened to the elbow?"

"I took a bullet in it landing on the beach at Caen. Shattered the elbow. My right arm has been useless ever since. They have just welded the elbow back onto my arm ... lots of metal. It doesn't straighten, but at least it doesn't flop around."

Sir Sussex gave a fleeting tut of sympathy and then turned to Alec. "Ballentine, I am pleased to have met you. Do keep in touch." He turned to leave but then leant in conspiratorially. "I regret you must not ever mention WASP to *anybody* at the moment, Ballentine. You certainly cannot write about it, for now, but you will get first dibs when it is safe to tell the tale, eh?" Sir Sussex winked at Alec and nudged Captain James. "Good seeing you again, James. Look after that elbow. We need you back in MI6. War's not over yet!"

As Sir Sussex left, he waved a cheery farewell at the barman who stood smartly to attention.

"What is your part in this business, Dan?" The men settled back down in their chairs, lit cigarettes and ordered more beer.

"Well ... bit of a story. When I was travelling back from Spain after I escaped—"

"Escaped? What happened?"

"A tale for another day, old chap. Anyway, I met an extraordinary fellow on the boat coming back home. His name was Deller. He said he was Austrian, but could pass for an Englishman from my club. He claimed to work for MI6. Showed me a letter saying as much – officially headed and stamped. I did not see who signed it, though.

"He was in his cups one night at sea. He was telling me about being 'made', he said, to become a member of this organisation WASP. It was all very secret, he said, so I asked him why was he telling me? He said he thought that I was a man called Ferdi Summers, or something like that. He must've mistaken me for someone else. He kept calling me Ferdi. He then looked panicked and clammed up for the rest of the trip, I suppose having realised I was not this Ferdi. I didn't think much more of it; he was just a strange drunk.

"Being debriefed in hospital on my return by Sir Sussex, I mentioned this to him, and he got very interested. He told me to keep it to myself. He asked me if I knew anyone not in the service who he could get to investigate WASP. I suggested you."

"Thanks," Alec said in despair. "Where is this Deller fellow now?"

"We have no idea. He stayed in Falmouth; I went off to Queen Alexandra Military Hospital to get my arm reattached."

Alec winced at the thought of his friend's pain. "No idea who this Summers chap is?"

"No."

"So, you are MI6 as well as SBS?" Alec was impressed.

"Yup! Quite a hero, aren't I?" They both laughed and clinked their mugs of beer.

*

Alec Ballentine, a successful journalist and war correspondent, was born during the Great War, in Chichester, West Sussex. His parents were both dead, and he had a twin brother who was a Hollywood actor of little note, who he saw every five years when they shared a milestone birthday. He had a mortgage on his Battersea apartment to worry about, but not for long as it was nearly paid off. He loved food and wine, but he preferred to drink whisky rather than beer as he thought it would keep him from getting any fatter. He was, after all, sixteen stone and getting to the point in his life where he found any exercise more of a bother than a benefit.

Being six feet four inches, Alec was a big man, taller than most. His height, broad shoulders and his confident bearing made him an imposing figure. His sparse mousy-blond hair was cut short, and he had a receding hairline at the parting.

During his National Service after leaving university, Alec discovered he was not a natural soldier, in shape or attitude. He hated being shouted at by narcissistic non-commissioned officers and having to do things in the middle of the night, always in an astonishingly unpleasant environment. Nothing in soldiering was comfortable, whether it was sleeping or being transported about. Because of his height, the beds were too short, and he kept banging into things.

However, training for the army helped him to serve as a war correspondent for *The Telegraph* newspaper in the Second World War. For a while, he assisted the celebrated journalist Christopher Buckley. He always seemed to be on a beach with sand getting into every crevice, sending back his copy and the odd roll of film from the front line. Everything was endlessly hazardous.

Alec was one of the last people to be rescued off the beaches of Dunkirk. To be precise, he was rescued along with two French sailors and a wounded Belgian soldier from a holed dinghy with a dead Seagull outboard motor, two miles off the French coast, in the early morning of June the third 1940. They rowed for about two hours after the motor conked out, convinced they would see land at any minute. They were beginning to become despondent until they were spotted by a *schuyt*, a huge ocean-going Dutch barge.

He got back to England, and after writing about his Dunkirk experience, he became quite a celebrity journalist – until the attention switched towards Norway's surrender to the Nazis the following week.

After peace in 1945, there was nothing really going on in the world war-wise. Alec was bored. He fell in love a couple of times, bought his apartment, and watched London slowly rebuild itself.

For the next ten years, he had a go at finding something out about WASP, but always hit a brick wall. He met Sophie Younghusband, an art historian from Christopher's of Bond Street, where they were first introduced. Alec was researching stolen Nazi art but knew nothing about the subject, and Sophie not only intrigued him but was also useful for his newspaper article.

In 1955, Alec got engaged to Sophie before going off to Spain on assignment. On a fleeting visit to London (he had to return to Spain to finish an article) he found Sophie had become tired of his absences and the lack of time with her fiancé. She said they would need to talk seriously when he next returned.

He had just finished researching a huge article to be serialised by *The Telegraph* about the pieds noirs in Algeria and the ongoing Algerian civil war for independence. The pieds noirs, or "black feet", were trying to preserve the Frenchness of a North African country, with little success.

After North Africa and Spain, Alec arrived back in London. He'd decided he would do nothing for a while other than enjoy eating and drinking in the restaurants that had opened whilst he had been away, try to track down some of his old, neglected friends and see a film … basically, catch his breath. And have that talk with Sophie. But it was too little too late for that – she had left his flat, where she had been looking after Benjy, the cat. He was not too upset; in fact, now he'd had a few days to get used to the idea, he was quite relieved that Sophie had called off the engagement.

However, his plan of relaxation was curtailed when Father Joe Dent pounded on his door that night and told his intriguing story.

2

Autumn 1955, Battersea

Alec was licking his wounds from the cutting words of condemnation in Sophie's letter. Words like "selfishness" and "uncaring" were underlined, and the engagement ring sat sadly in its velvet box, glinting in the centre of the coffee table. What she said was true, but he was a busy journalist; he could not stop his life – his assignments – for her. He tried to convince himself that if she loved him, she would have accepted that his job took him away for months at a time.

He was startled from his thoughts by a hammering on his front door. Who could be out on a cold October evening? He opened the door and a clergyman in cassock and dog collar fell in.

Alec didn't know the vicar well. He had nodded at him at a local council meeting and met him when he helped out at a Battersea fête in the park once, a duty forced upon him by Sophie, who had got to know the cleric rather well.

"Ah!" the clergyman gasped. He looked up at the tall, large man with some surprise. "Mr ... um ... Ballentine, I am sorry, may I come in? I must come in!" he panted, clearly upset and breathing heavily. He stood in the door, bent double with both hands on his knees, perspiration glistening over his prominent forehead and temples. He must have run up the eight flights of stairs and not used the lift.

"F-Father Joe?" Alec stuttered, only just remembering his name. "What on earth are you doing here? Are you OK?" Alec thought an element of concern was called for, even if he felt no charity for Father Joe at that moment.

"I need to talk to Sophie, please," he puffed. "It is terribly important." He looked around, hoping to see Alec's ex-fiancée appear.

"She's not here, I'm afraid ... doesn't live here ... and I have not seen her for quite a while. We are not together, you see." Father Joe seemed confused. "We split up," Alec clarified.

"She was here the other day." The vicar looked up at Alec accusingly.

"She was staying in my flat whilst I was away, trying to find a flat for herself. Anyway … is there something I can do to help you, vicar?" Alec stood at his open front door, still one hand on the handle; he was getting impatient and wanted to get rid of the man, but politely.

Father Joe stood and composed himself.

"A man has been killed," he gasped. After a long intake of breath, he added, "I've just killed a man."

"Christ!" Alec blurted, then remembered who he was speaking to. "Sorry, I mean …" He tried to collect his thoughts. His annoyance at being disturbed was tempered, and he was rather curious to find out what Father Joe was talking about.

"I've killed a man!" he repeated and walked jerkily – and uninvited – into the flat, where he collapsed onto Alec's light-brown leather sofa. Father Joe's cassock dragged over the arm and left a smear of dark red. He looked in alarm at the blood marks and stood up again, undid the belt that held his cassock about his waist and pulled it over his head.

"Oh, dear Lord – I am in a mess! All this blood on me." Under his cassock he wore an old grey shirt with the dog collar attached, and a pair of black trousers. Benjy miaowed and scuttled off the sofa when Father Joe took off his cassock, wrapped the bloody bit into the middle and threw it on the floor in disgust. He collapsed down on the sofa again, holding his head in his hands and rocking back and forth as he stared at the cassock with an appalled expression on his face. Alec was still at the front door, watching with some concern as the vicar removed his bloody cassock.

"Mr Ballentine—"

"Alec, please," Alec offered.

"Alec … I am sorry to burst into your flat with" – he gestured at the bloody cassock on the floor in front of him – "all this."

"Well … fine." Closing the door, Alec popped into the kitchen and found a damp cloth and started to wipe away the blood off the arm of the sofa. "I will get you a drink. Whisky all right?" Alec was calm. He thought this was an occasion that required composure.

"Do you want a drink, vicar?" Alec repeated.

The vicar hesitated before speaking. "Just water, please."

"Cigarette?"

"No … well … yes, please. I don't usually …"

"There is a box in front of you with matches beside it. Help yourself."

15

Alec was pouring the drinks when he suddenly came to his senses. He stopped and turned to the cleric.

"You say you've killed a man? Why me, Father? Why on earth have you come to me? Why have you not told the police?"

"Well, Mr … Alec, you were the nearest place that I could come, and I hoped Sophie might be here as she has always been so kind. I tried her at the gallery, but they have closed."

"It is Sunday, vicar, and eight thirty at night!"

"Oh, yes … I suppose it is," Father Joe said.

"Anyway, Sophie left a few days ago, when I got back from abroad. But why have you not contacted the police? Or have you phoned them?"

"Oh … I don't know!" Father Joe was exasperated. Alec thought he may even be on the verge of crying. "I have another dilemma. I know the man I am supposed to have killed."

"Supposed? For God's sake, they are never going to suspect you of doing it, not on purpose, are they?" He poured out a glass of whisky and water for himself.

"Well, it *was* an accident. I suppose I didn't mean to kill him, it just … happened." He was streaming with tears, and mucus was dribbling from his nose. Alec averted his eyes with disgust. "Will you come to the church and see what I should do? Help me. Please, Alec." He took a handkerchief from his pocket and wiped down his moustache, much to Alec's relief.

However, Alec was not going to go to any church to see a dead body. He was tired and wanted to curl up with a book in front of the fire. He had seen enough dead bodies during the war. He was about to tell Father Joe about his strenuous few weeks being a journalist, when Joe said, "It involves a friend of mine, a lovely girl. I do not want any harm to come to her."

"Oh yes?" Alec sneered. "One of your flock that has strayed into the path of darkness? Call the police, or I—"

"She's called Baroness Freya Saumures, otherwise known as Charlotte de Tournet."

Alec was stunned. His memory raced when he recognised the names, his interest piqued. He went over to the coffee table, took a cigarette from the silver-plated cigarette box, lit it and threw the match into the fire; then, as an afterthought, he picked up the box and offered a cigarette to the vicar. Father Joe looked at the contents of the box blindly, then realising what was being offered, shook his head.

The names were familiar to Alec. It took a little delving into his memory – and then it came to him.

"What – the girl who disappeared a few years ago, during the war? *That* Charlotte de Tournet?"

"Yes," the vicar said, somewhat hesitantly.

"And this woman, Freya, didn't she marry a baron something or other, and was on trial for treason not so long ago? Something to do with being a prostitute for the Nazis in Paris?"

"She was never a prostitute, and anyway, Freya was found innocent," Father Joe shouted in protest.

"The trial was dropped," Alec said scathingly. "How do you know Baroness Freya?"

Father Joe looked up, blinking back tears. "She is my ... she is a goddess. The goddess Freya." He looked wistfully at something in the distance, above the fireplace, as though he had seen a vision no one else could see.

Alec threw his hands in the air and gasped in exasperation. The man was deranged. How on earth this vicar thought Sophie could be of any more help was quite absurd. It was all getting rather weird. He didn't know what to do. One minute, a blood-soaked cleric was hammering at his door, saying he had killed a man, yet the next he didn't want the police to be involved.

"What has she to do with Charlotte de Tournet ... the goddess Freya?" Alec asked.

Father Joe looked hopelessly into Alec's eyes, tears pooling in his. "I told you: they are the same person," he said, as though Alec had missed the point.

Alec sat on the sofa beside him, amazed by what he had heard. The vicar asserted that there was a connection to one of the most extraordinary stories during the war: the incident of Charlotte de Tournet, who was left a huge house in Avenue Foch, Paris, by her grandmother, and some wonderful paintings – the Barrett Collection – and God knows what else. She then disappeared as the Nazis walked into Paris in 1940, much to the distress of her aunt and uncle who had brought her up. Then, the vicar alleged, Baroness Freya Saumures was the same person who had been brought to trial three years ago, in 1952, for war crimes and fraternising with the enemy, or something. The papers on both sides of the Channel and the Atlantic had a field day with the story. Every paper had a blurry image of the pretty young baroness wearing dark glasses on the front pages.

Charlotte, however, had disappeared during the occupation of Paris by the German army. Her tearful and slightly gaga aunt, Stella de Tournet, made heartfelt appeals to the Third Reich to return her much-loved niece but was told she must have died during the occupation. Now, it was alleged by the vicar that Charlotte, while calling herself Freya, had been running some kind of brothel in her house in Paris throughout the war and was not dead at all.

"What do you mean, a goddess?" Alec questioned irritably.

"She's staggeringly beautiful, wonderful, a vision of …" He petered out when he saw Alec looking at him strangely. Father Joe stroked his beard in thought, nervously eyeing Alec and then casting his eyes to the fireplace. Alec was beginning to sense Father Joe was regretting coming to his flat. He was also thinking that he regretted having anything to do with the vicar. He was quite mad … possibly.

"We've got to go to the police," Alec repeated. He wondered if somebody was actually dead or if the vicar had imagined it. But then there was the bloody cassock.

"Come with me," Father Joe pleaded. "It's just down the road in my vestry. And then we can decide what we should do about the police."

Alec thought he might as well. There might be a story in it if it was something to do with Charlotte de Tournet. Would people remember her disappearance? It was so long ago. But then there was the connection to Baroness Freya Saumures …

"OK," Alec said in a resigned way. "Then, if there is a body, we'll see about the police." Father Joe was about to protest but Alec put up a warning finger and he fell silent.

3

Alec Ballentine lived on the fourth floor, the top apartment in a red-brick Victorian mansion block in Prince of Wales Drive, South London. St Mary's Church, Battersea, was around the corner on the south side of Battersea Park Road. Alec had never been in the church, even when he was first trying to impress Sophie. It was a dull, blackened red-brick Victorian church, fake Gothic and grim. The sulphurous yellow street lamps cast a jaundiced light over the front of the church. There was ugly rusting chicken wire over the Gothic arched windows. Bomb-damaged houses, some cleared and replaced by hastily erected hut-like houses, were on one side of the apparently untouched church. The other side of the road, opposite the church, had rows of undamaged terraced houses and shops.

It took them ten minutes to walk around to the front porch of the main door of the church. Father Joe took out a key and unlocked it.

"I thought churches were never locked?"

"Not in this area," said Father Joe, looking cold in the dark porch. He was shivering, and his face looked even older and greyer, not helped by the street lighting. It was getting late, about nine o'clock in the evening, and Alec realised that Father Joe had walked from the flat without his cassock – there was still a cassock soaked in blood on the floor of Alec's flat. How was that going to be explained to the police? Alec felt a pang of irritation towards the man who had now complicated his life even more.

"Just through here." They passed through the door and a heavy black coarse wool draught-excluding curtain, and switched on a few lights. They continued past the font, turned and walked quickly down the aisle, their steps echoing around the cold, dark nave of the church. Beyond the rows of pews were the choir stalls, where Father Joe suddenly stopped, dropped onto one knee and crossed himself, his eyes fixed on the cross upon the altar in some kind of silent prayer. Just as Alec was about to say something, Dent stood up and turned left down a gap between the choir stalls and the large box that housed the organ pipes, to a door.

He unlocked the door and opened it very slowly, then switched on the light. He took in a long, shaky breath. "There he is, Mr Ballentine." Alec squeezed past him, through the door and down a couple of steps into a small, chilly vestry.

On the bare wood floor was the body of a thin man. He lay face down, and a puddle of dark red, almost black, blood spread across the floor from his head. His head was furthest away from the door, his splayed feet and slightly bent right leg just an inch or two from the steps that led down into the vestry. His right arm was bent, his hand by his neck, and as Alec circled the blood on the floor, he saw that his right hand clutched the handle of a knife. The blade was stuck in his neck, in the region, Alec surmised, of the carotid artery. Alec had once held an American GI's carotid artery, in an attempt to save his life when the soldier was shot in the neck during the war, so he knew roughly where the artery was, and how much blood it produced.

Alec had forgotten how uncomfortable he felt in the presence of a dead person, especially a body that had violently met its end. He had seen more than his fair share of violent death, and it still sickened him.

"Good grief," he said, tiptoeing around the corpse. "Do you know who he is?"

"His name is Ferdi – Baron Olivier Ferdinand Saumures."

"What, Baroness Freya's husband?"

"Yes," Father Joe said, trying to avoid meeting Alec's eyes.

"Bloody h ... heck!" Alec looked with interest at the body. "Is he German?"

"No." Alec thought he heard a note of deceitfulness in his voice. "He is ... was from Luxembourg. But he should not have come for me!" The last few words were blurted out in anger.

"How do you know the baron?" Alec said, trying to look at the dead man's face. There was a long pause, and Alec wondered if Father Joe had heard him.

"He was sort of blackmailing me," Father Joe said in a matter-of-fact way. He was now sitting on the step at the doorway, his face looking cadaverous.

The baron, who looked to be about the same age as Alec, was dressed impeccably: a dark tailored suit – a dark-blue satin lining could be seen where the jacket was folded back – with a bright white shirt, the modern attached collar soaked in blood. On his feet were a pair of shiny black brogues, bulled to a glossy shine like an infantryman's boot. Alec could see a coat of arms on the cufflinks, with a navy-blue-and-white striped background and the profile head of a roaring lion in gold. He also noticed what looked like a regimental or old school tie.

"What happened?" Alec wondered why he hadn't asked this question before.

Father Joe thought for a while. "Ferdi" – he indicated the body on the floor with a wave of his hand – "came into the vestry after I had said evening prayers, and demanded ..." He swallowed hard. "He demanded more money. I said I had no more money, that every penny had already gone to him and Freya, and I could not give him any more." Alec frowned. An unlikely tale, he thought.

"So, Freya – the goddess – was in on the blackmail too?" Alec said, slightly mockingly.

"No!" Father Joe exclaimed. "She couldn't have, she's so ..." He was getting more distressed.

"You just said that you paid all you had to Ferdi and Freya."

"That was a mistake. I meant just Ferdi." Father Joe was wringing his hands as though washing them. "Anyway, I told him to go away, I would not give him any money, and that I wanted to see Freya. He roared an awful word at me, then told me terrible things about Freya. He said I was to leave Freya alone and that I was not to come near her, and then he drew out a knife."

"So, that is Ferdi's knife?" Alec looked down in interest. It made sense, he supposed; why would a vicar be armed with a dagger?

"No, it's ... yes, it's his knife." Father Joe carried on miserably. "He lunged at me with the knife. I caught his arm but slid on my cassock. I fell back, dragging Ferdi down with me, and as we hit the ground, the knife went into his neck. I tried to stop him ..."

"Tried to stop who?"

"Ferdi ... Saumures." Alec could not work him out. The story was most confusing.

"What kind of money were they asking for?"

Father Joe looked at Alec with annoyance. "I'm not saying."

Alec sighed. He was starting to lose his patience.

"What did Saumures mean when he said not to come near her?" Alec asked, looking around the small vestry.

"I don't want to talk about that now. He didn't mean sleep with her, or anything like that, but something else." Father Joe was getting into a tangle.

He was lying and plainly regretting what he had said. "I just want to get rid of the body, and I want you to help me find Freya and protect her."

"I am not going to do any such thing. Protect her from what? You? Were you expecting Sophie to help you with all this?" Alec was angry. "She would also call the police. Does this work?" Alec pointed at the old-style candlestick telephone on the desk, picked up the earpiece and started to dial 999.

"No! You promised you weren't going to call the police," Dent sobbed.

"I certainly did not! I said we will see what the situation is. And in any case, the way you described it, it was an accident. It was *his* dagger, which explains the blood on your cassock ... which, incidentally, we must go and get out of my flat. And it seems he was not a nice man – he was blackmailing you."

"Precisely. He was blackmailing me," Father Joe said as though he was convincing himself. "An awful lot of terrible truths will come out, and I will never be able to preach in this parish again – or any parish for that matter."

"I think that is the least of your worries."

"Oh? You think so, do you, Mr Ballentine?" Father Joe stood and stepped down into the vestry, jinking around the body's shoes.

"Well, I am sorry, but I am going to call the police." Alec picked up the telephone once again. "I am not going to get myself hanged just to save your blemished character. Who do you think I am? I don't understand your religion. I thought Catholics were celibate."

"I'm not Catholic. Why do you think I'm Catholic?"

"You're called *Father* Joe."

"I'm a dean."

Alec was confused. "Anyway, I had no idea that you lot had 'relations' with dubious women. No wonder you are at the mercy of their pimps!"

"Oh God, you don't understand. Freya was not a prostitute, she's ... she's ... Anyway, they won't hang *you*. *I* killed him."

"Were you screwing her?" Alec said.

"Don't say that word," he pleaded.

"Did you have sexual relations with this girl, then?" Alec rolled his eyes.

"No! But ... Well, no."

"Did you pay to have relations with her?"

"No! I didn't. It was not like that."

"Then who did screw her – apart from her husband?" Alec gestured towards the corpse.

"Nobody!" shouted Father Joe, virtually in tears again.

"So, what was this money for? Did you pay her?"

"Not quite. Well, in a way, yes, but—"

"Then she is a prostitute, end of story, not a goddess. That was what she was tried for, a few years ago."

Father Joe gaped at Alec, clearly not sure what to say. "It was so long ago, and I didn't know ... and besides, he made me do it."

"Who made you do what?" Alec asked, his patience now lost with the dithering cleric, who plainly had difficulty in the art of lying.

Father Joe took a sharp intake of breath and looked down at the floor. He sat heavily back onto the step again and began to sob.

"Who is the baron, vicar?" Alec said gently.

"He's an artist. He is ... was married to Freya."

"And you say Freya ... Freya Saumures is also Charlotte de Tournet?" Father Joe did not answer. Alec regarded him with an expression of distrust.

Alec picked up the phone and when the operator asked which service, he asked for the police and ambulance. He was not sure Father Joe was psychologically able to go to a police station. But, he decided, it was not up to him.

*

Charlotte de Tournet, eh? Alec thought. Now that could be quite a story. And why was old Joe being blackmailed? He wasn't rich, just a sad bearded clergyman, a rather pathetic vicar of a shabby little parish in Battersea. And why had he chosen Alec? Sophie, he supposed. Alec was beginning to worry. Father Joe must have had other friends, closer friends, perhaps even friendly parishioners. Why me? he asked himself again. And who is – and where is – Charlotte de Tournet, or Freya, and what is her story?

Alec took a packet of Players from his tweed jacket pocket and lit a cigarette with a match. He looked around for an ashtray or a bin for his spent match but could not see one in the sparse vestry. He placed the dead match back into the box. Alec looked at the cleric sitting dejected on the steps of the vestry, with only a tiny bit of empathy. He did not feel very compassionate. He felt used.

Father Joe reached into his back pocket and withdrew a hip flask, much to Alec's surprise. Looking away from Alec, he took a long drink from the flask, screwed back the stopper and replaced it in his back pocket.

Alec was weary of drama, exhausted of adventure. He just wanted to go to bed, his nice comfy bed, after weeks and months of travel and discomfort.

At last, the police arrived. Alec and the cleric were ushered out of the vestry and into the body of the church. Alec was told to sit in the front pew, while Father Joe was taken to the back of the church. Another policeman stood in between to make sure they did not talk to each other.

A middle-aged man introduced himself as Detective Inspector Jack McMillan. He sat beside Alec and interviewed him, placing his well-worn bowler hat on his knee.

Alec told him everything that happened that night, from Father Joe crashing, uninvited, into his flat and asking for his help, and leaving his bloody cassock, to arriving at the church and seeing the body. He told the inspector everything except the names Charlotte de Tournet and Freya Saumures. If Father Joe wanted to put himself in a padded cell, Alec thought, it was up to him.

"Why did the vicar kill him, do you think, Mr Ballentine?"

"Well, I think he said he was being blackmailed by this chap Baron Saumures, but certainly, in my opinion, he did not kill him intentionally. It looks to me like a terrible accident. You will have to ask him for the details. I don't really know him."

"Thank you, sir. This is my detective sergeant, Sergeant Glass." Alec looked up to see a small, fat young man in a dirty black suit. He was writing something down and stopped and nodded at Alec. The senior police detective thanked Alec for his assistance in a somewhat disingenuous voice and let him go home. "My sergeant will accompany you to retrieve the cassock. We will need to take your fingerprints for elimination first."

On his way out of the church, as he wiped the black ink off his fingertips, he spotted Father Joe sitting on a pew beside the font with another police inspector. When Father Joe saw Alec, he shouted, "Mr Ballentine, find Freya for me. Protect her from … well, just make sure she is OK. Please! Tell her she's a goddess!" He was hushed by the inspector and made to sit down.

*

Alec got home. He and Sergeant Glass went in to retrieve the cassock. It was put into a foldaway shopping bag.

"Try not to walk all over the bit of blood, sir," Sergeant Glass told Alec in a heavy Cockney accent. "We'd need to have it looked at by them forensics blokes."

"Really?" Alec was surprised that they were going into it so thoroughly.

"Yeah. Well, I'll be getting on now, sir. Your mate will be in Battersea nick if you need to see him, unless Scotland Yard want him, that is."

"He is no 'mate' of mine," Alec mumbled.

"What was he saying about a fair?" asked the sergeant just before he left.

"Freya. He wanted me to find a friend of his called Freya."

"Do you know who that is, sir?"

"The dead man's wife, I believe."

The sergeant took a long look at Alec, until Alec, feeling uncomfortable, frowned.

"Ta, sir." The sergeant licked his pencil and wrote something in his notepad.

Bloody police, Alec thought. Always thinking you are lying.

Alec thanked Sergeant Glass, saw him out, fixed himself a drink and sat in the armchair with Benjy, who was a little put out as this was his preferred sleeping quarters – there was never usually a human sitting in it at night. His tail swished with discontentment.

What an evening. Poor old Father Joe, Alec thought. He must be a lonely old chap.

He thought about calling Sophie to hear what she thought of the situation, but it was getting late, and it was Sunday ... and he did not think, after what she'd said in her letter, she would talk to him anyway.

But why was Father Joe so upset? Killing someone might be a good reason, but he didn't *really* kill the baron; it was self-defence, an accident. His fixation about Freya was also intriguing. Who was she? Was she really this Charlotte de Tournet girl?

4

All night long Alec sat in his chair in his pyjamas and dressing gown, socks on his feet to keep out the cold, a cigarette in his fingers with a long ash hovering over a half-full ashtray. He attempted to go to bed but the incident with Father Joe kept his mind in turmoil. This girl, well, woman now – she would be around thirty – was a mystery during the war. She was kidnapped, it was thought, from her school, the day the Germans entered Paris. Her uncle, Sir Jason Barrett MP, was in England; her step-parents were somewhere else in France, on holiday, and found they could not get back; and Charlotte was being cared for by a Swedish couple, a nanny or housekeeper and her chauffeur husband.

Was Charlotte actually Freya? What had this baron fellow to do with Freya, apart from marrying her? Had she been a prostitute? And what was the old cleric babbling on about "finding her and protecting her"? From whom?

Alec was jerked awake. The room was cold, and he must have nodded off. Dawn was approaching slowly; a soft orange glow was coming through the window at the back of his apartment. It was eight o'clock, so he had managed three hours' sleep. He went to the bathroom to get washed, shaved and dressed.

He set off for Fleet Street. On the way, he decided to pop by Battersea police station to see if Father Joe was able to give him any more information about Charlotte de Tournet … Freya Saumures. He needed to find out more about who she was, and her dead husband, Baron Ferdinand Saumures.

"Yes, sir?" said the sergeant behind the desk, in that superior way desk sergeants have that really irritated Alec.

"I've come to see Father Joe Dent. Would it be possible to talk to him? I'm a friend and—"

"He's been sent home, sir," interrupted the sergeant, "on police bail. His lawyer sorted it out. He was put in the care of a Special Branch super, I believe. I was not on duty. You will find him at his house."

"Who was the Special Branch superintendent?"

"No idea," the sergeant said unhelpfully.

"Why did you send him home?"

"Are you a legal person, sir?"

"No, a friend."

"Well, you will have to ask him or his lawyer about that. The guv'nor is not here at the moment. He's in bed, I should think, a-kippin'."

"A-what?"

"Sleeping, sir. You're not from around here, are you, sir?"

Alec left the police station. He was perplexed about Father Joe being sent home with a possible murder charge hanging over his head. And a lawyer – how on earth did he get hold of a lawyer in the middle of a Sunday night? Who was this lawyer? And what had Special Branch got to do with things? Was it because the victim was a baron?

Alec was more and more intrigued with the unfolding story. He decided to go to Fleet Street, to the *Telegraph* building first, to look up all he could about Charlotte de Tournet's disappearance. Then he would try to find Father Joe. He was not entirely sure he knew where the vicarage was, or if there was such a thing as a vicarage in a run-down Battersea parish.

*

The Telegraph
30 July 1940
NAZIS TAKE ENGLISH SCHOOLGIRL HOSTAGE
By C. B. Snow
The Nazis have taken a British schoolgirl, Charlotte de Tournet, prisoner. Mrs Stella de Tournet (42) and her French husband, industrialist Jean de Tournet (48), appealed to the German High Command to return their 15-year-old stepdaughter. The de Tournets were in Madrid, Spain. Charlotte de Tournet was abducted by the invading German army as it entered Paris on 14 June 1940, from her school, the Lubeck Académie, in Paris.

When the German High Command made enquiries on the de Tournets' behalf, through the Madrid Embassy, they were unable to locate Miss de Tournet at her school, which they claim was abandoned. The family mansion in Paris – according to French intelligence,

19 Avenue Foch – had been taken over by the Nazis as headquarters for the Department of Information.

There was a picture of the family taken a good three or four years before the war, Alec judged, as from what little he could see, Charlotte looked very young – certainly not fifteen years old.

Alec scanned as many newspapers of the time as he could to see if there was any more information. There were lots of stories about the invasion of Paris, but not much on the disappearance of Charlotte de Tournet, apart from a bit about her family, about her mother dying when she was a baby, and plenty about Jean de Tournet and his steel empire, and how he would pay anything to get their beloved Charlotte back.

BODIES FOUND IN NAZI BROTHEL IN PARIS. ONE MAY BE BRITISH.
20 September 1944
Reuters Correspondent

If it was not for the headline, Alec would have just gone past it. He was surprised, as he read on, to find it was about Nineteen Avenue Foch.

Amongst 23 bodies found in a bombed-out mansion in Paris were several unidentified men, high-ranking SS officers, judging by the uniforms found at the scene. Two other bodies, one of which was in Savile Row tailored evening trousers, were discovered by French and Allied troops in the rubble of a mansion on Avenue Foch last week. The building was thought to have been either bombed or a victim of the French Resistance over a year before.

The building, 19 Avenue Foch, was the British ambassador's private residence during the Great War. The steel tycoon Jean de Tournet and his wife also lived there, when Charlotte de Tournet, their stepdaughter, was kidnapped in June 1940, now believed to be dead. The house became the notorious venue for visiting high-ranking Gestapo and SS officers and was known as 'Le Palais' – The Palace.

More evidence of Nazi atrocities surfaced after the German army were driven out of Paris on 24 August 1944 thanks to the heroic actions of the French Forces of the Interior (FFI), with the help of the Allied forces.

News of The World
29 September 1944
A NAZI HOUSE OF ILL REPUTE!

Rumours of 19 Avenue Foch – 'Le Palais' – in the centre of Paris being a high-class brothel could not be verified. The mansion was burned down, bombed by the Free French army in September 1943. Up to eight bodies of high-ranking SS officers were found in the ruins. The bodies are being examined for identification, and are believed to be high-ranking Nazi SS Officers. Another body was in British-made Savile Row suit trousers. An expert has informed us that one of the bodies is that of Heinrich Müller, head of the Gestapo. Another body may be that of Wilhelm Frick, interior minister, and thought to be Himmler's right-hand man.

That's a shame, thought Alec. It was not Frick. He was one of those who were actually caught, tried and executed in 1946. Heinrich Müller was never caught, so it could be him. But, Alec wondered, who was the suited person? A British spy who got left behind?

"You were looking for information about Freya Saumures, Mr Ballentine?" asked the custodian of the archives.

"Yes, George. Have you got something?" Alec looked up from his notes.

"I remembered a trial, three years ago, about that Swedish girl who turned out to be a prostitute for the Nazis in Paris." Clouds of cigarette smoke poured out of George's mouth like exhaust fumes as he spoke. "She was acquitted, though. That Mr Bing-Wallace, who writes for *The Times*, wrote something. You know Mr Bing-Wallace, don't you, sir?"

"Thank you, George, let me have a read. Very kind of you."

The Times
2 July 1952
WAS BRITISH BARONESS WORKING FOR THE NAZIS IN PARIS?
By Philip Bing-Wallace

It was alleged that Baroness Freya Saumures (who claimed to be of Swedish descent but is a British subject) was one of the many women that entertained the Gestapo and SS during the occupation of Paris, a jury was told. At the baroness's trial today, the Old Bailey heard Daniel Merrick-James QC, prosecuting council, astonish the jury by revealing that

Baroness Freya Saumures allegedly worked with the Nazis throughout the Nazi occupation of Paris.

There was a photograph of a woman in a headscarf and dark glasses, alongside a tall dark-haired man who had a protective arm around her, his face shielded by his hand. A description beneath the image read: *Baroness Saumures with her husband, Baron Ferdinand Saumures, outside the Old Bailey after her acquittal.*

Alec could not see her face fully, but the picture of the baron, even partially obscured, certainly looked very like the man lying dead in the Battersea Park Road crypt. Alec read on.

> *When Mr Merrick-James sat, a clerk of the court handed the judge, Justice Henry Folks, a note. The judge then asked the court to be cleared. Twenty minutes later, the court was reconvened. Justice Folks announced to the jury that the prosecution had dropped all charges and that Lady Saumures was acquitted.*
>
> *There was no explanation for the acquittal. The jury was dismissed with thanks. Neither Baron nor Baroness Saumures had any comment.*
>
> *Baron and Baroness Saumures live in West Sussex and are well known to a select group for their musical evenings and events. They are also well known for protecting their privacy.*

Alec rummaged on. It was getting close to lunchtime and his head was beginning to ache. The archive room was not the best place for research; it smelt of print, cigarette smoke and human beings. There was hardly any air, as for some reason the windows were never opened.

Alec put back the large blue folders. He wanted to know if anybody had identified the British-suited man in the fire at Nineteen Avenue Foch.

"Find what you wanted, Mr Ballentine?"

"Yes, I think so, George. I may have to return. Thank you for finding that piece on Baroness Saumures."

"If I find anything else, I will give you a call at El Vino's wine bar, sir."

5

Alec signed out of the archive room, thanking George again. He wandered over to El Vino to see if any of his old colleagues were there. He turned right, out of the mock-Gothic building that housed *The Telegraph*, crossed the road and up the slight hill of Fleet Street. The road was busy; the weather was cold, the sun desperately trying to peek through the grey milky sky.

Alec went through the old double doors, panelled with decorated, frosted Victorian glass. The long-standing wine bar El Vino was a fabled watering hole for barristers from the Inner Temple and journalists, a mainstay of Fleet Street professionals for just over seventy-five years. The smell of fortified wine and stale smoke wafted up Alec's nostrils like an elixir. It was early and the long bar, black with age, had only a couple of well-dressed chambers clerks chatting at the far end, next to a wood-panelled screen that divided the bar from the Smoking Room beyond.

The ceiling and the walls were dark amber, a yellowy brown obtained from years of smoke. Alec went to the centre of the bar and lit a cigarette from the gas-pipe flame that stood permanently lit for customers to light their cigarettes or cigars. He felt he had come home; all was familiar, the smells, the noises, the rows of wooden barrels of sherry and port along the back of the bar – nothing had changed. He ordered a Bual Madeira, one of his favourite pre-lunch drinks. A young pallid barman served Alec a small glass of the deep-ochre fortified wine.

"Mr Ballentine, how lovely to see you again," a broad-chested man boomed. He appeared from the tall desk at the end of the bar. Frank Bower, the proprietor, wore round-framed glasses and had thick silver-grey hair. He looked resplendent in black-tailed morning jacket, his thumbs in the pockets of his bright yellow-and-emerald-green paisley waistcoat. He strode over and gently pushed the young barman aside. "I'll do this, thank you, David. Nice to see you still enjoy the Bual, sir. We have only just managed to get it back in since the war." Alec proffered a pound note. Mr Bower gave it to David and ushered him to the huge till at the end of the bar. "I trust you are well. Not seen you for a while," he said, beaming at Alec.

"I've been in Turkey, Malaya, and Spain ... all over the place," Alec said, but Mr Bower was more interested in what David was doing. "And I am home for a while, for a rest." The change came back on a little silver tray and Mr Bower took it from David and put it on the bar in front of Alec. "Is Mr Bing-Wallace still around, Mr Bower? I wanted to have a word."

"He'll be in as usual at twelve forty-five, I should think." Bower looked at the fob watch. "Sit at his table in the Smoking Room, sir," Bower said, looking through the serving hatch to make sure Mr Bing-Wallace's table was free.

"Thank you, Mr Bower. Do you have a half-bottle of Pommery?"

"Oh yes, sir. The boy will bring the champagne over."

Alec wandered into the empty Smoking Room. He had not quite understood why it was called the Smoking Room as you could smoke everywhere. He sat at a table in the corner. A wooden screen turned it into a slightly more private area. The nine tables, made of dark wood, were each surrounded by four or five captain's chairs with cracked leather seats and leather arm padding, while some of the other tables had cheaper bent-cane chairs. A square glass ashtray, salt and pepper, and a menu in a little red leather folder were placed on each table. The whole room was bathed in light that came from a great skylight almost as big as the room. Alec was the only customer in the Smoking Room for the moment.

A lad in a black waistcoat and long white apron brought over a half-bottle of champagne in a small ice bucket and two glasses.

"On your bill, sir?"

"No, here you are." Alec held out some pound notes.

Just as Alec paid the lad, he heard the double doors swing open, and a loud sing-song voice hailed "Bordink!" Philip Bing-Wallace always announced himself, whatever time of day, with "Morning" – or, with his adenoid affliction, "Bordink". Bing-Wallace – the London *Times* cultural columnist, as he titled himself – had adenoid problems and his *M*'s turned into *B*'s, especially when he was nervous or excited.

"Good afternoon, Mr Bing-Wallace," boomed Mr Bower from behind his high desk.

Bing-Wallace was an elegant man. Today he was dressed in a well-cut black suit, the effect somewhat spoilt by a badly tied blue polka dot bow tie.

He strode down the centre of the bar area, his shiny black shoes and spats clomping on the floor. He had an umbrella hooked over one arm and a huge wad of newspapers under the other, and a black homburg hat in his hand.

"Balladtide, how lovely!" Bing-Wallace stopped at his table and threw everything he held onto a spare chair in an untidy heap, then sat heavily down beside Alec, still in his overcoat. "And Pommery – how delicious. Is this you?" he asked, seeing the half-bottle of champagne.

"Yes, Philip."

"How exceptional of you!"

Philip Bing-Wallace was sometimes *The Times's* theatre critic, but he mostly enjoyed covering juicy trials at the Old Bailey. He got most of his information from the barristers who regularly joined him at his table at El Vino. He also knew just about everything that was going on in "society". He had been a journalist for over thirty years, and with the help of an encyclopaedic memory, could muster up a story about virtually every scandal worldwide. His table was always occupied by one journalist or another, seeking information or wanting advice about a story, and Bing-Wallace rarely ended up having to pay for his daily half-bottle of Pommery champagne – sometimes two half-bottles.

He was thought to be well into his fifties – nobody knew his age. He had a full head of thick black hair, an apple face with no chin, neat round ears and a slightly hooked nose, always kept high and aloof. He often had a patch of unshaven chin or a small plaster on his face, because, he said, "I always use a cut-throat razor – you never know if those safety razors are actually shaving anything." And, as he was always in a hurry, bits would be missed on his chin or he would nick a bit of skin.

"My dear Ballentine, where have you been?" Alec opened his mouth to answer when Bing-Wallace turned around to the waiter and shouted, "I say! One could die of thirst, you know." The lad scurried over and took the half-bottle of champagne out of the ice bucket, opened it expertly and poured it into Philip's glass for tasting. "Just pour it out, could you? I am sure it is splendid." The boy filled the glasses, not hearing Alec say, "Not for me, thank you."

"Well, how have you been?" Alec once again started to answer, when Bing-Wallace interrupted. "I've had the most awful day," he said, taking a long drink of champagne. "My dear, I fell off the number nineteen bus this morning. Look!" He turned his back to Alec and Alec could see a little scuff on the left shoulder of his overcoat as he stood to take it off. "I had got on the bus and before I could grab the bar thingy, the conductor had rung the bloody bell and the bus leapt off and I fell out of the back … right in the middle of the King's Road."

"Were you all right?"

"Oh yes! I decided to do a theatrical fall so that the conductor would feel awful, but he didn't see me or my great performance. I got up and thought people would rush over to see if I was all right, but they just all strode on – one or two laughed! God, I hate the King's Road, awful people. That's why I am loath to go into Peter Jones. I always seem to bump into people one would rather not talk to. But they do have such nice things there." He finished the first glass of champagne and started on the second as soon as Alec pushed it in front of him. "So, Alec, what are you up to these days? Still going off with the soldiers into battle and so on?"

"Nothing at the moment, Philip. But, do you remember, during the war, when the Krauts waltzed into Paris in 1940, and there was that girl who was kidnapped?"

"You mean Charlotte de something or other?"

"Yes, de Tournet."

"That's the girl. Why?"

"She was the daughter of a steel mogul called Jean de Tournet. Apparently, they made a fuss from Madrid to try and get her out of Paris."

"I think, if my memory serves, he was her uncle *and* stepfather. Her mother was murdered by her German lover, you know." Bing-Wallace pondered for a moment. "Or was he Austrian? Can't remember if anything came of that. Very odd. She was left this huge house in Avenue Foch by her grandmother – vast it was, positively a mansion, in the middle of Paris. But the bloody Nazis took it over during the war as some kind of entertainment place, like a high-class country club. Some say it was a brothel." Bing-Wallace pulled a face of disapproval. "A brothel in Avenue Foch, would you believe? Only the Nazis would have the bad taste to do such a shameful thing."

"So, it was a brothel, not even a high-class—?"

"No idea. Damned Nazis did terrible things in Avenue Foch," Bing-Wallace said, appalled. "Anyway, a bomb – don't know whose – razed it to the ground." Bing-Wallace sat back in his chair, thinking and drinking, and then sat up again and asked, "Why on earth do you want to know about that? I doubt you will get any more from that story … it was ages ago, and it was all upheaval during the war. Nobody will remember."

He paused and looked contemplatively into the distance. "Dear Paris," he reminisced, "just wrecked during the war. Those wretched Nazis had no idea what they were destroying. The art! Oh, the art they buggered off with. Quite a lot of it, you know. We will never get it back." Why did he say "we" will never get it back? wondered Alec.

"Do you know a girl, possibly a high-class prostitute, called Freya?" Alec asked after a pause.

"Certainly not," Bing-Wallace cried indignantly. "What do you think I ... oh ... just a tick ... you mean Baroness Freya Saumures? She was a high-class courtesan, I think she called herself. One of the most beautiful women in the world it is said. No, I don't *know* her, I've seen her a few times. I was at her trial, you know." He paused to have a sip of champagne. "Why?"

"Are we talking about the wife of someone called Baron Ferdinand Saumures?" Alec asked, smiling conspiratorially.

"Well, yes." Bing-Wallace regarded Alec suspiciously. "They entertain a little in Sussex, but only a very select few get to go to their soirées, my dear, not the likes of you or—" Bing-Wallace suddenly looked excited. "Have you been invited, Alec? Would you take me?"

"Well, I think they may be one and the same. Charlotte and Freya."

"Charlotte de Tournet was killed ..." Bing-Wallace abruptly sat bolt upright. He looked around and then back to Alec, and whispered, "How on earth did you make *that* connection?" He put a finger up. "Both have something to do with the house in Avenue Foch?" Bing-Wallace then stopped, looking disappointed. "Hang on ... ages. She was only a young girl. What age was she when she was abducted?"

"Fifteen or sixteen?" said Alec. "Where can I find this Freya, anyway? And, no, I have not been invited to anything."

"Shame. Well, if she was fifteen in 1940, she would be around thirty now, so it could be her." Bing-Wallace was drumming his fingers on his lower lip, thinking.

"Do you know how I can track her down, Philip?" Alec repeated forcefully.

"A place called Burton Park Place, near Petworth in Sussex. It's a bit of a fortress, though. Unsolicited visits are vehemently discouraged," Bing-Wallace said, still thinking. "She's very beautiful, or have I said that? There are not many, if any, photos of her. I last saw her at an opera house in Sussex – that Christie chap is revamping ... again." Bing-Wallace cast his eyes up in wonder. "She was with her husband and a Moorish beauty, watching *Così fan tutte*. They caused quite a stir. He's very good-looking. Queer, you know." Alec spluttered on his Madeira; he was surprised to hear Philip so casually state that Saumures was a homosexual.

"When was this, when you saw them?"

"Oh, this last summer. They are opening a new bit of the stage this year. Glyndebourne – glorious for opera. Sit outside for picnics, you know, by the ha-ha. It's going to be a gorgeous place." Bing-Wallace went into a dream, away in another world, a contented smile on his face.

"Philip, how do I talk to her?" Alec was getting a little annoyed by his prevarication.

"I don't think I know anybody who knows the baroness. Though I have tried to go with Yehudi to one of the baron's evenings, a couple of times. Only way to get invited is when you are with someone like Menuhin." Bing-Wallace carried on. "She is one of those rare creatures, a celebrity who is not famous, only infamous, if you see what I mean." Bing-Wallace chuckled, and drained the last of his bottle into his glass. "She hangs around the sort of people that none of us have access to – the extraordinarily rich, titled and foreign. Like her husband, the baron. He owns property all over the place. In London, he owns the Adolphe Hotel off Piccadilly and—" He started waving at a waiter. "I say!" he shouted. El Vino was now getting hectic, the bar filling up with smartly dressed men, Mr Bower welcoming most of them by name in his booming voice from behind his high desk at the end of the bar.

"Yes, sir," said the waiter, looking worried.

"I would like a half-bottle of the Pommery, and two sardine and cucumber sandwiches, and another one of whatever Mr Ballentine is drinking." His adenoids made it difficult for the waiter to understand.

"But, Bing-Wallace, I've got to go," complained Alec.

"A bottle of what, sir?" asked the young waiter.

"A half-bottle … *half-bottle*!" Bing-Wallace turned to Alec. "Nonsense, I want to hear more about your story, Alec."

Alec could see the waiter looking worried and baffled. "Mr Bing-Wallace would like half a Pommery champagne, and two rounds of sardine and cucumber sandwiches, please." Alec helped the waiter with translation, for the boy was plainly new. "Bing-Wallace, I don't think I have very much more—"

"My dear boy, you are not telling me everything, are you?" Bing-Wallace leant forward. "Tell me all. I will not ruin the story for you, scout's honour. It just sounds rather fascinating. Especially this thing you said that Charlotte and Freya are one and the same."

"Oh, OK. Hang on …" They sat back in their leather captain's chairs as the waiter opened the champagne and another waiter placed a plate of two rounds of sandwiches of thick white bread onto the table.

"The famous El Vino sardine and cucumber sandwiches. How scrummy," Bing-Wallace said with excitement.

Alec could see his exclusive story dwindling away but decided that Bing-Wallace was the best person to help him put the pieces together. As soon as the waiters went, Alec and Bing-Wallace leant towards each other conspiratorially. Bing-Wallace took a triangle of sandwich and looked expectantly at Alec.

"Last night, a vicar, Father Joe Dent, pounded on my door at about half eight."

"Catholic, was he?"

"No, Anglican."

"But—"

"I know – no idea why he's *Father* Joe. Anyway, I let him in. He was wearing a cassock soaked in blood—"

"Blood? This is getting good, Alec … Sorry, carry on, old chap."

"As I was saying, he collapsed on my sofa, blood going everywhere, and he said that he had killed someone … this man." Alec stopped to collect his thoughts, thinking Bing-Wallace would interrupt again. "He implored me to go around to the church … his church in Battersea, near where I live. So I did. Saw the body, and said I would call the police."

"Quite right, dear boy. Do you know who the victim was?"

"Well, this is it. Father Joe said it was Baron Saumures."

Bing-Wallace gasped. "My God, Alec. How extraordinary. Are you sure?"

"Father Joe then said this de Tournet girl was involved and that the name she goes by now is Freya … and that she is a goddess." Both men looked at each other, Bing-Wallace taking in all Alec had said. Realisation put a smile on Bing-Wallace's face, and he wagged a finger of recognition at Alec.

"Oh, but yes," announced Bing-Wallace, "the Swedish goddess of love, Freya. How was she involved?"

"Well, he, the vicar, said that this baron bloke was blackmailing him. I mean, this is an impoverished-looking vicar in a run-down parish in Battersea, being blackmailed by a rich baron?"

"Was Charlotte or Freya blackmailing him too?"

"I don't know. Father Joe says not."

"Had he – the vicar – met Freya, or does he know her? How would he come to meet her in the first place?" Alec shrugged. Bing-Wallace tutted. "Not very professional of you, Ballentine, you did not ask enough questions. What were you thinking?"

"I don't know why I didn't pursue it in depth." Alec sighed. "I hoped to ask him this morning, but he was let out of jail."

"So he did get nabbed by the police?"

"Yes, I insisted we report it to the police. But the vicar was most upset that I did. There was a dead body, after all!"

"What was the blackmail about, do—" Bing-Wallace suddenly checked his level of speech as he realised that as he'd said the word "blackmail", heads turned on neighbouring tables. He carried on, slightly quieter. "Blackmail about what, do you think?"

"I don't know. I was annoyed, tired, fed up and just wanted to get the police to sort it all out so I could go to bed. But then he mentioned Freya and Charlotte de Tournet, and that the baron had said to him that he was 'not worthy to sleep with her', or words to that effect."

"Do you think she had sex with the vicar, as a kind of honeytrap?" Bing-Wallace then waved his hand to discount that theory with an expression of confusion. "There must be something more about this Father Joe chap."

"Well, that was my conclusion. I trotted down to the church, wondering if this chap was spinning a yarn."

"Or even setting a trap for you, Alec." Alec was surprised; Bing-Wallace may have a point, and he wondered why he might think it was a scam. But then he thought of his ex-fiancée, Sophie, Father Joe's original hopeful accomplice. She would have seen it as a trick … if it was. She knew Father Joe quite well.

"No, Philip, it never occurred to me. Anyway, there was the body in the vestry, blood everywhere. It looked like this Baron Saumures had the dagger and Father Joe somehow slipped and dragged Saumures onto his own knife – straight into the neck." Bing-Wallace winced. Alec carried on. "He was a smartly dressed chap."

"He was reputed to be a bit of a fruit," said Bing-Wallace. Alec had slightly suspected Bing-Wallace as being a bit of a fruit himself. The homosexual society in London was a closed network as it was illegal, and he thought Bing-Wallace may have known Saumures through that network, if there was one. He may have got Bing-Wallace completely wrong – although there was no Mrs Bing-Wallace. He did not press the matter further.

"Well, I decided to cover myself from any legal bother and called in the police. Possibly I should have pumped him more, the vicar that is, to see if it was a story, but I could not – unusually for me – be bothered."

"Never mind, Alec." Bing-Wallace went back to drumming his fingers on his lip in contemplation.

Alec carried on, "And they came along and hauled poor Father Joe off to Battersea nick. But the strange thing was I went to see Father Joe this morning, and I was surprised to find that a lawyer of some kind had arrived, along with a Special Branch police superintendent, and managed to get him out on police bail."

"Who was the lawyer? Did you get the name of the superintendent?"

"The police would not give me names. I think the desk sergeant knew me as a journalist and was just being bloody."

"That's a shame. I bet I could find out, if you give me a couple of hours. The one thing that bothers me, Alec, and don't take this the wrong way, is: why you?"

"It bothered me as well. He knew my fiancée, Sophie."

"My dear boy, are you getting married?" Bing-Wallace slapped Alec on the back.

"No, no, she buggered off when I went on another assignment abroad – can't remember which. She got fed up with not getting any attention … apparently." Alec shrugged in a "that's life" gesture.

"Never mind, she obviously did the wise thing. You'd make a bloody dreadful husband, Alec."

"Thanks! Anyway, I suppose he – Father Joe – also knew I was a journalist."

"A gung-ho journalist at that. He wanted someone like you for a reason, and I bet it was to give him protection from these blackmailers or to find someone." Bing-Wallace sat back in thought and then had another idea. "He wanted you to find this Charlotte de Tournet or Freya or whoever she is, for him." Bing-Wallace looked like he was hatching a plan. "I want to know who the lawyer was. You go and see if you can find the errant vicar."

Bing-Wallace stood up and drained the glass of champagne. They both picked up a triangle of sardine and cucumber sandwich.

"Hey!" said Alec with some alarm. "What do you think you're doing? Please remember that this is my story, Philip."

"Don't worry, old sausage, all in hand. This is far more interesting. Promise I will keep it quiet. Anyway, you are freelance; you could sell it to *The Times*, with my byline." This was very generous of Bing-Wallace; a piece in *The Times* under Bing-Wallace's byline would get more prominence. Alec would make sure, however, that it was a joint byline.

Bing-Wallace looked serious again. "We have a lot of questions to answer before we can put any kind of copy together. Who is Father Joe? Who is Freya? Where did she come from? I believe she was a Swedish beauty who infiltrated high-ranking Nazis during the war and may have worked for the British Secret Service." Bing-Wallace put up a finger as an idea came to him. "Which was basically why her trial ground to an abrupt halt. So, she can't be this Charlotte girl."

"Well, where has this Charlotte girl been since 1940?"

"Dead," Bing-Wallace said simply. "We've only got this chap Father Joe's word that Charlotte and Freya are one and the same."

"But why would he say it if they are not one and the same? Where would he get the idea? Why those particular two women?" said Alec.

"We just have to dig one of these people up, find out what is going on, won't we? No good surmising without evidence. No evidence, no story. No story, no pay – no pay and no Pommery!" Bing-Wallace then said, with concern, "But, Alec, won't the death of the baron be in the news by tomorrow, or even in this evening's news?"

"I am the only person, other than Father Joe and the police, who knows. Anyway, he's not that famous. I bet no one will bother with the story yet. Not unless what we've found out comes out."

It was two o'clock in the afternoon when they emerged from El Vino onto a dingy, still bustling Fleet Street. Bing-Wallace, even after a bottle of champagne, seemed perfectly sober. They bade each other a good afternoon and went their separate ways.

Alec had parked his precious silver Jaguar in Chancery Lane, which ran off Fleet Street, opposite El Vino. It was parked just outside the Law Society building. He was tempted to pop in to see if there was a way he could track down the lawyer who "sprang" Father Joe, but he had no idea who or what to ask. And was it the kind of thing they would know? He was not sure how Bing-Wallace was going to find out.

6

Alec drove over Chelsea Bridge and onwards with the vast green expanse of Battersea Park, edged with well-arranged trees, on his right. The towering edifice of Battersea Power Station rose up on his left, behind noisy railway lines mounted on brick viaducts, and dirty green trains rattling towards Victoria Station from the south coast.

He turned right at the bottom of the park into his road, Prince of Wales Drive. The park was looking very dishevelled, and the light-grey sky behind the trees threatened rain. The trees were shedding foliage, the grass long and covered in dry leaves of various shades of brown. The mild breeze was not warm or cold, just dank.

Alec parked the sleek silver Jaguar XK120 Drop Head outside his building and walked round to the church in Battersea Park Road as he'd done the night before. Outside the sad-looking church, the brick walls stained with black soot and grime, stood a corpulent policeman with a hard face, erect and properly at ease through military training, one arm with a rain cape draped over it like a waiter's napkin. He saw Alec approach the door of the church and he put up his hand to halt Alec, with an official frown.

"No one is permitted in the church. There has been an incident, sir."

"Mr Ballentine?" said a voice from behind the policeman. Sergeant Glass emerged from the shadow of the church porch with a notebook in his hand. He walked slowly over to stand beside the policeman. He had a smile that could only be described as smarmy on his round, badly shaved face. He looked a little absurd standing beside the tall policeman.

"Gent wants to go into the church, Sarge."

"No, Mr Glass, I just wanted to visit Father Dent," Alec interjected, "to see if he was OK, but I don't know where the vicarage is."

"The vicarage, if you could call it that, is just across the road, in that house next to the laundry, above the café – first-floor flat."

Alec looked across the road and saw Mancini's Café nestled between the Sunshine Laundry and a long terrace of virtually undamaged houses. The first-floor flat was behind two large Victorian windows recently painted white against the mottled red brick. The other windows in the terrace were cracked and peeling and the colour of coffee cream.

"Is he in?"

"No, he ain't, sir," said Glass, looking now at Alec with some interest. "Tell me, Mr Ballentine, being a journalist and all, is this visit professional or friendly?"

"Well, a bit of both really. I was surprised he was let out."

"So was we, sir." The sergeant stood beside Alec, the top of his trilby hat coming level with Alec's eyes. Alec thought policemen had to be a certain height.

Much to Alec's surprise, the sergeant took hold of Alec's arm and said, "I have something to show yer, Mr Ballentine."

He led Alec into the church. His grip on Alec's arm was surprisingly strong and left no doubt which direction he wanted Alec to go.

"Hang on," Alec protested. The sergeant released his grip as they went through the main door into the church and down to the vestry behind the organ. The detective removed his hat, revealing a dense crop of black spiky hair, and put it on a choir stall. In the vestry a large maroon patch was where the body and the blood had been. A chalk outline of the body was described on the wood floor.

They stopped at the back of the vestry at a dark-green draught-excluding curtain that Alec thought was the back door to the church. Sergeant Glass pulled the heavy curtain to one side, revealing a huge Gothic-style oak door, slightly ajar.

"This way, sir." The detective pushed the door open. Alec fully expected a creak, but it swung open silently. As he went through, he noticed that the huge lock on the door had been hacked out.

"Did you do that, Sergeant?"

"No, that's how we found it this morning." There were some wide stone steps and a light shone up from a room below. They descended into some kind of large windowless stockroom or crypt, about forty by thirty feet. The ceiling's thick joists were quite high. Sergeant Glass went over to the far corner of the room, his steps echoing on the stone floor, his shadow moving quickly with the single bright light bulb, and pulled back a fawn-coloured canvas dust sheet that covered a large pile of angular objects and piles of planks of wood.

"What do you think of that, then, sir?" Underneath the dust sheet were a few picture frames, all ornate gold, but mostly badly chipped, the white plaster moulding showing. There were no pictures in them. There were also what appeared to be smashed-up crates, lots of them, and all the markings on the crates were painted over with black paint.

"Very nice," said Alec, not sure why these were so significant. "I don't think they belong to this church, though."

"Nah – these ain't church property."

"Well, have you asked Father Joe?"

"He's not at home. Can't find him anywhere. Thought you might be able to help."

"What do you mean, I might be able to help?" Alec was not happy with what the policeman was insinuating. "How would I know where he is? Anyway, have you checked his flat?" Alec asked angrily.

"Yes, sir, we have." Sergeant Glass irritably covered up the frames with the dust sheet and stomped back past Alec. The policeman, followed by Alec, went back to the cellar door and started walking up the steps back into the vestry.

"DI McMillan and a constable are there now searching his flat to see if he's got any more gear stashed away – like this lot here."

"Can I go over and have a look? See the inspector?" asked Alec.

"No, you bloody well can't. You're not only a journalist but also a suspect." Sergeant Glass was now, for some inexplicable reason, getting angry. He strode out of the church with Alec hot on his tail.

"What do you mean by that, Sergeant?" Alec exploded when he caught up.

"Where have you been all morning then, sir?" enquired the sergeant, still a little terse, his usual composure steadily returning. "We know you went round to the nick this morning. Where did you go after that?"

"I went straight to Fleet Street. I was in the *Telegraph* building from about nine thirty to twelve thirty, then I was in El Vino's from a little after twelve thirty to well past two. Why do you want to know?"

"A police officer went round to collect Mr ... Father Dent for further questioning." Glass was back to his normal calm self, no trace of the earlier flare-up. "We then got a report from a Mrs Derby, the housekeeper to Father

Dent, saying there was a policeman with a head injury on her stairs and she'd called an ambulance."

"Bloody hell! Is he all right?" His immediate concern turned to anger. "Did you think I did this?"

"We don't know, do we, sir? You're a big gent. It could have been Father Dent, you, Mrs Derby, or any of the four and a half million people in Lon—"

"Oh, don't be ridiculous, Sergeant." Alec was now standing quite close to the little detective and hoped his height might intimidate him. "Now you know where I was all morning and there are lots of people to back me up … and in any case, why would I want to brain a policeman in a stranger's flat? I had no idea where Father Dent lives."

"So you say, sir," said Glass, looking up at Alec, unperturbed by him towering over him. He turned a shoulder towards Alec and stood side on, took out his notepad and licked his pencil and started writing notes.

Alec sighed angrily. "And I had nothing to do with the incident in the church, either."

"Thank you for that, Mr Ballentine. What was the places you mentioned?"

"The *Telegraph* building and El Vino."

"Are they both in Fleet Street, sir?"

"Yes, Sergeant, they are. You can talk to the records clerk at *The Telegraph* – there is a register I signed in and out of – and the owner of El Vino, Mr Frank Bower." Alec was not going to mention anything about Bing-Wallace. "Tell me, Sergeant, do you know who this Baron Saumures fellow was?"

The sergeant looked up at him, clearly weighing up whether to answer him or not. Alec noticed that the sergeant had intelligent, thoughtful grey eyes in his round porcine face.

"No, sir, we have not formally identified the deceased. He was not known to us. There is no information on him, no wallet, no identification. We've only a name that Father Dent gave us. We have no idea who he is … officially."

"Oh." Alec was stumped by this answer. "So, he could be anybody?"

"He's nobody we know, sir, and we know a lot of people. We will go to 'missing in action' and see what they have."

"Missing persons, I presume."

"Yes, sir. Thank you, sir. Will you be in your apartment if Detective Inspector McMillan needs you further today, sir?"

"No, I will be trying to find Father Dent and some other people for the rest of the day," said Alec tersely. "You can find me either at the *Telegraph* building or at my apartment after six this evening." Sergeant Glass put down his pad and pencil, and squared up to Alec with his hands on his hips. He talked to Alec's chest.

"Well, if you comes across Mr Dent, can you be so kind as to inform the police, and not approach him or warn him of our interest in him? I would be obliged." His eyes went slowly up to Alec's face.

"Very well, Sergeant, I will." Alec was about to walk off when he thought of something. "Has anybody informed Baron Saumures's wife of his demise?"

"No, sir, and they won't until the body is more positively identified."

"How are you going to do that, Sergeant? Surely it's the wife who will do that?"

"We have our ways, sir." Policemen could sound so condescending. "But we do not need any help from the press, Mr Ballentine. We will inform the relevant people in due course. Do *not* print anything about this, please."

Alec walked away. He regretted not fighting the sergeant at his own game. As he got to the edge of the pavement, he turned towards the sergeant, who was talking to the large constable, and shouted, "What was the name of the lawyer who got Dent released last night, Sergeant Glass?"

The detective waddled over to Alec, his forefinger rubbing his chin in thought. He stopped and looked up at Alec with a little grin.

"If I tell you, sir, will you do as I asked – if you come across Mr Dent, that is?"

"Yes, officer, of course." Alec tried to sound friendly, not bubbling over with anger as he was inside.

The sergeant riffled through his notepad and said, "He was called Eric Strider. We think he had a slight German or Jewish accent. But Strider is not a very Jewish name."

"Have you contacted him?"

"He does not seem to be in his office. Strider's offices are in Middle Temple Lane, where you're going now, ain't yer, sir?" He gave a little smile and a quick wink. Alec was indeed going to be very close to Middle Temple Lane as it was just off Fleet Street, in the area known as Temple – the centre of British law.

"By the way, sir, I don't think I am speaking out of turn, but Father Dent's fingerprints do not feature anywhere on the dagger. Did you see if he was wearing gloves?"

"No, he was not wearing gloves." Alec thought for a bit. "But the dead man's hand was on the hilt of the dagger. Was it a dagger?"

"Yes, it was. We think the victim's hand was placed there. There is another good set of prints on the knife, but they do not belong to any of the two men – the victim or Father Dent … or your prints, sir." Alec was about to say something like "Thank God" when Glass said, "Did you notice anything strange about the dagger, sir?"

"No, why?"

"Just wondered," the policeman said offhandedly.

Alec looked at the little man then lit a cigarette, not quite knowing what to say or make of the last statement. He decided not to pursue the subject any further. Alec gave Sergeant Glass a nod of farewell. He looked up and down the road for cars and strode across.

"Don't forget, sir, to tell Father Dent," shouted the detective.

"No, I won't!" shouted Alec back over his shoulder.

As he turned, Alec saw, out of the corner of his eye, a man fifty yards up the street, leaning against the wall of a ruined house. He was dressed nearly all in black, with a hat and scarf, his face in shadow. As Alec took another look at the man, thinking that he may have been watching Alec and the policeman, he had gone. Vanished into thin air.

*

As soon as he got into his flat, Alec called Philip Bing-Wallace at the London *Times*.

"Philip, I know who the solicitor was," Alec announced.

"So do I," Bing-Wallace batted back, much to Alec's disappointment. "He is Eric von Strider – except he does not use the 'von' bit any more – and guess who his principal client is? Baron Ferdinand Saumures of Luxembourg – Ferdi to his friends."

"Well, fancy that." Alec was even more intrigued. "Fancy the lawyer of the murdered man rescuing his alleged murderer. This is organised, Philip; secret service stuff, I reckon."

"How exciting!"

"Philip, we must see this chap and ask for a comment on the baron's murder."

"Absolutely, old thing."

"Then I must track down the baroness and get a comment from her."

"Could I come too? I would love to see the house," Bing-Wallace implored.

"No, Philip, I need you in London. And be discreet; we do not want the rest of Fleet Street getting this. By the way, I have been warned off publishing anything about this by the police. So no story, at the moment."

"Don't worry, dear boy, I am a professional." Alec cast his eyes up to the sky; Bing-Wallace was a huge gossip, a professional rumour-monger. "The lawyer is not in his office in Middle Temple, so I am going to try and track him down this afternoon in El Vino or the Wig and Pen. If he is not a regular at either of those, I will go down to Davy's Bar."

"What about the Cheshire Cheese?"

"Lawyers never go to the Cheshire Cheese, unless Mr Bower has thrown them out of El Vino for a misdemeanour."

"They will all be closed," Alec said. "He will not be drinking; he will be with a client. I will go to the library and find out more about von Strider. How did you find him, anyway?"

"Got a friend in the Law Society."

"I was going to go in and try that, but I don't have a 'friend'. What on earth did you ask?"

"Oh, it will take too long to explain. Who told you, come to that?"

"I asked a policeman." There was a sigh on Bing-Wallace's end of the line. "I will see you around Fleet Street at some point later this afternoon, Alec. Did you find the cleric?"

"No. That is why I am getting a bit fed up. He's disappeared. His flat – which seems to serve as a vicarage – is being searched by the police, and there were some empty picture frames and crates in a cellar storage room in the church."

"Picture frames? That doesn't sound very sinister. I would have thought that all churches have pictures. What kind of picture frames?"

"Rather ornate, but some a bit damaged. And broken-up crates. The crates must have held some large paintings. And the frames, though damaged, were beautiful, nothing like the kind of things a Battersea church would have. Anyway, I don't think churches have pictures, do they?"

"I am just as irreligious as you, dear boy. Haven't been in a church since the coronation, and only then in my professional capacity."

"And another thing, Bing-Wallace: the police don't know or have not heard of Baron Ferdinand Saumures. I don't think the baroness has been told of his death."

"Well, that's a rum show. Not surprising, though. Anyway, I'll get on. Good luck."

He rang off before Alec could tell him to be careful about what he said to von Strider – if he found him.

7

Philip Bing-Wallace found Eric Strider's name described in creamy-white paint on the black entrance board beside the doorway of Twenty-Three Middle Temple Lane, a narrow, cobbled, carless lane that came straight out of a Dickens film set. A handcart containing files obstructed most of the entrance. He went up some narrow steps and knocked on the door marked "Clerk's Office". The door was thrown open by a young ginger-haired worried-looking youth with spots. He was putting on his coat and trying to gather up a thick pile of buff files, some folded and tied up with pink or white ribbons.

"Yes?" he said breathlessly and looked a little alarmed.

"I have a three-thirty appointment with Mr Eric Strider," Bing-Wallace lied.

"Yes, sir. Well, he isn't here at the moment."

"Oh." Bing-Wallace tried to look put out. "Can I wait for him?"

"I am afraid I must get these files over to King's Bench Walk for counsel to review. You will have to wait in the clerk's office, if that is all right." The boy had a West Country burr and he was thinking of more than one thing at a time – he was plainly unfocused.

"If that is conducive to you. Presumably Mr Strider won't be too long? I will look after the place whilst you are away," Bing-Wallace said as pleasantly as he could. The lad took a cautious look at Bing-Wallace, eventually saying, "Thank you, sir."

"Well, cut along, young man." Bing-Wallace ushered the boy on with what he thought was an assuring smile. The boy seemed racked in indecisive thought and hovered on the threshold of the office door.

"Mr Strider will be back in one or two minutes, sir. I won't lock the door." The lad looked hesitantly at the key in the door.

"Thank you, young man."

Bing-Wallace watched the boy scurry off down the narrow stairs. He then walked into the clerk's office, hurriedly took off his coat and hat, and hung them up with his umbrella on a dark wood hatstand. He arranged the chair in the clerk's office so that he could quickly dart out of Strider's office if he heard someone coming up the stairs.

"This could not be more propitious," he said aloud. He went to Strider's office door and found it unlocked. "Good gracious – very opportune."

The office was tidy, except there were some empty file drawers open that Bing-Wallace closed. He suddenly thought of fingerprints and took out his hanky and wiped the front of the drawer, and drew them out again gently. Trespassing and snooping in a lawyer's office now, Bing-Wallace, he thought. How exciting! There was nothing in Strider's office he could see that related to his quest. Bing-Wallace went back into the clerk's room and sat down at one of the two desks in the cramped room. He looked around for an address book or client list, or anything about Baron Ferdi or Freya Saumures. A cursory rummage in the drawers found nothing of significance. The in tray had a few sheets of paper about property, and stocks and shares advice from a stockbroker, addressed to Strider. The papers were in a bit of a mess, and Bing-Wallace neatened them up, then wondered if it was wise to tidy. The drawers of both desks were unlocked but empty. Well, for heaven's sake, no wonder he felt safe to dash out to King's Bench Walk; the place had no interesting files, he thought.

Then Bing-Wallace saw a correspondence file with letters written waiting for signature. They were all bills for various legal work that had been done: advice, conveyancing, nothing startling. The client file read: "Baron Olivier Ferdinand Saumures, Burton Park Place, Duncton, Petworth, West Sussex: advice for planning required for Burton Park Farm, thirty-nine guineas".

The phone on the desk suddenly rang. It was incredibly loud and made Bing-Wallace jump – so much so, he threw the correspondence file up in the air. Pieces of paper went everywhere.

"Bugger!" he gasped with his hand over his heart. The phone rang twice and then went silent. Bing-Wallace gathered the documents that had landed on the floor and saw another invoice, for services rendered to Sir Jason Barrett MP, Alston House, Wimbledon. Bing-Wallace started to write down the address but as soon as he put the pen to his notepad, he heard someone coming up the stairs. He slammed the drawers shut, regretting the noise, and rapidly put back the correspondence file. He hoped he had not disturbed anything to make the clerk suspicious. He dashed out from behind the desk and managed to sit in the chair he'd prepared for this emergency. He just succeeded in composing himself to look as innocent as possible when there was a slight tap on the glass panel and the door opened.

The head of Alec Ballentine popped around the door.

"Philip! Fancy seeing you here." He was grinning as he must have gathered Bing-Wallace was ruffled and feeling very guilty.

"For Christ's sake, Ballentine, you gave me a fright." The nervous adenoids were kicking in again.

"What were you doing, and where is everybody? Did you break in?" Alec stood in the clerk's office, his large body making it feel even smaller.

"No, the clerk let me in. But I found something quite interesting. Strider not only represents the baron, but also Sir Jason Barrett MP."

"Who the bloody hell are you two?" thundered a voice with a slight accent from behind Alec. Alec whirled round in surprise to see a bald man with thick black-rimmed spectacles. "Come on! Who are you?" he shouted again.

"My name is Philip Bing-Wallace. I am the theatre critic for the London *Times,* and this is my colleague Alec Ballentine."

"How did you get in?"

"Your clerk let me in."

"My clerk?" Strider turned around and spoke to someone outside the office. "Did you let these men into the office, Baker?"

"No, sir," answered Baker, who had an older, refined voice and no West Country accent. Bing-Wallace looked around the door at Baker.

"No, your other clerk."

"My *other* clerk?" Strider said in alarm. "I don't have another clerk. Get out of my way!" Strider pushed past Alec and Bing-Wallace and looked at the desk.

"Oh, good God, we have been burgled. Baker, call the police. You two will come into my office." He took a key from his waistcoat pocket and went to unlock the office door, but he found it unlocked already. It was a much larger room, with bookshelves covering nearly every wall. The desk was uncluttered and tidy, as was the rest of the office.

Strider gasped at the open file drawers and slammed them shut. His cheeks red with vehemence, Strider pointed a bony forefinger at two chairs in front of the desk, indicating for Bing-Wallace and Alec to sit, his temper plainly rendering him speechless.

"What do you want with Sir Jason Barrett?" Strider's little black pinprick eyes glared angrily through the thick lenses of his spectacles at Bing-Wallace and Alec. Both sat hurriedly as though they were naughty schoolboys in front of the headmaster.

"I really don't know what you are talking about, sir," Bing-Wallace blustered belligerently, approaching indignity.

"Come, come, I heard you talking to your colleague about finding Sir Jason Barrett. Do not lie to me or you will be arrested and charged for breaking and entering. Now, what do you want with Sir Jason?" Alec put his hand on Bing-Wallace's skinny arm and squeezed it to stop him from talking.

"We are trying to trace the whereabouts of Father Joe Dent."

Strider gaped and sat heavily in his chair.

"Father Dent? I do not know him, and I do not represent him," Strider said less heatedly, his eyes cast down at his desk rather than at the journalists. "You are not the police and you are not a legal officer, are you?" He was beginning to look nervous.

"No, Mr Strider, but I am a witness to the alleged killing of Baron Ferdinand Saumures by Father Dent. And the police would like to talk to him." Strider remained silent and eyed Alec, shocked, his mouth opening and shutting, undecided what to say.

He then said, "As I say, Father Dent is not one of my clients." He frowned at Alec. "Did you see Father Dent kill this man? How do you know the victim is called Baron Saumures?"

"What do you mean, you are not Father Dent's lawyer?" Bing-Wallace chirped in.

"Just that. I have never heard of the man." He was plainly lying; he was blinking rapidly and his tone had changed, slightly defensive now. Bing-Wallace's and Alec's eyes met, incredulous brows furrowed. "Who told you that I was representing this person?" Strider demanded.

Bing-Wallace said, "I was told by a friend of mine in the Law Society."

"And I was told by the police at Battersea police station, a Sergeant Glass. We were trying to find Father Dent after his release from Battersea police station in the early hours of this morning. I was told, when I went to interview him, that a solicitor had been called and had got him released to a Special Branch superintendent. Would you know who that superintendent would be?"

"Certainly not!" said Strider unconvincingly. "Anyway, it was not me. I do not do criminal law – my firm only deals with private clients and their estates in Great Britain and Europe. My conclusion is that a person posing as me presented adequate credentials and, along with this young special policeman, put up a good argument and posted a suitable bail."

"We did not say he was young," Alec said. "Is he a young man? We've never met him, you see."

"Good heavens, Alec, what is going on?" Bing-Wallace sat back in his chair, shaking his head. "Mr Strider, where do you think Father Dent is?"

"I don't know the man. Have you tried where he lives?" Strider was searching his office and desk whilst talking.

"Father Dent is not at his apartment, sir. How do you know the superintendent is young?" Alec asked again.

"I don't know!" Strider blustered. "I presumed. When did you last try to see Dent?"

"Last night."

"I can't help you, then. Anyway …" Strider put the palms of his hands on the desk and, now composed, leant over to scowl at the two journalists with his sharp little eyes; he was extremely angry and plainly trying to control his emotions. "What has happened to all my client files?" he asked, as though he was addressing a witness in court.

"No idea," Bing-Wallace and Alec said in unison, leaning back in their chairs, trying to distance themselves from the angry solicitor.

"Baker!" shouted Strider to his clerk.

The spindly clerk in half-moon glasses shuffled in and said, in a distressed voice, "May I have a word in private, Mr Strider?" Strider marched out of the office with Baker.

"Alec, we are going to have to somehow get out of here. Is he calling the police to clap us in irons or is it just to report a break-in?"

"It seems not to be a break-in. It looks like someone else had the keys. All his files on – I think – Sir Jason Barrett have been lifted. Is that *the* Sir Jason Barrett, do you think?"

"When I came into this office, there were a few drawers open that were completely empty. Should I tell Mr Strider?"

"Did you say all the drawers were empty?"

"Some … those drawers there, the ones he slammed closed." Bing-Wallace indicated a wooden four-drawer file cabinet. "They were open and empty, and I think the one next to it was pretty empty too. Come to think of it, there was a little handcart full of files at the bottom of the stairs."

"So, it can't be just one client, Philip. I mean, how many files on one person does a solicitor gather?"

"Will Strider give us any more information, or should we fend off as soon as we can decently extricate ourselves?" said Bing-Wallace, unable to grasp what Strider had in mind.

"Christ, I don't know—"

Strider came back into the office. He sat behind his desk, linked his fingers and spoke quietly. "Can you describe this second clerk you saw for me?"

"Only one of us saw him – he had gone by the time Ballentine here arrived." There was a pause, and Strider looked at Bing-Wallace, annoyed.

"What language are you speaking? Have you a speech problem?" Strider asked bluntly.

"No." Bing-Wallace was a little hurt. "But I have a bit of a cold."

"I see, a cold." Strider sighed impatiently. "The clerk?"

"Yes, of course." Bing-Wallace got the point and spoke carefully. "He was sort of ginger, a pointy-faced youth with spots. Thin, tallish, sounded like he came from Bristol or Cordwall … Cornwall … West Country anyway," Bing-Wallace enunciated slowly. There was another pause whilst Strider squinted at each of the journalists opposite him.

"I would like your details for the police who are about to arrive. I will not detain you as I would rather we did not discuss the missing files with them. If I see a hint of this in a newspaper, however, I will descend upon you like the wrath of God and his angels. I can very easily put a case of breaking and entering together and theft of confidential material, jeopardising the security of the nation – *exempli gratia*, treason."

"Could you?" Bing-Wallace was astonished and quite horrified.

"Do I make myself clear, gentlemen?" Strider said.

"Yes, sir," they said in unison. "Goodbye, sir." The journalists handed over their visiting cards and left. Bing-Wallace collected his coat and hat. They both darted down the narrow winding staircase and out into Middle Temple Lane. Two men, unmistakeably police detectives, were marching down the cobbled lane from Fleet Street in military step. They were both dressed in trilby hats and dark-blue suits under unbuttoned fawn raincoats. Alec and Philip turned the opposite way and hastened downhill, left into Crown Office Row, and into King's Bench Walk.

8

"Christ, I feel like a naughty schoolboy again," said Alec as they walked into King's Bench Walk. "We have just had a dressing-down by the headmaster. Strider could easily be a man handy with a cane."

"That man Strider is a crook," said Bing-Wallace. "His utterances are like the product of a performance of Joseph Pujol ... Le Pétomane!"

"Who is Joseph Pujol?"

"He is a well-known French flatulist performer."

"What?"

"A fartist, dear boy, a performer of farts." Bing-Wallace began to giggle, as did Alec. "Isn't this fun! Much better than going to review *The Clemency of Titus*!"

"The who?"

"*The Clemency of Titus* – Mozart, you know. One of his last. Quite agreeable, really, but not a *Magic Flute*."

"Is that what you were meant to be doing today?"

"Well ... yes, I suppose so."

"Philip, I hope this has not taken you away from more important stuff."

"Don't be too silly, Alec, I would not miss this for the world. I am dying to meet the baroness in person."

Alec's thoughts turned from the mysterious baroness to Sir Jason. "Philip, what has Sir Jason Barrett – an MP – have to do with things? I've just been reading about him at the library."

"He's Charlotte de Tournet's other uncle. Her mother's older brother," said Bing-Wallace.

"And owner of the *Sentinel* newspaper, ex-diplomat, et cetera, et cetera?" Alec said, surprised.

"The very same."

"Heck, Philip, you are a font of … Anyway" – Alec stopped walking – "I found a little more in the newspaper library."

"Oh yes, do tell."

"It appears that de Tournet's steel company, DTS, was amalgamated just after the war with a German steel company. They are still going strong. Don't know about Mrs de Tournet, Charlotte's aunt."

"Charlotte's aunt!" Bing-Wallace exclaimed. "A good title for a play, don't you think? I can see it now." His hands swept towards an imaginary billboard. "'*Charlotte's Aunt* – a tale of love, lust and a murdering vicar' – it'll be a sell-out!"

The journalists, still laughing, arrived at the back entrance to El Vino, walked straight into the Smoking Room and sat down at Bing-Wallace's table.

Alec said, "As to the Barrett family, we never really got much out of Strider about them."

"We didn't get much about anybody, really. Except, he didn't ask us anything more about what we were saying about Sir Jason, did he?"

The Smoking Room was dark and devoid of customers. "What's going on?" Bing-Wallace was alarmed.

"They haven't quite opened yet. Couple more minutes," Alec assured him.

"I will wave madly – like an Italian – when it is time for a drink. The waiters are very good to me."

"Why, Philip?"

Bing-Wallace looked proud of himself. "I've a bit of a reputation for tearing strips off the waiters if the service is slack. I'm legendary, you know. My admonishments are even sometimes written down and published in the comment pages." He looked around to make sure he was not overheard. "I once reduced a waiter to tears for spilling a whole glass of my champagne."

"I remember that. You left him a huge tip because he poured it onto your lap when you set fire to your crotch with a cigar!"

Bing-Wallace looked embarrassed. "Oh … that was it … yes. I got another waiter to resign and join the Royal Navy – as recommended by me – so he would be as far away from El Vino (and me) as possible. I even paid him a month's wages. Mr Bower was not at all happy. And then there was the time I was thought to have died after it was reported I was involved in an accident whilst riding my pushbike – I don't drive, as you know."

"I didn't know you rode a bicycle."

"I don't *now*! When the young waiters heard of my supposed demise, they held an impromptu party in the Smoking Room, before Mr Bower came down from his office upstairs. As they celebrated with lemonade and a small cake, I entered as usual, at my customary hour. The waiters were stunned and pretty shocked to see the apparition of Mr Bing-Wallace." He threw his arm up as though a stage entrance. "I strode to my table in the Smoking Room. I looked like a maharaja, you know, with a large white dramatic bandage about my head, and both my hands were strapped up. 'What is this party for?' I asked. 'It's for you, Mr Bing-Wallace, sir,' a quick-thinking waiter said, 'to celebrate your survival of the accident, sir.' The waiter thought he would then elaborate, unwisely, with 'You're a legend, Mr Bing-Wallace'. 'Well,' I said, taking a stance not unlike the Duke of Wellington, 'to quote … somebody … that makes one a legend in one's own lunchtime, doesn't it!'"

"That explains it." Alec chuckled.

"I am pleased to report the whole incident was reported in the *Daily Mail* and in *The Times* the following day."

Alec brought the conversation back down to earth. "Sir Jason Barrett, I have just read, was, as you know, a senior British diplomat at the beginning of the war. He decided to give up the service, it seems, under a cloud of some kind. I can't find out what or why. He is now the proud owner of that newspaper to the businessman, *The Sentinel*, as you said. I forgot he's an MP as well."

"He's been an MP for quite a long time, but he has only recently been made a junior minister, when Mr Churchill got back into Number Ten again. He's a junior Home Office minister, I believe."

"And he is the owner of a newspaper? Is that allowed?"

"A very boring journal in my view." Bing-Wallace sighed. "A newspaper for insomniacs; you start reading it and you will drop off to sleep with dreariness."

"And" – Alec put his forefinger up to make a point – "on top of all that, he is uncle to Charlotte de Tournet, or Baroness Freya Saumures, if we are to believe Father Joe."

"Indeed." Bing-Wallace was looking up at the skylight, wrapped in thought. "A shame *The Sentinel* is so tedious, I would love to liven it up." Alec looked at Bing-Wallace, wondering what he was going to come up with next.

"What is this vicar like, Alec? Churchy? A holy God-botherer? What?"

Alec thought for a moment. "He's very grey – you know, sort of pallid, huge grey beard. Not much backbone, blubbed a lot."

"Nothing wrong with a bit of a cry. He had just knifed a man. I would blub."

"S'pose so. And I think he enjoys his drink, by the looks of him."

"Bit of a lush, is he? Aren't most vicars apt to take a tipple too many?" Bing-Wallace remarked. Says the man who has at least a half-bottle of champagne every lunchtime, thought Alec, let alone what he might consume in the evening.

"Yes, but a *vicar*, Philip, getting overemotional. I thought they are meant to be made of stronger stuff: caring, courageous, feet firmly on the ground. He was the opposite. A mess. And selfish. I could not see this man being a vicar. Didn't like him, I'm afraid. I don't know why Sophie had anything to do with him."

"Your ex-fiancée?"

"Yes," Alec sighed.

"What did Sophie do? Nurse or something? Possibly why she was so compassionate."

"No, she is an art historian. Works for the fine arts department of Christopher's of Bond Street." There was a long pause. Bing-Wallace kept looking around, waiting for the bar to open. "Nonetheless," Alec said, trying to get back to the point, "if Sir Jason is the owner of *The Sentinel*, I will trot down there in a minute to see if I can see him."

"Not a hope, dear chap. I think he lives there quite a lot of the time, and never comes out, unless he goes to the House. He's a monk!"

"Well I'm going to have a go. I think I should go down to Sussex tomorrow and see if I can find Burton Park Place."

"What do I do? Twiddle my thumbs whilst you find all the juicy bits of the story?" Bing-Wallace said. The lights started to come on in the bar. "I will wave my hands about – don't be alarmed, I am getting a waiter." A waiter came over on seeing Bing-Wallace's hand gestures.

"Yes, Mr Bing-Wallace?" the waiter said, trying in vain not to sound exasperated.

"Oh – are we open?"

"Nearly, sir."

"Half a bottle of Pommery and an Upmann corona, if you would be so kind."

"Half-bottle Pommery champagne, two glasses, and the cigar. Thank you, sir." The waiter repeated back the order.

"Do you want a cigar, Alec?"

"Oh … well … that would be nice." Alec turned to the waiter. "What would you recommend? Nothing too big."

"Well, sir, most of our clients—"

"My dear chap!" Bing-Wallace exclaimed in disgust at the waiter. "Lawyers and prostitutes have clients! You have *customers* in El Vino's."

"Actually, Philip," Alec said, "on second thoughts, I'd better go and see if I can meet Sir Jason. I'll go on my own tomorrow. What I might do is get you to see him tomorrow if I can't. You are more respectable than I am."

"Thank you, jolly decent and all that." Bing-Wallace accepted the false modesty but, Alec knew, had to agree. Alec, after all, was dressed a little like a tall, scruffy school sports master in his striped blue-and-grey tie, moleskin trousers, and a tatty green sports coat that had leather patches on the elbows. "I'll look forward to hearing from you this evening, Alec. You've got my home telephone number, in Chelsea?" Bing-Wallace then waved at someone. "Caesar, my dear old boy!" he shouted as a huge man with an impressively substantial girth wandered over, proffering his hand. "Do join me. Ballentine is buggering off. Have a glass of Pommery."

"Remember, Philip, this is between us, old chap," Alec hissed as he got up from the table. He was worried Bing-Wallace was about to tell everybody about his exploits of the day.

"Don't worry, Alec, not a body shall I impart our adventures to."

"What adventures, Philip?" said the large man.

"Nothing, Caesar." Bing-Wallace tapped the side of his nose. "Just a story Ballentine and I are cooking up. All lies, of course!" He laughed.

9

Alec walked out into Fleet Street again, took his baker-boy cap out from his pocket, slid it on and buttoned up his brown overcoat. It was getting dark already; the lights in the shops were being switched on. It still had not rained and it was getting a lot cooler. Alec strolled down Fleet Street towards Ludgate Circus. He could see the imposing dome of St Paul's commanding the top of Ludgate Hill. The light-blue railway bridge that ran over the bottom of Ludgate Hill obstructed a view of the front of St Paul's. Cars and lorries were now queuing up and down Fleet Street, trying to get home or conveying their last delivery of the day. Newspaper sellers were crying out the evening news at each major road junction.

Alec turned right into Bouverie Street, a narrow, cobbled street that echoed his every step, then past the *Daily Herald* building, and the *Sentinel* building at the corner of Bouverie Street and Tudor Street. The heavy swing doors led into a large lobby with *The Sentinel* in large black letters set into the cream-and-amber marble on the floor, along with the logo: a clock face set at eight o'clock with the legend "Jonathan's Coffee House 1680" around the edge of the clock.

At the reception desk, Alec asked to see Sir Jason Barrett.

"Do you have an appointment?" asked the receptionist, a substantial middle-aged woman with a tight cloud of blue-rinsed coiffured hair that made her look far older than she probably was.

"No, but I would like him to confirm a story I am writing about his niece, Charlotte Barrett."

"Who? He doesn't have a niece." She seemed a little too knowledgeable, Alec thought.

"Can you tell him Alec Ballentine would like to confirm some new information about his niece, Charlotte de Tournet or Charlotte Barrett?"

"I'll ask his secretary and see what she says. She may have gone home, though. He never sees people without an appointment." She had an affected voice that Alec found comical. She did, though, look slightly flustered, an emotion she was plainly not accustomed to.

The receptionist rolled her chair on little casters over to a wall of switches, plugs and wires. She put on some headphones and flicked a few switches.

Alec looked around the lobby. There was an elderly gentleman in a black commissionaire's uniform who gave Alec a smile and a gentle salute when Alec went over to the floor plan to see where he would find Sir Jason.

"He will see you, sir," the receptionist called over the glass barrier that separated her from the public. There was an element of surprise in her voice. "Take the lift to the top floor and Mr Alderson will meet you."

"Thank you." Alec was also somewhat surprised. He was used to powerful men turning him away when he asked for an interview. The technique of asking them to confirm an embarrassing story usually worked, but not always. Really powerful men, the ones who flirted with the underworld, could be a little dangerous if they didn't want a story to be told in the newspapers; they would stop at nothing to prevent it, including maiming or even murdering. Alec's journalistic sixth sense felt that Sir Jason Barrett MP could be one of those – a powerful man who came under the maiming and murdering category.

He went to the lifts. The commissionaire had pressed the Up button and again gave Alec a little salute. The man smelt of tea, and his false teeth rattled as he smiled at Alec.

He tried to smarten himself up and took off his hat. He'd been totally prepared to be told he could not see Sir Jason, so he was not quite ready for this meeting. All the way up to the fifth floor he straightened his tie and brushed down his crumpled brown coat. He decided it was too scruffy, so took it off and folded it over his arm, leaving his patched green sports jacket on show.

Whilst tucking in his shirt and checking his tie for the third time, he thought of how he was going to phrase his questions. He had to be delicate, not anger Sir Jason or alarm him, and yet he had to get the story. And there were a few mysteries to clear up: Father Joe, Baron Saumures, Baroness Freya Saumures and Charlotte de Tournet; what happened at Nineteen Avenue Foch, who owns it and what is it now? Christ, Alec thought to himself, I am going to be here all night. Will he answer these questions, or will he just have me shot?

The lift doors opened and a neat young man in a shiny black three-piece suit, made of one of those new materials that Alec hated, stood before him with his hands behind his back and a polite smile.

"Mr Ballentine? My name is Alderson, Sir Jason's colleague. He's expecting you. This way, please."

They came to a pair of heavy oak doors set in a wide Tudor arch, and after Alderson gave a brief knock, they went through.

Sir Jason was a graceful-looking, tall and erect man, with white-grey hair slicked down to a shine with pomade. If you wanted the definition of old and distinguished, Alec thought, this is he. He stood as Alec entered. Sir Jason Barrett was in his fifties, possibly sixties, Alec calculated. The huge office was lit by two twelve-armed chandeliers and the residue of evening light coming through a vast twenty-foot-wide by ten-foot-high window. Panoramic views could be seen of St Paul's in the distance, round to Blackfriars Bridge and the Thames. Alec's steps on the stone floor echoed around the high ceiling as he walked across to Sir Jason. Vincent Price and Charles Foster Kane would be right at home in this office, Alec thought.

"Good afternoon, Mr Ballentine," said Sir Jason in a low, pleasant voice. He sounded tired. He came around from behind his beautiful oak leather-topped desk. He wore a tailored black single-breasted jacket with a fawn waistcoat. A fine platinum – it would not be silver – fob chain draped from his waistcoat pockets, and his striped trousers had a sharp crease in them. He walked with no stoop but slowly. He proffered his hand to be shaken by Alec. It was cold and bony. He indicated they should sit in the four sumptuous brown leather armchairs, set on a dark-red and gold-yellow Persian rug. The chairs were placed either side of a wide walnut coffee table in front of an open fireplace where a fire burned with a rigorous flame.

"Lovely pictures, Sir Jason," Alec said, spotting four large landscape oils on the walls of the office.

"Do you enjoy art, Mr Ballentine?" Sir Jason asked.

"I don't know much about art, I'm afraid, but I am sure these are very fine. I had a friend who was more of an expert." Alec thought of Sophie.

"Please sit down, Mr Ballentine." Sir Jason indicated one of the leather chairs and lowered himself gently into a chair opposite Alec. He kept his right leg straight as though the knee did not bend. Alderson slipped into the chair beside Sir Jason. He looked pensive, until he met Alec's eye and smiled ingenuously.

"Drink? John, if you would be so kind." The neat man in the black suit stood to get the drinks tray. Alec wondered who Alderson was. He couldn't be Sir Jason's secretary as the receptionist had said they were a woman. Manservant? Bodyguard, maybe? No, too thin, and he looked too clever to be either.

As whiskies were poured into wide cut-glass tumblers and soda offered, Sir Jason said, "You are enquiring about my late niece, Charlotte Barrett."

"You believe her to be dead, Sir Jason?"

"She went missing in August 1940 and we have not heard from her since. We believe she was taken to a prison camp in Poland in 1944 just before Paris was retaken, where she was killed by the Nazis." Sir Jason talked quietly and calmly. "What is this new information you have, Mr Ballentine?"

Alec took a sip of his whisky and soda, and seeing a heavy ashtray was placed on the coffee table before him, he lit a cigarette, blew out the smoke, considering how to ask the all-important questions.

"Have you heard of a person called Freya Saumures?"

"Possibly."

"Or Father Joe Dent?"

"Again, possibly." He looked up at Alderson as though conveying his impatience or irritation of this journalist.

He looked angry and was about to comment when Alec asked, "Or Baron Ferdinand Saumures?"

Sir Jason shifted uncomfortably in his seat. He turned to look at Alderson again, sitting silently beside him. "John, I would be grateful if I could be left alone with Mr Ballentine." Alderson stood and bowed slightly, his expression indicating no surprise or dissent, and quietly left the room after a tilt of the head of farewell to Alec.

The old man paused, stared at the fire for a minute and then said, in the same quiet, steady voice, "A woman, who I am told claimed to be my niece, was accused of being a Nazi collaborator. I offered information to the contrary. That is as far as I can go on that matter," he stressed with the widening of his eyes at Alec. "Baron Saumures was an operative in the British Secret Service during the war. He was part of a special unit of the SIS, the Special Intelligence Service. I did not know him; I only knew of him in my capacity as one of the operations directors in MI6 during the last war, as I am sure you know."

"Do you know where the baron is now?"

"I have not heard about Sir Ferdinand since 1942. I believe he was working covertly in a Paris gallery when last I heard. As far as I know, he is now married and lives in Sussex. They are part of the aristocracy set that I and my paper are not very interested in. He was, I gather, a very good artist."

"He *was* a very good artist?"

"He's a very talented portrait painter. You still have not answered my question, Mr Ballentine. I have answered quite a lot of yours. What is this new information you have?"

"Sir Jason, a vicar in Battersea – where I live – came to me last night claiming he had killed a man in his church. After going with him to the church, and seeing the body of a man, the vicar claimed that the man was Baron Ferdinand Saumures ." Sir Jason sat passively in the armchair, his eyes disconcertingly unblinking, his right forefinger tapping impatiently against his left-hand knuckle. Alec gave a nervous cough and straightened himself up. "He then said he was being blackmailed by the man he alleged to have killed."

"How did the vicar claim he killed the man?"

"By mistake, he says. I concur, by the way. It looked like the man came at Father Dent with a knife or a dagger. Father Dent tripped on his cassock and dragged his assailant down on top of him, and the dagger went into the assailant's neck. Father Dent pulled himself from under the man and managed to cover his cassock in blood. He then came up to my flat."

"Why did the vicar come to you?"

"He was looking for my former fiancée who was living at my flat whilst I was away on assignment."

There was a pause as the old man looked at Alec in a way Alec could not read. There was no emotion; he did not seem to be expecting Alec to say anything. He sat with his hands cupped together resting on his upper lip; only his steel-grey eyes with yellowing whites could be seen, observing Alec. "And how did my niece's name come up from this?"

"Father Dent – the vicar – claimed that the man, Ferdinand Saumures, and his wife, Freya – the baron and baroness – were blackmailing him. He was, however, reticent to say Freya was involved in the blackmail."

"And?" Sir Jason asked, now starting to lose his patience.

"And …" Alec decided he should stand at this point, for no apparent reason. "Father Dent claims that Freya is your niece, Charlotte de Tournet."

Sir Jason stood up stiffly, his face impassive.

"I have correspondence and some proof that my niece was killed in Poland, and therefore this person cannot possibly be Charlotte Barrett. Do you propose to write a story with these" – he paused to find the right phrase – "unsubstantiated claims about my niece, or Baron Saumures and this woman Baroness Freya Saumures?"

"No, Sir Jason, I don't think we can with the facts as they stand … at the moment. However, there is the evidence from the trial of the baroness."

"What of it? I don't think there is much more to say at this stage." He put out his hand for Alec to shake. They shook hands, but Sir Jason did not release Alec's hand; instead, he tightened his grip. Alec looked into his eyes. He could see the shape of Sir Jason's skull under his skin, dappled with age spots. Sir Jason said in a steady and exacting low voice, "I would be grateful if you could keep me informed of your research at all times. I would also be grateful if you could direct me to where the body of Saumures is being held; I would like to pay my last respects to a brave man. Further, I would use caution about using Saumures's name in any story. You may find yourself – how can I put this without being melodramatic? – in a great deal of trouble with certain governmental departments. Good afternoon, Mr Ballentine."

"But at the trial and acquittal of Baroness Freya Saumures, you were the person who said she was a collaborator."

"According to whom, Mr Ballentine? Philip Bing-Wallace? He is not exactly a reliable source and, frankly, should stick to being an arts critic. The War Crimes Commission made the accusation, not I."

Sir Jason released Alec's hand and walked over to the door and opened it for him. Alec was desperately trying to think if there was anything else he should ask about, but he was too shocked.

"Good day, Mr Ballentine," Sir Jason said more forcefully, seeing Alec hesitate.

"Thank you for seeing me, sir. If I hear anything more, I will be in contact with you for comment. There is nothing more you can tell me about the victim, Baron Ferdinand Saumures?"

"No. I regret not," Sir Jason mumbled. As Alec ambled through the heavy oak door to leave, Sir Jason closed the door behind him so that he had to speed up to avoid it colliding with his back.

Bloody hell! thought Alec. That was a definite hint for him to find out more about Ferdinand Saumures. Who was this man? He must have been something for Jason Barrett to know him.

10

"Bing-Wallace, I'm calling with news." Alec was home in his apartment with a whisky and a cigarette. Benjy the cat rubbed against Alec's leg to get attention – he wanted some food. "I managed to see Sir Jason."

"Bloody good show, Ballentine. What did he say?"

"Not a lot. Only that he is convinced Charlotte de Tournet is dead. I need to find someone who was in the British Secret Service during the war."

"Why on earth … good God, Alec, I would have thought the one person who would know anybody in the secret squirrel stuff would be you! All your army-fying and being a war correspondent. But why?"

"I just wondered if you knew someone – not an actual spy."

"But why?"

"Well, apparently, it looks like our friend Baron Ferdinand Saumures was in MI5 or MI6 and was a spy during the war."

"The baron?" Bing-Wallace sounded incredulous.

"Yup!"

"That may explain why Freya Saumures got off at her treason trial," Bing-Wallace said quietly. "He turned out to be a dark horse. And possibly why Father Dent got released. It's all hush-hush stuff."

"How would they know so quickly that Dent had killed someone, let alone *who* he had killed?"

"They know everything." Bing-Wallace put on a dramatic, conspiratorial voice. "The police would have informed someone, I should think."

"But, Philip, do you know anybody else who knows about the secret service? A journalist rather than an operative – if you see what I mean?"

"There was quite a lot of secret stuff going on during the war." Bing-Wallace paused. "What about Jeremy Tillett – wasn't he something cloak-and-dagger?"

"Do I know him?" Alec asked.

"Yes, he's the crime correspondent for *The Express*, bad hips, walks as though he is trying to suppress a fart." Alec chuckled and thought of the tall barrel-chested man who came into El Vino every now and then. He wore huge bushy sideburns and talked like a Guards regimental sergeant major, loud and precise.

"He will smell a story and start interfering, won't he?" Alec cautioned.

"'S'pose," Bing-Wallace said. "Didn't you do a piece, a long time ago, on the secret service during the war?"

"Yes, with Sir Sussex Tremayne. He sadly died earlier this year."

"Wasn't he SIS? He must have had a number two, surely?"

"Yes, he did, but I never met him. I could look him up." But then Alec thought of Captain Dan James. He had not seen him for ten years, since that last meeting with Sir Sussex Tremayne.

"I do have an old friend who was in the SBS, he may know something."

"What would someone in the Special Boat Services know? They took their orders from these intelligence people."

"This chap was also MI6," Alec said. "I will call him when I get back tomorrow."

"Where are you off to tomorrow?" Bing-Wallace asked.

"I told you. I'm going to find Burton Park Place."

"Well, that's great," Bing-Wallace puffed. "I get all the boring jobs!"

"Do you drive, Philip? Do you have a car?" Alec said, knowing the answer would be no to both questions.

"Oh, very well – you win! I will dig up stuff on Sir Jason. I am sure he is more than involved. Keep me informed about the baroness."

"I will, Philip, I will." Alec was relieved as he dearly wanted to do this alone. Bing-Wallace could be a little thoughtless.

*

The following morning, Alec searched the newspapers for any reference to the death of Baron Ferdinand Saumures. There was no mention anywhere, which was a relief as well as surprising. He thought Bing-Wallace might have sneaked in something, but he had, after all, honoured their agreement about keeping it quiet until Alec could get more from his visit to Sussex. Not even *The Sentinel* had anything. But then the lacklustre *Sentinel* wouldn't have anything exciting or gory like that.

*

It was a bright, mellow morning, and the trunk road to the south coast seemed quite busy coming into London, but was virtually clear the way the Jaguar was heading. Alec found the drive uneventful and glorious; the roof was down, the wind was cool but not cold. The North Downs and Box Hill looked lush and green, and the remaining leaves on the trees were turning from amber to shades of gold to deep maroon.

As Alec turned off onto the Petworth Road, the tarmac was wet with dew and the sun glistened and sparkled off the surface of the road. The smell of fresh, watery grass filled Alec's senses as he took in the lovely fragrances of the countryside. He was away from the fumes of car exhausts, sewage smells, chimney smoke and smog that pervaded in and around London. In Sussex, there were villages of flint and brick houses, clustered around little ponds. He loved driving through the downland areas, the peace and the beauty of the hills covered in old deciduous woods, and acre upon acre of rolling green pastures looking as smooth as a billiard table. Bent willow hedges, plaited by skilled craftsmen, surrounded the fields and lined the roads.

Petworth, a historic town, with Petworth House proudly perched on the top, was sleepy and not at all busy. Alec weaved through the narrow cobbled streets, out the other side, and on towards the South Downs.

As he passed the little village of Duncton, just before the road rose up the side of the Downs the map showed a turning to the right. And there it was, a narrow road with grass growing in the centre of the metalled lane. It meandered along, following the base of the Downs. Alec was going slowly so that he did not go past the entrance to Burton Park Place. There were high willow and hazel hedges either side of the road and it was virtually impossible to see the countryside apart from a glimpse every now and then.

Suddenly a horse and cart with bales of straw piled high appeared before the Jaguar. Alec braked hard. An angry-looking farmhand in leather boots and high leather puttees glared at Alec from under his oil-cloth hat, puffing at a pipe that had virtually no stem.

"What du're wan – you." He barked at Alec.

"To get past!" Alec yelled back over the windscreen.

"Back 'are'n' then – you." The farmer batted the back of his hand, indicating for Alec to back into a gateway to let him pass.

In Sussex, the country folk had this strange way of putting "you" at the end of a sentence, an affectation some Sussex people – like the old cart driver – put on as heavily as possible to people they regarded as London folk. Alec, however, was born in Chichester, the county town of West Sussex, so was used to the accent, no matter how put on it was.

Alec backed the Jaguar into a gateway fifteen yards back and waited for the horse and the heavy cart to pass. As the old farmhand passed, he shouted down to Alec, "There's a tracker as well!" and jerked his thumb over his shoulder. Alec was going to ask the old man about Burton Park Place, but he was gone.

The "tracker", or tractor, was following up behind with another trailer stacked high with straw bales. A young lad was driving and as he drew level to Alec, he yelled, "Nice Jag!" with an admiring smile, clearly delighted to see such a car.

"Do you know where Burton Park Place is?"

"Just round the corner," he said, still gazing at the sleek, sporty Jaguar. "Can't miss it – you." Alec thanked the lad and as the way became clear, he gunned the engine so the lad could hear the powerful motor, and shot off down the lane.

Sure enough, just around the next bend, the thick hedge turned into a long, tall wall with panels of flint framed in red brick, and then a wide entrance with two tall brick and flint gateposts and two large black iron gates that were thankfully open. Alec turned into the drive. Before him was a tarmac narrow road, recently laid. To the right of the drive was a grass bank gradually sloping down to a wide meadow with an avenue of poplar trees down the centre. To the left was a wooded copse bordered by black iron estate fencing that followed the long drive as it swept along, slightly curving to the right, for about a quarter of a mile.

As Alec drove around the extensive drive, a magnificent and enormous red-brick Queen Anne house gradually came into view from behind the avenue of poplars. Wooded hills surrounded the area behind the house, framing it with autumn colours of russet, evergreen and gold. As he approached the house, he drove through a second set of tall ornate iron gates and crunched onto a large gravel area with a white stone island and an Italian fountain in the centre, which was not gushing out water. He parked and got out, looking up at the splendid three-storey elevation of the front of the house. He approached the shiny black double doors enhanced by a classical white portico.

He was grateful that he had thought to put on his best dark-blue suit – he'd left his tatty brown overcoat in the car but kept his new black homburg on. He made a mental note to buy a new overcoat – a decent one. Alec was not a vain man, but he felt that he should invest more in his appearance, considering the type of story he had lately landed.

Alec was expecting a butler to appear at the front door at any second, and if he had been in his usual old schoolteacher's outfit, he would have been shown either the way out or, at best, the tradesman's entrance.

He pulled the brass bell pull and heard a distant chime somewhere inside the house. The glass panels in the doors showed no movement, light or life for at least two very long minutes. As he reached for the bell pull again, he saw a dumpy elderly lady with a white day cap and a white apron over a dark-blue dress. She looked like a hospital matron except she held a duster in her yellow rubber-gloved hand. She looked flustered when she saw Alec smiling as charmingly as he could at her through the glass panel in the front door. She turned and looked about to see if there was someone else that could deal with him. She eventually opened one of the double doors slightly and poked her head out.

"Yes, sir, can I help you?" she asked. Alec could see she held a large square silver tray in her other hand.

"Good morning, madam. Yes, may I please talk to the lady of the house?"

"What do you want?" She had a Scandinavian accent.

"I write for *Country Style* magazine, and we would like to feature—"

"Thank you, Christina, I can deal with this," a voice boomed from behind the lady, and a man, the archetypal butler, appeared at the door. He was quite young, and thin except for a small belly paunch, which was putting a strain on the buttons of his black waistcoat. He opened the doors fully and stood firmly in the centre of the opening. "May I help you, sir?" This might be a little harder, thought Alec, and decided to go the direct route again.

"I would like to talk to Baroness Freya Saumures, please."

"Do you have an appointment?" Here we go, thought Alec, the usual brush-off. He decided to get straight to the point, as he had with Sir Jason.

"I am researching an article I am writing about the war in Paris. I would like a word with the baroness to ask her if she had known a Charlotte Barrett or de Tournet."

Alec heard a long intake of breath and then the crash of a metal tray onto the floor from somewhere behind the butler. "I also have some important news to impart regarding the baron."

"Who do you represent, may I ask, sir?" He said "sir" somewhat acerbically.

"My name is Alec Ballentine, and I am the war correspondent for *The Telegraph*." Alec was trying to sound as important as possible.

The butler's expression gave nothing away – he was, however, stumped for words; his mouth hung slightly open. He then said, "There is no one of that name here. Good day." He slammed the door and strode off, leaving the old woman standing in the middle of the hallway. She saw Alec looking at her, picked up her silver tray from the floor and scurried off after the butler. Alec had no time to protest or try another angle.

He rang the bell again and waited, but there was no movement at all. Alec looked through the glass door panel and could see a wide hall with a polished wood floor. A tall, flowerless vase of blue glass sat on a round table, and above that hung a massive lantern-style light that was unlit. The light came from the windows either side of the portico.

Alec strolled back to the car, muttering aloud about "bloody stuck-up butlers" and "who do they think they are?" He looked up at the windows, hoping, as they do in films, to see a curtain twitch or a face suddenly disappear. Instead, the front door opened. The butler reappeared and strutted up to Alec. Alec thought the butler was going to hit him. He had not noticed a big black car come charging up the drive until it slewed to a halt beside him. He stood in slight alarm as two large men in cheap blue suits got out of the car. Both had military haircuts and were heavily built, and both looked exactly the same: twins.

"Thank you, gentlemen," the butler shouted at them. "I have sorted out this gentleman; he is wanted in the house. However, could you keep close by, in case we need you? He's a journalist."

"Can you tell me what this is all about?" Alec said angrily to the butler, grinding his teeth and squaring up to him. He did not like being threatened, especially by an arrogant lackey feeling secure now that he had two thugs behind him.

The butler wagged a finger at Alec to follow him back into the house. Alec was about to say something when the butler said, "Please do not speak." Alec was taken aback.

Alec followed the prancing figure, trying not to lose his temper and ruin his chances of an interview.

In the dark hall, Alec was shown a seat to one side of a large oak door.

"I will call you when Lady Saumures is available," said the butler.

Hovering in a doorway at the back of the hall was the Scandinavian lady, looking worried. She hissed at the butler to come near, presumably to ask about Alec.

Ten minutes passed in the silent hall. Alec could just about hear voices, along with the shutting of doors and the buzz of a bumblebee trapped behind the glass by the front door. He was about to help the bumblebee when the butler appeared and indicated to Alec to follow him with a flick of his forefinger.

"Leave your hat," the butler said abruptly.

From the hall they went through a tall, polished oak door into a sitting room, and through to another, smaller room with a piano, the rooms lit by the windows looking out at the gravel driveway. After going through more doors, they came to a passageway. The butler pointed to a door to their right and said, "Toilet." Alec smiled to himself.

At a large oak door, the butler knocked and they entered a large, dark study – it may have been a small library. Alec was indicated to sit in a high-back leather chair that was placed in front of a desk. The butler waited to see that Alec did as he bade, then left without a word, softly closing the doors behind him.

He looked around the room before him. Behind the desk was a wall of books on deep-ochre-coloured bookshelves. The wood-panelled room smelt of cedar, as though a cigar smoker inhabited it most days. There was also a sweeter, gentler fragrance in the background. The sun had come out strongly and light streamed through the window, dust particles dancing in the shards of light.

"Who exactly are you?" a soft woman's voice said behind him. His mouth went dry and for a split second he had a metallic taste on the sides of his tongue. He stood, turned, and gulped. A vision had appeared from somewhere. Was she real? She was tall, with long, glossy light-gold hair surrounding a perfectly shaped face. The front of her silk white robe was open down to a delightful cleavage where a long silver cross hung. As she walked slowly past Alec to sit at the desk, the robe parted for a fleeting glimpse of her leg. A scent of lily of the valley meandered over him. A hand with long graceful fingers indicated for him to sit again in his chair. She was real!

She was, without doubt, the most beautiful woman Alec had ever seen.

"Well? Who are you and what do you want?" She was stern but not angry. She seemed, Alec detected, slightly curious.

"Would I be addressing Freya – Baroness Saumures?" he managed to ask after a few more seconds gazing at this unfathomably beautiful woman.

"Who are you, I asked, and what do you want?"

"I am sorry. My name is Alec Ballentine. I am a journalist for—"

"I do not like journalists. You have a couple of seconds to tell me why you are here." She picked up the telephone on the desk and was about to dial.

Alec said hurriedly, "Your name came up when I was asked to help a vicar with a predicament. He had an accident and in his distress, he mentioned your name, and that of Charlotte de Tournet." The lady slowly replaced the receiver and stared at Alec with a mix of curiosity and distress in her eyes. Alec could see why Dent called her a goddess – she really was.

"What was the vicar's name?" She was now composed.

"Dent. Father Joe Dent."

She sat in the desk chair, seeming somewhat distressed. "And what was his predicament?"

"It is a little difficult to say." Alec thought that he should just come out with it. "Father Dent was confronted by a man with a knife. As he tried to defend himself, the assailant tripped or something, stumbled onto Father Dent, and the knife, in the assailant's hand, ended up in their neck. The attacker died of his wounds."

"Oh! Why do you want to know who I am?"

Alec thought for a moment. "The vicar or priest mentioned your name, Freya, and then he said that you were also Charlotte de Tournet." She appeared unmoved, her arms folded, her body sitting stiffly on the edge of the chair. "He also mentioned that she, Freya … you … were a goddess." He laughed nervously as he told her what Dent had called her.

At those words she stood up suddenly and whisked around the desk. Alec stood as the woman came up close in front of him. She was surprisingly tall, only three or four inches shorter than Alec. Their eyes met, her wonderful violet-blue eyes wide, her long eyelashes fluttering.

"What did you say?" she asked in a low voice, her eyes drilling into his. He was overwhelmed by her closeness, her sweet breath, her scent, her flawless skin bar a small scar above her right eyebrow. Her face was so close he could have kissed her on her lips. He felt her robe brush up against his leg. "I repeat, Mr Ballentine, what exactly did the vicar call me?"

She's confirmed who she is, thought Alec. "A goddess," he said, "and I quote: he said you were a goddess."

"Do you know who the dead man was?" she asked, now looking nervous, a shake in her voice.

Still transfixed by her eyes, Alec said hesitantly, "The vicar said, I regret to say, it was Baron Ferdinand Saumures—" Before he could finish, the lady's hands shot up to her mouth and stifled a gasp. Her eyes pooled with tears. Alec reached out to support her descent onto the desk in a mild gesture of comfort, the most he considered proper in the circumstances. He searched around the room for some water and could see a decanter of something amber. He rushed over and took off the stopper and smelt – it was brandy.

"Can I give you some brandy, err …" He did not know what to call her.

"My name is Freya Saumures, and yes, I would like a large one." She sat in the desk chair again, her head down, her hair covering her face. "I will just have a few minutes, Mr …"

"Ballentine, but call me Alec."

"I prefer to keep it formal, Mr Ballentine." Alec stood in front of the desk as the lady sat drinking her brandy.

"I am Baroness Freya, wife to Baron Ferdinand Saumures." The baroness swung the desk chair around so she faced the window. All Alec could see was her profile.

"Would you mind if we did not speak for a while?" she asked, her voice cracking.

"Do you want me to go?" offered Alec, instantly regretting the proposal as she could very easily accept. To his surprise, she said, "No, stay and talk to me. I don't talk to many people nowadays." Alec could not imagine why.

"What happened to the priest?" she asked.

"The vicar, Father Dent? He was hauled off to the police station after I called 999."

"So he is in custody?" The light caught her face, and he could see that her cheeks were shiny with tears.

"Well, no, as it happens. He was released by a lawyer called Strider of Middle Temple Lane."

"Really?" she said, swinging round and leaning forward on the desk, an element of anger creeping in.

"I visited his offices and met a clerk who was clearing out files. When Strider arrived, I asked why he had got Father Dent released and he claimed he did not know him. He said that you were his clients – you and the baron. Why would Father Dent want to kill Baron Saumures?"

The baroness inhaled a sharp breath. Alec winced and chastised himself for being too direct.

"I don't know ... not sure," she said. "Who else knows about this, other than you and the police?" She placed the half-drunk glass on the desk. She sounded calm again.

"A colleague, Philip Bing-Wallace."

"Do I know Mr Bing-Wallace? The name seems to ring a bell."

"He did a piece on your abortive trial," Alec said cautiously.

"Oh that. A farce. How do you know the vicar?"

"I don't really. He is just our local vicar. I live in Battersea."

The baroness was quiet, anguish over her face again, the fingers of her right hand delicately resting on her lips.

"What are you going to do with this information?" she asked with a slight tremor.

"Nothing at the moment. All I am doing is trying to clear up a mystery. Father Joe Dent has gone AWOL. The police are looking for him."

"What is AWOL?"

"'Absent without leave'. It's an army expression. Sorry. He has disappeared." The baroness sat in contemplation. Alec gazed upon her whilst she was not looking at him, trying to read her thoughts, looking through the shadows, struggling not to stare, which was difficult.

"But are you writing an article?" she asked eventually, eyes back onto Alec.

"Baroness, the last thing Father Joe said to me before the police put him in jail was to find Freya. To find Freya and protect her – you. When he said that he knew you, and then said that you were also Charlotte, I was naturally curious. He has now disappeared."

After what seemed an age, the baroness stood up, and so did Alec.

"Do sit, Mr Ballentine." He sat and watched the baroness walk slowly around the desk. When she spoke, her voice was hollow and full of sadness.

"Between just you and me, Mr Ballentine, I am Charlotte de Tournet." At last, thought Alec. "I tell you this, Mr Ballentine, but I will deny it if asked by anybody else."

"But why, Baroness?"

"That is my business, no one else's. And because I do not trust journalists and avoid them at all times. We ... I ... have guards around all the time to prevent journalists getting anywhere near us." Alec thought of the two thugs at the front of the house. "The fact that you have brought devastating news is why I am talking to you."

"But your uncle, Sir Jason, owns a newspaper."

She flashed a look of despair at Alec. "Have you met Jason?"

"Yes, yesterday. He says you are dead."

"I am to him. Oh, I wish you had not seen him."

"Why don't you want him to know you are alive?"

"I don't like him." She sighed. "He was, according to my aunt Stella, a bully to my aunt and my mother. He was not at all nice to me when I inherited the house in Avenue Foch, and" – she thought for a while – "I just wanted to disappear. I had always thought him dangerous. That's it." She was emphatic and, Alec thought, losing her temper for some reason. Maybe he was being too intrusive – he needed to hold back a bit.

She pulled out a man's handkerchief from her sleeve. It had a coat of arms in one of the corners. She looked at the coat of arms for thirty seconds then wiped her face.

"I have not seen my uncle since the beginning of the war. I believe he thought Charlotte was dead, but it seems that I have been found after twenty-odd years. However, I also think he was behind the trial." She went quiet.

"You think Sir Jason was behind your arrest?"

"He's a very dark man, my uncle. Did he send you here?" she said, eyeing Alec intently, her eyes narrowing.

"No. As I said, I met him yesterday. I repeat: he said you were dead. But he knew Ferdinand Saumures, said he was part of MI6 during the war."

"Yes," Charlotte said flatly. Alec wondered if she was confirming that the baron was MI6 during the war, or that she knew what Uncle Jason said was true.

Charlotte stared at the reflection of Mr Ballentine's face in the mirror. He was not aware of her fixed gaze. She was trying to work out what to do with this journalist. He was not the nosy type, or unscrupulous, as far as she could judge from such a short acquaintance. Not out for a story whatever happened. He was a handsome man, tall, with good manners. He had looked genuinely concerned when she was distressed. His grey-green eyes were wise, slightly sad spaniel eyes – very attractive, she thought. His hands were large, with long, unmanicured fingers with short nails. His shoulders were broad and so was his chest, which gave an attractive bass-baritone timbre to his voice. He spoke in a cultured accent with no affectations. She liked this man. He seemed trustworthy, intelligent and, above all, kind … a gentleman.

Charlotte had been surrounded by men most of her adult life. Only one attracted her, only one had she fallen in love with – and he turned out to be cruel and broke her heart. But he was dead. She had killed him. He was a Nazi, an SS officer, dashing and charismatic. But Jost Krupp was an evil person.

After the war, she and Ferdi had settled in Sussex. She met all sorts of men – artistic, musical, gushing, and some conceited peacocks. Some men were shy and guarded, mostly politicians; some were minor royalty out for a good time. They all enjoyed Charlotte's company. The women that accompanied some of the men were wary of Charlotte, jealous of her beauty, frightened of the power she could command over their husbands.

However, she had very little experience with the type of man like Alec Ballentine. She'd become weary of her last lover, Cecil Bainbridge – he used her. Mr Ballentine reminded her of Ulrich Fuhrman, the blond secret service man who'd worked for Ferdi at the gallery in Paris during the occupation. Yes, she liked this man, despite him being a journalist and the bearer of awful news.

"I am sorry about the baron," he said.

"Not only is he … *was* he my husband, he was also my friend. Are you sure it is Ferdi?" Charlotte sniffed and choked slightly on the last few words. The knot in her stomach when she first heard the news was not going away. She thought that after all her experience of tragedy, she would be used to devastating news.

"No – I can't say that I am sure it was him."

"Why have I not heard anything from the police?"

"They are waiting for some kind of positive identification, I think."

"Then how do I know he has been killed? You could just have made it up to gain entry."

"I am sorry, that may be true. I have only Father Dent's word that the body was Baron Saumures. You seem to think that I am telling you the truth, though. Why's that?"

"You mentioned my codename during the war: 'Goddess'."

"Do you know Father Joe Dent? Was he part of the secret service?"

"Yes," she sighed hopelessly. "Dent's my father." Ballentine's face turned to shock. "And one of Ferdi's greatest friends. His real name is Franz-Joseph Deller." She lowered her head. "'Delle' or 'Deller' is German for 'Dent'. He's Austrian."

11

Alec found himself speechless … again. That name: where did he know it from? And then the mist parted and his recall was clear – the meeting in 1945 with Commodore Sir Sussex Tremayne. His friend Dan James had travelled back from Spain during the war with a drunk who talked about a mysterious group called WASP. *His* name was Deller. Was this just a coincidence … same name … a common name? Alec felt a flutter of excitement again.

"I am sorry, Mr Ballentine, my life has been a series of deaths, murders, war and sadness. Most of my family have died." She took the handkerchief from her sleeve again and wiped her eyes. She brought her robe together as though she felt the cold.

"I am going to get changed, if you would excuse me." She walked to the study door and looked back at Alec. "Come with me, I want to show you something." Alec followed her out of the study, back through the sitting rooms, into the front hall. She moved so beautifully, Alec thought. Just the merest hint of a sway, the silk robe tight over her body, the heavy waves of her golden hair moving slightly, like ripples on a still pond …

"This a lovely house," Alec said. "It is very …" Every now and then the robe would part to the side as she walked, enticingly revealing a shapely leg, distracting him.

"What?" the baroness asked without looking at him.

"A lot of history," he said weakly. For a journalist he could have been more erudite, imaginative. He averted his eyes for fear she would spot his admiring furtive glances.

She glided over the dark wood floor to the other side of the hall. They went through some double doors into another large, sparsely furnished reception room. Further on, they came to a set of ornate double doors as big as barn doors: chalk-white with dusty light-blue panels and gold mouldings of harps in the centre, bordered by gold and light-blue frames. Huge gold-and-white wooden doorknobs in the shape of a stylised flower were in the centre of each door. Charlotte pulled on the doors with all her weight. Alec rushed forward to help her, but it was too late; the doors swung majestically open to reveal a vast ballroom.

Along the right-hand side were four expansive, vaulted windows, thirty-foot high, with swathed curtains the colour of deep sienna gathered back with thick gold tasselled ropes. The windows reached high up to the domed ceiling decorated with ornate square-patterned mouldings. The ballroom was quite cold, and the baroness held her robe together to keep warm.

Through the window the view was breathtaking. Beyond the wide red-brick terrace, the lawn sloped down to the avenue of poplars. The grass looked to have been naturally mown by grazing deer or sheep – there were no lawnmower lines as far as Alec could see. Beyond the avenue of poplars were the Sussex Downs, flawless green snooker-table meadows, rising gradually up and up to woodlands in autumn colours running along the hill crests, stretching as far as the eye could see in either direction.

"This is what I wanted to show you." Charlotte's voice was tense. She stood beside two oil paintings amongst a barrage of art. Two excellently crafted modern portraits hung beside each other: one of a man in summer clothes lounging in a deckchair in a hot garden; the other of a beautiful lady who was seated in an easy chair in a bright, airy room. She had auburn shoulder-length hair that was pulled back on either side of her head by silver or ivory combs, and a striking face with a slightly large, angular nose and a thrusting chin. Her eyes were large and attractive, with long eyelashes.

"This is my mother, Alice Barrett, and this is my father, Franz-Joseph Deller."

"Oh!" Alec was astonished and went up to the portrait to see if the curly haired, clean-shaven thin man in the portrait bore any resemblance to the bearded man he knew as Father Joe.

"How did you find him in Battersea?" Alec asked.

"Ferdi discovered him, by accident. It was last Friday. He was in a traffic jam in Battersea and saw Deller walking out of his church. Ferdi was not sure it was him, with the beard, but Deller spotted Ferdi in his car and ran. Ferdi could not follow him."

"Why did he run? He said you were blackmailing him."

Charlotte gave Alec a long stare. "He had stolen the Barrett Collection."

"What is the Barrett Collection?"

"Fifteen priceless works of art. Artists like Caravaggio and Constable. Why would *we* be blackmailing *him?*"

"That is what he said – not so much that *you* had anything to do with the blackmail, just the baron."

"Ferdi went back up to London on Sunday to confront Deller about the collection – and got killed for his trouble."

"Tell me more about this collection of paintings," Alec asked. Charlotte hesitated and eyed Alec again, assessing his honesty, Alec supposed. He tried to look as sincere as possible.

"I inherited the Barrett Collection, along with the house in Avenue Foch, when I was ten years old. Most of the important works were stolen by Franz-Joseph Deller from my house in Paris in 1940."

"How did the baron know that—"

"They were friends before the war. They were at art school together in Paris."

"But that is incredible, Baroness," Alec said and turned back to the portrait of Father Joe, or Franz-Joseph Deller. "I am not sure I see the likeness," he said, scrutinising the portrait. "He didn't sound German." Alec was not convinced.

"Austrian ... he's Austrian. He spent most of his early years being educated in England. He went to an English seminary, I think."

Alec looked back at the portrait. "It is very difficult to see this man being Father Dent."

"Both these portraits were painted by Ferdi," she said sadly. "If that man has killed Ferdi, I will hunt him down and kill him myself!"

"Your father?"

"He was no father to me. He killed my mother and now you think he killed Ferdi. One of the most talented—" She put her handkerchief to her eyes, covered her face and sighed a long sigh.

"Freya, what has happened?" Alec heard a low female voice with a heavy accent from the door of the ballroom. A dark, elegant woman entered.

"Ferdi has been killed by Franz-Joseph Deller," Charlotte said bluntly.

"Oh, my dear ... but that is impossible!" The woman went to Charlotte and held her, seemingly unaware of Alec's presence.

"Theodora, I must get changed." Charlotte broke away from the woman's embrace and turned to Alec. She was just about in control of herself.

"Mr Ballentine, this is my very good friend Theodora, a Turkish empress." She smiled as she looked at Theodora. "Can I leave you in her hands? Coffee, or something?" Charlotte started towards the door and then turned. "Do you want to hear a story, Mr Ballentine? One that, one day, you will want to print?"

"I don't know." Alec shrugged.

"Theodora, we will meet back in the study. I am going to find Christina and tell her the news."

With that, she left.

*

Alec's mind was racing. The name Deller was jumping about in his memory. Was it the same man?

"What happened to Ferdi?" Theodora asked, snapping Alec out of his thoughts. She looked at him as though he'd committed the murder. "Where is Ferdi's body? Why have we not been told?" They were back in the study, and she was pouring a coffee for Alec and herself.

"The police will have his body, I suppose. They do not know who he is, only that his name is probably Ferdinand Saumures."

"How do you know Franz-Joseph killed Ferdi?"

"Well, I don't know if ..." Alec suddenly felt apprehensive.

"You can talk to me about anything. Freya won't mind." She paused. "It's probably best to wait for Freya, anyway." She handed Alec a cup of black coffee without offering milk or sugar. "Who are you?"

"My name is Alec Ballentine. I am a journalist."

"Really," she said, casting a critical eye over him from head to toe. He was grateful he had thought to bull his shoes to a military shine.

Theodora was stylish, her black silky hair cut fashionably short. She was what Alec's mother would describe as a Latin beauty.

"How do you know Joseph, Mr Ballentine?"

"I don't. He knew a friend of mine. We know him as a clergyman called Father Joe Dent."

Theodora made a strange rasping sound in her throat. "He's a foolish donkey, that one! An idiot and a drunk." Alec was surprised by Theodora's intimate knowledge of Dent.

Eventually Charlotte came through the door, much to Alec's relief. He was seldom intimidated by people, but Theodora was beginning to make him uncomfortable.

The baroness was dressed in a black skirt and jacket with a high fur collar, her gold hair swept up in a French roll, revealing the long neck of a ballet dancer. Her face was still a little pale.

Alec stood and offered her his seat. She took the desk seat again. Theodora had switched on a lamp on the desk, to Alec's surprise, proving there was no power cut. Charlotte's face was now lit by the desk lamp. She wore, as far as Alec could see, scarcely any make-up.

Together, she and Theodora made a very attractive pair of women. Why they were not the centre of society, on the front of every glossy magazine, was beyond Alec's comprehension. The baroness was plainly very rich, married to a wealthy, good-looking man. She would inherit all this, he thought, so the stuff of gold for the likes of *Tatler* and *Vogue* magazines. Rich, attractive, and a baroness. No wonder she had a staff of thugs to keep nosy journalists away.

"Tell me, Mr Ballentine, all that you know," the dark, mysterious woman asked.

"About what, Mrs …?"

"Madam Theodora, or just Theodora," she said, lighting a cigarette.

"Her real family name, Mr Ballentine, is a national secret. She has a British passport with 'Theodora Smith' on it. Something Ferdi arranged." Charlotte smiled for the first time and it brightened the room.

Alec was hopelessly in love.

Charlotte turned to look at Alec and her smile switched to concern. "Are you all right, Mr Ballentine?"

"Yes, I am, Lady Freya, or should I address you as Lady Charlotte?" Alec said with a sigh. Theodora gave Charlotte an alarmed look.

"He knows?"

"He does," said Charlotte. "And we are going to hear more about Mr Ballentine's story, aren't we, Mr Ballentine? Who knows what, and what happened to who. First of all, we want to know everything you and Jason talked about. I want to know how long it will be before he comes knocking at my door."

"I didn't really talk to him about you. I talked mainly about your husband. He was not very forthcoming. Well, he wouldn't be, would he?"

"But was he interested in Charlotte de Tournet?" Charlotte asked.

"No, not really," Alec said. The women looked at each other. "He just said you died in Poland in 1944."

"Were you followed on your way down this morning?" Theodora asked.

Alec was a little shocked by the question. "I'm afraid I was not looking out for anybody following me. However, I cannot remember seeing another car behind me from Petworth, if that helps. Why would I be followed?"

"Jason," Theodora and the baroness said in unison.

"Oh?" Alec said. "Why would Sir Jason want to follow me? Your whereabouts is not exactly a secret."

"He has taken over my estate in Paris and has assumed authority of my aunt Stella's estate since the disappearance of Jean de Tournet, her husband. Stella is housed in a private hospital in London."

"What is the matter with her?" Alec asked with concern.

"She had a breakdown when her husband did not come back after the war."

"Do you know what happened to him?"

"Yes." Charlotte looked at Theodora who was shaking her head slightly, an expression of warning on her face. "But I cannot tell you how I know."

The women sipped their coffee, looking at each other again as if with some kind of telepathic communication.

"Mr Ballentine, would you like to stay to lunch?"

"Freya!" Theodora hissed.

"That would be delightful, Baroness."

Charlotte went to the bell pull next to the fireplace and rang it. A few minutes later, there was a knock at the door, and the small round woman Alec had first seen through the front door came into the study.

"Mr Ballentine, can I introduce Mrs Jorgensen, one of my mothers." Charlotte placed a loving arm over her rounded shoulders and gave her a gentle hug. Christina Jorgensen giggled and shyly went up to Alec, who leapt to his feet.

"How do you do, madam," Alec said charmingly. He took the elderly lady's hand in both of his and gently shook it, looking into her eyes and smiling. Alec knew how to charm ladies of a certain age. He remembered his father had advised him that charming mothers in front of their daughters would always win the daughter's heart.

Christina had obviously been crying; her eyes were puffy and red.

"Christina, would it be all right if Mr Ballentine stayed for lunch?"

"Yes, of course – there is plenty," she said in a heavy Swedish accent. "Very nice to meet you, sir." She gave Alec a pleasant smile and did a little bob-curtsy.

"Alec, please call me Alec."

"By the way, my lady" – Christina turned just before she got to the door – "shall I send the Tanner boys back to the farm? They are getting under my feet and distracting the maids. Mrs Tanner and Rupert keep tutting at them."

"Send them back, Christina. And you don't have to call me—" But Christina had gone out the door before Charlotte could finish.

"She has been through a lot, Mr Ballentine, my surrogate mother. Her husband, Bo, was murdered in front of her by the Nazis in a prison camp just outside of Paris. She was repatriated to Sweden without him."

"Why was he killed?"

"He and a few other men – all Jews – attacked the guards when they tried to escape the prison. Bo was not Jewish but hated what the Nazis were doing in the prison, and being an ex-soldier, helped with the escape attempt. He and twenty-one other men were executed by a man called Jost Krupp, an SS Nazi officer and mass murderer. They were shot in front of everybody."

"How did Christina become your surrogate mother, Baroness?"

"It is a long story."

12

Charlotte told the story of her war to Alec. She told it in a slow, wistful way, with no unnecessary embellishments. He was on the edge of his seat throughout, enthralled, regretting he had no way of recording the story aside from his notepad, which he felt he could not use.

She told him of the death of her mother, and how Franz-Joseph Deller – Father Joe – had killed her when Charlotte was a week old. He disappeared and turned up fifteen years later as an SS colonel in Paris, when it was occupied by the Nazis.

"It was Deller who sent Bo and Christina to Drancy prison," Charlotte said. "He wanted to make sure I stayed, I think."

"Did he know who you were?" Alec asked.

"Don't think so – how could he? But Bo and Christina were Swedish, and they tried to protect me by saying I was their daughter, Freya."

"And Father Joe was an SS colonel, you say?" Alec said disbelievingly. "But how on earth did that happen? How in God's name did a Nazi colonel – an SS colonel – become a vicar in a London suburb?"

"It was all to do with Ferdi." Charlotte carried on. "He and Ferdi were something to do with the secret service during the war."

"Whose secret service?" Alec asked gently, not wanting to sound disparaging.

"Ours," said Theodora indignantly. "The British!" she clarified, trying to sound British, but it did not work. Charlotte smiled condescendingly at Theodora, who threw her arms up and said, "Well, I try to be British nowadays."

"But I have only just heard about this," Charlotte said sadly, back to being serious. "Deller not only killed my mother, but he also stole the Barrett Collection, on the pretence of taking it for what was called – back then – Nazi cultural improvement."

"We think he stole fifteen priceless works of art," Theodora said.

"And he stole them from your house in Paris?" Alec asked.

"Yes, Nineteen Avenue Foch – Le Palais, as the Germans called it during the occupation. The collection was left to my mother, and then it came to me when I was only ten." Charlotte looked up, as though seeking inspiration. "I lived in Boston, Massachusetts, for quite a lot of my first ten years, then moved to Paris when my grandmother died. There, I lived with my stepmother and stepfather, my mother's sister and brother-in-law, Jean and Stella de Tournet."

"Hence why you were caught up in the occupation," Alec said.

"It was so fast." Charlotte stood and started to pace. "I met Theodora, and Jost Krupp." She stopped pacing and looked at Theodora with a slight smile at the recollection. "I was basically some kind of hostess, a 'courtesan'."

"When did you change your name to Freya?"

"Bo, our chauffeur, and his wife, Christina" – she pointed at the door that Christina had earlier exited – "quickly decided to make me Swedish so that it was not discovered that I was technically British and the owner of the house the Nazis had just occupied. They said that I was their daughter, Freya Jorgensen."

"I see," Alec said quietly, like a psychiatrist, waiting for Charlotte to say more.

"Then I met Baron Ferdinand Saumures … Ferdi."

"How did that come about?" Alec asked.

"I saw that portrait of my mother, the one I showed you in the ballroom, in the window of an art gallery in the Opéra district. It was there I discovered that Deller was my father, because Ferdi was one of his best friends, I think."

"Really?" Alec was somewhat surprised. "Is Deller a …?"

"No, he can't be, he fathered me! And, according to Ferdi, he loved my mother – but that's doubtful," Charlotte said huffily.

Theodora stroked her shoulder. "Do you really want to do this now, darling?"

"Yes, I do." Charlotte suddenly turned to Alec, taking him by surprise. "I will insist that you do not write anything about this until we confirm that it is Ferdi who is dead, and why he died."

"Of course," Alec assured her. "What happened with the baron at the gallery?"

"He had files on the Nazis and the SS in Paris. These were very secret files." She stopped and swept a look at Alec with an expression of alarm. "I don't think I can talk about the files."

"Don't worry. I am not permitted to write about anything to do with national security. I am, however, an official war correspondent." He produced a little booklet with an embossed crown. "I am very discreet. What happened at Le Palais?"

Charlotte told Alec of her and Theodora's encounter with Heinrich Himmler at the first dinner, Heinrich 'Gestapo' Müller, *Kriminalkommissar* Karl Hueber of the Gestapo and General von Ardle, who was in charge of Le Palais. She also told Alec of her stepfather's traitorous sudden appearance at Le Palais in 1943. "He seemed to be working for the Germans during the war," she said. "We managed to escape before he could tell the Nazis who I was."

"Who did you work for, Madam Theodora?" Alec turned to the dark woman who looked cautiously at him.

"I don't know you well enough to tell you that," she said coolly.

After a pause, Charlotte said, "You will know, I suspect, that some bodies were found in the remains of Nineteen Avenue Foch, Mr Ballentine. I can tell you, I think, who they are."

"Be very careful, darling, remember Mr Ballentine is a journalist," interjected Theodora.

"Madam Theodora, the story is too fantastic to believe. It should be a book," insisted Alec.

"Do you not accept the story as being true, Mr Ballentine?" asked Theodora.

"On the contrary, I certainly believe all that you tell me is the truth. Most of this is still forbidden for me to publish under the 1911 Official Secrets Act. Being a war correspondent, I had to sign that act – and a lot more besides."

"Then I will tell you more," continued Charlotte, "because, when Jason catches up with me – which he will – I will need all your help. That night, the fourteenth of September 1943, I nearly died, not from the bombs but from a nasty little shit called Hueber, a horrid Gestapo man."

"Is there any other type?" Alec said, hoping to lighten the mood. Charlotte looked back at him blankly. Alec regretted the jibe.

"Anyway, Hueber was about to rape me when Theodora put a bullet in his head." She stopped. She was getting gradually angrier with the memory. She took a deep breath. "The bodies I know about are: Jean de Tournet, my treacherous uncle" – the body in Savile Row suit trousers, thought Alec – "Heinrich Müller, *Kriminalkommissar* Karl Hueber, a German businessman called Wagner, and General von Ardle. And two other SS officers – both majors – who I did not know."

"Really? One of the dead may have been Gestapo? Müller? That would explain a lot."

Charlotte looked down to the floor sadly and carried on with the memory. "There may have been the remains of *SS-Hauptman* Wil, who was the head of the household – a nice enough man but, being an SS captain, he could quite easily have been another bastard. Also, Ulrich Fuhrman, one of Ferdi's men, but dressed as an SS captain. There were two girls: Agatha, and I can't remember the other one." She looked up at Alec, her eyes shimmering with tears again. "I was so innocent then, Mr Ballentine, young. I had no idea what these people were capable of, or what was actually happening in the war."

"You were fifteen," Alec said kindly.

"But she told us she was a few years older," Theodora said. "And she looked it."

"May I ask how old you are now?"

"I was thirty earlier this month, on the fifth of October. Ferdi and I had been married for twelve years on my birthday."

There was a hush, an uncomfortable silence. Nobody knew what to say. Alec longed to give Charlotte a hug.

"Have you been back to Paris? Have you had a look at Nineteen Avenue Foch?" Alec asked.

"I don't want to go back yet. Paris holds too many memories. I will one day, I suppose." She looked wistfully at Theodora, who reached out and stroked her arm in a knowing kind of way. "I love Paris. I spent nearly ten years there, was educated there, spent most of the war there, fell in love and lost my virginity there …"

"Charlotte!" Theodora chastised but could not conceal a little smile.

Christina returned and announced lunch was ready. Alec, Theodora and Charlotte went into the dining room. Charlotte linked her arm through Alec's, much to his surprise and delight.

"Do you mind, Mr Ballentine? I like a man to take me into the dining room. It's very old-fashioned of me."

Theodora raised an eyebrow and smiled slightly as she followed them.

The dining table was set up for three at one end.

"We normally eat in the kitchen, but Christina has decided that you should be treated as an honoured guest," Charlotte said, indicating that Alec should sit at the head of the table and the ladies on either side.

"How did you manage to get Christina out of Paris?" Alec asked.

"Ferdi went back to Paris after D-Day, in late 1944, to bring back his files from the gallery. He found some records of her deportation back to Sweden in a house on Avenue Foch that the Nazis used to keep records in. I went to Sweden when the war was over. I found her in Gothenburg. She was very lonely and near destitution, working in a bakery. So she came back with me. All she wants to do is look after us. She is a sort of housekeeper, but I don't let her do much. I have plenty of staff."

"On another subject, and I hope this is not too inappropriate," Alec asked gently, "why did Sir Ferdinand go to see Father Dent?"

"Well …" Charlotte thought for a while. Christina had brought in some cured salmon – gravadlax – and brown bread, and some pickled cucumber, lettuce, a potato salad, and a bottle of sharp Muscadet white wine. Charlotte helped Alec, placing a selection on his plate. She was spooning a little dill and mustard sauce onto the salmon when she stopped, looked at him and said, "I don't quite know where to start."

"From the row, I would, darling," Theodora said matter-of-factly.

"Do you know, Mr Ballentine, I have known Ferdi for over thirteen years. We have seen most of the war together, and we've lived here in Sussex since the end of the war, having concerts, entertaining all his friends and acquaintances. And I only discover the day after my birthday that he has been lying to me all these years."

"A big lie," Theodora chipped in.

"Part of my mother's legacy," Charlotte carried on, "was the Barrett Collection. Franz-Joseph Deller was instrumental for not only stealing the collection but stealing it for *himself*!"

"It did not end up in Germany, then?" Alec said, his fork loaded with gravadlax and salad not quite making it to his mouth.

"No. My husband … our marriage was one of convenience. I never wanted to have children – I am not sure I can, actually – and my husband, well, *was* a homosexual." She paused for a reaction from Alec but he chose not to react at all, instead keeping eye contact with her and nodding gently. "He was very nervous about being caught and so we married in Spain, on my birthday."

"They did not make it a real marriage, if you see what I mean," Theodora interjected. Alec coughed into his glass of wine just as he took a drink. Charlotte frowned at Theodora.

"This is lovely salmon," he said, before asking, "I presumed you loved him in some way?" He hoped it was not too personal as he saw Theodora scowl at him again.

"Well, at first it was more admiration. He was so caring and lovely towards us – Theodora and me."

"He was very good-looking," Theodora said.

"Yes, and he was wise … and a good friend, to all of us – we thought." She talked nervously, avoiding meeting Alec's eyes. "He had a few jobs during the war, one of which was to build files on all Nazi and SS personnel in France, in particular in Paris. These files were codenamed 'Wasp Trap' – I don't know why."

Alec looked up, astonished. He felt uneasy. "Have you ever heard of, or heard Ferdi talk about, WASP?" he said cautiously.

"Just 'wasp'? I think so. Can't quite remember. Ferdi seldom talked about the Wasp Trap files, just a couple of times during the war and a couple of times after. He and our friend Bernard had to go over to Paris to collect—" Charlotte looked up. "I don't know if I should be talking about this." Seeing the concern on Alec's face, she said, "Why, what is WASP to you?"

Alec placed his knife and fork down on his plate and looked at the salmon for a few seconds, composing his answer. He licked his lips. "WASP was …" He stopped and looked up at the ceiling, thinking, and then back at Charlotte. "WASP *is* – because we think it still may be going – a powerful group of people, from mainly conservative countries: the USA, Spain, Italy, Britain, Germany … They formed just after the Russian revolution, thirty-two years ago, mainly to stamp out communism." Alec sighed. "That sounds quite tame. They are basically a political espionage organisation, and we think they were in league with the Nazis before and during the war."

"I've heard of this group, through Ferdi," Charlotte said, frowning. "What are you trying to say?"

"Well, I just wondered if Ferdi had anything to do with—?"

"No!" Theodora and Charlotte said together.

"Why would he? He was neither powerful or political, as far as I know." Charlotte was getting angry.

"Or Deller?"

"I have no idea about him," Charlotte said. "I have not seen Deller for, must be, fifteen years. Anyway, what is WASP to do with you, Mr Ballentine?"

"WASP stands for" – Alec searched his memory – "I think, for War Against Socialist Parties. But I don't know much about them, other than they were powerful during the war and work like the mafia."

After a brief silence, Theodora said, "Well – all I can say is they have not exactly succeeded. There are commies everywhere."

"Theodora!" Charlotte looked shocked at her friend. She turned to Alec. "Mr Ballentine, what is a 'wasp trap'?"

"A wasp trap is a simple device to trap wasps and flies. You put a cover over a jam jar full of water, with a little hole in the middle; the wasps crawl in with the promise of some delicious jam but can't fly out again, and drown in the water in the jar."

"Oh, how horrid." Theodora winced.

"So, you know about the Wasp Trap files?" Charlotte asked.

"Yes, I did a small piece on it a year after the Nuremberg trials, but I could not interview anybody, didn't know who was responsible for compiling it – it was shrouded in secrecy, you see. All I could write was that they existed for the Nuremberg trials, and no more, so I gave up. I am bitterly disappointed that my best contact now seems to be dead." Alec looked at Theodora, and then back at Charlotte. "How much do you know about the files?"

"I was one of Ferdi's contacts. As was Deller," Theodora said.

"Really, Madam Theodora?" Alec was excited. "Do tell me more."

"I will, one day," Theodora said and kept on eating her lunch.

"OK." Alec looked at Theodora in some surprise, the door of further information slammed in his face. He turned to Charlotte. "So it was the baron who put the Wasp Trap files together?"

"Yes. I can also tell you – now he's dead – that Ferdi was an agent with the Abwehr. A triple agent, I think he was."

"He was a Special Intelligence Service double agent, and a double agent for Abwehr? A very dangerous game to play."

"Yes," Charlotte said with an impressed note. "It took us ages to work out what Ferdi was up to when he told us. His secret stuff became a nuisance," Charlotte said sadly. "This is why we had a row. Ferdi had, unknown to me, recruited Franz-Joseph Deller—"

"A Nazi SS colonel, for God's sake," Theodora interjected and then made a strange strangling noise in her throat.

"He wasn't then." Charlotte flashed a glance of annoyance at Theodora. "He was recruited as one of Ferdi's informants. I was incensed. Ferdi had recruited him in 1925, a few weeks after I was born! He had known Deller for ages – we didn't know."

"Why were you incensed? Because he was your father?" asked Alec.

"No! Because he had stolen the Barrett Collection." Charlotte threw her hands up in frustration. "Every day for the past twelve-odd years, I have asked Ferdi to help me find my paintings, stolen by Deller, and get him to find Deller. And Ferdi knew where the bloody man was. He may have known where Deller was all the time."

"Deller is a real liar, a stinking Nazi liar." Theodora was getting worked up. "He said he did not have the paintings, but he does – or did."

"Well, this is where I may be able to help," Alec said calmly. "This is my job, after all. I can investigate. Was the baron capable of killing? Did he go to see Dent or Deller to threaten or to kill him?"

"I very much doubt he went intending to kill." Charlotte paused for a moment. "Well, he was trained during the war, but so was Deller, I suppose, when he went into the SS. He was a soldier, after all. But he – Deller – was … is weak, a drunk. He may not be now. What did Deller look like, Mr Ballentine?"

"Well, nothing like he looks in the picture in your ballroom. He has thinning curly hair on top and lots of hair on his chin. I think he still drinks, though." Alec felt a little uneasy confirming Dent's drink problem from just a few hours' acquaintance. "Sorry, I should probably not say that."

"A beard?" Charlotte was surprised. "Yes, Ferdi said he was looking hairy. And pretending to be some kind of priest as well? How long had he been there as a priest?"

"Well," Alec said hesitantly, "he has been an Anglican vicar in Battersea since just after the war ended, I think. He got to know a friend of mine. She was a churchgoer. I'm not. She brought him back once or twice for drinks whilst I was away …" His explanation petered out when he found he was being scrutinised by the women.

"Who is this woman?" Theodora asked abruptly, as though she was his mother demanding to know more about her son's latest conquest.

"She *was* my fiancée. She is not any more. She got fed up with me, I think."

"She knew Deller well?" Charlotte asked softly.

"I honestly don't know. He wanted to see her that evening, not me. I had only met him once or twice before."

"What does she do?" Charlotte asked.

"She is an art historian and works as an adviser to—" Alec halted, and a feeling of realisation sneaked in.

"An adviser to whom?" Theodora said.

"To Christopher's art auction rooms in Bond Street," Alec said, slightly to himself.

"Good God, they could be in cahoots," Charlotte said. "They could have sold all the paintings already."

"I very much doubt it," Alec said, slightly too emphatically.

There was another uncomfortable silence. Theodora sat back in her chair and drained a glass of white wine and lit a cigarette. Charlotte was looking at her plate of hardly touched gravadlax and salad.

"So," Charlotte said in a low, controlled voice, "Deller came to you, as this, er ..."

"Vicar," Alec finished for her.

"He told you that he had murdered Ferdi by mistake. He took you back to his church, and you saw a body – that he said was Ferdi. Did you have a good look at his face?"

"He was lying on his front, his head to one side. I could see most of his face, yes."

"Is that the man?" Theodora said, pointing to a picture behind Alec. He turned to look at the painting behind his chair, an accomplished oil portrait: an intimate study of Charlotte seated on the floor, looking up at a man seated on a chair, her arm over his knees. He was looking out from the picture and Alec imagined it was a self-portrait. It was the same man, virtually down to the clothes. He had a cravat rather than a tie, the same jacket and trousers, a different shirt but the same shape of cufflinks.

"I am afraid they look the same, yes. Did the baron paint that portrait?"

"It will now be his final work – it took him ages," Charlotte said quietly, resigned.

"I am so sorry, darling." Theodora reached over the table and stroked Charlotte's hand.

"Oh, Theodora, what a mess! I am going to have to tell Bernard, find out where Ferdi's body is and go and see that awful man Strider about what happens to the estate."

"There was one thing that may interest you," it occurred to Alec. "When I went back to try and find Father Dent, I was asked by the police to have a look at a pile of old discarded crates and picture frames in the cellar of the church."

"What kind of crates?" Charlotte stood and walked over to the portrait of her and Ferdi.

"They were, I suppose, the kind that would hold large works of art, but they were all smashed up. The picture frames were damaged but looked quite valuable."

"No pictures?" Theodora said, watching Charlotte running her hand down the frame of the portrait.

"No, I am sorry."

"Where can Deller have gone to?" Charlotte returned to the table.

Christina came into the dining room with a telegram in her hand. She looked sombre. Perhaps it was the reputation of bad news that usually came from a telegram, or she was grieving for the baron.

"The boy says is there an answer?" Christina said in a quiet, solemn voice.

"Thank you, Christina. Just say no answer." Charlotte went over to Christina and lightly held her and kissed her on the side of her head – she only came up to Charlotte's shoulder. She took the telegram, opened it and started to read as she walked back to the table. She stopped abruptly.

"Well, your enquiries have already started a flurry, Mr Ballentine … from Jason." She waved the telegram at Alec slightly crossly and then went back to reading it. It was a long one; Alec could see lots of tape silhouetted on the page.

"Well?" Theodora was fascinated. "What does he want?"

"*To Baroness Freya Saumures* – he addresses me not as Charlotte – *I believe we may be related and that you have recently suffered a bereavement STOP My condolences STOP I would be grateful if we could meet at your convenience at my country house in Wimbledon STOP Would tomorrow 5pm for tea be suitable? STOP My address is Alston House, Wimbledon Parkside, Wimbledon Common STOP*. Well! What an assumption," Charlotte said still looking at the telegram. "And what is more, he signs it *Sir Jason Barrett MP*. God, what do I do?" Charlotte looked at Theodora.

"Go, darling, tell him all, get your Paris house back."

"It's your house, Theodora, I keep telling you."

"It is my house when you are dead, darling. You are not, technically, dead."

"Not now, apparently," Charlotte said, looking at the telegram. "I think we – you and I, Mr Ballentine – will go to London and see what we can discover."

"I would be delighted, Baroness. When?" Alec was thrilled.

"What about now – today?" Charlotte turned to Theodora. "Darling, you stay here and try and find Bernard. Tell him everything. Tell him to meet us in London; he will help us. I will be in our suite at the Adolphe Hotel."

"I will pack you a case, Charlotte— I mean ..." Christina flapped her hands in confusion, distressed she had used Charlotte's name in front of strangers. She scuttled off.

"Who is Bernard, may I ask?" Alec asked hesitantly. Both women eyed him, clearly still cautious that he was a journalist.

"He is a friend of ours. He helped us escape France during the war," Charlotte said in a tone that was business-like. "He worked in the SOE and was part of the secret team Ferdi was involved with. He was injured rather badly, though. But, Mr Ballentine, he is off limits when it comes to writing anything about this. Do you understand?"

"Yes, of course. But I should say, if he is Major Bernard Trent, codename 'Bertrand', I know quite a lot about his war." Both women were astonished by Alec's knowledge of Bernard. It seemed, at the same time, to reassure the ladies; Alec was plainly a well-informed journalist, not one of those newshounds.

"You are quite a man, aren't you, Mr Ballentine?" Theodora said pleasantly.

13

The journey back to London was, for Charlotte, an adventure. She rarely went to London, not since the abortive trial nearly three years previously.

Thinking about the trial, Charlotte was convinced Deller had somehow got to the authorities and wanted Charlotte to be put away so she would stop pursuing him about the collection. That was Ferdi's theory, anyway. When Ferdi had said he had found out where Deller was hiding, Charlotte demanded – she remembered guiltily – that Ferdi go and confront Deller about the art collection. If she had just asked him nicely, Ferdi might still be alive, as he would have gone there with Bernard.

In the car, during the rare quiet periods, Charlotte thought about her husband. Ferdi's death had not affected her as badly as she thought it would. Was it because, unforgivingly, he had kept from her the secret of Franz-Joseph Deller being in London? He'd even encouraged her endless search for the Barrett Collection, not least her trips to Germany after rumours that artworks had been found in caves in the south of the country. Ferdi had told Charlotte that he was convinced the collection was not in England, but in Germany or America.

Charlotte's gaze unconsciously rested on Alec's face as he drove. He had a classic profile, conventional straight nose, square jaw, laughter lines in the corner of his eye. He was large and filled up the driving seat of the car. His left muscular upper arm lay very close to Charlotte's right shoulder. She liked this man. His sense of humour, when he allowed it to surface, was dry and intelligent. She liked the car, even with the roof now up as it was threatening rain. The conversation was about everything other than Ferdi, Jason or Deller. They talked about what Alec did during the war, Dunkirk, and his exploits throughout the years that followed.

They laughed. He told stories of his colleagues in Fleet Street, the El Vino gossip, and about Philip Bing-Wallace, which was the only time they gently touched on the subject of Ferdi.

As Alec and Charlotte arrived in London, the sky was getting darker and the afternoon was closing in. The wind was getting stronger, and leaves were scudding across the road as the Jaguar drove past Battersea Power Station.

Charlotte turned her thoughts to her uncle Jason. She had never been especially fond of her uncle. She believed he thought she was dead, then somehow found out that she was alive after all, and may have made the accusations about her time in Paris and at Le Palais during the war … and of being a traitor. If it was not Deller who gave the police and the War Office the evidence that Freya Jorgensen was a Nazi sympathiser, it had to be Jason. Thanks to Ferdi and the secret service authorities, the charges were quickly suppressed.

Everything was now in turmoil. Ferdi had been killed by Deller. The prospect of finding her art collection, now that Deller had been found, was becoming tangible. She needed to confront her uncle and talk to him about the collection. He might not know that it was Deller who stole it for the Nazis. But he might want it for himself and make it complicated for Charlotte to claim that the pictures were hers … because she was technically dead. Thankfully, it looked like Alec was willing to help. However, she was worried whether he was helping her, or just doing all this for a story. Either way, she decided not to care … for now.

*

Alec took Charlotte to the Adolphe Hotel. It seemed to have taken the staff slightly off guard. Arno, the manager, welcomed Charlotte warmly and loudly so all in the reception lobby could hear that a titled and very important person had arrived. He hardly looked at Alec. Alec whispered to Charlotte that he would be in the lounge and would arrange tea for them both. Arno whisked Charlotte up to the suite, talking animatedly as they left.

Alec took the opportunity to see if he could get hold of Philip Bing-Wallace at his office in Fleet Street whilst Charlotte was being taken to her suite.

"Philip? Alec here."

"My dear boy. Did you have a lovely time with—?"

"Hold up for a second, Philip – don't have much time," Alec said. "I am at the Adolphe Hotel with Charlotte de Tournet, or, to be precise, Baroness Charlotte Saumures."

"Good God, Ballentine, well done. Jolly good show." Adenoids to the fore.

"She has just booked in. I gather she and the baron own the place, would you believe!"

"Told you! Well, you will get a good tea there."

"I am here for an hour or so if you need me. Then we must try and find Father Dent – who turns out to be her father, by the way."

"Really? Her father? The vicar chap is Charlotte's father? Bloody—"

"She wants to find the Barrett Collection, which she suspects is not only in London but was brought here by Father Dent, whose real name is Franz-Joseph Deller." Alec paused; all he could hear on the other end of the phone was breathing. "Are you all right, Philip?"

"Yes, it is just quite a lot to take in." Bing-Wallace coughed, then said, "I think I know where Dent is, by the way. He went to Wimbledon, to Sir Jason's house."

"How on earth do you know that?" asked Alec, astonished.

"I decided to follow Sir Jason from his office. I just happened to be passing when I saw him."

I doubt he "happened" upon Jason, thought Alec. I bet he was staking out *The Sentinel* all day.

"I followed him in a taxi. He was in a chauffeur-driven car, and I took a taxi and told the driver to 'follow that car'. Terribly exciting – until the taxi driver said he was not going south of the river. I had to bribe him, Alec, with ten shillings!"

"He lives in Wimbledon, doesn't he? Charlotte got a telegram from him."

"Saying what?"

"That he was her uncle and he wanted to meet her at his house tomorrow."

"Bugger that – go now, catch him out."

"You saw the house?" Alec asked.

"He lives on the Common – lovely house, walls all the way round and a massive iron gate with a little gatehouse. Like a mini Kensington Palace. It cost me over a pound to get there!"

"How did you know Dent was there?" asked Alec, seeing Charlotte going to the tea table and looking around for him. He waved and pointed to the phone.

"He was in the car with him, didn't I say? Dog collar, beard, couldn't be anybody else."

"OK, well done, Philip." Alec was distracted.

"Are you all right, Alec?"

"I will explain later but I must go, she is back at the table," Alec hissed.

"Well, I must say!" said Bing-Wallace, sounding hurt. "Can't I come with you?"

"Can't. Only room for two in the car. Good bit of sleuthing, Philip … talk this evening … or tomorrow. Bye." He replaced the receiver before Bing-Wallace could say any more.

As Alec walked back to the table, he could not help but allow his eyes to slowly wander over every part of Charlotte. Charlotte sat sipping from a teacup, her slim stockinged legs elegantly together at an oblique angle, her ankles crossed. Her long, graceful arms were accentuated by the long sleeves of her black dress. He admired her elegant fingers holding the teacup, a single plain wedding ring on her left ring-finger. She wore a black pillar-box hat on her golden hair that was gathered up in a chic roll, a small net veil covering her eyes. He was conscious that she was aware of his scrutiny and he quickened his step towards the table, looking away from her to the cake stand on the table beside her. She smiled at him, he hoped enjoying his attention.

"Will you permit me to call you Charlotte? You must call me Alec."

"OK, Alec," she said quietly, still with a slight smile.

Alec took out his cigarette case and offered her a cigarette, which she refused but she indicated that she did not mind him having one. Alec lit a cigarette and leant closer in.

"My friend Philip Bing-Wallace thinks he has discovered the whereabouts of Father Joe Dent, or Deller," Alec declared.

"How wonderful. Where?"

"He's at your uncle's house in Wimbledon."

"Really? Why is he there?" She looked shocked. "Does he know Jason?"

"He must do. It is all a bit of a coincidence, isn't it?"

"It seems. They are probably all spies. Jason was." She looked thoughtful and then asked, "How does your friend know Deller is with Jason?"

"He saw him drive off in Sir Jason's car. They drove to Jason's house together, according to Bing-Wallace."

"Is he there now?"

"I believe so."

"Well, let us not waste time. Let's go and find him."

Alec was excited that she was so positive, full of action. She did not seem to be brooding or mourning over her husband's murder any more; she just wanted to get going.

"Should we not go to the police and make a formal identification of your husband's body first?"

"No, he's not going anywhere. But Deller may disappear again, especially if he knows that I know who and where he is." She added, "You don't suppose he is dangerous, do you? Should I find a pistol?" Alec was shocked.

"No!" he said a little too loudly, and then lowered his voice. "No. I will be there. He will not be dangerous." Alec pictured the tragic figure in the vestry the night before. "But I promised to tell the police where he was, if I came across him."

"Well, if he is at Jason's house, you can phone them from there. I just want to know why he killed Ferdi, and where my paintings are. I hope he has not sold them all."

"Let's hope," Alec said, helping Charlotte on with her coat and enjoying her scent.

He put some money on the table and went to the cloakroom, retrieved his hat and his coat, and they set off in the Jaguar to Wimbledon.

On the way, Alec thought about Deller and what his friend Dan James said about meeting him on a fishing boat. Was it the same man Dan travelled back from Spain with? Was this Sir Sussex's contact to do with WASP? Did Sir Jason have something to do with Deller's release from Battersea police station?

"What do you know about your uncle Jason? Why is he a knight?"

"My great-grandfather was a baronet, and Jason succeeded the baronetcy when his father died in the Great War. I suppose it disappears when Jason dies."

"And he was something to do with the diplomatic service before the war?"

"Yes, in Paris. My grandfather was the British ambassador, and I think Jason wanted to be ambassador as well but the war came along – the Second World War."

"I gather he was also in MI6 during the war," Alec said.

"Ferdi said he was. I don't really know. I never knew what his role was, or what he had to do with Ferdi. He's a bit of a mystery altogether." There was a long silence as they drove past the All England Lawn Tennis Club. "Jason was such a cold fish. Never married, never really talked to me or my stepmother when I was a child. I cannot actually ever remember him smiling."

"He was pretty impassive with me," Alec said.

"Did you like him?"

"Didn't really have time to get to know him. Strait-laced, severe, but looking good for his age."

"He must be in his fifties," Charlotte said.

"Really? Then he looked old for his age." Charlotte smiled at him. "He had a chap working for him, in what capacity I'm unsure, not a secretary or a servant. Called Alderson. Know him?"

"No, I wouldn't know. Though Ferdi mentioned a young man not long ago. He thought he was part of Jason's MI6 team."

14

As soon as Charlotte and Alec left Burton Park Place, Theodora looked up Bernard Trent's number.

"Bernard, it's me," she gasped over the phone, gripping the mouthpiece with both hands.

"Theodora, what on earth has happened? I haven't heard you like this since the war. In fact—"

"Listen, Ferdi has been killed."

"What! Who by?"

"You will not believe me, but by Franz-Joseph Deller, you know, the—"

"The SS colonel at Le Palais? The bastard! Charlotte was desperate to find him."

"Yes, but what we did not tell you was" – she took a breath – "he is also Charlotte's father."

There was a long silence, broken by, "Christ! I'm coming over."

"Yes, but I need you to take me to London."

"Why? Don't answer. I will come and pick you two up in about half an hour."

"Just me – and I want to go up tomorrow. I have got to stay here with Christina for when Charlotte calls with news. Rupert and the maids have gone off for a few days." Charlotte had given them the weekend off as she was meant to be away with her husband.

"It sounds complicated. I am on my way. In a bit." After a pause, Bernard said, "Theodora, are you still there?"

"Yes. What is it?"

"Remind me to tell you about an envelope Ferdi gave me in case he was killed. I must get it to Freya – or are we calling her Charlotte now?"

"Where is it?" Theodora asked, hurt that she was not the one with such an important task.

"Hidden in the house. I will show you when I get there. See you soon. Bye." The phone went dead.

There was a time during the war when Bernard and Theodora were more than friends, but they never became lovers. Bernard loved Theodora but found he came second to Charlotte and Ferdi and the house at Petworth. Theodora was happy to be Charlotte's companion and live at the magnificent Burton Park Place. Bernard thought he could turn his hand at being a tenant on one of the four Burton Park tenanted farms, but he knew nothing about farming, and he had no money.

He then tried shipping wine again, but that all fell through. He had trouble finding winemakers, and getting the wine shipped became impossible; there were very few merchant ships, and what ships remained were full of more important, vital supplies. He even tried to get Ferdi to buy him a merchant ship that was being sold cheap in Southampton. But it was a "bucket", full of rust, and it had a bent keel from a sea mine – no wonder it was so cheap. Due to his injured leg, he was unable to do anything physical anyway.

And so, when Arundel Hall preparatory school advertised for a maths and general subjects teacher with a good knowledge of cricket coaching, Bernard applied, lying about his qualifications in all subjects – he was always very good at maths, however, and he had coached cricket; he used to captain his college at Oxford, where he failed his mathematics degree, and took over the coaching when the current coach was injured in a high-speed cricket ball accident.

His charm and his injuries – sustained in France in his escape during the war – made good his application, and he had been teaching the boys at Arundel Hall for three years.

He was a very good teacher, which helped. The boys admired him hugely and enjoyed his tales of the war, when he'd served as an SOE agent codenamed "Bertrand".

He arrived at Burton Park Place in his elderly Morris Minor and limped into the house. Theodora ran to greet him in the hallway.

"Tell me all," Bernard said, putting his arm around her shoulders. She was not crying but looked haggard and distressed.

"I've got drinks in the study."

Theodora told Bernard everything in hushed tones, just in case Christina could hear.

"I am so worried, Bernard. Charlotte has gone off with this journalist, a stranger, which is very much out of character. She keeps well away from journalists, as you know, and here she is going off to London with one."

"She probably fancies him." Bernard chuckled, but seeing an expression of realisation cast over Theodora's face, said, "Was he good-looking? Nice? What?"

"He was relatively good-looking," she said. "Big, you know, like a rugby player; nothing like the men she has been around for the last few years. He had a nice smile … nice eyes."

"But the baron, for heaven's sake." Bernard changed back to the subject. "What a mess!"

"She has asked me to stay here and look after Christina and to be on the end of the phone."

"OK," Bernard said, rubbing his hands together. "What do you want me to do?"

"Get us both another drink." Theodora was deep in thought. "Bernard, did you know that Deller was a vicar in Battersea all this time?"

"No, why would I? Was he?"

There was a crash and the sound of broken glass somewhere in the house.

"What was that?" Bernard asked.

"Christina dropping something, I should think." She watched Bernard pour two gins. "You and Ferdi were both involved in secret stuff during the war, I just thought …"

"Different sections. I was head of an SOE section, he was an agent in Paris. He was the Paris contact of an escape line that we ran. And anyway, Charlotte asked me each time I came here – in various different ways – if I knew where Deller was with her paintings." He paused. "What's this rubbish about Deller being Charlotte's father?"

"He *is* her father. I have known for quite a while. Charlotte wanted to keep it quiet."

"Not surprised she wanted to keep that under her hat. Those two, Charlotte and Ferdi … what a couple," Bernard said, and then remembered something. "I must get in touch with the SIS. Ferdi left me instructions in case he was killed." They heard a faint cry from Christina. "See if she is OK, Theodora."

"I had better see what—" Theodora was interrupted by a scream.

Theodora raced to the study door, shouting "Christina!" The door burst open and in walked a man, holding Christina up by her hair.

"What the bloody hell is going on?" Bernard cried angrily. Christina was whimpering, her eyes shut, her hands shaking in front of her face. The man threw her to the floor then raised a black walking stick and levelled it at Theodora's throat so she did not come any closer to him. She turned and went to Christina, who was sobbing on the floor, nursing her shoulder.

"Who the hell are you?" Bernard rushed up to the man but stopped abruptly as he saw he had drawn out a wartime Luger pistol and brought it up to shoulder height, aiming it directly at Bernard's forehead. Bernard stared at the ugly scar running down the man's cheek to his mouth, which was set in a cruel grin.

"Hello, Theodora," he said in German. "I thought you were dead."

Theodora stood, leaving a prostrate Christina on the floor. She looked aghast and pale as horror and realisation sank in. "Krupp! Jost Krupp! We thought *you* were dead!"

"What?" shouted Bernard. "The bastard who did my leg in?"

Krupp turned to look at him, flicked up the safety and fired the Luger. A split second before he fired, Bernard dived to the floor and the bullet sank into the bookshelf, sending fragments of paper up in a puff of confetti. Christina screamed and hid her head under her arms as she lay on the floor like a frightened spaniel. Krupp re-aimed.

"Jost, stop ... just stop!" Theodora screamed. "What are you doing here?"

"Go and sit over there," Krupp barked, waving his stick at the chairs and the small sofa in the corner of the room. He kicked the chair in front of the desk; it slid to a stop next to the sofa. He limped heavily over to the desk and sat on the corner, perched like a rook on a fence. He kept his eyes on Theodora and Bernard as they picked Christina, who was shaking with shock, up off the floor and onto the sofa. Theodora sat beside her with her arm around Christina's shoulders.

Krupp took hold of the telephone cable and ripped it out of the wall. He looked sharply at Bernard, who was still standing. He aimed the Luger at him. Bernard quickly sat in the chair, anxious.

"Jost ...!" Theodora cried.

"Be quiet!" he snapped back. He sat in the desk chair and pointed his pistol at the door.

"Jost, there is nobody else here."

"Be quiet, I said. Say anything else and I will shoot the woman, then the man!"

105

Theodora closed her mouth. She patted Christina on the lap to quieten her moaning.

Bernard sat frozen on the chair.

15

Jost Krupp watched the door intently. He felt the man's gaze and knew he would be thinking of ways to grab the gun. Krupp wondered who he was, how he knew him. And Theodora: she'd hardly changed in all these years – shorter glossy black hair, still a striking-looking woman with those full lips and huge, slightly oriental brown eyes. He did not know the old woman, but she was no trouble, and Theodora was occupied comforting her.

They waited for fifteen minutes – it seemed like fifteen hours – but nobody came through the door. With the sound of the shot, if anybody else was in the house, they would have appeared by now, Krupp thought.

"Where is she?" he said. "Where is your friend?"

"Who, Jost?" Theodora said quietly.

"Freya – the baroness," Krupp snarled acerbically. "Who do you think?"

"She has gone to London. Her husband has just been murdered by … someone," Theodora answered coolly.

"Yes, I know. By me," Krupp said in an unemotional way.

The old woman gulped. Theodora's mouth gaped open.

"What do you mean, *you* killed him?" Theodora yelled. "Why did you kill him, you bastard?"

"He was a nasty little queer and got a lot of my friends shot or put in jail. And he would not tell me where the files were," Krupp hissed. "Where are the files? He said they are here."

"No, he didn't say that. What files? You're making it up. Why did you kill Ferdi?" Theodora looked confused.

"Deller was going to be next, but he said he would take the blame for killing Saumures. I agreed. If he said anything, I would kill him, and then Freya."

"What do you want with Freya?"

Krupp bent down to his right boot, felt around the rim and pulled out a syringe. He placed it on the desk.

"I just want to see her again before I kill her. She crippled me; she stabbed me in the leg and there is still a bullet in my back where she shot me. And then there is this." He pointed at the scar on his face.

There was a silence. Theodora's attention was taken with the syringe on the desk. Then her gaze turned onto Krupp with revulsion. He felt uncomfortable. He had always liked and admired Theodora. It never seemed to bother him if people didn't like him, but somehow it was unsettling to see his old friend glaring at him with such contempt.

"How did you evade capture after the war, Jost?" Theodora asked. "How did you get away with it?"

"I didn't. I was captured just at the end of the war. I had a nice little vineyard in France. I have only just been released."

All this time Krupp kept looking over at the man. His Luger followed where his eyes went. He looked at the man's leg. "What happened to your leg? Did Freya slice you as well?"

"No, *you* broke it with the butt of a rifle," he said in a low, threatening voice.

Krupp was taken by surprise. He thought for a bit, looked at the man and then shook his head slowly. "No, can't remember you. A while ago, eh?"

"In the Gers, France, in the Free Zone!" The man shouted the last two words. Theodora shushed him, gesturing to calm down with her hand.

"Well, I can't remember you," Krupp said. He was suddenly aware that the old woman was watching him, studying him out of the corner of her eye.

"What are you planning, Jost?" Theodora asked gently.

"I don't know, I—"

Just at that moment, Christina leapt from the sofa and launched herself at Krupp, screaming something in Swedish and then in English: "You killed my Bo, you killed my Bo!" She rushed around the desk, her hands aimed at Krupp's neck. He aimed the Luger at her, but she hit it with her elbow just as he shot. Theodora dashed over to stop Christina. A second shot was fired, and the round went into Christina's eye socket and exited out the back of her head. Blood and small pieces of bone and brain sprayed over Theodora's face. She jinked away, covering her face with her hands.

Christina crashed heavily to the floor, her head cracking like a coconut on the edge of the desk as she fell at his feet. Krupp was astonished. Then he saw the man charging towards him, propelling himself at Krupp's Luger. He stepped a pace back and the man crashed on top of the desk. Krupp brought the weapon down hard, and the butt of the pistol hit the side of his head and knocked him unconscious. Theodora saw the man being knocked out and screamed, then saw the pistol was levelled at her head and threw up her hands in surrender. Her face was splattered in blood, her eyes wide in shock. Krupp was breathing heavily, confused. "What was that all about?" he shouted, pointing his pistol at Christina's body.

"You killed her husband in Paris. He was in the Drancy prison during the war. I think she recognised you."

Krupp was losing his patience. "Sit down there!" He pointed to the sofa. He picked up the syringe from the table and went to the study door. "Do not move, Theodora. I mean it. I am going to look around." He glanced at the man on the desk and put the pistol to his temple. "I will just finish this off first."

"No, Jost, don't. I will stay with him. I will tie him up. Don't kill him, please." Krupp was taken aback by Theodora's entreaties.

"Is this a boyfriend, Theodora?"

"Something like that."

"If you are not here when I get back, he dies, and when I find you, you'll die." She nodded her head, looking like she was about to cry. If he left the man alive, it would mean Theodora would stay with him and not jump out the window.

Krupp left the study, locking Theodora and the man in. He had to find these files.

Theodora sobbed, holding her arms tight around herself, trying to relieve the pain in her stomach. There were no tears. She looked down at Christina's body. She cried very rarely, if ever. She did not like crying; it never achieved anything. But seeing Christina – quiet, demure, unassuming, timid Christina – dead on the floor, with a horrible wound to the back of her head, and Bernard – gallant, heroic, dashing Bernard – looking as good as dead, draped over the desk, something turned inside her, memories of the war and the terrible things that happened then. A great surge of sadness welled up into her chest and she found herself weeping.

Thirty minutes had elapsed and Bernard was still unconscious. Theodora was worried. How badly was he injured? Had Krupp damaged Bernard's brain? He was still breathing, but erratically, and had not moved. Mucus was coming out of his nose. Theodora tried to turn him over but was worried she would drop him off the desk and damage him some more. She went over to the window, opened it and looked out, hopelessly working out a way she and Bernard could get out. It was pouring with rain, Bernard was unconscious and Krupp would be back at any time. The prospect of any escape was bleak.

She heard the limping gait of Krupp's return. She quickly closed the window and went over to the still body of Bernard. She felt fear as the door was unlocked. She looked around for a weapon, something she could knock Krupp out with. She tried not to panic, tried desperately to stay calm.

As Krupp came through the door, he kept the pistol in front of him. "Step back!" he commanded. He looked at Bernard, and then back at Theodora. "Where would she hide the files, Theodora?"

"I don't know. They would be in here if anywhere." She tried to sound relaxed. "Can you give me a hand with Bernard? He should not be unconscious for this long."

"Leave him! Turn out all the drawers. Pull them out, see if there are any files stuck to the bottoms."

"No, Jost! Help me with Bernard first. You did this."

Krupp slapped her hard on the face. She drew in a long breath and looked up at him, furious.

"You be careful, Jost Krupp! I will kill you for what you've done here," she shouted. All fear had gone, replaced by anger. She pulled out the drawers. Krupp kicked each drawer over to see if anything was stuck to the bottom.

"You can't kill me! How would you, I wonder?" Krupp said angrily, waving the pistol at her face. "I have had enough of this. Where is Freya? And where are the files that Saumures brought back from the war? Tell me now or I will finish this man off." He pointed the Luger at Bernard's head. Bernard groaned slightly when the barrel of the pistol pressed on his temple. Theodora rapidly thought through some options. There were not many, she realised. Krupp had started twisting the barrel into Bernard's head, so she had no time to think of a plausible lie.

"OK! She has gone to see her uncle in London. I don't know anything about the files. If there are any files here, they would be in this office. But, Jost, all the Paris files would have gone to somewhere official ages ago."

Krupp cast his eyes around the study. Surely he must see it was obvious there was no other place where files could be stored or hidden. He looked behind the paintings, tapped on the walls.

"There were some other files that the queer did not submit. Freya knows," he shouted. "She knows and is hiding them."

"How do you know? What files?" Theodora was genuinely bewildered.

Krupp slapped Theodora without warning with the back of his left hand. Theodora staggered back a pace. She was shocked, hurt by such violence from someone who was once a good friend.

"Don't you lie! I know you and Freya are thick as thieves. If she knows, you know."

"Well neither of us knows, Jost, and—" Theodora winced as she stroked her cheek where she'd been hit.

"Who is her uncle?" He drilled the barrel into Bernard's head.

"Sir Jason Barrett."

Krupp's jaw dropped in amazement. "Really?"

"Do you know him?" Theodora asked, distressed at the barrel drilling into Bernard's head. The hammer was cocked, Krupp's finger on the trigger.

"Sir Jason Barrett? Franz-Joseph's friend who owns the newspaper? The politician?" He lifted the barrel of the gun away from Bernard's temple, leaving a crisp white circle in the skin. Theodora's mind was racing. She was astonished Krupp seemed to know who Jason was. She was confused by his comment about him being Deller's friend. "Right then, we will go there now," he said almost jubilantly, which confused Theodora even more. He must be mad, insane, or something.

"We?" she said, looking at Bernard.

"You and I ... We don't need him." Without warning, Krupp shot Bernard through the head. Theodora gasped.

"No! You bastard!" She bent down, her eyes level with Bernard's. She put her hands on either side of his face and watched saliva dribble from his mouth, his eyes wide open in surprise. They slowly blinked at her, unfocused, a smile forming on his lips. The surface of his eyeballs clouded over, the lids slightly closed. Life drained out of his face in Theodora's hands.

"Bernard!" she moaned.

She felt a sharp prick in her shoulder, near her neck. She put her hand up to her neck to swat away the sting and her hand collided with a syringe. Then, a kind of darkness grew from her chest to the top of her skull. She felt herself fall, and then ... nothing.

16

Theodora woke to find herself lying on her left shoulder in the foetal position, her hands tied with telephone cable. A belt tied her ankles together, along with some cable to prevent her from being able to straighten out. A thick wool scarf was tied tightly around her head, with a large knot stuffed into her mouth. There was no light except for a thin sliver of grey above her head. She was in the boot of a car. It smelt of petrol and oil, and, every now and then, exhaust fumes. The car was travelling at great speed. It was a wet road as the tyres sloshed through puddles, and a drop of water would drip onto her cheek intermittently.

The belt around her ankles was extremely painful, but at least she was wearing slacks so the belt was not biting into her skin. She was finding it hard to breathe; her nose was full of mucus and when she did manage to clear her nose a little, the smells from the boot of the car made her feel sick. The knot left only a little space to breathe through the corner of her mouth, and her jaw started to ache. She felt cold as well as clammy, and completely wretched.

Theodora remembered what happened just before she passed out, and she felt her heart squeeze with sadness. In a matter of days, three of her most cherished friends had been cruelly killed by a man she thought she may have loved at one stage – as had Charlotte.

She was completely immobilised and unable to do anything. And Krupp was set to murder her greatest friend and companion.

The car stopped a few times and Theodora thought she could hear voices, so she tried to kick out at the boot lid, but it was almost impossible; the belt and the telephone cord restricted any kind of movement.

What seemed many hours went by. The little chink of light gradually disappeared as it got dark outside. The car eventually stopped, the engine switched off. The suspension went up slightly as the driver, presumably Krupp, got out of the car and slammed the door. There was an echo, as though they were in a tunnel or an alleyway. The boot lid was suddenly opened, and the driver stood over Theodora. Her back was towards him and she tried to look over her shoulder. He turned her over roughly and pressed the Luger muzzle against her head. "You're awake." He smiled, then bent down and hissed into her ear, "I may be a bit of time. No point in shouting, nobody comes down here."

He was about to shut the lid again but was distracted by a noise. As he looked away, Theodora slipped the cord that bound her hands over the boot latch. As Krupp slammed the boot lid, the latch snipped the cord. At the same time, the lid smashed into Theodora's fingers and her knees. She desperately tried to stifle a cry. The gag helped, but she was still heard by Krupp, who opened the boot again and looked at Theodora. She kept her hands together, hoping he would not check the bindings.

Krupp saw her fingers were covered in blood from the boot smashing onto her knuckles. He smiled as he looked into Theodora's frightened eyes. He roughly rolled her back onto her other shoulder and slammed the lid shut again. She heard Krupp's uneven, limping steps echoing, getting quieter as he walked down the alleyway. She waited for the steps to disappear. She pulled the cable off her hands and took the gag out of her mouth. She felt as though she was going to be sick with each action. She then tried to turn herself around so that she could bring her knees up to unfasten the belt around her ankles. She kept getting something caught up on her clothes in the darkness, but eventually managed to turn herself, bring up her knees and unbuckle the belt.

She felt around the floor of the boot for the latch to open the lid. As she was doing so, the lid suddenly moved a bit, then opened. A piece of wire had kept the latch from locking.

The sky was murky with dark grey clouds. It had been raining. She had no idea what the time was; she was not able to focus onto her small watch. She felt cold and shivery.

As she swung both legs out of the boot, she saw her shoes had fallen off and she had to juggle the heavy boot lid with retrieving them. Theodora stood, the lid slamming behind her. She looked at the car, an old grey Morris Oxford – not a car she knew.

She unknotted the dark-blue scarf that had served as a gag and tied it around her neck, stuffing it down her blazer for extra warmth. A cold shiver went through her as a gust of wind blew up the narrow alleyway. She still had no confidence that she was able to walk. She looked around, blinking rapidly to get her vision to focus. On one side was a high, windowless wall, and on the other side was the back of what looked like a warehouse, with metal fire escapes snaking down from the floors above. The road was cobbled and a single pavement ran parallel with the tall wall. There was an archway a few yards away, but it was blocked to cars by a bollard in the centre of the road. In the other direction, which she thought was where Krupp had limped off to, was a T-junction to another narrow road that then joined a busy road junction about a hundred yards away.

This is London, she thought. She looked around for a street sign and found one beside the archway. With the help of the wall, she staggered towards the archway – only five yards away, but every step made her feel giddy and sick. What did Krupp inject me with? she asked herself and took deep breaths through her nose. She got to the street sign; it said, in black lettering, "Bride Lane EC4".

Theodora swung round to the other direction. He must have gone to Jason's office in Bouverie Street, she realised and smiled to herself. She went through the arch and along a passageway. She looked at her watch and took time to focus onto the tiny dial; just after five thirty in the afternoon. She was sure that Inner Temple and Fleet Street must be close because she had sent letters to EC4, to the lawyers. But where was Fleet Street? Could she remember the address of the lawyer, Strider? Or should she try to get to Charlotte at the Adolphe Hotel? How far was it to the Adolphe Hotel from here?

She went through another archway and a church appeared on her right, surrounded by a tree-lined courtyard and some houses. She went around the church to find a way in. She pushed open the main heavily studded door. It was a new door, not what she expected from such an old façade. Inside there was a long aisle with a magnificent shiny black-and-white tiled floor. Light wood stalls for parishioners ran down each side of the aisle to the altar, and there was a little man in a black cassock polishing the immaculate wood. The crisp white walls had arches decorated with gold plaster flowers.

The man did not see Theodora come in, so she decided that she would sit in one of the stalls and rest. She still felt sick, but her head was clearing. She was desperate for a cigarette.

"Hello," the man said gently when he saw Theodora sitting in the stall through his wire-rimmed glasses.

Theodora spotted he wore a hearing aid and shouted, "Do you mind if I rest here a while?"

"I am not deaf, madam, I have a hearing aid," he said with a slight smile, pointing to the device attached to his belt with a wire running up to his ear.

Theodora saw his expression change to one of concern. "I am sorry, sir, I am a little lost. I was in an accident, you see."

"Golly! Yes, you do look a little …" He decided not to finish the sentence.

"Where am I?" Theodora asked. The man was surprised.

"St Bride's Church, just beside Fleet Street, madam." Theodora was confused. "The City of London, you know." His head tilted with unease.

"Oh, I see. Do you have any money I could have? I can leave you my watch and my earrings." She felt her earlobes and remembered she had not put any on. "I am not wearing any – but I have a diamond ring." He shook his head as she spoke, still with a gentle smile on his face. "I must get a taxi to the Adolphe Hotel," she said in desperation.

"I will take you there on a bus in a moment," the little man said kindly. "I have finished here for today, but I do not have any money – well, not for a taxi."

"Oh," she said, trying not to sound ungrateful. She looked at her watch; it was a quarter to six and she needed to warn Charlotte about Krupp urgently. "Do you have a phone I could use?"

"There is a box at the top of Fleet Street, and one—"

"Don't you have a phone here?" Theodora said incredulously. She looked at the little man and realised she was being rude. She mellowed her voice and said, "It is just that I must warn—"

"We are still waiting to be connected. We have not had a telephone since the renovation."

The little man disappeared off somewhere, and she wondered if she had offended him somehow. Theodora could hear his droning voice talking to someone else. She then heard two sets of footsteps approach. The little man, now wearing a gabardine mac and holding a flat cap in his hands, was accompanied by a tall, thin man with a white dog collar, a tweed jacket and cavalry twill trousers. They moved towards her, looking at her cautiously.

"Are you all right, my dear?" said the vicar in a deep, melodious voice. "Only Frank was concerned."

"Thank you, sir, but I must get back to my hotel. I must tell my husband about the accident."

"Are you hurt? Do you need to see a doctor?"

"Thank you," she said impatiently, "but I must get to my hotel. I will be fine when I get there. My friends and my husband will help me." She suddenly felt tearful, the vision of Bernard dying in her hands. If anybody was to be her husband, it would have been him.

"Very well." The vicar backed away, looking uncomfortable. "Don't distress yourself, my dear. Frank will take you to the bus. Here is a half-crown for the fare." The vicar gave Theodora a coin, which she accepted with a smile of gratitude. The vicar blushed slightly.

"Don't suppose you have a cigarette?" Theodora asked hopefully. The vicar smiled and found a cigarette case in his jacket. He sprung the lid open and offered her a filterless cigarette and a light from a silver lighter. She drew in a long draw of smoke and released it out slowly.

Frank coughed and looked at the vicar somewhat sternly.

"Quite right," the vicar said, "we better take this outside. Frank does not approve of smoking in the church, not with St Bride's history." He chuckled nervously.

Theodora had no idea that the entire church had just finished being completely rebuilt after the whole building was virtually burned to the ground during the war.

17

The evening was fast closing in when Charlotte and Alec arrived at Alston House on Wimbledon Common. The house was set back a hundred feet from the road, behind tall, imposing black metal gates. A side gate with a modern intercom speaker was set into the twelve-foot brick wall that surrounded the house and grounds. The red-brick mock-Edwardian mansion beyond was surrounded by trees on each side, and a honey-coloured gravel drive ran up to a huge, empty parking area. Close-clipped lawns spread either side of the wide gravel drive.

Alec went around to the passenger door of his Jaguar to let Charlotte out. She swung her legs elegantly out of the car. She smiled up at him in gratitude for opening the door and offering a hand. She could see a little blush, and wondered why Alec seemed nervous – or was it embarrassment?

She looked out over the common that Alston House faced. It was a little scrubby, but in autumn that was not surprising. There was no traffic noise. You could be in the middle of the country, not eight miles from Marble Arch. It was still cloudy but darkening, and it was getting quite chilly. Charlotte buttoned up her coat to the fur collar and adjusted her little pillbox hat.

"What shall we do now?" Charlotte asked in a hushed tone.

"Let's see if anyone is in first. We should ring this intercom thing, I suppose." Alec pressed the button beside the speaker. A faint buzz was emitted.

"Can I help you?" a cultured voice of indeterminate sex said from the speaker, surprising both Charlotte and Alec. They looked at each other and the intercom said, "Speak clearly into the speaker, please."

Charlotte went up to the speaker and shouted:

"My name is Baroness Saumures and I would like to talk to Sir Jason." As an afterthought, she said, "We are related."

"One moment, please," the thin voice over the intercom said.

"Was that male or female?" Alec asked. Charlotte giggled lightly. She would have laughed but she was too anxious. What was she going to say to her uncle? What if Deller was there? How would she react? How would he react, for that matter?

"Please come in," the voice said. "Push the side gate when you hear the clicks."

There was a series of metallic clicks from the lock on the gate and Alec pushed it open. He allowed Charlotte through first and then he stepped through. The gate swung shut and there was an ominous click as the gate locked again. Charlotte was relieved to see a button in the centre of the main gate post, which must be the way to release the gate on exit.

As they walked towards the shiny black front door, it slowly swung open and a short, thin lady with a severe but handsome face stood at the threshold with her hands clasped together in front of her. She wore a black dress with long sleeves. Her dark hair was cut like a boy's. She reminded Charlotte of Mrs Danvers in *Rebecca*, but prettier. She offered a thin smile and spoke with a low, precise voice.

"Good afternoon, Lady Saumures. May I ask who this gentleman is?" She did not move from the threshold as they approached.

"This is a friend and adviser, Alec Ballentine."

"Thank you. Would you like to come in?" She stepped aside and allowed them into the hallway.

"My name is Jane Gardener, and I am Sir Jason's housekeeper. May I take your coats?"

"No, thank you, I will keep mine on. I am a bit cold," Charlotte said.

"I will keep mine too," Alec said and slung his coat over his arm.

For some reason, Charlotte took an instant dislike to this woman. She seemed cold, untrustworthy, and possibly dangerous.

"Would you follow me?" Jane Gardener said, turning swiftly on her heel and toe like a trained dancer.

She took them to a large light-oak door just off the hall and knocked gently before opening it. "Baroness Freya Saumures and Mr Alec Ballentine," she announced. As Alec and Charlotte walked in, Charlotte heard an utterance like a gasp of alarm from a lady somewhere in the room.

She scanned the room as she entered. There was her uncle, Sir Jason, standing at the large white marble fireplace with a cup of tea in his hands. Standing up from a high-backed sofa beside the fire was Franz-Joseph Deller, now bearded and wearing an expression of nervous expectation. He held a large tumbler of whisky. He was in his vicar's garb, without the cassock. When he saw Charlotte, he sat down hard on the sofa, his mouth gaping in astonishment. Charlotte glared at him. She desperately wanted to say something, but nothing came into her head. She was aghast at how Deller looked, hardly recognisable; but for his eyes, he could have been anybody.

On the sofa with Deller was Mr Strider, the lawyer, who stood as they came in, looking sheepish and embarrassed.

"So, Mr Strider," said Charlotte in surprise, "you seem to be everywhere. Do sit down." Sir Jason was about to say something, but Charlotte interrupted him. "Hello, Uncle. We have not seen each other for a while." Jason said nothing, just kept looking at Alec and Charlotte with a mixture of irritation and uneasiness.

On the other side of the fire was another high-backed sofa with its back towards Alec and Charlotte. A young, attractive woman with mousy hair rose from the sofa and turned slowly towards Alec. When her pretty blue eyes met his, he exclaimed:

"Sophie! What on earth are you doing here?"

*

After a long, silent ride on the nineteen bus from Fleet Street to Piccadilly, with Frank in attendance, Theodora at last walked through the door of the Adolphe Hotel in Albemarle Street, just off Piccadilly. It was a long walk for Theodora, and she was exhausted. She still felt unwell from whatever Krupp had injected her with.

She staggered up to reception, where a young man in a morning suit and black waistcoat came out from behind the desk and rushed over to her. He said in a low, gruff voice, "What do you want, madam? This is the Adolphe Hotel, and unless you have booked you will have to leave immediately."

"Madam Theodora?" said another voice with a clipped German accent. The young man looked amazed at Arno, the hotel manager. "It is Madam Theodora, is it not?"

"Arno, you godsend," Theodora exclaimed in German.

"Ah so, it is our Madam Theodora. Madam, what has happened?" His chubby frame waddled over towards her in front of the reception desk, his plump hands extended towards her as though to take her into his arms, which they both knew would never happen. They carried on in rapid German, to the bewilderment of the young receptionist.

"Arno, is Lady Saumures here?"

"Yes, but—"

"Oh, thank God, I must see her. Is she in her suite?"

"No – she has gone out with a gentleman, a man I have not seen before," Arno said discreetly.

"My God, where?" Theodora panicked.

"I have no idea, madam. They had tea at that table there and—"

"I must go and find her. Arno, how can I find out where Sir Jason Barrett lives? I know it is in Wimbledon, but I have forgotten where exactly – Wimbledon Common, I think?" Theodora was rambling. She put her hand to her forehead and Arno inhaled sharply as he saw the scrapes on her knuckles.

"Madam! What has happened to you? You must go to the baroness's suite and clean up. I will find out the address." He turned to the lad at the reception desk. "You," he said, beckoning him to come over.

"I was in an accident, Arno, and desperately need a cigarette and a drink. I had no money for a taxi and came here by bus." She raised her hands high in the air, angry and upset. "By bus, would you believe? I have never been on a bus!" Theodora stood in front of the shocked hotel manager, one hand on her hip, the other holding her forehead.

Arno went into action and barked at the young man beside him. "Assist madam up to Lady Saumures's suite and let her in, and be quick about it! Madam – call down for *anything*."

"*Vielen dank*, Arno." Theodora thanked Arno as she went to the lift. The doors opened, and the young man stood to one side to let Theodora in. As she went into the lift, she saw herself in the mirror and nearly screamed. What she saw was a woman with matted hair, freckles of dried blood over her face and smears of dark mahogany on her forehead. As her hands came up to her mouth to stifle the scream, she saw that her knuckles were covered in clotted blood. Her clothes were filthy, the shoulders of her jacket covered in dust and dirt. She turned to the lad in the lift with her; he was looking at her from the corner of his eyes, plainly unsure what he was doing with this mad woman.

"I can see now why you were concerned about letting me in, young man. I look a terrible sight."

"Yes, madam," he said automatically and then, realising what he had said, "I mean no, madam. Sorry, madam."

"Don't worry." She patted him on the arm as she got out the lift and they went into the suite. Theodora went straight to the drinks cabinet and poured a half-glass of brandy and took a French cigarette from the silver box on the glass-topped table beside the cabinet. She lit the cigarette and inhaled deeply.

*

Twenty-five minutes later, the young man at the desk saw, Theodora hoped, a glamorous lady in a dark-brown dress and a fawn overcoat over her arm. The mirror in the lift showed her black bobbed hair was shiny, but her face looked a little pale and drawn. She put on some gloves to hide her chapped knuckles.

Arno bustled up to her, his head to one side, a huge fat grin over his apple-shaped face. "Now, that is the Madam Theodora we know," he said in English. "I have found the address; I have a friend who works for *The Sentinel*. Here are some of your Gauloise cigarettes, an Adolphe Hotel lighter, and I have taken the liberty of putting twenty pounds at your disposal, which you can return at your convenience." He handed over the cigarettes and an envelope.

"You are simply divine, Arno." Theodora was about to give him a huge kiss on the forehead, but she thought it may demean his authority in front of his subordinates, so she just clasped his hand in both of hers, offered him her sweetest smile and mouthed "*Vielen dank*". His face flushed from his neck upwards like a wine glass filling with red wine.

"Michael will find you a taxi." Arno took her coat and held it up for her to put on.

It was nearly seven o'clock when she got into the taxi. The driver complained about going as far as Wimbledon. Theodora said that she would tip him two pounds if he stopped muttering – which he did, happy to take quadruple the fare.

Theodora was able to reflect on the events of the past few hours. Her headache had gone, and she felt a lot better after a brandy, a bath and a clean set of Charlotte's clothes. As she smoked her cigarette, and feeling a little more normal, she played back the horror of what had happened in Sussex. Watching the murder of her close friends, the horrendous way they had died ... How was she going to tell Charlotte? Not only about the slaying of Christina and Bernard, but also that Jost Krupp was responsible – not just for the murders of Christina and Bernard, but also, it seemed, for Ferdi. And to crown it all, that he was still alive! Charlotte was convinced she had killed him in Auch in 1943.

Perhaps I should have gone to the police, she thought. They would find the bodies and catch Krupp. But she had to warn Charlotte about Krupp before she did anything. Would Alec Ballentine help? As the taxi went over

Wandsworth Bridge, the street became quite dark. The gas street lights were gradually being turned on, a task still done by a lamplighter, and were being lit as they passed Wandsworth town hall.

The grey sky now turned blue-black, the noisy taxi clattered on, and the craggy face of the driver with a stub of a cigarette hanging out of the corner of his mouth, illuminated by a ghostly light from the dials on the dashboard, was still muttering about something Theodora could not hear. Theodora's mood went from frightened anticipation to verging on panic as they steadily drove through the murky streets of South London. Perhaps I should go to the police, she thought as they drove past Wandsworth police station, but then it might be too late.

She thought about the bodies of Bernard and Christina, left at the manor on their own. That stupid butler would not be back until after the weekend. Perhaps she should have called the local police or the Banner brothers? Oh, why did I not just think more at the hotel? she castigated herself.

Theodora was wracked with guilt, frightened about confronting Charlotte with the awful news – and making things even worse for her as Charlotte was meeting her uncle for the first time in over twelve years, and she might also confront her father.

But what was it that Krupp had said about Deller being Sir Jason's friend?

18

"I could ask you the same thing, Alec. Why are you here with this woman?" Sophie looked Charlotte up and down.

"Charlotte" – Alec turned to face her – "may I present Miss Sophie Younghusband. We were to get married, but we had to call it off." Alec looked at his ex-fiancée. "Miss Younghusband, may I introduce Baroness Charlotte Saumures."

"Oh!" said Sophie, slightly taken aback.

"May I intercede, touching as this reunion is?" Sir Jason said, walking slowly over towards Charlotte. "My dear, I am so glad to see you. We all thought you were dead." Jason spoke in an impassive way. He extended his hand to shake hers. He made a quick sideways glance at Alec. "You know this man is a journalist, don't you?"

"Yes, Uncle, I do," Charlotte said icily, and then looked at the inadequate man on the sofa shifting his nervous glances from the fire to Charlotte and then rapidly back to the fire.

"And that man, I believe, is my father and the man who stole my family's art from Avenue Foch." She looked at her uncle, ready for him to be astonished … disbelieving. To her amazement, he was neither.

"My dear" – Jason walked back to the fire in thought – "this man, who is indeed your father—"

"And the man who murdered my mother – your sister!" Charlotte said loudly, her voice trembling in fury.

"Well, let us leave that for now." Jason was sounding like the politician he was.

"I did not kill your mother," Deller said quietly, still looking at the fire, his words slightly slurred. "It was an accident. I should have—"

"You ran away, you gutless bastard! No balls. A drunk!" Charlotte strode up to Deller. She stopped and took a long look at him. His red-rimmed eyes slowly looked up into hers. "And then you had the gall to steal the Barrett Collection."

"I say," Sophie said in surprise. "You think he did what?"

Charlotte whisked around and looked at Sophie. "Are you in on this? Aren't you an art expert or something?"

"Well, yes, but I am not a … What do you mean?" Sophie turned, suddenly angry. "I hope you are not accusing me of any dishonesty. Remember there is a lawyer here," Sophie said indignantly, pointing at Strider.

"I can't get involved in this kind of thing, you know," Strider said meekly.

"Sophie." Alec went around the sofa and stood in front of his ex-fiancée. "Have you any idea where this collection is?"

"No, Alec. And what is it to you, for heaven's sake?" Sophie shouted back.

"I did not steal the collection, Freya." Deller stood up and gestured in Jason's direction. "I was—"

"And you killed Ferdi. He used to be your friend. Why did you kill Ferdi?"

"Who is Freya?" Sophie said. "Who are all these people you have killed, Father Joe?"

"How well do you know this man?" Alec said to Sophie, pointing at Deller.

Everybody was now standing and shouting at each other, until Sir Jason shouted in a cracked voice, "Quiet, all of you!" It fell quiet. "Will you all take a seat. Mr Ballentine, please sit here between Miss Younghusband and Lady Charlotte – or do you like to be called Freya?" Jason did not give her time to answer. "Father Dent, stay put," he said firmly. "Mr Strider, I wonder if you would get young Gareth to fetch some drinks." Jason was plainly used to taking control of a situation.

Charlotte was still seething with anger and glowering at Deller when Strider left the room. Whilst he was gone, Jason said, "Mr Strider is here to ensure any legalities that may arise from this meeting are acted upon. He will also offer any advice needed. My niece, Baroness Saumures, was supposed to be here tomorrow, but she evidently decided to change her plans and is here now." Charlotte was about to say something when Jason carried on. "Mr Ballentine here is a journalist." Jason strode over to Alec and looked down on him. "I trust that you realise, Mr Ballentine, that anything that is said in this house this evening is not to be published. I regret if you are unable to give me this undertaking, you will have to leave." Jason had one eyebrow raised, waiting for Alec to promise.

"Uncle, Mr Ballentine is a friend, my guest—"

"My dear, you only just met him this morning. How could he possibly be a friend? He is just out for a story."

"I can assure you, Sir Jason," Alec said, "that nothing will be written about this meeting unless it is legally and ethically approved by you and Mr Strider. I am here as support for Lady Saumures, who has just lost her husband. I am not here primarily as a journalist."

The door opened and a spotty red-haired youth entered the room. Strider came in just behind him with Jane. The housekeeper went around the silent room and gathered the tea things.

"Thank you, Jane. Gareth, would you get everyone a drink, quickly please, and then we are not to be disturbed."

"Yes, Sir Jason," said Gareth with a West Country burr. Alec wondered if this was the clerk Bing-Wallace came across who cleared out Strider's office of files.

The drinks trolley was produced and everybody except Sophie had large whisky and sodas. Sophie stuck to just soda water.

"I am going to conduct this like a meeting in my boardroom or my constituency surgeries," announced Jason. "I will be chairman and I would be grateful if you would address the meeting through me." Still standing at the fireplace, he surveyed the room. "First of all, I would like to welcome my niece, who I have not seen for many years and thought was dead." He bowed slightly towards Charlotte. "Secondly, the main purpose of this meeting with Miss Younghusband, Father Dent and Mr Strider was to establish how we can reduce the damage that has been done by the attempted sale of the Caravaggio, *Portrait of a Courtesan*."

"What?" Charlotte blurted. "So *you* have my collection, Uncle?"

Jason sighed impatiently.

"My dear, we will come to that eventually, but if you listen, I will explain the situation and everybody's part in this mess."

"Too bloody right you will," she said angrily, "and then we will see what the police have to say about this."

"Perhaps. As I was saying ..."

Charlotte slumped back into the sofa, feeling like a child who had been told off.

"Charlotte, I should explain something that you will not have known."

"Yes?" she said, her interest piqued.

"During the war I was head of a small division in MI6 that recruited Germans to act as double agents."

"I heard about this from Ferdi ... a little about it, anyway," Charlotte said. "He was very cagey, though."

"Franz-Joseph Deller here was one of those we recruited."

"Oh!" Charlotte was surprised.

"He studied religion, here in England. He spoke excellent English. He had very powerful parents that he did not get on with, however, and using them as referees – in a fashion – he was able to get recruited into the German secret service to spy on us, you see."

"Was he part of B1A, run by Colonel 'TAR' Robinson?" Alec said. For the first time, Jason looked surprised.

"Well ... yes ... but I am bewildered as to how you would know about it, Mr Ballentine."

"Listen," Charlotte interrupted. "I am getting very fed up with all this secret stuff during the war. Ferdi was up to his neck in it. Are you trying to tell me that this man" – she pointed at a dejected-looking Deller – "has been working for you and Ferdi all this time, as a vicar in Battersea?"

"Yes ... well, sort of," Jason said.

"Well, he not only killed Ferdi, when Ferdi wanted to know where my paintings were, he also—"

"I did not kill him, Freya ... Charlotte," Deller said.

"You did, you murderer, and my mother. You have killed most of my ..." She took a sobbing breath. "And you stole my paintings. You told Alec you killed Ferdi, and the police."

"I did not kill him," Deller said plainly. His attention went back to the fire, ending any further comment. He sipped his drink.

Charlotte stood up in exasperation. Jason strode over to her, waving his hand to get her to sit again, making shushing noises to her to calm down. As she sat, she swiped a tear of anger away with the back of her hand.

"My dear," Jason said, gently interrupting Charlotte, "Franz-Joseph did take the collection from Avenue Foch, but he did so for *me*." There was a few minutes' silence for Charlotte to take this statement in.

"What do you mean, for you?" she said crossly.

"He managed to forge a requisition document for the paintings to be taken to Germany for the German Culture and Enlightenment programme. I could not allow the collection to be shipped to Germany, and Franz-Joseph managed

126

to get the important pieces of the collection, almost totally unscathed, back to England with my help." Jason then turned to look at Deller and said angrily, "To some degree." Charlotte was amazed.

"But where is the collection now, Uncle?"

"In my newspaper storerooms in the London Docks."

"Then what is the problem that requires this woman and the lawyer?" Charlotte gestured widely at Sophie and Strider.

"I regret Franz-Joseph decided that he would like to realise some money behind my back and put one of the paintings from the collection up for auction. Greed got the better of him." He scowled at Deller.

"Ah." Charlotte began to understand. "Well, what do you expect from a—"

"That, I am afraid, was not the main problem."

Deller was still gazing into the fire, visibly cringing in anticipation at what Jason must be about to say. Everybody else seemed to be slightly embarrassed for some reason.

Jason sat in the deep armchair opposite the fire, between the two sofas. He held his tumbler of whisky in both hands and examined the glass as though finding inspiration.

"Charlotte," he began, "your grandfather, my father, was a collector of art as you know. However, the collection … has one major flaw."

"Oh?" said Charlotte. Jason licked his thin lips and said:

"The paintings … virtually the whole collection … are fakes."

It took quite a few seconds for the significance of what Charlotte's uncle had said to sink in. In her surprise, she had grabbed the sleeve of Alec's tweed jacket tightly with both hands. She looked past Alec to see Sophie, her eyes cast down at the floor, her head gently nodding.

"You mean *all* the paintings … the whole collection … the Sisleys … the …?" Charlotte shook her head in disbelief. "All fakes? But why? *How?*"

"*Nearly* all are fakes. The only genuine paintings were a portrait of your grandmother by Sir William Orpen that I commissioned, and there was one other. They were all painted by a counterfeit artist called Gerard Dagmar. A genius—"

"What do you mean, a genius?" Charlotte said furiously. "And how do you know they are fakes?"

"Your grandfather told me. I was the only person who knew," Jason said, beginning to look embarrassed. "This was why I was more than upset when the collection was left to you in my mother's will. I thought she would have left the collection to me. That is why there was a proviso in the will that stipulated that the collection should never be sold. It had been added just before her death."

Charlotte's eyes met Alec's, her mouth wide open in astonishment. Realising she had her hands clenching Alec's jacket, she released it and sat with her arms folded.

"That is why I had to get the collection back here when the war broke out."

"You used British Secret Service resources to smuggle out your personal art collection?" Alec said scathingly.

"It is not his collection, Alec, it is mine," Charlotte shouted.

"It became my responsibility to ensure the collection was protected, Charlotte." Jason was stern.

"How did you manage to get the collection to England?" Alec asked.

"This man" – Jason pointed at Deller – "Franz-Joseph Deller, arrived in Falmouth with the collection from Spain – or was it Portugal? – and decided he was going to keep a painting from the collection for himself."

"Well not quite, Sir Jason." Deller suddenly spoke. "I kept the painting in lieu of payment. You had never—"

"Mr Deller," Jason countered, "you stole the painting to sell. You and Miss Younghusband there decided to sell stolen paintings."

"I was not aware they were stolen!" Sophie shouted, which stunned the room. "Let me make this quite clear, I did not know they were stolen." She looked at Strider, then to Sir Jason. "I was the one that found them to be fakes and potentially averted a scandal! Father Dent – or whatever he is called – said he was an agent for the paintings: your agent, Sir Jason." When she had finished, she stood up and walked towards the drawing room door. "I will not be party to this. I thought this was just a case of poor judgement on Father Dent's part. I was not aware that these paintings were stolen, or part of a collection, or who they belonged to. I was asked for my professional advice. I will refer this to the police in the morning. Any future dealings with me or Christopher's auctioneers, you will have to—" She stopped suddenly. The door flew open and the spotty youth, Gareth, stumbled into the room, tumbling Sophie backwards. She squeaked as she was pushed backwards, her hip striking a table. She turned angrily at the boy who had pushed her. Behind him, a man in a long black coat, a scar under his eye and a stick in his left hand, was aiming a pistol straight at her.

"Christ!" Sophie gasped.

"Everybody remains seated. Anyone standing will be shot," the man said in a heavy German accent.

Jason stood. "Krupp, how dare you—" A shot rang out. A vase at the back of the room exploded. At the same time, Jason spun around, a spurt of blood bursting from his left upper arm, and he crumpled heavily back into his chair. Sophie screamed and dropped to the floor in panic. Charlotte felt faint as she realised who the man was.

19

"I am sorry, driver, but I must find a police station," Theodora said through the partition window inside the taxi.

"You want to what?" said the driver, looking round at Theodora.

"A police station, please, and hurry."

"Why, what have I done?"

"Nothing. I just need to go to the police station. It's urgent."

"Well, make your bleeding mind up, woman," he shouted sullenly and then, not quite under his breath, "Bleeding foreigners."

Theodora took a five-pound note out of the small handbag she'd borrowed from Charlotte and shoved it through the gap at the driver. "Will that cover it?"

"I should think so, madam," he said, with slightly more respect.

"Then get on with it and stop being so rude."

The driver's attitude changed instantly. He stopped the taxi and did a U-turn in the middle of the road.

*

"Sir Jason," Gareth shouted in alarm and began to run towards his employer. Jason was gritting his teeth and holding his arm, slumped in his chair.

Krupp tripped the lad up with his stick and shouted, "Sit on the floor and shut up. And you – sit." He pointed the pistol at the little man in glasses who was standing, ready to bolt for the door in terror. He sat quickly down on the sofa again.

"Jost?" a husky voice said in astonishment.

Jost Krupp turned and looked down at the sofa. Sitting there, her head turned towards him, was the beautiful face of the girl he knew as Freya Jorgensen. He took a deep breath and exhaled slowly. She looked a little older but was still the most beautiful woman he had ever known. He was spellbound for only a moment and then suddenly realised the circumstances. She looked as though she was about to faint or vomit; her hand was firmly over her mouth, her face the colour of window putty, her eyes frightened, her brow furrowed.

"Well, Freya. This is a moment I have been waiting for, for a long time," Krupp said in a shaky voice he would have preferred to sound more menacing. He coughed, casting his eyes over the big man sitting next to Freya. The big man was looking up at him with a blank expression. He looked around at the others. He saw Deller about to push himself up from the sofa with his hands, looking distastefully at him, his liquid eyes showing anger as well as a little fear.

Pointing at Krupp, he shouted, "This is the man who killed Ferdi, Freya. He is a wanted criminal, a Nazi criminal."

"Now where is that painting you kept for me?" Krupp said loudly to Deller. "Or have you sold it?"

"They are no good to you, Krupp, they are fakes. Ask" – Deller's eyes rested on the big man on the sofa – "that man there. He is some kind of authority."

"You bastard!" Freya stood and strode over to Deller. Red with fury, she had no fear. She slapped him across the face. Krupp watched with a thin smile.

"Sit down, Freya," Krupp warned.

"For Christ's sake, I need my arm …" Jason said, blood seeping through his fingers where he held onto the wound.

"Now you." Krupp pointed at the big man with his pistol and waited for Freya to sit back down. She sat as close to the man as possible. He must be a reassuring presence.

"Alec has nothing to do with this, Jost," Freya said.

"You like this fellow, do you?" Krupp said, levelling his pistol at him.

"No!" Freya said with alarm. "He is just an acquaintance who is helping me with … things."

"My name is Alec Ballentine. I am a journalist and I specialise in art and the art world," Alec said calmly. "We have just discovered that the Barrett Collection is all faked."

"Really?" Krupp said with disinterest, looking down at Jason in his armchair, then to Strider who was keeping very quiet and trying to be as small and unnoticeable as possible. "And who are you?" Krupp asked Strider.

"My name is Strider, Sir Jason's lawyer."

"Find something to stop your client's bleeding." Krupp looked nervously at the wound on Sir Jason's arm. He stood back so he could keep as many people in view as possible. Strider put his handkerchief over Jason's wound.

"And you? Who are you?" He pointed at the young woman with his pistol. She was still on the floor, beside the sofa that Freya and the big journalist sat on.

"Sophie Younghusband. I am Mr Ballentine's … secretary."

"What do you want, Jost?" Freya said angrily. "Are you going to kill us all? Or do you just want to frighten us for a while?" Krupp rounded on Freya. He limped up to her and, dropping his stick, sank onto one knee, grabbed her by the throat, and shoved the barrel of the pistol in her open mouth. It was so quick it took Freya by surprise. It felt good; he was in control.

"*Du gottesfürchtige hündin!*" he spat in German loudly in Freya's face. "You and that Turkish bitch. What has that queer done with the files?"

"Get this out of my mouth!" Freya spluttered, finding it difficult to talk. The expression on her face then suddenly changed and her eyes were distracted by something behind him. He turned his head, tried to re-aim the pistol, but his arm was being held. Something struck the base of his head. He shuddered as a fist hit his jaw. A flash of light, a sharp pain, followed by darkness.

When Alec saw Krupp grab Charlotte, he quickly bent down and picked up Krupp's discarded stick whilst he was shouting at her in German. Alec then brought the stick down onto Krupp's neck. Krupp tried to swing the pistol round to shoot Alec, but Charlotte had grabbed his arm. The barrel crashed against her top teeth as it was torn out of her mouth. Alec swung a powerful punch across the side of Krupp's head that rendered Krupp unconscious. Krupp rolled onto the floor, the weapon clattering to the ground.

Alec saw Jane Gardener peering around the door. "Miss Gardener, call for the police and an ambulance." Alec took charge. "Father Dent, would you find something to tie up this man?"

"If I go anywhere near that man, I will kill him." Deller's words were slurred. "You have probably killed him anyway."

"Mr Strider, sir? Will you help me tie this man up?"

"Yes … well … I am not used to this sort of thing, you know," Strider spluttered, virtually in tears.

"Who is?" Alec said, frustrated. He examined Jason's wound; it was not bad, just a graze on his upper arm. "Sophie, would you help with Sir Jason's arm?"

"Charlotte," Jason said in a hoarse voice, "I really would not do that."

Alec turned to see Charlotte sitting on the sofa, looking at Krupp's unconscious body and holding the pistol to his head. She had the hammer cocked and her finger on the trigger.

"I do not think that is wise." Alec placed a hand gently on the hand that held the pistol. She was plainly weighing up the consequences of blowing Krupp's head off.

"I killed him once. I should have shot him in the head, though. I will kill him now."

"Go and see your uncle. He wants to talk to you." Alec gently levered the pistol out of her hand. His heart ached to see her enraged face. She plainly wanted to pull that trigger. "I am sorry, really I am. But it is ... you'd be hanged."

She went over to her uncle and knelt beside him. Sophie was holding a towel over the wound on his arm.

"You wanted to see me, Uncle?" Charlotte said. She seemed insensitive to his injury.

"Do you know what happened to de Tournet after the war?"

"Is this really the time to ask me questions? Why do you want to know about my treacherous stepfather, Uncle?"

"Strider has a document that basically leaves everything to you if he is not found. Your aunt is provided for, apparently. She is in an asylum."

"I know she is, Uncle, we ... I pay for it."

"I see," he said, as though something had been solved. "But do you know where de Tournet is?"

"He is dead, Uncle," Charlotte said flatly.

"How do you know?"

"I killed him in 1943. He was doing business with the Nazis. He tried to rape me" – she stopped and shivered – "but I killed him before he could."

Jason and Sophie both looked at Charlotte with horror. This was the first time Jason had showed any genuine emotion throughout the evening. It was fear. Everybody in the room was staring at her. It was such an extraordinary statement, said with hardly any sentiment or drama.

Strider and Gareth had heard what Charlotte said and stood with lengths of curtain cord in their hands, both with utter disgust over their faces. Alec stopped tying up Krupp's hands. He'd been about to take Krupp's pulse as he thought he may have killed him, when Charlotte spoke. Deller looked at Charlotte, nodding approval.

133

"But then, I thought I had killed this man," she said, pointing a thumb at Krupp, "and he seems to be very much alive. If Jean de Tournet managed to survive a stiletto blade into his brain and a bomb from the RAF, who knows?" There was a lengthy silence. Nobody spoke.

"Tell me," Jason said at last, in a hoarse voice, "do you know where the missing Wasp Trap files are? The files your husband had in Paris?" Alec wondered why her uncle was asking about the files.

"I have no idea, Uncle. He went to Paris after it was liberated, but I have no idea what he did with the files. I am not interested, frankly." She stood and wiped away a tear and looked back at Krupp.

Alec sat Krupp up on the floor, his back against the sofa, and trussed his hands and legs together. He was gradually coming round. Jane Gardener came into the room.

"The police are on their way, Sir Jason." She knelt down in front of the semi-unconscious Krupp, an expression of fascination on her face. "I have opened the gates." There was a sharp hammering on the door. "That was quick."

The police entered. Behind them was Theodora.

"Freya?" she called loudly as soon as she entered the house.

20

Back in the Albemarle Suite in the Adolphe Hotel, Charlotte was prostrate on the sofa, her head on Theodora's lap. It was late evening and it was pouring with rain outside. As Theodora stroked her hair gently, Charlotte lay silently, her face covered by her golden hair. A blanket covered her body and legs, placed there by Alec just before he went off with the police, Krupp and Deller.

Charlotte and Theodora had left Alston House after Jason had been attended to by his doctor. The bullet had only grazed his arm.

Alec accompanied Detective Inspector McMillan, who had appeared fifteen minutes after Theodora arrived with the Wimbledon police. Father Joe Dent was with them but in handcuffs, looking relieved that Krupp was under guard in the Black Maria and on his way to Scotland Yard. Krupp was accompanied by Sergeant Glass and two uniformed police officers.

"That man has successfully killed nearly everyone I have loved," Charlotte said softly. "The sooner he is hanged, the better. How is it he seems to appear wherever I am, and then try and kill everybody? Is it me he wants to kill?" Theodora shrugged, there was nothing she could say.

Theodora had just told Charlotte of the massacre back at Burton Park Place and Charlotte had not taken it well … understandably.

"My heart is heavy," Theodora said. "My head aches and so do my shoulders and the back of my neck. God knows what Krupp has done to me."

"He nearly killed you." Charlotte looked up at Theodora, who was nodding in agreement but distracted. "What are you thinking, Theodora?"

"Darling, tell me about Mr Ballentine. Did you get on with him?"

Charlotte raised her head. "Theodora, he would not let me kill Jost. If it was not for Alec, that man would be dead. Anyway, I don't think this is the time to—"

"I just think the English police are not prepared for a weasel like Krupp, and I wondered if Mr Ballentine would help us ensure Krupp is … how can I put this … got rid of. For good. Before he escapes, or talks his way out."

Charlotte viewed Theodora for a long time, trying to understand what she was saying. "He is never going to escape. He is going straight to the gallows," Charlotte said emphatically, although Theodora did have a point.

"I truly hope he does, darling, but it will be after a trial, which could take a long time," Theodora said, her voice building in anger. "He will slip away somehow, he always does!" Charlotte sat up and put an arm around her friend.

"Theodora, he is never going to get out. Apart from anything else, he is ill, injured after what I did to him. We know an awful lot about him and who he was during the war."

"I just would be happier if he was dead," said Theodora.

"We all would. But he will be dead soon, hanged by British justice. And I very much doubt Alec would help kill him, if that is what is behind your original question." There was a long silence.

"No, I think not," Theodora said considerately, looking away. "I am going to have a bath." She got up quickly. "Are you going to be all right, darling?"

"I am fine." Charlotte gave a tired smile of assurance. "I am going to bed with a pill, and then tomorrow, we have the identification and police questions … endless questions, I should think. We will probably see Alec too," she said, looking forward to seeing the large, reassuring frame of the journalist. She realised that the thought of Alec Ballentine made her feel a little more at ease, even though he had stopped her from killing Krupp.

She thought about the next day and all that it held with dread. Identifying her husband's body and sorting out the mess back home at Burton Park Place. She needed to think about what to do about Rupert the butler, the maids and the Banners. She lay back on the sofa, listening to Theodora's bath being run. Her head was throbbing and her eyes felt gritty.

What was she going to say about the collection? She thought back at the revelations about all those lovely paintings. Were they *all* fakes? Was it illegal to own counterfeit art? She could not help but feel slightly sorry for her uncle. He looked rather pathetic.

Apparently, according to the Sussex police, the study at home had been virtually destroyed by Krupp in his search for something. He had gone through the whole house, taking out wall panels, breaking into the few locked rooms. God, what a mess!

*

The small, confined interview room was full of smoke as the policemen chain-smoked to keep themselves awake and to help concentration. Inspector McMillan was interviewing Franz-Joseph Deller, and Sergeant Glass was taking notes. Deller felt exhausted. He wore a coarse grey blanket provided by the police as he complained of being cold. He could see his reflection in the mirror in the interview room. He had grey rings under his eyes and his skin was washed out and waxy.

"Let us start from the beginning, sir," the inspector said, his hand pushing his hat back on his head, an expression of exasperation on his face.

"Your name is Mr Franz-Joseph Deller and you are a citizen of Austria—"

"*Originally* a citizen of Austria," Deller interrupted. "I am now a British subject under the name of Joseph Dent."

"And you're a vicar?" the sergeant asked bluntly.

"Oh but yes! I was ordained just after the war, on the third of July 1945. A lovely sunny—"

"So what do we call you?" the inspector asked.

"Joseph Dent or Father Joe or Mr Dent, even just Joseph, I suppose."

The sergeant asked, "After your release from Battersea nick ... police station ... where did you go?"

"I went with Mr Strider, the solicitor, first to his office and then an hour later to an apartment at *The Sentinel* newspaper in Fleet Street. I believe it's Sir Jason's private suite."

"Did you go to your flat before that?" The sergeant was watching Deller closely.

"No. As I said, I went straight to Fleet Street – to Bouverie Street, I think it's called."

"Are you sure, Mr Dent? Because we think you may have gone home to get some cloves."

"Cloves?" said Deller, then realised what was being said. "No – I have been in these same clothes for the last two days and nights. In fact I am becoming quite smelly!" Deller gave a nervous laugh.

"Mr Dent," the inspector carried on, "what happened in the vestry at your church the evening of Sunday last?"

"I believe I told you all this—"

"You claimed responsibility for killing the gent, when questioned then. Now you assert the German – you named him as Jost Krupp – killed him on Sunday evening."

The policeman's wise, kind face showed no judgement, no anger, nor really any emotion. His deep voice was measured and composed. His sergeant, however, chose not to hide his feelings of contempt for the prisoner, and his squashed porcine face scowled at Deller. His hand holding a short pencil hovered over his notepad.

"Well, I had just cleared up after evensong, when this man, Baron Ferdi Saumures—"

"The victim?" the inspector asked.

"Yes—"

"Did you know this man – the victim – previously?" the sergeant asked brusquely.

"Well ..." Deller tried to compose himself and to think about what he was going to say, but the inspector interrupted his thoughts.

"Mr Dent, you must answer truthfully. You have yet to be charged, but anything you say may be used in evidence. Remember, sir, this is not the time to lie or prevaricate."

Joseph looked at the inspector, his eyes moist and blinking back tears. The sergeant tutted. The inspector gave him a look of warning. "Sorry, guv," said Sergeant Glass.

"Carry on, Mr Dent. Did you know the dead man, Baron Ferdinand Saumures?"

"We were students in Paris together before the war. He recruited me into a branch of the British Secret Service. Unfortunately, I am unable to tell you much more about that," Deller whispered.

He saw the incredulity in Sergeant Glass's face. Plainly, the sergeant was unable to see how he could be part of the secret service.

"I see, Mr Dent. And when was the last time you saw the deceased before that Sunday night?"

"Oh ... sometime in 1943 – the last time I was in Paris. He had hardly changed, whereas I must have been very different."

"What did you do in the war, sir?" the sergeant asked.

"I was a colonel in the SS, responsible for collecting artworks for the Reich—"

"Bleeding hell, you was a Nazi, what stole the art out of France? *And* a bleeding SS Nazi colonel?" Glass said, astounded. McMillan coughed another warning to his sergeant.

"Well, yes, but I was also spying on the Germans for the British."

"Did you take the Barrett Collection for the Germans?" the inspector asked, looking slightly shaken by what was being revealed.

"No, actually. I was asked by Sir Jason."

"What has Sir Jason got to do with this?" The inspector's eyes turned towards the mirror on the wall.

"He was sort of in charge of us all, I think."

There was a sharp double tap on the door to the interview room, and the door burst open. A dapper man in his forties with long, unmilitary black hair strode in with a police sergeant behind him. He wore a red buttonhole carnation in the lapel of his modern grey houndstooth suit. The inspector and his sergeant leapt to their feet. Deller followed suit, feeling worried. The man entering had the unmistakable air of authority, despite his young age.

"Good evening, Father Dent, my name is Adams. Assistant Commissioner Jeremy Adams. I am in charge of your case here at the Yard."

"The Yard?" Deller was confused.

"Scotland Yard," Adams corrected.

"I am in Scotland Yard?" Deller became agitated and felt he was being misled for some reason.

"Do sit down, gentlemen. Father Dent," Adams carried on, kindly, "you can talk freely in this company. We are the police, and I am part of the security services."

"I have only your word for that, Mr Adams. Come to that, I have only your word that I'm in Scotland Yard."

Adams produced his warrant card and Joseph craned his neck to read the contents. Adams then pointed to a black plaque under the large mirror that said in white letters, "Interview Room 2, Scotland Yard", beside which was a large red button with "ALARM" written on it.

"Please sit down, sir, there is a lot to get through." Adams sat in the chair next to McMillan, which meant Sergeant Glass had to stand next to the large uniformed policeman.

"Father Dent," Adams said less cordially, "what I specifically need to understand is if you killed Baron Saumures, whether it was by accident or—"

"No, I did *not* kill him," Deller said emphatically. He sat down, wrapping the blanket around his shoulders. "That man, Jost Krupp, who is a wanted Nazi criminal, killed him. He suddenly appeared in the vestry when I was talking to Ferdi." Deller took an inward breath. "He threatened me with a knife."

"Why did this man you refer to as Jost Krupp threaten you with a knife, sir?" Adams asked in his clipped, military voice.

"He wanted to know the whereabouts of Freya Jorgensen, the baroness, and some paintings, and" – Joseph paused and his head dropped – "money I owed." Joseph raised his eyes, anticipating more questions, but the policemen allowed him to carry on. "He and Freya Jorgensen were once lovers in Paris during the war and he wanted to find her." Joseph coughed nervously. The policemen seemed less accepting of this story.

"What are the paintings you refer to?" Adams asked.

"Sir Jason Barrett's collection. Jost Krupp thought, wrongly, that I was keeping the collection in France for myself. I was, in fact, bringing it back to England under Sir Jason's instructions. I promised Krupp money or the Caravaggio for his silence, or he was going to go to the Gestapo. I escaped with the paintings before he could report me."

Deller stopped and focused on a cigarette burn on the table. Adams whispered something in McMillan's ear. McMillan nodded and got up. He and his sergeant left the room. Adams's attention went back to Deller and he asked simply, "Who killed the baron?"

"He did … Krupp, not I."

The deputy commissioner removed a piece of paper from a buff file in front of him and glanced at it, then passed it to the sergeant.

The sergeant licked his lips and said in a grave voice, "The man who was arrested at Sir Jason's home in Wimbledon has identified himself as Günther Wolff, not Jost Krupp. Why do you think this man is Jost Krupp?"

Deller eyed the policemen opposite him, appalled.

"He *is* Jost Krupp, without doubt," he said emphatically. The sergeant looked at Adams with a slight nod and made a note on the piece of paper.

"Why did you tell Mr Ballentine and the police inspector that you killed Baron Saumures?" Adams asked.

"Because he threatened to kill Freya if I did not take the blame. He was … is … a terribly dangerous man, and I am glad you have him behind bars."

"How did Mr Wolff or Krupp kill the baron, and why?" Adams did not seem to be as convinced by Deller's story as much as he had hoped.

"He threatened me with a dagger, and Ferdi stepped in front of me to prevent him from stabbing me. When Krupp struck out at the baron, the baron tried to step back out of the way, but I was behind him and he tripped on my cassock. He slipped forward. Krupp thrust the dagger into his neck. The baron swung round, holding the dagger – I suppose trying to get the dagger out of his neck – and fell on me and died." Joseph tried to remember the awful event and hoped he had not left anything out. "Krupp then placed a gun at my head and threatened to kill Freya unless I took the blame for the murder."

"So, the man, Krupp, or Wolff, had the knife or dagger in which hand? And where was the gun?" Adams asked. Joseph screwed up his eyes in thought.

"He had the dagger in his left hand, and the gun ... no wait, he ... yes, that's right. He had the knife in his left hand."

"Why didn't he just shoot you with his pistol?" Adams asked.

"I don't know!" Deller said incredulously. "Why don't you ask him?"

"Now, where does the baroness, Freya, come into things?"

"Well ..." Deller felt nervous. What was he going to say? He eventually blurted, "She is my daughter. Her real name is Charlotte."

Deller could see Adams viewed him with an element of sorrow, as though he was some kind of fantasist.

"And how do you know she is your daughter? Why do you think she is your daughter, sir?"

"She just is! It is very difficult for me. I have only just met her for the first time since the war."

"When did you see her in the war?"

"It is too complicated ... I really can't ... It's just too complex," Deller yelled, exasperated, his head beginning to throb. He rubbed his temples with the tips of his fingers, his eyes tightly shut.

"I have plenty of time, Mr Dent," Adams said, seemingly unmoved by Deller's outburst and distress, but then he said somewhat kindly, "Can I get you a cup of tea – coffee?"

Deller wondered about the possibility of getting a large whisky but dismissed the likelihood and shook his head. He carried on with his story. "Her mother and I were lovers in 1925, the year Freya was born, except she was called Charlotte. She became Freya so that she would not be discovered as being British when the Nazis took over her house in Avenue Foch, Paris, in 1940."

"What happened to Charlotte's mother?" How did Commissioner Adams know the very questions he did not want to answer?

Deller lied.

"I don't know. I left France just after she was born and went back to Austria."

"So, you saw her in Paris, during the war?" Adams sat up and placed his forearms on the table. He looked sceptical.

"Yes," Deller said. He was feeling very weary. Adams sat back, his arms crossed. There was a period of silence. Deller focused on the cigarette burning in the ashtray.

"We shall leave the war for the moment," Adams said, to Deller's relief. "Tell me about the paintings you were" – he thought for a word – "acquiring for Günther Wolff or Jost Krupp."

Deller thought. Should he make up a story, or just tell the truth? Was it too late or unwise to prevaricate? They would find out in the end, somehow. He would tell the truth. "I had to get a Caravaggio painting back from Sir Jason's collection, or Krupp was going to kill everybody else!"

"Well he has, just about," Adams shouted, shocking Deller. "A body in Battersea, possibly a grievous assault on a police officer at your rooms, a wounding in Wimbledon and two bodies in Sussex. Why did you not contact us immediately?"

"But I did!" Deller shouted.

"No, you did not!" Adams shouted back. "Mr Ballentine did. You just wanted him to help you dump the body. Your actions have resulted in three people being shot. Two are dead … three, counting the baron!"

"Who else is dead, for heaven's sake?" Deller stood up, distraught. The police sergeant moved in closer.

"A woman called Christina Jorgensen and a man called Bernard Trent."

Deller sank back onto the chair, wrapping his blanket around himself again. Adams carried on with his tirade. "This is a wanted and highly dangerous war criminal. He kidnapped and assaulted a woman, Theodora Smith, and threatened half a dozen people with a pistol, and finally, he shot and wounded Sir Jason Barrett. All because you did not contact us directly to warn us of this dangerous man's existence."

"Where is he now?" Deller asked, hoping he was in some highly secure dungeon with chains attached to each limb.

"As he is an alien – from Germany – he is being taken to the Aliens Department, a secure police station in Holborn," Adams said and stood to leave. At the interview room door, he turned, calm now, and said kindly to Deller, "I am afraid you will have to remain here, Father Dent. Your flat is a scene of crime, and in any case, it is late."

"What do you mean – a scene of what crime?"

"One of our police officers was assaulted on the stairs to your flat. We believe the perpetrator was Günther Wolff, trying to find you."

Deller felt sick yet grateful that he was staying in the relative safety of Scotland Yard. Deller went up to sergeant, and plucked at the sergeant's sleeve and whispered, "Would it be possible to get a whisky, for my throat, you understand? Just half a bottle ..." The sergeant smiled sympathetically.

"'Fraid not, sir. I will get a cup of tea and an aspirin to you."

*

It was well past midnight and Jost Krupp sat in the back of the police car. Beside him, in the back seat, sat an old uniformed police sergeant, and driving was a detective constable. Krupp was handcuffed, his hands in front of him. He pretended to be groggy and exhausted, and hardly moved throughout the journey.

As the police car turned up a wide, deserted street, the sergeant leant forward to ask the driver for a cigarette. As he did so, Krupp quickly and deliberately leant forward too and stretched his handcuffed hands down his trouser leg.

"'Ere, what are you up to?" the sergeant growled.

"*Ich bin nur mein knöchel kratzen,*" Krupp said lazily. "My ankle – it has itch, I think you say." When the old sergeant looked back at the driver to get his cigarette, Krupp pulled up his trouser leg, revealing his right boot. Inside the boot were three small syringes – there had been four of them.

The sergeant took hold of Krupp's shoulder and pulled him back to sit upright. As he did so, Krupp swooned towards the policeman as though in a faint. When the sergeant pushed him back, Krupp swiftly sank a syringe into the policeman's leg and depressed the plunger.

"'Ere, he's stuck me with something!" he said incredulously. "You bastard, you've stuck me with ..." He passed out before he could finish the sentence.

The driver slammed on his brakes as he heard the sergeant shout. He could not see Krupp, who was sitting behind him, so he went round to the sergeant's door and opened it. The sergeant fell out onto the pavement as Krupp pushed him hard with his shoulder. The driver ran around the back of the car, furious. Just as he opened the door, Krupp pushed his good leg against it so it burst open, smashing into the detective constable's face. He sprawled across the road. Krupp quickly got out and finished off the detective with another syringe full of dope. A shaft of pain went up his injured leg and back, and he cried out an oath in German. He leant up against the car and gritted his teeth, waiting for the pain to subside.

Krupp looked up and down the wide pavement to see if anybody had seen anything. It was deserted. First, he went through the detective's pockets and took out his wallet, but found no keys. He checked the sergeant's pockets, and found the key to the handcuffs and unshackled himself. He pulled the rest of the sergeant's body clear of the car, then retrieved the syringes. Then he slammed both rear doors and clambered into the passenger seat. Seeing his error, he cursed and shifted over to the driver's seat, and drove off.

He calculated he would have at least two hours before the authorities would realise he had escaped. He was astonished that they – the police – had not only failed to search him thoroughly, but they had transported him in a car and not a prison van. Now he had over four pounds in notes and change from the policemen, a fast police car, and a nearly deserted London ahead of him.

He started to laugh at the stupidity of the English police.

"How did they win the war?" he cackled.

21

Alec sat in the police station for hours. He had, unwisely as it transpired, phoned Bing-Wallace to tell him the news. Bing-Wallace said he wanted to sit with Alec at the police station and get all the gory details. Alec was tired and just wanted to go to bed, but nothing would dissuade Bing-Wallace from joining him in the police waiting room.

"What is happening?" Philip Bing-Wallace asked in a whisper.

"Philip, I am too tired." Alec sat thinking what he was going to do. He wanted to file the story but felt that he might endanger his relationship with Charlotte, and, perhaps, a bigger story. He wanted to keep in her good books, not only so he could write her story about her war, but also so he could get closer to her. He was very taken with her, but was under no illusion that the relationship – if it could be called that – could ever be a romantic one. He was annoyed that she had affected him so badly, that all objectivity had basically gone. She could ask him to do anything and he would have to comply.

"Philip, you are going to have to write the story."

"Oh, Ballentine, how lovely of you. But why not you?"

"Because I want to get even closer to the baroness – I want her to tell her whole story. She will not approve of me breaking this news. I will write it, but you will have to put it in *The Times*. *The Sentinel* will certainly run it."

"Where is everybody anyway? Who is in clink here?" Bing-Wallace asked, but Alec was thinking of something else. "Is Father Dent Joe here? Alec, what's going on?"

"Sorry, Philip, a lot on my mind." Alec described the events of the evening to Bing-Wallace.

"The baroness has certainly aroused something in you, Alec."

"Well, she's quite something. You will fall for her charms as I did, I guarantee you. Her friend Theodora is also very attractive but slightly severe. A little older than Charlotte. And, it turns out, Father Joe is not only Charlotte's father but also an Austrian called Franz-Joseph Deller."

"I'll be jiggered," was all Bing-Wallace could say. "So he's not a real vicar?"

"Apparently he is." Alec continued with the evening's events to Bing-Wallace's ever-dropping jaw.

"What are the files Sir Jason was asking about, do you think?" Bing-Wallace asked when Alec told him about Jason getting shot.

"Well, during the war there was a division of the SIS that compiled a dossier on almost all of the high-ranking Nazis in Paris. These files were used at Nuremberg. The files were called the Wasp Trap files, which you may remember – I did a small and rather inadequate piece on them a few years ago."

"No, I'm afraid I missed that," said Bing-Wallace, sounding confused.

"Well anyway, these secret files were compiled by Baron Ferdi Saumures's team in Paris during the war."

"Do you think it was those files that boy was taking from Strider's office?"

"No," Alec said. "I'm not sure what those files were. That is a very good point. What were those files? That boy, I think, is called Gareth and I met him at Jason's house in Wimbledon. He is working for Sir Jason as some kind of servant, I think." Alec thought more and then said, "I bet he was gathering all the legal files that were on Sir Jason. Nothing to do with the Wasp Trap files."

"So, where are these missing files, do you think?"

"Nobody seems to know. The baron hid them."

"And the baroness claims not to know where they are?"

Alec was in deep thought again. His rump was becoming uncomfortable on the bench in the police station waiting room, so he stood and strode about, puffing at his cigarette. Why would Jason want to know about the files? Was it because he was responsible for running the operation? Surely they would have gone to the head of the security services – the baron would not have them.

"Does Sir Jason know this Wolff or Krupp character, Alec?"

"Well, on reflection, I think he may do. He called out his name when he burst in." Alec swung round and beamed at Bing-Wallace. "Well, Philip, this is shaping up to be a fascinating story; I hope you are taking notes. In the morning, I will go to the Adolphe Hotel and see the baroness. Perhaps we can do a little sleuthing."

"Good idea," Bing-Wallace said. "You are on, dear boy," he added, gesturing with his chin. Alec turned to see the sergeant coming into the room.

"It is a bit late now, sir. Can you come back tomorrow morning?" said the sergeant.

"You mean this morning, Sergeant, or do you mean Wednesday morning?"

"Yes, sir, sorry, sir, this morning. About ten o'clock. The inspector needs to get some kip. He's had very little lately. You will be seeing Assistant Commissioner Adams, sir." The sergeant quickly ducked out of the room.

"Well I haven't had much in the way of sleep either!" Alec shouted angrily after the sergeant. He turned to Bing-Wallace, his arms outstretched. "What a bloody nerve. Keeping me here for hours and then just brushing me off."

"Never mind, dear thing. Go home and have a whisky. I will go and give them a piece of your mind."

*

Alec got back to his flat at well past two in the morning. Benjy the cat was still out patrolling his area or snuggled up in another flat, more than likely curled up with Mrs Ash, the concierge who also cleaned for Alec. Alec was convinced he got fed by other people and acquired new owners with his charm. It was quite true what Philip Bing-Wallace said about cats and dogs: that "dogs have owners; cats have staff".

Thinking about the long day, he was thankful to have driven to Sussex and to have met Charlotte. He was totally captivated by her. Her face, her smile, her legs were constantly flashing into his brain each time he thought of her. She was quite a character as well as gorgeous. She had a quick mind, and temper, and a lovely sense of fun. Her moods could swing, however, quite rapidly, from cheerful to gloomy. But on hearing her story, he was not too surprised.

She was a complicated woman living a complex life. Art theft and forgery, an estranged uncle, and a murdered, homosexual husband. Alec was used to war, politics, natural disasters – tangible stories without too much mystery. He wondered if he was capable of writing a story with so much passion going on.

Charlotte's friend Theodora was a completely different story: enigmatic, even a little scary. Charlotte was so beautiful, in body and personality, easy and approachable, but also short-tempered, whereas Theodora had a hard beauty, austere and rigid. She had a low, near masculine voice with a thick accent, but she was wonderfully elegant; every movement was with balletic poise – except when she had arrived at Alston House with the police, she looked haggard and drawn. When she told Charlotte of her terrible adventure with Krupp, Alec was there, Charlotte held onto his hand, her grip getting tighter and tighter as the horrors unfolded.

Charlotte had never had a traditional childhood, Alec supposed. She had no parents as such, a surrogate mother in Christina, and a sister in Theodora. Did she say her stepfather tried to rape her? Alec had no idea how she'd coped as a child, and he was interested in finding out.

The German, Wolff or Krupp, was dangerous, a typical Nazi, but Charlotte plainly was able to dilute his scariness. He could not bear to hurt her, even with his hand about her throat, his gun in her mouth. Alec had seen a flash of uncertainty on his face as he gazed into Charlotte's wide violet-blue eyes, before Alec hit him with the stick.

And Sophie: how – or more to the point, why – did Sophie get so deeply involved in this? She was so staid and sensible, not really one for adventure or spontaneity. Would she survive professionally? Alec felt slightly sorry for his ex-fiancée.

As for Strider, he was just a treacherous, lying lawyer. Why did Sir Jason seem to trust him? Alec mused. He wondered if anyone in that household could be trusted. Strider worked for not only Ferdi and Charlotte, but also, unbeknownst to Charlotte, it seemed, her uncle Jason.

The austere housekeeper, Jane Gardener: where was she when Wolff was threatening everyone with a pistol? Calling the police, Alec supposed. But was it normal that housekeepers wore seamed stockings and high-heeled shoes, as she did? The boy, Gareth, did not strike Alec as a sharp blade. He looked slightly frightened all the time. But then, it was not as if it was a particularly joyous occasion, and Alec had only seen him fleetingly, pouring drinks and tying up Wolff; not really an opportunity to gauge Gareth's sense of humour.

Farther Dent: poor old Father Joe. Plainly put through the ringer by Sir Jason, possibly by Sophie as well, and then by Charlotte. The man had the most extraordinary past: a former SS colonel, art thief, murderer and, more than likely, an alcoholic. And a vicar, which Alec found somewhat unbelievable now he knew more of Father Joe's story. Charlotte had accused him of killing her mother. Just looking at him, you would never believe he was capable of any of the things he was supposed to have done.

And then there was Sir Jason Barrett MP. Alec wondered if Sir Jason was a credible person. Why did he feel Jason was a bit dodgy? How did he recruit an Austrian – a Nazi SS colonel, no less – to steal and transport a whole collection of art – counterfeit art at that – to England in the middle of the war? Using his influences in the intelligence service, his friendship with Winston Churchill? And it looked like he was after the same files Günther Wolff was searching for. What were these files?

*

"Look at this, Charlotte." It was Tuesday morning. The rain was lashing down in high winds, but it was warm and cosy in the Albemarle Suite. However, Charlotte felt a cold chill run through her bones at the thought of the things she had to do that day. She felt run-down, as though she was getting a head cold.

"At what, Theodora?"

"*The Times* has you all over page four. There's a rather nice picture of you and a very old photo of Ferdi. No idea where they found that. It says: *Baron Ferdinand Saumures of Luxembourg was found murdered …*"

"Not now, Theodora. I will read it later. I want to get today over and done with first, and then go home … and see what is left of it."

"Oh, all right, darling. I thought you would want to stay a little longer in London."

"No, not really. Sorry. You stay here if you would like. See a show."

The women were told they had to be at the Chelsea mortuary by eleven o'clock for the identification, and then they would be going back to the Adolphe Hotel for an interview with the police. As they went down the stairs, Arno raced up to them, his head tilted to the side with an expression of deep condolence on his face.

"Oh God," whispered Charlotte in despair, "Arno's going to be intolerable." She managed to rustle up a sad smile at his approach.

"Lady Saumures, our deepest condolences."

"Thank you, Arno," Charlotte said without sentiment. "Arno, we need a car to take us to the Chelsea mortuary, please. We have to be there by eleven."

Arno's chubby hands shot to his mouth at the thought of her going to see the body.

"I have Jack waiting to take you." A thought suddenly came to him. "My lady, I regret you will have to go through the kitchens to get to the car. The press are everywhere outside. Jack will take you. I am sorry," he said, as though it was his fault the press was intruding.

"How on earth do they know where we are?" Charlotte cried.

"Mr Ballentine, darling, I am afraid," Theodora said unkindly.

"No, I don't think it could be him. I think the police told them."

They waited in the tea salon until it was time for them to go. One or two other guests in the room were stuck behind their newspapers. All Charlotte could see were photos of her on the front page, the one of her and her husband after the abortive trial a few years ago. *The Times* had a photo that was taken when she was at Ascot with a friend, Cecil Bainbridge, the year before. Cecil had ducked out of the photographer's way when he saw a lens pointing in his direction. She looked so happy, she thought. Why did they have a photo of her looking happy when they were writing about the death of her husband?

Arno appeared looking distressed with two men behind him, one tall and one round and chubby – he could have been Arno's twin. Both men wore damp fawn raincoats and held their wet hats on their chest as though in salute. With a shaking hand, Arno indicated Charlotte to the men.

"Lady Saumures?" the taller man asked gently.

"Yes?" Charlotte was alarmed. Arno trotted off, shaking his head, his hand over his forehead. She recognised the man as the policeman she had met the day before.

"My name is McMillan. We met yesterday. I am the detective inspector in charge of the case of the murder of your husband." Theodora stood and went to stand behind Charlotte.

"Yes?" said Charlotte with dread. McMillan looked up at Theodora. "Oh, this is Madam Theodora Smith, Inspector. You can say anything, she is my closest friend. Please, carry on."

"I am afraid Günther Wolff, or Jost Krupp, escaped from police custody last night—"

"Bah!" Theodora exclaimed loudly in disgust. "What did I say! These bungling fools. I knew that man would get away."

"Mrs Smith—" McMillan started sternly.

"Madam Theodora, if you don't mind. We'll go now, back to Sussex, build a fortress, get the Tanners armed—"

"Madam Theodora!" McMillan was shocked. "It is not that serious."

"It bloody well is, Inspector Milligan," Charlotte said in some distress and got up from her seat.

"McMillan, milady," McMillan started, with a shocked expression at the ripe language.

"How did he get away?" Theodora demanded as they walked together to the stairs to go back to their room.

"He overpowered the driver of the police car he was in and escaped in the car." McMillan was beginning to sound rather embarrassed.

"Christ!" spat Charlotte. "So he could be here any second now. You'd better come with us, Inspector, and make sure he is not lurking in our suite."

"But the identification, Lady Saumures."

"Until that man is dead, I will not stay in London a single moment longer. He is a Nazi. He has killed – to my knowledge – ninety-two Jews. He not only tortured our friend Bernard Trent, but he has now murdered him, my dear friend Christina, her husband … my husband, for Christ's sake!" She stopped at the bottom of the stairs, throwing her hands up, absolutely furious. "I could have put a bullet in his head last night but I didn't." She and Theodora stormed up the stairs, McMillan and Sergeant Glass following behind. McMillan tried once or twice to interrupt her tirade. "This man, Inspector" – she stopped halfway up the stairs and wagged a finger at the inspector – "this man has a bullet in him that is killing him. He could not care less who he kills to get what he wants."

"What does he want, Lady Saumures?"

"I don't bloody know! It may be me, either dead or in his clutches, or a painting he was promised by Franz-Joseph Deller."

"As to Deller, or Dent, he—"

"I hope you have him safely locked up somewhere in a deep secure dungeon, or you will get him killed as well!"

"I am sure this Herr Wolff is not that—" McMillan spluttered.

"He will have gone into hiding, milady," Glass chipped in.

Charlotte flashed a searing glare at the sergeant, as did Theodora, who was about to say something. Charlotte put up her hand to stop her talking just as they got to the suite door.

"Don't bother, Theodora, just let us get packed and out of here. I am going to try to find Mr Ballentine and see if he will take us home. Here is the key, Inspector." Charlotte dangled the key in front of him and waited for him to go in.

Theodora said, "Your man here can wait with us in case the *ficken drecksack* is on his way up the stairs."

"The what? Madam, please! Your language," the sergeant said.

"*Madam, please*," Theodora sneered. "Madam, please, you understand German now? I will give you *madam, please*! Get your gun out and look competent, for God's sake!"

151

"We are not armed, madam. Very few British police are. Anyway, he will not be armed."

"How do you know?" Theodora thundered.

"He was thoroughly searched when he was taken into custody," the policeman said.

"Then how did he 'render the driver helpless'? With a syringe full of some drug, I would bet."

McMillan, who had just gone into the suite, came straight out again when he heard Theodora's theory.

"How did you know it was a syringe, miss ... I mean, madam?"

"Because that was what he did to me, fool! I told the other policeman yesterday." Theodora snatched the key out of McMillan's hand and strode into the suite with Charlotte in tow. As she passed McMillan, she hissed, "Stupid police. Your incompetence is ... is ..." She couldn't find the word, so slammed the door, bumping McMillan's shoulder.

"Quite a couple of women, eh, guv?" Glass said.

"You could say that." He was feeling embarrassed. "How did the Yard police not find the syringe? The foreign woman has a point about incompetence. Who searched him and Dent?"

"Didn't we search them, guv?"

"No, I left it to the Yard – they were there first."

"Looks like nobody searched the suspects, guv."

"Bloody hell, Sergeant. Somebody is going to swing for this."

"Should we finish interviewing them women, guv?"

"No, Sergeant, leave them be for now. The baroness, it transpires, is niece to Sir Jason Barrett. I think I will go and see Mr Ballentine at the Yard first. I will warn him that these ladies are looking for him." McMillan then had a thought and knocked on the door.

"Who is it?" said Theodora from the other side.

"Inspector McMillan, Madam Theodora. Just to say we will be interviewing Mr Ballentine at Scotland Yard this morning, in about an hour. Would you like me to get him to contact you here at the hotel?" There was a pause. The door slowly opened, and Charlotte put her head around the side.

"I would be grateful, Inspector McMillan, thank you." She gave him a small, pretty smile and closed the door.

22

Charlotte picked up the phone and dialled reception.

"How may I assist you, Lady Saumures?" the female receptionist said on the other end.

"May I talk to Arno, please?"

"One moment, please … putting you through."

"My lady," Arno said, sounding annoyingly tragic, "how can we be of assistance?"

"Arno, if you see a man with a heavy limp and a large scar on his face anywhere near the hotel, you must first alert the police …"

"Immediately, my lady!"

"… and then us. Instruct the staff. I would be very grateful, Arno, if you would do this for me, and I am so sorry to have put you through this."

"Quite all right, my lady, I will ensure this man never gets near you or Madam Theodora. The inspector has left a policeman here for your protection."

"Thank you, Arno. We are expecting Mr Ballentine to come and collect us."

"Very well, my lady. By the way, my lady."

"Yes, Arno," Charlotte sighed.

"The baron's Bentley is still parked in the hotel garage. Would you like me to get a driver to take it back to—?"

"No, thank you, Arno. It may be useful to keep it here."

*

"What do you mean 'escaped'?" Alec exploded. He was in an office at Scotland Yard.

"He had a syringe of what we think was concentrated sodium thiopental, a pretty strong knockout drug," McMillan said, exasperated. "He had it concealed in his boot, we think."

Alec sat shaking his head. "What about Lady Saumures and Madam Theodora? Do they know?"

"They have been informed. Unfortunately, they have refused to go to the identification of the body of Baron Saumures."

"Well, I am not surprised. Perhaps I should get in contact. Do you know where they are?"

"They did ask for you, Mr Ballentine." Alec's heart leapt with pleasure at the thought of being wanted by Charlotte. A knight in shining armour. "I think they would like you to drive them down to Petworth, to the manor." Or just a glorified chauffeur, he thought, slightly disappointed. "They're at the Adolphe Hotel."

"I will go now, Inspector." Alec eagerly jumped to his feet.

"Just a few things first, sir."

"Of course, Inspector."

"Do you know much about Sir Jason Barrett?"

"Not a great deal, I'm afraid. He's a cabinet minister, MP, was in MI6, and quite senior, from all accounts. Apart from being the proprietor of *The Sentinel* newspaper, he was an official at the British embassy in Paris before the war. I think he was quite senior there as well. He is also Lady Saumures's uncle – her mother's brother."

"Well, this is where it gets complicated. From what I gather from official records and the secret service themselves, they say that he was not a senior part of MI6 ... or MI5 for that matter. He was, or is, a friend of Mr Churchill's, and has quite a lot of influence in government."

"What? Really?" Alec sat slowly down again, most perplexed. "He was certainly a high-ranking British diplomat."

"As was his father, Mr Ballentine."

"It was his father that started this mess about the collection."

"Yes?" McMillan said, jotting down notes. "Who told you he was in the secret service?"

"Lady Saumures, when she was telling me about the Wasp Trap files," Alec said.

"Now the Wasp Trap files: according to the secret service, they do exist and were delivered around the end of the war to the War Office. Some of the files have gone missing, apparently. Their theory is, the files may have been sold or acquired by the Simon Wiesenthal Trust or other Nazi hunters." The inspector stopped to see Alec scribbling down some notes. "Mr Ballentine?" he asked, waiting for comment.

"Do you think the baron sold these files, Inspector?"

McMillan became cautious. "Perhaps you should direct that sort of question to Assistant Commissioner Adams, Mr Ballentine."

"I have got to go. Have you finished with me?" Alec stood and put on his hat and coat.

"For now, sir." The inspector also stood and put out his hand, and said, slightly sardonically, "Don't leave the country, sir." Alec detected a sly smile.

All Alec could think of was Charlotte and Theodora sitting in their suite in the Adolphe Hotel, twiddling their thumbs. But he must find Philip Bing-Wallace first. He headed for the nearest phone box and called Bing-Wallace's office.

"Philip Bing-Wallace." He answered the phone breathlessly.

"Bing-Wallace, it's me, Ballentine."

"Golly, Ballentine, I have only just got in!"

"Sorry, but I need you to go out again. I want you to go and see Lady Saumures and Madam Theodora. They are holed up at the Adolphe Hotel."

"Why? I thought they were identifying the baron."

"Jost Krupp has escaped the law."

"Good Gad! That's a very poor show."

"And they feel he will be heading for the mortuary at Chelsea to make bother, so they have decided to postpone the identification."

"Golly! I will go to them right away." There was a slight pause. "What sort of questions should I ask, Alec?"

"Don't ask any, just entertain them if they feel like it. Be a reassuring presence."

"Heavens! Not sure how reassuring I can be though. I'm not a great big thing like you!"

"No, but you have charm, Bing-Wallace." Alec heard Philip laugh.

Alec next called the hotel.

"Charlotte, Alec Ballentine," Alec said in haste on the phone. "I have asked Philip Bing-Wallace, a great friend, to come and keep you company. I cannot come over immediately. I must go and see someone first. Is that all right?"

"Fine, Alec. I will warn Arno that Mr Bing-Wallace is arriving, and we can expect you at what time?"

"I hope at about one o'clock. I will take you and Theodora back to the manor, if that is where you would like to go."

"Oh, thank you so much. I will be eternally grateful." Charlotte's soft, sweet, lightly accented voice sent a tingle down Alec's spine.

*

"Alec Ballentine, you old bugger!" shouted the athletic, stylishly dressed man. "When are you going to get shorter?" He strode over, hand extended, his elbow locked at a right angle, a huge smile beneath his opulent pepper and salt moustache, a pipe jutting out from between his teeth. Alec was waiting at the reception desk of the In and Out – as the Naval and Military Club in Piccadilly was affectionally called.

The man striding towards him, Captain Dan James MP MC, was the only person Alec knew who had not only served with the Special Boat Service during the war, but also with MI6, having been recruited from the SBS in 1945.

"Dan, it has been far too long. How's the gammy elbow?"

"It's fine. Stuck fast at right-angles but I can still get to my pipe. Come and have an early drink and tell me all. Are you still scribbling?"

"I can't have a drink, Dan, I'm in a bit of a rush, but I have a strange question to ask you: are you still part of MI6?"

The captain's eyebrows shot up in surprise. With a good head of short, greying hair he looked around forty, but Alec knew he was well into his fifties. He was a Liberal MP for Bermondsey and Old Southwark, in London, and still part of the Ministry of Defence.

"Good God, Alec, why on earth …?" James looked around the reception hall and then pulled Alec into the empty billiard room. He gave the clerk behind the desk a wink as they went past.

"That's quite all right, Captain James, sir."

"What's this about, Alec? And no, I'm no longer spooking."

"Well basically …" Alec told Captain James about his adventures of the past few days: the vicar killing Baron Saumures; meeting the beautiful Baroness Saumures; the Nazi, Jost Krupp; right up to the fake collection of paintings, and especially Sir Jason's role in the affair. "You told Sir Sussex about the man you travelled back from Spain with, on a fishing boat."

"Deller, yes. Strange chap."

"Well, it turns out that the vicar, Father Joe Dent, and Franz-Joseph Deller are one and the same."

"Good God. Are you sure?"

"He was coming back to England with some boxes … large crates, right?"

"Yes, that's right."

"They were full of valuable … well, possibly valuable paintings that Sir Jason had arranged to get shipped back from Paris by this chap Deller. Bit of a lush? Had curly hair and a beard?"

"Yes! No beard, though. What an extraordinary story. But Sir Jason … what was he thinking, getting this chap to—"

"Sir Jason claims to be MI6. Was he? Would he recruit Deller as a German double agent?"

"Sir Jason wasn't a field agent – at least, I don't think he was. He was only a minor part of MI6, I believe. I know he irritated Sir Sussex Tremayne. But, Alec, I was not that senior in the service, I was only part of the SIS, gathering naval intelligence at the end of the war. Sir Jason had Winston's ear. He's now a cabinet minister, but not my colours." Alec clearly looked confused. "I'm a Liberal, Alec, or had you forgotten."

"Sorry, Dan. Can you remember what kind of 'minor part' he played?"

"A sort of liaison officer between the Foreign Office and secret services, I believe. He was part of the team that advised the government about the possibilities of the Germans taking Paris. But Paris was taken very quickly and, as we now know, virtually unchallenged. In retrospect, we were badly advised by Sir Jason Barrett. But you can't quote me, Alec. Club rules, you know." Dan smiled.

"I see," Alec said. There was something nagging at the back of Alec's brain but he could not work out what it was.

"Dan, do you know anything about an operation during the war called the Wasp Trap?"

"I do. It helped with a lot of evidence for the Nuremberg trials."

"I am on the verge of finding out more about the Wasp Trap files, I hope. Apparently, it was Ferdi Saumures who put most of the files together. Do you remember our meeting ten years ago with Sir Sussex Tremayne, about WASP – W-A-S-P?"

Dan James looked alarmed. "Yes, vividly. This Deller chap claimed to be in MI6 and was *made* to be a member of WASP. Where did you hear about WASP? Was this recently?" He paused for a moment. "Has Deller said anything about WASP, Alec?"

"No. But I am going to try and sound him out, when I can get to him."

"And we think it's the same Deller? Isn't Deller quite a common name?"

"Possibly. But this Deller is a drunk, like your Deller. He's Austrian, speaks English with no accent, like your man, and was transporting the collection for Sir Jason Barrett. All a little coincidental to say the least. It also turns out, would you believe, Deller is Charlotte's father."

"Really? Did you know Sir Sussex Tremayne was Baron Saumures's godfather?"

"I did not know that!"

"I believe it was Tremayne that recruited Saumures in the first place. Do you think Saumures was a member of WASP?"

"I don't know," Alec said, shrugging. "It's all a bit confusing now, Dan. Thank you for turning my brain inside out."

"I am sorry I could not help you more about Sir Jason. Loved to have met the gorgeous Baroness Freya or Charlotte."

"I had better shove off, Dan, I am going to meet the said gorgeous Baroness Charlotte. This Nazi Krupp is loose. He's calling himself Günther Wolff now."

"Dangerous cove, is he?"

"The worst, Dan, the bloody worst."

"I bet he will go to ground for a few months to take the heat off him a bit."

"Perhaps he has scarpered, but I would not bet on it." Alec and Dan James shook hands.

*

Alec drove the short distance to the Adolphe Hotel. All the way there he thought of the strange coincidences that had occurred in the past few days. Were they coincidences? He could not think how they could be anything else. It all started with Sophie knowing the vicar. If she had not got to know Father Joe – Deller – none of this would have happened. He would not have met Charlotte.

He arrived at the hotel and went to the reception desk and was shown up to Charlotte's suite. He had decided he was not going to talk about Sir Sussex Tremayne to Charlotte for the moment.

"Dear thing!" Bing-Wallace said on opening the door to the suite. "I was elected to open the door, ensuring that you were not a bounder." There was some laughter in the suite, which reassured Alec that the women had been well entertained by Philip.

"No, just me," Alec said, walking in to see Theodora and Charlotte on their knees around the coffee table with a pack of cards.

"Been teaching the girls Racing Demon. A very noisy game."

"We have had fun with Philip, Alec." Charlotte looked as though she was successfully recovering from flu, still pale, but full of smiles. "Alec, is it possible to drive Theodora and me to Sussex?"

"I've only a two-seater, I'm afraid. I could hire a car."

"You can use Ferdi's Bentley," Charlotte said. "It's in the garage below. Leave your car for Arno to look after."

23

"*Jou bliksem*, Krupp! *Boudkapper*! You gave me a terrible shock," yelled the tatty, saggy-looking man in Afrikaans, puce with anger. "Where the hell have you been? And what have you done with my car?" He wore a dirty grey fisherman's smock and brown corduroy trousers. The sixty-year-old man swiped one of the few straggly long black hairs back over his sweaty bald head. His unshaven double chin wobbled as he stormed over towards Krupp. "And what is this? A police car?"

"Shut up, Jaffery. I have replaced your car for another, slightly newer one. Unlike the heap of junk lent to me," Krupp said tersely. "I need to get back to Germany, quickly."

"Why, what's happened?" Jaffery now looked concerned.

"I got arrested by the police." Krupp slammed the door of the police car. He had driven up the muddy drive to Jaffery's run-down farmhouse, just outside Newhaven in Sussex. It was nearly dawn, cloudy and dank. The only light came from the outside light above the wood pile, where Jaffery had been collecting wood when he drove up.

Albert Jaffery owned the farmhouse and barns, and about twenty acres of scrubland and reeds that ran down to the sea. The farm used to grow reeds for thatching, but ever since the Jafferys took it over, it had been nothing but an eyesore and left to wrack and ruin. Krupp wondered what Jaffery spent all his money on, all the thousands of marks and gold he had been paid throughout the war, before and after.

"I can't pay you anything, Jaffery, but our mutual friend in WASP can. I will telegram him as soon as I get to Emden."

"Like hell you will. You know the rules, Krupp."

Krupp stuck his hand into his trouser pocket and Jaffery suddenly stepped back and snapped out a pistol from his trousers.

"Just you hang on, Kraut. I have been dealing with you lot too long to get whacked."

"Calm down, Jaffery, I was getting out a notepad. I was just going to write down his details."

"No, I just take gold or silver, as you know, or fuel. Forget it. You can bugger off to Shoreham or Portsmouth and hitch a lift from there." He started to walk back to the farmhouse, then stopped and turned round, his pistol levelled at Krupp's stomach. "Keys!" he spat.

"Come on, Jaffery, have some charity. All the money WASP and the Nazis have given you in the past, all through the war."

"Give me the keys to that abortion of a car, you Kraut bastard, and … *voetsek*!" Jaffery tossed his arm towards the drive, indicating to Krupp to get lost.

Krupp leant against the car, his arms folded in silent protest. He wished he had his stick in his hand, but he'd left it in the car. He thought for a bit, looking at the held-out hand. It started to drizzle, but the two men remained in the same positions in the muddy farmyard.

"Listen, Jaffery, I cannot walk anywhere with my bad leg. I could drive, but there will be police looking for this car."

"That's my car now, so you cannot have it anyway."

"Well, there it is," said Krupp angrily. "You are going to have to kill me, and then you will never get any more money from WASP. Or, come to that, the files held on you."

"What would I want with the files? They have nothing on me." Jaffery spat onto the ground in front of Krupp.

"Don't you believe it. You forget who your main benefactor is." Krupp had an idea. "However, I can also get a lot of fuel for you." Jaffery looked interested.

"Where is this fuel? It can't be any old fuel, you know."

"Good marine diesel. German diesel for your German S-boat. It is stored at Emden in large bulk tanks and I have access to them."

"Bollocks. You would say anything to get me to take you over."

"I will also pay you some money in gold, but you will have to melt it down yourself."

"Where is this gold, and why do I have to melt it down?"

"It is also in Emden. The gold comes from teeth, Jewish teeth."

Jaffery looked aghast.

"Teeth?" He lowered the pistol.

"Yes, teeth. Will you take me now?"

Jaffery thought a while, squinting at Krupp, his mouth open.

"If I get any wind of a double-cross, Krupp, you will die. I will chop you up into pieces and throw you overboard. And don't think I haven't done it before."

Krupp would not put it past him. He hoped he would have disposed of this odorous fat man before Jaffery realised he was being duped.

"Come on then, Krupp," Jaffery said with contempt. "We'd better get going now. The tide is about to turn."

Krupp was quite surprised but said nothing, not wanting Jaffery to change his mind. He'd thought the stand-off was going to take a lot more time.

He followed Jaffery down to the river inlet. It was surrounded by reeds tall enough to hide the large boathouse where a motor torpedo boat was stored. It was a German S-boat, or, as the British called them, E-boat, slightly altered to disguise it as a large pleasure craft. It was moored in the boathouse next to a smaller fishing boat covered in camouflage netting.

Getting to and from the boathouse was perilous, well-guarded as it was by hazardous bogs and marshland. On the rare occasions the police visited Albert Jaffery, he used a hidden getaway path from the farmhouse to the boathouse, from which he could escape in the converted motor torpedo boat he'd acquired from the Germans after an unsuccessful raid off the Channel Islands.

"When are you coming back, Krupp?"

"After Christmas. Why do you ask?"

"I thought I would stay with you, just to keep an eye on you."

"You can't," Krupp shot back angrily. The last thing he wanted was this dreadful South African hanging around for the next two months. "I will send a telegram when I return, and there will be a lot more money." Jaffery pulled on a rope, and the netting that covered the boats lifted in one up into the roof space of the boathouse. Krupp scrambled with difficulty onto the boat deck. His leg was hurting and all he wanted to do was to sleep on the smelly bunk in the cabin once they got under way. He also was trying to think how he was going to get the fuel he'd promised Jaffery. That was another worry to face in about sixteen hours.

"I should hope it is substantially more … the money. Perhaps I could have some in advance so that I can get you a Christmas present." Jaffery laughed at his own joke. "I am just going to lock up the house and get some things. Back in a tick."

Part Two

24

December 1955, Burton Park Place, West Sussex

"I am so grateful to you for inviting us for Christmas, Charlotte. A happy Christmas to you, Madam Theodora." Alec raised his glass of Madeira to the two ladies as he stood, like lord of the manor, at the fireplace in the opulently furnished and absurdly named "small drawing room" at Burton Park Place.

"Here, here!" Philip Bing-Wallace said from where he had sunk snugly into a huge deep-red armchair, raising his glass of champagne. It was after ten in the evening, and they had just come back from Christmas dinner served at the Cricketers public house and hotel.

"I have so few friends left," Charlotte said sadly. "They have all been killed or forgotten."

"Darling," Theodora scolded, "don't be like that on this joyous day."

"I'm not being sad – it's the truth. It is lovely of Alec and Philip to join us." She saluted Alec with her glass and then said seriously, "Where are your parents, Alec?"

"Both dead. Dad was killed in London in the Blitz, and Mum died just after the war, we think of grief. She was a nurse, in Chichester, so was very busy during the war and had no time to grieve. But then she retired after the war and never really got over my father's death."

"What a shame," Theodora said with absolutely no feeling. "Any brothers or sisters?" Theodora asked, now sitting, her feet tucked up on the sofa.

"A twin brother who lives and works in America. He is trying to be a film actor … Adam Ballentine."

"Really?" Charlotte perked up. She was still wearing black, a chic black silk strapless Chanel dress with a fine mesh see-through jacket with huge black polka dots scattered across it. "Do we know him?" she asked eagerly.

"No, I'm afraid not yet. He is very good-looking – we are not identical, I hasten to add. He is working his way up. He was a soldier in *The Day the Earth Stood Still*, a science fiction with that lovely girl …"

"Patricia Neal, wasn't it?" Charlotte was getting quite relaxed now. "Did he have a speaking part?"

"No, but he did say a line in *White Christmas*, remember, Alec?" Bing-Wallace said. "He said, 'Take a seat, General'. He was a soldier again – got the shoulders, like Alec." Bing-Wallace pointed at Alec's shoulders. "He came in near the end when they sang to their admired general and sang 'White Christmas'. Quite apt, really, considering it's Christmas today."

"Yes, that's right," Alec said. "But you have to wait all the way through the film before you get to him. Adam said you can see him in the middle of the film but he is amongst lots of other extras."

"That is a lovely film," Charlotte said thoughtfully. "Ferdi and I went to the first showing in Brighton last year. Did he fight in the war?"

"Yes, for the American forces. He was a GI, a corporal. He fought through Italy, and then France. We met up in Holland at the end of the war."

"What does he do now – in between films?" Theodora asked.

"I don't know. We haven't talked for a while. I think he's writing."

They all sat in silence for a while in the small drawing room, looking at the fire that Alec had built with some small assistance from Philip Bing-Wallace – he just handed Alec kindling and a couple of logs.

"What about you, Philip?" Theodora looked at Bing-Wallace, wide-eyed in mock anticipation. "Are you a belted Earl of something?"

"Good God, no!" Bing-Wallace sprang to his feet and balletically swept an arm over his head. "Mother was a ballet dancer, for the Royal Ballet and Sadler's Wells. Father was a writer of historic essays or something. Frightfully boring. Both dead." He fell back into his chair. "Bugger," he said as champagne splashed over his face.

"We are all orphans," Charlotte said quietly.

"Not quite, darling," Theodora said. "You at least still have a father, of sorts." The group fell silent.

There was one other guest: Bonzo was a black Labrador, a six-month-old puppy, and was a Christmas present to Charlotte from Sir Jason Barrett, presented to her the month before. She adored him from the moment he sprang from the back of a Land Rover into her arms and promptly urinated all over the front of her dress whilst enthusiastically licking her face. Theodora was horrified and was on the verge of instructing the man who brought the dog to take it back.

Bonzo broke the silence that Christmas evening with a little bark and a whimper as he got up from in front of the fire and sat at the drawing room door.

"Oh, good boy." Charlotte raced to the drawing room door to let him out, then through the door that led out onto the terrace and the garden.

"I'll join you if I may, Charlotte," Alec asked.

"There's still not been any news of the whereabouts of Jost Krupp since he escaped police custody," Theodora warned. "He could turn up at any time."

"I doubt it, Theodora." Charlotte looked unsure. "I have Bonzo to protect me if he turns up."

"I'll stay here and entertain Madam Theodora," Bing-Wallace said, lamely half standing as Charlotte and Alec left the room.

"How thrilling!" Theodora said, not hiding her sarcasm.

"Now, Theodora, you do find me entertaining, don't you? Don't break my heart," Bing-Wallace pleaded. Theodora laughed. She adored this eccentric old man, ever since he came to sit with Charlotte and her in their suite in the Adolphe Hotel after Jost Krupp escaped. He was terribly funny about how he said he would protect them from the Nazi beast – he would pounce on the cad and hold him down and spout Shakespeare sonnets at him whilst he dots his nose.

"The Germans hate Shakespeare," Philip generalised. "They get bored quite easily."

"Who doesn't get bored of Shakespeare?" mocked Theodora. Bing-Wallace overacted shock and disgust.

"Germans don't ever seem to get bored of Wagner's interminable operas," he said. "Come on, let's have some music on that big machine there." He went over to a radiogram and opened the lid. "This is a splendid piece of furniture, Theodora. Does it get very loud?"

*

It was a crisp, chilly evening, the moon was out and stars twinkled. Charlotte had a shawl around her shoulders. Alec looked back at the house and through the window into the small drawing room. He could see Philip and Theodora waving their arms around in some kind of strange dance.

"What are they doing?" Alec asked, enjoying the amused smile on Charlotte's face.

"Listen," she said, cocking her head. "Can't you hear? It's Mozart's clarinet concerto. They are conducting the orchestra!"

"So they are." Alec wondered how loud it must have been in the drawing room. "It's all that Pommery champagne."

"I still can't get used to seeing the light streaming out from the house in the evening," Charlotte said softly, as though she did not want to wake anybody sleeping. "After all those years of blackout, it still seems funny."

"I know what you mean," Alec said. "I still carry a torch in London in the evening even though we have street lights again. Habit, I suppose." Alec watched Charlotte's breath turn to vapour in the cold. Bonzo, still young, squatted to take a pee; he was not quite old enough to cock his leg. He loped off after a scent, his strong tail wagging happily.

"Have you ever been asked to act in a film?" Alec asked Charlotte.

"No, not really. Why?" she said, self-consciously brushing her loose hair from her eyes.

"Well ..." Alec felt embarrassed. "You are so very ... err ... attractive."

"Thank you, Alec," she said. She seemed amused by his awkwardness. "You should be in films as well as your brother. You could be a British Rock Hudson."

Alec chortled at the absurdity. "Would you want to be one of those glamorous film stars?"

"No, not really. I would not want to be an actress. I don't think I can act." Then she remembered, "Well, I was asked by a German film crew to be in a film they were shooting in Le Palais, but they were told they could not film inside Le Palais for some reason. So, I was *nearly* in films."

"There are hardly any photos of you. I mean, I would have thought you and Theodora would be prime subjects for *Tatler* magazine, or *Vogue*."

"Ferdi hated any publicity. He was pretty secretive, as you know. And I was not too keen on being seen as I was still trying to avoid my uncle. Anyway, I am a little shy. I don't really like being gazed at, if you see what I mean."

"Why did you want to disappear?"

"I just did. To get away from my stepfather. And to some extent, Uncle Jason. I hated my uncle, he was ... Jason was just too ... confining. He, with my stepfather, drove Aunt Stella to madness – she was the only nice ..." She shook her head, wanting to change the subject. "I have plenty of money, anyway, with Ferdi. I don't need a film or acting career."

"What about your house in Paris? You may have lost your house in Avenue Foch," Alec said, watching to see if he had gone too far with the questioning. Charlotte smiled at him. "I bequeathed it to Theodora in my will."

"Oh, I see. Has she done anything about it?"

"No, we have not yet returned to Paris. But they know that it now belongs to Theodora."

"They?"

"The lawyers, in Paris." Charlotte suddenly stopped. She turned to Alec, concern over her face. "Strider is part of the French firm of solicitors. The same lawyers my stepfather used."

"Well, that is why he is a little put out, I should think, that you are still alive."

"We must talk to him about Avenue Foch after Christmas," Charlotte said and then turned towards the light coming from the small drawing room. "Poor Theodora."

They both walked slowly on, following Bonzo as he sniffed along the edge of the terrace.

"How long have you been a journalist, Alec?" She came near to him, walking close beside him, watching Bonzo.

"Ever since leaving university, just before the war. I did my bit of National Service and then went straight into the war as a correspondent."

"Were you frightened – during the war?"

"I was. And I was always uncomfortable; nothing was built or designed for my size. So, I seldom had time to be scared. But you must have been frightened?"

"I was, a bit." She smiled up at him. "But I rather enjoyed it."

They strolled on, their hands nearly touching.

"Charlotte, do you feel lonely ever?"

"No, not really. Theodora is always there – when she is not pursuing a man, that is."

"Does she pursue men?"

"She is a hot-blooded Turkish woman. She sometimes goes off with a man, stays with them, uses them and then returns complaining that he was dull or too pretentious. She lived with one, here, for nearly a year, but Krupp killed him."

"Bernard Trent, I presume?"

"Yes." Charlotte sounded sad. Alec was disappointed he never met Bernard. He admired Trent's courage during the war, his work with the French underground, running escape lines, being part of the SOE.

"Is Bing-Wallace going to be OK with a hot-blooded Turkish woman?" Alec said in mock alarm, changing the subject. Charlotte turned to look at him as she giggled. God, she was lovely.

"I am sure Mr Bing-Wallace can look after himself." Charlotte was walking slowly towards where Bonzo was sniffing busily under a large planter, and looked down at what had caught his attention. "Bonzo, leave it now!" She turned to Alec. "Alec, do you know what has happened to Jost Krupp?"

"He's buggered off back to Germany or even to South America, I should think. He's a marked man here. How well did you know him, anyway?" Charlotte's face suddenly turned gloomy. She hugged herself, looking self-conscious. "It's only," Alec carried on, "we never really understood who he was and why he did those terrible things. What has he got against you?"

"He was my first lover, you know."

She came up close to Alec, measuring his reaction, he thought, for expressions of judgement or shock. He ensured there were none, but the nauseous taste of jealousy in his throat made him cough slightly as he said, "Oh."

"I was fifteen or sixteen, he was a glamorous SS officer, charming, oh-so handsome, and … anyway, he came to Le Palais with Theodora the first night I was 'Freya'."

"Oh, I see, that long ago," Alec said. "Was that the first time you met Theodora as well?"

"Yes. She was so kind. I was so innocent … about everything. The war, the Germans, the SS." She finished quietly with "Men."

"Is Günther Wolff his real name or one he has acquired?"

"He acquired it, I should think," Charlotte said. "He more than likely stole it – killed a Günther Wolff to avoid being prosecuted for war crimes."

"Really?"

"Ferdi had a huge file on him."

"I wonder where that file is now?" Alec was concerned.

"It must have come over with the rest of the Wasp Trap files, I presume." Charlotte looked at Alec curiously. There was a thoughtful silence. "Would his file be one of the files Ferdi hid?"

"That would explain some of his actions, yes."

"But to kill everybody just for a file? He killed Ferdi, the only person who knew about the files." Charlotte covered her mouth with her hand. "Enough now. Let's have a pleasant walk with Bonzo," she said virtually to herself.

"You must have been constantly afraid in Paris," Alec said. "I mean – if you were discovered, you would be killed."

"I don't know why I was never really scared, only once or twice when my stepfather appeared. He suddenly turned up at Le Palais, warmly greeted by the Germans. It was not *that* that was worrying. I was just worried he would find me and ..." She went quiet again.

"What?" Alec asked gently.

"... rape me again." Alec pulled back unintentionally; he was not expecting that answer. "Which he did. Well, he tried, so I killed him."

"I ... I am sorry to hear that," Alec said, he thought, rather inadequately. "When was the other time? Or should we leave it at that?" He found that he was in journalistic mode, which he was not sure was appropriate. He needed to know more about this woman. He wanted to know her better. Something, he was sure, that was going to take a very long time to achieve.

"When Jost Krupp found us in Auch and took me away from Ferdi, that was scary." Their eyes met. "I thought that was the last time I was going to see Ferdi alive."

"But he escaped."

"Yes," she said. "I was young, Alec. Perhaps you are not so frightened when you are young."

"How was he wounded, to get that scar?"

"I tried to put his dagger into his eye when he kidnapped me. It ended up dragging down his cheek and into his leg ... into the bone." Alec winced. She carried on, with a little pride in her voice. "Then I shot him with his pistol. I seem to have missed all his vital organs. So, he did not die." Alec tried to hide his shock.

"Was that the first time you've seen him since then? At Sir Jason's?"

"Yes. It was a hell of a shock. A ghost sent to haunt me. I suppose I was frightened then as well. I felt sick when I saw him."

She turned her back on Alec and looked up into the dark night sky. Stars were desperately trying to shine through high, thin cloud; some did, but only the brightest.

"Well, you were only sixteen, you said. I didn't know anything about girls when I was sixteen. I had no idea of life. Only a lot of hormones buzzing around." He looked at Charlotte from behind. Her figure was exquisite. He loved how her hair tumbled over the back of her black shawl. He had certainly never seen a girl like her when he was sixteen. "Didn't you know about Krupp's reputation whilst you were at Le Palais? His misdeeds, his reputation as an SS officer?" Alec pursued.

"No," she said in despair. She held her hand up to her forehead, still with her back to Alec so he could not see her face. "Not until I met Ferdi at the gallery in Paris. But then Krupp disappeared. It seemed he had taken over as SS commander of the south-west of France when the Germans reoccupied the Free Zone. He killed Bo, Christina's husband … and now Christina as well. And poor Bernard." Her voice cracked.

There was a long silence. Alec looked up at the stars, trying to remember which constellation was which so he could change the subject.

"He was … is a bloody terrible man." Charlotte kicked at blades of grass growing between the red bricks on the path.

"Would you go back to Paris?" Alec asked tentatively. "Now you have the collection back?"

"Huh! The collection! Well, Theodora thought of starting an art gallery of fakes."

"Is that legal?"

"I really don't know … or care. You should ask your ex-fiancée."

Alec felt a blush. Luckily the light from the huge ballroom windows was too dull to show any detailed reddening. All he could see was the elegant form of Charlotte in front of him, crouching down, trying to stop Bonzo from digging in the planter.

"It's the chicken poo," Charlotte said with a giggle, wiping a tear from her eye.

"The what?"

"The chicken poo. The gardeners always put chicken poo onto the planters during the winter so when it rains, or the snow melts, it gradually permeates through the soil. It's very good for the plants."

"Oh," Alec said lightly. Bonzo was now bounding off to another interesting scent and Charlotte strolled after him. Alec slowly walked with Charlotte, aware that she was hugging herself in the cold. He removed his jacket and draped it over her shoulders. She started, then smiled up at him, pulling out her hair to make it fall over his jacket.

"Thank you, Alec, but we should be getting back soon. Now *you* are going to get cold," she said, rubbing the top of his arm.

She seemed suddenly aware of her closeness to Alec. She pulled her hand away quickly and stepped back.

"Sorry," she said. Alec wondered what she was sorry for. When he felt her touch, he'd sighed inwardly. He held his breath as he watched her stroke his arm. He was a boy again, not sure what to do, how to react, how to progress this obvious sign of affection … and then it was too late, she pulled away. A light scent of lily of the valley hovered around her, making it hard for Alec not to take a huge intake of breath to savour her perfume.

Bonzo came back from his digging, noisily panting. All that could be seen coming out of the darkness was a wide, smiling mouth, a pink tongue lolloping out the side of his jaw, a shiny nose, and two glistening dark eyes like black marbles. Charlotte crouched down to stroke his head and was rewarded with a huge lick on her cheek, which made her squeal with delight. Alec watched the scene, his heart yearning to draw Charlotte to him and kiss her.

She looked up at him. Her smile changed to an expression of concern. She must have recognised his feelings. She stood, then hesitated, and to Alec's great amazement, wrapped her arms around his neck and softly drew his lips to her mouth. Her lips felt like velvet, warm, soft and welcoming. Alec's jacket slid off her shoulders. Their bodies pressed together. Alec could feel every curve of Charlotte's body. His arms surrounded her thin waist. One hand went to the small of her back, the other to just above the curve of her bottom. She felt soft but muscular. It was a heavenly feeling. There was a fluttering in his chest, as though a bird was trapped inside his body.

When the kiss was over, Charlotte looked up into his eyes. He felt so much elation that he was fearful of speaking. She held the embrace, her head on his shoulder. Bonzo then panted up to the couple and jumped up onto the back of Alec's thighs.

"I think Bonzo wants to join us, Charlotte."

"Come on," Charlotte said to Bonzo. "Let us go in. It's cold."

Alec put his jacket back over Charlotte's shoulders. They strolled into the house, hand in hand.

*

"Well I'm off to bed. Goodnight, both of you," Theodora said with a small knowing smile.

"What have you done with Mr Bing-Wallace?" Charlotte asked.

"He said he was going to fill a hot water bottle and go to bed. Goodnight, you two."

"Goodnight. Happy Christmas," Alec said, about to stand up.

"Don't move, Alec," Theodora said, patting him on the shoulder. "*İyi geceler*, and *mutlu Noeller*," she added in Turkish and went out the door.

"I suppose we should go to bed, Alec."

"Yes, of course, it's getting late." He went to the fireplace and put the guard over the front of the grate.

"I mean, together," Charlotte said, standing behind him and taking his hand.

Alec swung around to face her, half in shock, half in wonder. The fluttering bird in his chest returned.

"Oh," he said, "I see." He coughed. It was rather brazen. He was surprised and delighted at the same time. It must be her strange continental upbringing, he thought. How far did she want to go? Just sleep together? His mind was racing. He had only made love to one other woman before. He hoped he would be OK. What about contraception?

They patted the sleeping Bonzo on the head.

"Don't worry, everything will be fine, Alec," she said soothingly – she must have seen some apprehension in his face. "I just need you with me, you see."

25

They woke late morning on Boxing Day 1955, a typical English winter morning. The view from their bed was of the sun intermittently emerging through large cotton-wool clouds that cruised resolutely across the blue sky, the sunbeams spotlighting large areas of the Sussex Downs. There was a slight frost on the window.

The bedroom was cold outside the sheets and blankets, but Alec and Charlotte were cosy in their bed, nestled together, she wrapped up in his arms, her head cushioned on the light down of his chest hair. She felt safe, and happy, but there was a nagging doubt; should she have encouraged Alec into her bed so quickly?

"You are … so lovely," Alec said croakily.

"You must be careful, Alec," she warned. He stroked her gold hair away from her eyes, taking no notice. "Alec?" Her eyes met his. She patted his chest. "I mean it, darling, you must not fall in love with me."

"How can I not?" he whispered.

"I am no good. Every man I have loved has been hurt and things have turned ugly."

"Do you love me then?" Alec asked. He closed his eyes, his head resting on the pillow. Charlotte dragged her fingers through the light hair on his chest.

"I would like to love you, but I dare not," Charlotte said softly. She could hear his heart quicken. "But do you get jealous, Alec?"

"If I know you love me, I cannot be jealous. When you say you don't love me, I will …"

"What?" She looked up at him with concern.

"I don't know." He opened his eyes. He bent his head down and kissed her on the lips. "I will run away to sea and never step on land again, like an albatross."

"You wouldn't, you know. You will want to kill me, like Jost Krupp!"

Alec looked shocked by this. "No, I would not. I like the idea of spending the rest of my life at sea, though. Would you come with me?" Alec smiled. Charlotte tried to smile back but was not convinced by his bravado. "You can't turn off love, anyway," Alec pointed out. "You either are, or you're not."

"True, but you could just be besotted with me – not in love."

"Not sure if besotted is the same thing," Alec said. "True love can come in many forms, some dangerous like obsession, possessiveness … possibly besottedness – if there is such a word. I don't think I come under any of those headings. This is mutual, isn't it?"

"You writers. Love is love, and you can either be in it, or out of it. An intelligent person should be able to end their love for someone, otherwise it just hurts too much if they are told they are not loved."

"Possibly. But I am sure it hurts terribly to be told you are *not* loved by someone, when you know they do," Alec said.

Charlotte struggled to understand why she was unable to end her love for Jost Krupp. Seeing his scarred face, the cruelty he had committed, had doused any love she had for him – except, that was not the man at Le Palais. She longed for *that* man, the man she still loved. The dashing SS officer.

She was comfortable with Alec. He was handsome, a gentle man, a big man. Could she love him? Very easily. But not now. There was little room in her heart for love. He plainly adored her, and she him, but not by the same amount, she suspected. She hoped he was not going to be too … too loving. Or demand more than she could give. At the moment, though, she was more than content.

They lay together, watching the sun battle to shine through the clouds. It was well into the morning.

"Do you know," Charlotte said, "I can't think of anybody who knew me as Charlotte, other than Jason. All my friends have disappeared, family gone or mad … no one."

She slid down into the warmth of the bedclothes and Alec's body.

"Theodora calls you Charlotte."

"Only for the last year or so, and only when we are alone."

"Why the pretence?"

"To keep Jason away. I don't trust that man! Never have," Charlotte said angrily.

"Why don't you trust him? He's an important man, an MP, a minister. He gave you Bonzo. He seems OK, if a little dour." There was a pause. Charlotte kept quiet. "Tell me about your house in Paris. What is it like?"

"I don't know. It is still in ruins. We – me, Ferdi and Theodora, that is – are finding it difficult to get funds from the German reparations."

"Do you get any?"

"No, I don't think we do, for some reason. Something to do with the bomb being Allied, not German."

There was another pause.

"Why aren't the radiators working?" Alec asked. The bedroom was cold outside the blankets.

"We don't have central heating in this part of the house, yet. There is a fire in the grate, ready to be lit." Charlotte giggled and slid further down into the bedclothes, covering her head.

"Christ, it's like being in the army! I will light the fire then," Alec volunteered with a tone of fake harassment.

"The only reason I invited you into my bed." Charlotte chuckled.

"Why don't you have a room with heating?" Alec put on some underpants underneath the bedclothes and reached out for his vest and jacket that were on the chair near the bed.

"I love the view from this room." Charlotte sat up and looked out the window. Her hair was ruffled up one side where she had laid her head on Alec's chest. "This bit of the house is the last to be centrally heated. We had just not got around to it."

"Well, I am going out, into the cold." He paused dramatically. "I am going out now. I may be some time."

Alec got out of bed. He grabbed the eiderdown to wrap around him as he quickly finished getting dressed. He went over to the fire that had been laid by one of the maids on Christmas Eve.

Christina would have lovingly laid the fire for Charlotte, she thought sadly. She would have loved Christina to have got to know this big man. He was quite like Bo.

"Matches on the mantelpiece," Charlotte said from the bed. She watched the way he moved, agile for a big man, elegant, sure-footed – almost feline, like a male lion.

Alec reached up to the high and ornately carved oak mantel. He found the matches and lit the fire.

"Is that Gustav Klimt?" he said, pointing at the picture over the mantel in a plain dark wood frame.

"Probably. My grandfather gave it to my mother. I smuggled it out of Paris when we escaped. I doubt it's genuine, though."

"There is a red chalk mark on it. Bottom left corner."

"Is there? Take it off the wall. There will be something on the other side, in the frame."

"It's a very good painting," Alec said, looking at the face of the girl on the pillow of gold.

"It's called *Girl on a Golden Pillow*. Do you know about these things?" Charlotte propped herself up in the bed, covering herself up to her neck in blankets waiting for the room to warm up.

"I don't really. My friend Sophie Younghusband knows a lot about art. We should get her to …" Alec stopped. He must have forgotten that Charlotte had already met her, that Sophie was cataloguing the fake works of art for Charlotte and her uncle Jason.

"Perhaps we should send this one up to her in London as well," Charlotte said with a sigh. "See if there is a message on the back."

Alec took down the picture from the wall and studied it. He flipped it over to look at the back of the canvas.

"Something here. Stuck on the wood of the frame with masking tape. A long piece of white folded paper – new paper." Alec gently peeled off the masking tape.

"Let's see." Charlotte was now beside him with a blanket wrapped around her naked body.

"It's a piece of headed writing paper, folded over and stuck to the frame. Here, read it, it's in French," Alec said.

"It's from Ferdi and it is to me and Theodora." Charlotte took the sheet of paper. "Let me see."

Charlotte translated:

"My Dear Freya – Charlotte – and Theodora.

"If you are reading this, I am probably dead, and Bernard has told you where to find this note." Charlotte's hand went up to her mouth. Alec stroked her hair, but Charlotte drew away, staring at the letter. She wondered if she would rather Alec was not there. Alec placed some more wood on the fire and returned to her side.

She carried on reading:

"Over many years, I have put together a large file of Nazi criminals, British, French and some Dutch collaborators and members of the SS and Gestapo. Most of the information came from a network of agents and undercover operatives recruited by me. One of which is you, Theodora." Alec and Charlotte looked at each other again, eyebrows raised.

"Did you know Theodora was a spy for the baron?" Alec asked.

"Sort of. I had not realised that she worked for Ferdi for so long. She is a secretive old bird. They were all secretive, I suppose." She stopped herself from thinking too much about it. "I'm going to get Theodora. I'll get dressed first."

"I would – you will give Bing-Wallace a treat if he is up."

"That is a point, and I think Rupert is in this morning, with Mrs Tanner."

She shrugged the blanket off as she walked quickly to the wardrobe and put on some underwear and a long white satin robe.

"I love that robe. I will never forget the first time I saw you in it," Alec said.

Alec watched her as far as the bedroom door. He sighed with a flutter of joy in his chest, not believing he had made love, for most of the night, to that woman. Was he out of his depth? Would she just play with him for a couple of weeks and then cast him aside?

When she was out of the room he turned back to the concealed letter. He wished his French was better; he could only guess at half of what was being said. The door was flung open and Theodora flew in. She was wearing scarlet silk pyjamas and her dark-blue silk robe was flying like a cape as she virtually ran at the piece of paper Alec held.

"Let me see," she said, putting on some half-moon glasses and holding out her hand. She saw Charlotte conceal a smile. "I have to wear glasses now, I'm getting old." She took hold of the paper. "I forgot that Bernard had said he had a message for us, in case Ferdi was killed." She started reading it.

"Translate it for Alec, Theodora."

"Have you not read it yet?" she said, aghast.

"Only the first paragraph," Charlotte said. She got a cushion and held it to her body, looking nervously over the top of the ornate piping.

Theodora sat on the edge of the bed. Alec and Charlotte huddled on the rug in front of the fire, looking up at Theodora as though she was about to read a bedtime story. Theodora lit a cigarette after offering Alec one, gave a little cough and started to translate:

"*Over many years, I have put together a large file of Nazi criminals, British, French and some Dutch collaborators and members of the SS and Gestapo …* blah blah blah.

"*These files were brought over from France just before the end of the war by Bernard and I, in a boat belonging to a man called Albert Jaffery, a smuggler who worked mainly for the enemy, it transpired. Using some dubious contacts, we managed to get the files, called the Wasp Trap files, into England. These files were presented to Colonel Sir Geoffrey Lawrence, who was president of the Nuremberg Tribunal.*"

Theodora looked up at Charlotte. Their eyes met, and Alec saw that she asked an unspoken question with a raise of an eyebrow and a slight sideways glance towards Alec. Alec only saw the slightest movement of Charlotte's head, then Theodora went back to the letter.

"*These files will be, or may have already been, used to track down war criminals and bring them to justice. There are five files that were not included in the Wasp Trap files. These can be found, in the event of my death, in my bank, C. Hoare and Co. of Fleet Street. The key to the strongbox is in the safe, taped to the top of the left-hand drawer. However, there is also a file on a top-secret project that I have been working on the past fifteen years. There is – or was – a movement called WASP. This is what Krupp was going on about, Charlotte. I bet you.*"

"Five files?" Alec said in wonder. "Does the letter say which five?"

Theodora looked up from the page.

"No. But there is more about WASP: *It is imperative that the file on WASP is taken directly to Sir Sussex Tremayne, or his successor.*"

26

Philip Bing-Wallace returned to London on Boxing Day. There were lots of hugs and kisses. Bing-Wallace was a huge success and helped turn what could have been a difficult Christmas into a happy few days. It was decided that nothing would be mentioned to him about the files or the letter. Charlotte had insisted that Bert Tanner take him home in the Bentley.

"My dears, what thorough luxury," Philip Bing-Wallace exclaimed. "I feel like the Pope." Then he paused. "Does the Pope go anywhere?"

"I don't know, Philip, but I doubt he would go in such style," Alec said, opening the back door to the silver-grey Bentley. "Get in and bugger off. I need to see you bright-eyed and bushy-tailed tomorrow."

"Very well, old thing. Charlotte …" He smiled at her and tilted his head as an unspoken thank you. He got into the car, and they all waved as he drove off.

*

"Why had Ferdi kept these files from the others, do you suppose?" Charlotte asked Alec as they strolled through the arcade of poplar trees in front of the house. The cold, cloudy day was now threatening snow. Bonzo was scurrying back and forth as Charlotte and Alec ambled behind him, hand in hand. The smells were all new and enticing and as they approached the wood on the east side of the concourse of poplars, Bonzo started to chase an interesting spoor into the woods.

"Bonzo!" Charlotte shouted. "Ah well, he can't get lost." She stopped at the edge of the wood and looked over the well-cropped field. "I suppose Ferdi thought he should protect some of the people in the files." She sounded reflective.

"I imagine they must be files of sensitive names," Alec said with a sigh. "We must retrieve these files before someone else finds them."

Charlotte came up close to him. "I know you are a journalist. This must be making your life very difficult. Give me a kiss, Alec," she said nestling up to him, her face turned up to his and her eyes beseeching, her body supplicatory. Alec put his arms around her.

Suddenly Bonzo came rushing out of the wood with his tail between his legs and a cross between a growl and a whine – he had been frightened by something. A blinding flash followed. Bonzo turned and started barking. Alec and Charlotte broke away from each other, confused and momentarily blinded. Alec guided Charlotte behind him, putting himself between the flash and Charlotte. There was another flash, and in the split-second flash of light Alec spotted a man with a camera in the shadow of the woods. He lunged in the photographer's direction, fighting the large spots that danced over his vision from the flash. He could just about see the man leaning, half hidden, against a sycamore tree.

"Oi, you! Stop there!" yelled Alec. "Who are you?"

"It's all right, guv, I'm press," said the man with a nervous smile.

"It's the Christmas holidays, for Christ's sake," Alec shouted as he walked quickly towards the man, who started to back away into the shade. The man seemed to be in two minds whether to sprint down the slope of the bank and run back to the gates or take another photo of Alec striding towards him, just in case he was someone famous.

"I know it's Christmas. I was sent here by my editor," the man said, raising his camera.

"Well, I'm a journalist too. Don't take any more shots." Alec put his hand up to block the flash from his eyes. The man lowered his camera, confused.

"Are you? Who for? Have you wangled an exclusive?"

"Never mind me. Who are you working for?"

"Jack Flowers of *The Sentinel*."

"Flowers?" Alec gestured towards Charlotte. "Do you know who that is?"

"The beauty? Yeah – Lady Saumures, Sir Jason's niece."

"And who are you?" Alec asked gruffly.

"I am only a staff photographer. I'm the bloke that usually does these things for the paper," said the man with a sly smile. "Er, is that dog safe? I 'ate dogs." Bonzo came running up to the man and started jumping up at him.

"Well, you should not be creeping around private property. What is your name?" Alec got hold of Bonzo by the collar. He was aware of a smell of damp, dirty wool coat and looked more closely at the man. He wore a peaked cap, long greasy dark hair sticking out the edges. He had a thin pencil moustache, and when he talked, Alec could see gaps in his stained teeth. If it were not for the very expensive Zeiss Ikon Contaflex camera, Alec would think he was a tramp.

"For the last time, what is your name and why are you here?" Alec said, grabbing hold of the man's upper arm.

"Or what are you going to do?" the man countered. "The wood is public land, according to the—"

"It certainly is not," Charlotte shouted. "It all belongs to the estate."

"Well I am sorry," the man said, looking only marginally contrite. "There is nothing much you can do to me, anyway."

"I can leave you to the security men here, who, I suspect, are not pleased to be bothered on their Christmas holidays." The Tanner brothers suddenly appeared behind the man and grabbed the camera.

"Er! You can't do that!"

"What is your name, sir?" Alec repeated.

"Dougie … Douglas Spencer. I'm freelance and … Er! Don't open that, it will—"

One of the Tanner brothers had taken the camera out of the brown case and pressed a button on the side, and the back of the camera flipped open, revealing the film, which Albert Tanner whipped out. He stuffed the exposed film in his pocket and threw the camera and the case separately back to Dougie.

"Thanks a bundle," said Dougie. He turned to Alec. "And who, may I ask, are you? And does Mr Saumures know you are snogging his missus?"

"He is dead, and you are trying my patience." Alec turned to the Tanner brothers. "Thank you, gentlemen. I think Mr Spencer needs to be escorted off the property; he is trespassing. Ensure he is put on his way back to London. We do not want Mr Spencer missing his deadline. I would be grateful if you did not break any of Mr Spencer's bones."

"Er! They can't touch me! Ow!" Dougie exclaimed as Charles Tanner cuffed him over the head. "I will report this back to the guv'nor when I get back."

"You do that, Mr Spencer. We will have you up for trespass if you report anything of this in the papers."

"Just one question before I go." Dougie shrugged off Charles Tanner's hold and looked at Charlotte.

"Are you the prostitute who worked at Le Palais in Paris during the—"
A Tanner brother cuffed Dougie over the head again, knocking his hat off.

"Oi, stop that!" he said as he got another cuff from the other Tanner brother.

Alec saw a flash of anger cross Charlotte's face. He could see she was restraining herself from confronting Dougie.

Dougie was hauled off by the Tanners to the drive, where he was unceremoniously bundled into the back of the Tanner brothers' Morris Thousand van and driven to his car parked on the main road.

"Who was that?" Theodora asked, walking towards them. Bonzo went up to greet her. "I saw him out of the window and called the boys, who were very quick to respond."

"A journalist," Alec said. "The lowest kind of journalist, I should say. An embarrassment to my profession." He watched Charlotte wander back towards the house. He imagined she must be disturbed by what the man had asked.

27

Charlotte was sitting on the floor of the small drawing room, in front of the fire with Theodora, nursing brandies. A whisky had been poured for Alec by Rupert, who, much to Charlotte's annoyance, still sported a black armband on the left arm of his black jacket.

When Rupert left, Charlotte got up from the floor, sat on the sofa and patted a cushion beside her for Alec to sit on when he had finished on the phone. Theodora sat with Bonzo, who was fast asleep to one side of the fireplace, his head on Theodora's lap. It had taken a bit of time for Theodora to accept Bonzo; however, he had managed to charm his way into her affections.

"What did *The Sentinel* have to say, darling?" asked Theodora.

"There is nobody there bar a doorman, apparently." Alec sat beside Charlotte, put an arm around her. Charlotte rested her head on his chest and sighed. The events earlier had upset her.

"He says he was a staff photographer, and that he was also freelance – you can't be both," said Alec. "He's called Douglas Spencer."

"Nasty little man. Why did he ask that awful question? How did he know about Le Palais?" Theodora asked. Charlotte was quiet.

"Jason, I should think," Alec ventured.

"Why would he? He is Charlotte's uncle. Her only relative. Sorry, darling."

"Well, he more than likely was the source for the court case," said Alec in a hushed voice. "I don't think it would have been Deller."

"The Tanners were good," Charlotte said quietly.

"Yes, they were wonderful," Alec said. "They will get rid of him."

"That man is up to something," said Charlotte.

"Yes, I think he is."

"What man?" Theodora asked.

"My uncle Jason. He must have known about me, got it all from my so-called father. What does he want?"

"The files, I would say," Alec said, "and I think he is going to make it difficult for you to do anything without getting those files to him."

"But what is in the files that is so important?" Charlotte stood and began to pace. "He has a collection of fakes – my collection. Surely that is why he wants it hushed up."

"But would a collection of counterfeit paintings be so terrible? What if one of the files is about him?" Alec said.

"Why did he give me a lovely dog if he was going to then plan to make my life a misery?"

"I don't think he thought Dougie would be caught and if he did, he probably thought Dougie would not talk."

"Are there more Dougies out there, gunning for me?"

"There probably are, I'm afraid," Alec said with a slight note of shame. "It could be that Sir Jason wants to somehow discredit me."

"Why would he want to discredit you?" Charlotte asked.

"To dilute the validity of anything I should write about you, or the files, or Ferdi ... I'm not sure, really. But you are right, Sir Jason is up to something."

Theodora said, "Darling, you have got to go to the police and get them to protect your house, your privacy. You must not go out without Alec."

"Alec has a job, Theodora. I will get the Tanners to sort something out. They will be back on duty officially tomorrow. In any case, I think we should go to London tomorrow, get the files out of the bank, and see what Jason is up to."

"Go and see him, you mean?" Alec sounded cautious.

"Well, why not? In any case, I have got to find out what is happening to the collection. I wouldn't mind finding out if my Klimt is a forgery and—"

"Will you talk about anything else with him, I think Alec is asking, darling."

"I don't know, Theodora. I want to know about my art collection ... *my* collection of paintings, not *his* collection, being counterfeit. And what are his plans about my half-destroyed house in Paris? And whether it is he who is damaging my reputation ... I mean, being asked if I was a whore at Le Palais! Who knows this?"

"You were never a whore at Le Palais, darling," Theodora said.

"I know I wasn't. But who knew I was there in the first place, as Freya Jorgensen, other than you and Jost Krupp? Franz-Joseph Deller? Possibly. My stepfather? He and Jason were pretty close. Who knew Charlotte de Tournet was still alive other than you and Ferdi?"

"There's Bernard Trent," Alec said.

"Why would Bernard tell Jason that I was Charlotte? It doesn't make sense. I think Jason knew all along somehow."

Charlotte stopped pacing and stood still. She was startled when Bonzo farted loudly and everybody started to laugh. Bonzo was fast asleep on Theodora's lap, blissfully unaware that he had lightened the mood. Theodora quickly got up, gently lowering Bonzo's head from her lap and waving away the smell.

Alec said, "Now that Bing-Wallace has gone back to London, we will leave it to Bonzo to keep our spirits up. And he seems to have charmed you, Theodora."

"He's a nice dog. A bit smelly, and chews too many things. He chewed a whole pack of my cigarettes the other day and was sick."

"He got one of my shoes last week, chewed through the heel. It snapped off when I put it on. I could not get cross with him, though." Charlotte laughed.

Alec said, "I have a few questions about things that have bothered me over the past couple of months."

"Well, thank you for bringing on the tension again, darling!" Theodora flicked the ash off the end of her cigarette with her thumbnail aggressively, making a clicking noise.

"What questions, Alec?" Charlotte said with a sigh.

"Well ..." Alec was gazing at the floor between his shoes, thinking about what he was going to ask, Charlotte supposed.

"I have three questions, two about Jost Krupp."

"I wondered when you were going to ask about him, Alec. Theodora will—"

"No – it is not about his relationship with you. It is when he crashed into Sir Jason's house. Sir Jason called him 'Krupp' or 'Wolff' – 'What do you want, Wolff?' or 'What are you doing here, Krupp?' I think he said. Something like that. Jason called him by his name. Did they know each other?"

"You are right, Alec!" Charlotte said. She tried to replay the scene at Alston House and went over to the window and looked out at the view. "He said, 'What are you doing, Krupp?' – not Wolff. I don't know anybody called ... They must've known each other!"

"Didn't Krupp announce who he was when he forced his way in?" Theodora said.

"No," Alec said. "I did not know who this man was until Jason called him by name."

"But Krupp shot at Jason," Theodora said. "Why would Krupp shoot Jason if they were not enemies?"

"I don't know," Alec said. "It just seemed odd that Jason knew who Krupp was."

"I cannot understand how they would know each other, unless Krupp was one of Jason's spies," Charlotte said. "What was the other question?"

"Why did Krupp kill your husband?"

"He's just a killer?" Theodora surmised.

"He is a killer, but perhaps not an indiscriminate killer," Alec replied. "Ferdi would be useful to him to find these mystery files. And who do we think is paying him? And why is he not still in jail or even hanged for his war crimes?" Alec put his hands behind his head and stared up at the ceiling. "There is a lot to work out."

Charlotte went over to Alec and knelt in front of him, looking up into his eyes.

"I don't know why Jost is trying to kill me. I wish you had let me kill him at Jason's. Then you would have a story."

"That would've been a mistake," Alec said, "and you would die, by the hangman." He gazed down at Charlotte and held her face in his hands.

"I will not write anything without your specific approval." His brow furrowed. "Lastly, why didn't Jason come to Ferdi's funeral? Did he say anything?"

"I was pleased he didn't," Charlotte said.

Ferdi's funeral was a small affair at the tiny chapel at Burton Park Place. It was attended by just Charlotte, Theodora, Alec and Philip, that bloody man Strider, and Arno, representing the Adolphe Hotel, along with an elderly man from the Luxembourg embassy. There was also a man in naval uniform.

Theodora asked, "Who was the man in the Royal Navy uniform? He did not stay on for drinks."

"That was Commander Stanley. He was Ferdi's godfather's aid," Charlotte said. "We did not really know him. He was all to do with Ferdi's secret stuff, I think."

"Sir Sussex Tremayne?"

"Yes. Do you know about him as well, Alec?" Charlotte asked, starting to feel annoyed.

"I met him just after the war. He asked me to do something for him."

"Oh, for God's sake, Alec," Theodora shouted. "We don't want to know." She turned to Charlotte. "Why could you not find a man that is normal, darling!"

"Is that why you came to see me, Alec? When Ferdi got killed? Because of Sir Sussex?"

"No! I didn't know of the connection until the day I brought you down after Krupp escaped. I was at Sir Sussex's funeral. Were you?"

Charlotte looked sadly down. "No, but Ferdi was." She rested her head on Alec's knee, her arms draped over his lap. The same pose she adopted in the last portrait of her and Ferdi.

"I am sorry, Charlotte. It was just my job. Sir Sussex wanted me to research WASP." Charlotte looked up into Alec's face. She wondered if he was being deceitful. Alec sighed as he gazed at her. "You are so lovely, you could—"

Fuming, she stood and backed away from him. There was a look of surprise on his face. "This is all I have, Alec. I don't want to be placed on a pedestal!"

"But I was not ..." Alec looked shocked. Theodora sat quietly, watching them.

"I don't have a writing aptitude, or an artistic talent. I do not think I am a very nice person. I spent most of my childhood being spoilt, most of my teens with people who turned out to be psychopaths, and did not realise it. If it were not for Theodora, I would probably have been a prostitute!"

"A bloody rich one," Theodora said quietly behind her. Charlotte turned on her friend and seeing her smile, started to laugh. "Yes, even richer than I am now. But I have never used myself – my face – as a weapon, to seduce anyone." She felt defensive for some reason. She sat down on the floor beside Bonzo and stroked his soft black ears whilst he chewed frantically at a bone.

Noticing Alec's confusion, Charlotte said quietly, "I got a lot of attention – male attention. I hated most of it. It started with my uncle Jean de Tournet." She paused and gave a little shudder. "Just saying his name now makes me queasy. I tried to keep out of the press, out of the public eye – not to be fashionable, or ..." She sighed. "I did not want to be an Audrey Hepburn or a Liz Taylor, always being pursued."

"I wanted to launch her into society," Theodora said proudly, "but Ferdi and she have always wanted to be private."

"Apart from anything else, I wanted to work," Charlotte said.

"Doing what?" Alec said, clearly surprised.

"Oh, I don't know – open a nightclub for dangerous men, or a brothel for old Nazis and despots. That is all I am qualified for. I am not particularly charitable. In fact, I think I am rather selfish. Like, apparently, my mother."

After a few minutes of silence, Alec said, "Let's go and get those files from your husband's safe box. Do you want to come too, Theodora?"

"Yes, I think I will. The last time you two went off, that dog Krupp came and murdered everybody."

"I will phone the Adolphe," said Charlotte.

"No, stay with me in my flat, it's safer. Plenty of room. Can I borrow Ferdi's Bentley again?"

"Yes, the Bentley's yours. I will call Jason and tell him what we are doing." Charlotte went to the door.

"I wouldn't, darling. Just surprise him. Don't give him too much information," Theodora said. "I don't think we should trust him too much. Remember, Dougie was one of his."

"That is true." Charlotte pondered for a moment. "If you are sure, Alec."

"It will be my pleasure."

28

"I got your telegram only a day or two ago, Krupp, not exactly very good notice," shouted Jaffery. Krupp was sitting on a bollard on the dockside, feeling majestic, looking down at Jaffery mooring his boat. "It was Christmas only a few days ago."

"Shut up, Jaffery. You are getting paid enough. In any case, I doubt you remembered it was Christmas." Krupp stood. Jaffery was at least four metres below, tying up his boat. "I gather you have failed WASP again." Jaffery jerked his head up from tying up the stern mooring line. Krupp, in his black full-length trench coat, his hands resting on a walking stick, glared down at Jaffery from the quayside in Emden docks, north-west Germany.

"What are you trying to pull now, Krupp?" Jaffery shouted angrily, his South African voice echoing across the still icy water of the dock. "I thought WASP was wound up after the war."

"Who do you think you and I are working for, Jaffery?"

"Whoever has money for the fare. Don't care who they work for. I work for nobody."

"Do you remember taking two men across the Channel to pick up a wounded Royal Marine soldier?"

"Possibly, if he had the right paperwork and plenty of real money, not fake money. Why?"

"Did these men instead come back with a quantity of file boxes?"

"I can't remember …" He stopped. "Yes – that's right, a few months after the invasion. They wanted me to go over to Le Havre and back to Newhaven." He paused in thought whilst scratching his buttock. "No, we ended up taking the boxes to Littlehampton."

"Do you know what was in those boxes?"

"I didn't ask. Why would I?"

"They contained details of most of the SS and Gestapo officers that were in France, members of the SD – the SS secret service – and WASP, and people who spied for the SD – like you, Jaffery. A lot of whom have since been tried and murdered."

Jaffery scampered up the quayside ladder, fast for a big man, to face Jost. He was puce with rage. His blotchy bulbous nose came angrily up to Krupp's face.

"I didn't spy for you lot!"

"Jaffery, you were not exactly a British loyalist, were you? That is beside the point." Krupp leant even closer to Jaffery's face and said in a low voice, "I have just gathered that you took these men from Newhaven to Le Havre, picked up these boxes and brought these men back again, but not to Newhaven. They worked for the British government!"

"Well, how was I to know? They said they were Royal Marines … except they weren't. They paid very well, came through a mutual contact. I am a businessman, not an idealist."

Krupp was surprised at Jaffery, who he regarded as a complete moron. He had plainly underestimated him, making him lose his temper.

"You are a stupid waste of a human being, and you have not only made a mess of your life, but mine as well," Krupp snarled. He grabbed Jaffery by the lapel of his jacket with his left hand, holding onto a rope attached to the bollard with his right, and pushed him to the edge of the dock. Jaffery looked frightened. His eyes cast down at his boat four metres below. Krupp only needed to let go and he would crash onto the thwart that lay across the well of the boat and probably break his back.

"If you let go, Krupp, you will never get back to Newhaven." Panic made Jaffery sound as though he was whining, which made the threat almost worthless.

"Why would I want to go back to England?"

"To get that girl you wanted … and to get the WASP file?"

"That you took over in the first place." He relaxed his hold on Jaffery's coat and Jaffery slipped a little. He waved his arms around, looking down at his fate. Krupp could see tears were forming in his eyes. "Feeling a little emotional, are you?"

Across the dock a man shouted at them, *"Alles in Ordnung?* Are you all right?"

"*Ja, wir sind ok, danke,*" Krupp shouted back at the man, and reluctantly hauled Jaffery to safety. He would have loved to have let Jaffery go, but there were witnesses.

"Payment," Jaffery spluttered. He quickly moved away from the edge of the dock, putting Krupp in between, his hand stretched out.

Krupp took out a small black purse. Jaffery grabbed it out of Krupp's hand, stepped away, checked the contents of the purse and found six gold coins. He tried to conceal his delight but failed when he licked his lips. He quickly pocketed the purse.

"Get me back to Newhaven, Jaffery. And when I return, I'd return with me, if I were you, and join me in Argentina."

"What? Who's going to pay for that?"

"You've got plenty of cash stashed away, you old miser. I know you. You are like Scrooge." Krupp gestured at the purse.

"No, I'm not." Krupp could see he was plainly lying. "Anyway, where is Argentina?"

"South America. Come on, get going." Krupp shoved Jaffery towards the ladder down to the boat.

"Don't push. Why Argentina?"

"You will have some friends there, Jaffery, if they have not been murdered already." Krupp dropped his bag over the side of the dock. It landed with a thud in the well of the boat.

"Hang on." Jaffery turned on Krupp. "Are you armed?" Krupp put up his arms. He smiled to himself as Jaffery patted down his coat. He also patted Krupp's ankle boots. Krupp noted that Jaffery was wearing shoes, with nowhere to conceal syringes.

The two men carried on bickering as they descended the ladder down to the old torpedo boat. Krupp felt quite a lot of pain in his back as he climbed down, and regretted not getting Jaffery to arrive when the tide was higher.

As they cruised slowly out to sea – to conserve fuel, Jaffery insisted – Krupp kept a surreptitious eye on the chart and the compass reading.

Jaffery was still whining about money, Argentina, and how he was not a German spy, when Krupp said, "Can you see the sun trying to poke through the clouds up there?" They had just passed between the small Dutch islands of Boswachterij and Vlieland before heading south, well out in the North Sea. It was fast approaching midday, and the sea was quite calm for a cold winter's day.

"What are you talking about, Krupp, what sun?" Jaffery went to the side of the boat and looked up. Krupp slipped a Luger out of his bag and shot Jaffery in the back of the head, the bullet exiting through Jaffery's right eye socket. He slumped over the edge of the boat. Krupp pulled off Jaffery's coat, took out the black purse from Jaffery's pocket, drew his feet up and sent Jaffery overboard.

Jaffery routinely searched Krupp before he ever took him aboard his boat – he did not trust him. Krupp knew this and had put the pistol in his bag, which he threw down into the boat before they cast off. He'd kept Jaffery so worked up about Argentina and spying that Jaffery forgot to search the bag.

Krupp took the controls of the boat and thrust the throttles to full speed, and hurtled towards the White Cliffs of Dover and Newhaven beyond.

29

"Good morning, Mr Strider," Charlotte said on the phone. Alec, Charlotte and Theodora were in Alec's flat and sitting at the dining table in his kitchen, regretting they had not, after all, gone to the Adolphe Hotel.

"Good morning, and compliments of the season, Lady Saumures. How can I assist you?" Strider sounded flustered.

"I am sorry to bother you so near to the end of the holidays, you must have a lot of work."

"Not at all, my lady."

"Mr Strider, I need to get into my husband's security box at Hoare's bank and I require a letter to prove that he is dead."

There was a long moment of silence. "In Hoare's bank you say, my lady?"

"Yes. He has left some things there." Another long pause followed. "Are you there, Mr Strider?"

"I am sorry, Lady Saumures. I will see to it today. When do you plan to come to town?"

"I plan to go to the bank this morning; we are already in town."

"You are in town? At the Adolphe?" He sounded incredulous.

"No, I am staying with friends. Mr Strider." Charlotte was losing her patience. "We will be with you in half an hour, and I would be grateful if you would see that the letter is available when we arrive at your office. Do I make myself clear?"

"Yes, yes, Lady Saumures," he blustered.

"And, Mr Strider, I am having difficulty locating my uncle. Would you know where he is?"

"I will try and locate him, my lady, and let you know when you come to my office. But I am not sure I can get a letter ready in time."

"I am sure you can, Mr Strider. Good morning." Charlotte slammed down the phone.

"Well?" Theodora asked.

"Firstly, he was surprised that I was in town. Secondly, he was very interested that Ferdi had a box at Hoare's bank, and thirdly, he does not know where Jason is – or says he doesn't know."

"Why are these facts all significant, darling?" Theodora asked.

"I suggest, Madam Theodora," Alec said whilst making some porridge on the gas stove, "that firstly there may be someone at the Adolphe Hotel who is informing Strider of Charlotte's movements – which suggests that she or we are being followed – but they missed our journey last night up to London. Secondly, these missing files have been searched for, and they – whoever *they* may be … and I bet Strider is one of the *theys* – had not considered Ferdi had a strongbox somewhere." Alec started spooning out three bowls of porridge.

"And thirdly?" Theodora asked, declining a bowl of porridge with a shake of her forefinger and an undisguised expression of disgust on her face.

"You have got to have some porridge, Theodora," said Alec. "It will put hairs on your chest and keep you warm."

"Is that what porridge looks like? It will probably kill me."

"Go on, Theodora," Charlotte entreated, "it is so good for you. With a bit of evaporated milk and brown sugar."

"No, stop, you are making me ill. I will just have my coffee and a cigarette. I would rather stick a pencil in my eye than eat that stuff. Anyway, Alec, what is significant about Strider not knowing where Jason is? He is his lawyer, not his nursemaid."

Alec started serving the porridge, Charlotte putting up a hand when he had put enough in her bowl.

"Strider and Jason are certainly hand in glove. To what end, I have no idea. I am not sure how trustworthy Strider is," Alec surmised.

"In which case, are we to assume Jason is *not* trustworthy after all?"

"Yes, I think so," Alec said.

"How is he not trustworthy?" Theodora asked.

Alec said, "There may be something in the files he is trying to conceal. Possibly he has a buyer for the fake paintings, presuming Charlotte was dead."

"You don't kill people for that," Charlotte said.

"You think Krupp is killing people for Jason?" Alec sounded doubtful. "A respectable politician, and a—"

"Then it must be Strider who is ordering all these people to be killed," Charlotte said.

"Why, Charlotte?" Theodora seemed confused.

"Strider must be hiding something." Charlotte looked up at Alec, who was eating his porridge propped up by the work surface.

Theodora was shaking her head. "He is such a little man, no backbone. He's not calling the shots."

"All the more reason to get someone like Krupp to do his dirty work," Charlotte said, drizzling evaporated milk over her porridge from a tin, Theodora regarding the procedure with disgust. "I am going to ask him when I see him. It's about time we sorted out Ferdi's will anyway."

*

It was a crystalline, crisp, sunny late December morning, and Twenty-Three Middle Temple Lane was deep in shadow. Charlotte and Theodora went up to Eric Strider's office.

"Good morning, Lady Saumures," said Strider rising from his chair, his little pinprick eyes looking worried through his thick glasses. He could not conceal his suspicion of Theodora's presence.

"You remember my good friend Madam Theodora Smith?"

"Yes of course, from the Alston House incident."

"Yes, indeed," Charlotte said. She was trying to sound as dippy as possible. She did not want Strider to consider her as a threat or a person who knew what she was doing. "That awful business, I did not sleep for weeks after that. That dreadful man!"

"Lady Saumures, I have the baron's death certificate."

"Oh!" Charlotte gasped, putting her hand up to her mouth. Theodora glanced at Charlotte curiously.

Strider carried on. "The will, it seems, is being held at our Paris branch, with Monsieur Russe."

"Oh? Why is it taking such a long time getting here? The baron was killed nearly three months ago." Charlotte took out a handkerchief from her sleeve and held it to her eyes as though she was about to cry.

Strider was embarrassed and slightly alarmed. "It seems, my lady, that they had lost the will momentarily. It was drawn up just after the war, but they had moved offices as the main office was badly damaged by a fire."

"Why was the will lodged in Paris, and not with you?"

"Your husband's request, after you introduced us to your husband, I believe."

"But the war was over when he had …" She paused, fashioned a look of distress. "Well never mind about that. I trust I am not going to run out of money in the meantime?"

"No, my lady, you have your own account at the Lombard Odier bank that is well within credit and should keep you and the house in Petworth in funds for the next year. But under the name of Lady *Freya* Saumures. The business accounts for the farm tenancies and the estate are also there under your husband's name. However, he had arranged power of attorney for you." Charlotte pretended she was confused. "Power of attorney, my lady, means that you have access to these accounts, with the approval of the directors of the estate."

"I just hope I will not need to go to the directors and that the will is available before long."

"Yes, yes, my lady." He sat down and started straightening up sheets of paper and his pens, his mouth open as if preparing to speak but unable to say anything. At last he said, with a hint of embarrassment, "As to this strongbox, how do you know about it?"

"Ferdi wrote me a letter. Why?"

"It is the first I have heard of it."

"Why would Ferdi tell you?" Charlotte said indignantly.

"Oh, I just thought he might, if there were important business files in the box." He licked his lips before he said, "Would you like me to trot up to Hoare's and bring the box back here?"

Just then the phone rang and everybody jumped. "Excuse me," he said and snatched up the receiver. "Strider … Are you sure …? You checked all his contact numbers? Thank you." He replaced the receiver, looking most perplexed. "I regret we cannot contact your uncle, my lady, and he is the only person who can help you get into your husband's strongbox."

"What absolute rubbish, Strider," Theodora said, taking charge. Charlotte and Theodora both stood, so did Strider. "Where is this letter?" Theodora demanded. "The one that says that Ferdi is dead?"

"It is here, my lady, but …" He pointed to a buff file on his desk. Theodora swiped it from under his fingertips and handed it to Charlotte. Charlotte took it, read the contents and marched out of the office.

At the door, Charlotte turned and glared at Strider. "My understanding of a lawyer – in our employ – is that he acts entirely in the client's interests *only*, in utmost confidence and ensuring our concerns are kept secure within this firm."

Strider sat heavily back into his chair. He was about to speak but Charlotte carried on, in a softer, slightly pitying voice. "Mr Strider, you and your London firm will be reported to the Law Society if I find that you have been acting against my husband and his estate in preference of Sir Jason Barrett or anyone else." Strider looked hopeless. "I believe, Mr Strider, that you are involved, somehow, in my husband's death."

"No! I … How dare you!" Strider blustered piteously. He tried to take control of himself, but it was too late. Charlotte walked out of the office. There was nobody else there, no clerks or secretaries – or witnesses.

*

Fleet Street had reawakened after the long Christmas holiday. C. Hoare & Co bank was an ancient institution, going since 1672. Alec was standing outside waiting for Charlotte and Theodora. He had news. "Bing-Wallace has turned sleuth again," he said. "He has found out where Jason has gone – well, he thinks he knows."

"Where does Philip think he's gone?" Charlotte asked with a little smile.

"He thinks he's gone to the country."

"Why would he think that?"

"Bing-Wallace says he was wearing his tweeds," Alec said, trying and failing to suppress his amusement.

"Well, that is sleuthing indeed." Charlotte giggled. "How does he know Jason is wearing tweeds? Is he stalking him like a deer?"

"I think he must be, but he cannot drive, and one cannot follow Jason's motor car on a bus; plus he hates taxis."

"Some sleuth, darling," Theodora said tritely.

Charlotte tried to think why he would go to the country without telling everybody. Businessmen always told people where they were going.

"Strider was also particularly interested in Jason's whereabouts for some reason," Theodora said, pulling her fur collar around her face. "You should have seen this one, playing the dizzy flapper. She basically told Strider that we don't trust him."

"Did you, by God!"

"Well, not in those words," Charlotte said. "Just that he seemed to be connected somehow to Ferdi's death."

"Christ! He must have had a seizure. Why did you confront him? What had he said?"

"He was so evasive, wasn't he, Theodora? He said he did not have Ferdi's will – which is nonsense. He could not find Jason, and said that Jason was the only person who can help us with opening Ferdi's strongbox."

"He's not a good lawyer, darling." Theodora shivered. "Can we go in? It is far too cold out here for a Turk!"

*

Charlotte proffered a slip of paper that had the reference number for the personal security vault in the name of Baron Olivier Ferdinand Saumures of Luxembourg. Charlotte also handed over her passport and the death certificate.

"Strider is plainly worried about what is in this box of Ferdi's," Charlotte said quietly. They were in a small ornate office, with windows looking over Hare Place and King's Bench Walk, areas steeped in Dickensian-style history and hardly changed since the eighteenth century. "He even offered to collect the box himself and bring it back to his office."

"Really?" Alec wondered how involved with Jason Barrett Strider was. "He is plainly up to something with Jason."

"Yes, I think he must be. And then we see him at Jason's," Charlotte said. "I think we need to go down to Wimbledon and see Jason. His tweeds were probably for Wimbledon."

"No, that is where Bing-Wallace had followed him to. He was *leaving* Wimbledon in his tweeds."

"Philip followed Jason to Alston House?" Theodora was aghast. "Isn't he taking this sleuthing lark a little too seriously?"

"He loves it. He has always wanted to be an investigative journalist; you know, the type that write for the *News of the World*."

The liveried clerk arrived in the office with a steel security box, about a foot wide by a little over a foot and a half long, and six inches deep. There was a lock on the front with two keyholes. The clerk was followed by a thin, grey-suited man who was rubbing his hands together. He came up to Charlotte and bowed in obsequiousness. "Lady Saumures, I am so sorry neither of the Messrs Hoare are here to meet you. I know you will forgive them," he grovelled.

Charlotte replied as imperiously as possible. "That is quite all right, Mr ...?"

"Stevens, milady."

"Mr Stevens." She offered him her sweetest smile.

"They would have wanted to send their condolences personally; however, they are in Switzerland at the moment." On seeing Theodora and Alec, Stevens asked who they were. Charlotte introduced them to Stevens, who politely asked them to sign a visitors' book and then took out a key and unlocked one of the two locks. Charlotte took out the key that was taped to the safe drawer in Ferdi's study and unlocked the other lock. Stevens then left the little office, virtually reversing towards the door like departing royalty.

"Right, then," Charlotte said. The lid was a little difficult to open. Alec stood well away from the box, not wanting to get in the way or look too eager to see the contents. At last, the lid opened and Charlotte took out a letter addressed to her. There was another one addressed to Theodora and Bernard Trent. Charlotte and Theodora both looked at the envelope sadly.

"Ferdi still thought of me and Bernard as a couple," Theodora said. "Perhaps we should have been, given time. What else is there? Let us see the files."

Charlotte was already lifting out six manila files. Each had a name on it in Gothic-style script.

"Jost Krupp," she read on the top file, followed by a sharp intake of breath in surprise at the formal photograph of Krupp as a captain, sporting an iron cross. He looked handsome, charming. She managed to tear her eyes away from Krupp's photograph and went to the next file. "This file has two names, Albert Jaffery and Hildegard Baumgartner – no photos. He doesn't sound like he is German. Here is Franz-Joseph Deller – no beard, in SS uniform! And Jean de Tournet." She felt a shiver as she saw the photo of her stepfather seated with her aunt Stella standing behind.

"Look at this." Charlotte glanced at Theodora and then showed Alec the final file name.

"Jason Barrett," Alec read, "and then … what is this? WASP! He *was* part of WASP!"

"Really?" Theodora said. "These are files on Germans and Nazi sympathisers?"

"Well," Charlotte said, opening the file on her uncle, "I think that is what Operation Wasp Trap was about. And we now know why it was called 'Wasp Trap'."

"Let us go back to my flat," said Alec, "and sift through all this. Charlotte, you need to read the letter first, I think. We have to get out of here before Strider alerts someone."

"Like whom?" Charlotte asked.

"I have a feeling," Alec said, packing up the files into a briefcase, "that Jason knows what the files are about."

"That is a thought," Charlotte mused. "You had better see if Philip can come and help."

"Good idea," Alec said.

As they emerged from the bank into Fleet Street, they hurried into Chancery Lane where the Bentley was parked.

30

"Alec, I will translate my letter for you," Charlotte said, back in Alec's flat in Prince of Wales Drive.

"Are you sure, Charlotte?" Alec sat beside her on the sofa.

"Yes, I am sure." She opened her letter. "I want you to get to know Ferdi. He was a complicated person, and I admired him.

"Chère *Charlotte*." She took a long pause, scanning the letter. "*I am so grateful to you for being my wife, when you could have had a proper husband and possibly children.*" She stopped. Her eyes cast miserably up at Theodora, and then to Alec. "I cannot have children, and I think he knew that." Alec was surprised that Charlotte should know this. He would have asked why she was so sure she was unable to have a child, but she quickly carried on. "*I am constantly in admiration of the pretence of your love for me in front of people. I regret that I was unable to offer you a man's love – a real lover – but I have always cherished you in the best way I could. Our friendship was wonderful and our companionship, though unconventional, was very strong.*" Charlotte stopped and took a handkerchief out of her sleeve. She dabbed a small tear from her cheek. "I'm sorry."

"Charlotte, I really think this letter is for you alone."

"No, Alec, I want you to share this with me." Charlotte stroked his cheek with her hand, tenderly, gazing into his eyes briefly, and then carried on with the letter:

"*The war had taken a toll on you, as it did on all of us, and I truly hope you will carry on with your life in a more conventional way. You will have no worries about money. I have left instruction that both you and Theodora are cared for through to old age and beyond. There is also something for Christina and for Bernard.*

"*In this box, you will find some files: records of individuals that I leave you, Theodora and Bernard to judge as to what should be done about them. There is* one file on your uncle Jason and his involvement with the WASP movement." Charlotte took a long inward breath, her brow furrowed. *"I recommend that his file is presented to Michael Stewart, the Secretary of Foreign Affairs (or whoever is in the position at the time of you reading this letter), and also the police and the War Crimes Commission. If Sir Sussex Tremayne is still alive and in action, he should be notified. He can be contacted via the Foreign Office and MI6.*

"There is one thing you must do as soon as possible, as I have not been able to do so. You must reclaim Nineteen Avenue Foch. I tried to ensure that the house was passed on to Theodora, in accordance with your will, but as there was no written will available, I think you will find your uncle Jason has acquired the house and is thinking of developing the site as his own. My God – this is getting … That man is …" Charlotte shook her head in hopelessness. "What are we to do, Alec?"

"We will sort it out, Charlotte. Sir Jason no longer has a right to Avenue Foch and he knows it. However, we are going to have to ensure you are not registered as 'dead' and that a valid will is drawn up. What else does Ferdi say?"

Charlotte carried on with the letter, angrily swiping away a tear. *"If, or when, you release the information in these files, you will have to make sure you are protected. That you ensure you, Theodora and Bernard, Christina and anyone else close are kept out of danger. There will be reprisals. I truly hope that I will have reduced the danger by the time you read this letter."*

The room fell quiet. All eyes stared at the files on the coffee table, apprehensive of what they were about to reveal. After a good couple of minutes, Theodora opened her letter from Ferdi.

"Charlotte," Theodora said after reading the letter, "Ferdi talks here about a man, Albert Jaffery. He is a South African who lives in Newhaven. Apparently, he was the man who brought Ferdi and Bernard over from France in 1944 with the files, but he worked for WASP. If anyone needed to secretly get to England from France or Germany, Jaffery was the person to do it. Ferdi thinks contacting the police and handing over his file should be our first action."

"I wonder why." Charlotte picked up the file with Jaffery's name on it.

Alec said, "I imagine if anybody wanted to escape England clandestinely – like Krupp – it would be with this chap."

"We need to look at Jason's file first," said Charlotte. "I would love to know why he warrants a Wasp Trap file. And what is he to do with WASP?"

Alec was thoughtful. "Sir Sussex Tremayne asked if I could look into WASP in 1945."

"What do you know?" Theodora was abrupt.

"The information is still quite sketchy. I crashed at the first hurdle when I tried to find a member of WASP. There were no documents or evidence that such a group existed. Then in 1951, I met the wife of an American journalist called Greg Schneider at an American news awards dinner. She accepted a recognition on her late husband's behalf, for his insights on the Nazis before the war that she had published as a book. It was revealed in this book that during the Duke of Windsor's visit to Adolf Hitler in 1937, the duke was overheard offering every success to Admiral Canaris for something called WASP. Unfortunately, the duke was not too circumspect and did not realise that he could be overheard by Greg Schneider. When Schneider asked the prince what WASP was, in an interview a day later, the interview was stopped instantly by the duke. Schneider was inexplicably imprisoned and told he was going to be deported for subversion."

"But this is fantastic!" Charlotte said. "The ex-king?"

"Schneider was put in the same cell as two German journalists. When he asked if any of them had heard of WASP, one of the German journalists had found out that WASP stood for 'War Against Socialist Parties' and that it was very powerful, highly secret, and very few people knew about it. And, he said, it was a British organisation, not, as Schneider surmised, a German group.

"On further research, I found that the German journalist was shot for treason. The American journalist was badly injured in a car accident, in Germany, after being released from prison, and died on the ship that took him back to America. He had concealed a notebook in the lining of his suitcase with the beginnings of his article. All it said, amongst other stuff about the Nazis, was: *The Duke of Windsor, with his wife and Adolf Hitler, is involved in a political group called WASP – War Against Socialist Parties. What is WASP?* There was a bit about the German journalist Helmut Krull, and then nothing. Mary Schneider showed me the very notebook and asked if I would like to write her husband's biography. Sadly I had to decline because of other commitments.

"I reported back to Sir Sussex in 1951, but he was very ill. His office told me to drop the research on WASP and to stop any further investigation, for my safety – which was slightly worrying. I was sorry not to have carried on with the inquiry."

There was a pause.

"Are there any other revelations you might come up with, Alec?" Theodora spat.

"No, I don't think so," he said defensively. Charlotte flashed Theodora a look of annoyance. "Bing-Wallace is popping over to help go through the files, if that is all right by you." Alec tried to change the subject.

"I think it would be a great help if Philip assisted us with the files. I need to see what's in Jason's file though," Charlotte said, reaching over to get it.

"Does Ferdi say much more in his letter, darling?" Theodora asked.

"No, just a bit more about his thoughts on me," Charlotte said self-consciously.

"It is so sad that he assumes Bernard is here, still alive, Alec," Theodora said. "You are going to have to take Bernard's place, darling." It was the first time Theodora had been pleasant to Alec all day.

The doorbell rang, and Philip Bing-Wallace appeared at the door with a bright smile. "Morning, everyone!"

*

Philip Bing-Wallace read Jason's file in depth, after Alec and Charlotte.

"I am shocked, my dears, simply shocked." Bing-Wallace stood up as though he was about to recite a poem. "Basically, as far as I can gather from this document, Sir Jason was working with the Nazis all the time – all through the war. The utter bounder!"

"It looks that way," Charlotte said, embarrassed. "I am sorry."

Everybody's attention swung towards Charlotte.

Theodora went over to her and said simply, "Not in the least your fault, darling. How can it be?"

"I have this list," Bing-Wallace said, holding up a sheet of paper. "It is basically a list of the people involved in this … WASP. It's horrendous, and," he huffed, "all run by Sir Jason."

"Are there any names we know?" Alec asked.

"Lots! It's endless," Bing-Wallace said. "Viscount Rathmore, to name one of many. His newspapers are poisonous. General Franco is another."

"I danced with the general on his birthday in 1944," Charlotte said quietly.

"Crikey," said Bing-Wallace, hesitating before going back to his summary. "Franco was basically rescued by WASP from his enforced confinement in the Canaries, and they encouraged him to root out the leftist government … it looks like the Spanish Civil War was started by WASP!"

"Hang on, Philip." Alec turned to Charlotte. "You have danced with General Franco?"

"She did, Alec," Theodora said proudly.

There was nothing anyone could say for a while. Alec was amazed that so much had happened to someone as young as Charlotte. To see and experience so much, meet such people, such dangerous people. Charlotte sat on the sofa with him and stared at her letter from Ferdi, thinking about something. She seemed bothered by what the files were revealing. Alec stroked her hand. She pushed his hand away.

"Sorry, Alec," she said replacing her hand for Alec to take, a sad smile on her pale face.

"Do you know, Alec," Bing-Wallace said, "there should be a book on these two gals."

Alec said, "Perhaps, Philip, one day, when this is all a distant memory."

"It looks like Sir Jason, according to that file, was the director general of WASP. And," Bing-Wallace said, a conspiratorial smile on his face, "the reason he was in London when the Nazis invaded Paris is because he basically let them in. It is as though he left Paris without locking the front door, so the Nazis could just waltz in and burgle the city. How on earth has this not come to light before?"

"It explains a lot," said Alec.

"How did Ferdi find out, when Alec and the secret service or MI5 could not?" Theodora asked. "Does the file say anything?"

"Well …" Alec held a piece of paper with more names on it. He felt uncomfortable.

"Well, what?" Charlotte plucked the paper from his hand. She started to read. As she read, her mouth fell open. "Franz-Joseph Deller!"

"What do you mean, Franz-Joseph Deller?" Bing-Wallace asked. "The vicar chap?"

"He was recruited into WASP by Jason in 1939," Alec said. "He was Ferdi's informant in Adlerhorst – Hitler's general headquarters. Jason was there in 1939, just after the war had started, and wanted Joseph to help him further the cause of WASP within the Nazi Party."

"This is too fantastic to believe," Theodora said. "Why is this man still alive? Why has he not been silenced by Jason?"

"He had the paintings?" said Alec. "He had some kind of back-up plan, perhaps? We will have to ask him. But he is going to be in danger when these files are published. We will have to be careful."

"Does Jason know about this, do you think, Alec?" Theodora asked. "Does he know Deller worked for Ferdi?"

"No, I don't think he does," Alec said. "That is why Jason has been keeping an eye on Deller, I suppose, getting him the job as a vicar. However, I don't think Deller knew much. It seems a lot of information came from Admiral Canaris and the *Abwehr*, before he was killed by Himmler."

"Ferdi said *he* was part of the *Abwehr*. Canaris and he were quite close. He told us all when we were in Spain, waiting to return to England," Charlotte remembered.

"Yes, darling," Theodora said. "Remember Bernard was quite put out. There was confusion as to who Ferdi was actually working for: the British or the German secret service."

"Presumably the British Secret Service knew Ferdi was recruited by the *Abwehr*?" asked Alec.

"Yes, I think Sir Sussex Tremayne encouraged it." Charlotte was getting distressed. "But why did Ferdi keep these files about Jason a secret? Why had he kept this from coming out? Surely it is a criminal thing to do?"

"I think," Alec said, "to protect you. I bet Ferdi was being threatened that you would be harmed if he ever released the information. That is why he kept the files. Look at what he said in his letter."

"And that is why Krupp is trying to kill me?"

"Yes," Alec said sadly, "and under Jason's instructions, *and* to get hold of these files before we do."

"But why now?" Theodora asked.

"Because Krupp has only just been released from prison-of-war camp, I should think," Alec said, tapping Krupp's file. "He had changed his identity. Günther Wolff got released early."

"There is an awful lot to get through," Bing-Wallace said, reaching over to take Krupp's file. "Well, Alec, any revelations about Krupp?"

"Not as much as I had hoped. It says he was killed at the village of Oradour-sur-Glane in 1944 – which is plainly wrong – and that he was badly injured in 1943, but there are no details."

Bing-Wallace said, "Wasn't that that terrible massacre in France? The whole village torched, every soul within murdered? It cannot be countenanced."

Charlotte said, "That was Krupp. This must be when he assumed another identity."

Alec carried on. "After a lot of research by Ferdi, he thinks that Krupp – under the name of Günther Wolff – was captured in Paris, claiming he was a wounded soldier."

"How on earth did Ferdi come up with that information?" Theodora asked.

"Krupp, Ferdi thinks, met Wolff somewhere, bribed him, or more than likely killed him to allow him to assume Wolff's identity. Ferdi found that the officers responsible for the Oradour-sur-Glane atrocity were a Major Adolf Otto Diekmann and Major Jost Krupp, Krupp having been killed there. Günther Wolff was arrested on the streets of Paris with an SS colonel and a woman prisoner. When he presented his papers, he was arrested and tried. He was sentenced to twenty years for his part in being in command of a Jewish labour camp construction team at Schirmeck, in Alsace, *not* Oradour. Which means he should be released in 1966, ten years' or so time. Why he was not executed, I have no idea." Alec looked at Krupp's file incredulously.

"So, if Krupp is Günther Wolff, he would have charmed his way out for some kind of parole." Theodora made a guttural noise of disapproval.

Alec said, "I do not see how, frankly, he could have got help. From Sir Jason, perhaps?"

Silence. They all continued reading the files, except Charlotte.

"Who is this Jaffery character, Charlotte?" Alec asked. Charlotte was in a kind of dream, looking out of the window over Battersea Park. "Charlotte? Are you OK?" Alec went over and stroked her shoulder.

"I'm fine," she said quietly.

"I say, you will never believe …" Bing-Wallace started with glee and then went quiet when he saw everybody's concern directed at Charlotte. He was halfway through Jaffery's file.

"I gave Philip the files on Jaffery and Baumgartner," Charlotte said. "I don't think I can do this. I think I want to go back home."

She looked exhausted and drained. Theodora went over to her and put her arms around her.

"Come on, darling. Would you like a drink? Alec, have you any—?"

"Cup of tea would be nice," Charlotte interrupted. "I'll go and make it. You read the files. We must get to the bottom of this. Anyone else for tea?"

"Love some, my dear," Bing-Wallace said. Charlotte went to the kitchen and prepared tea.

"Speak loudly, so Charlotte can hear," Theodora said.

"Jaffery," Bing-Wallace started, "was one of WASP's soldiers, as Ferdi describes him – like Krupp."

"A WASP soldier?" Alec started hunting through the WASP file. "I wonder who else is a WASP soldier, and if they are still active?"

Bing-Wallace took off his reading glasses and said, "Do you know, this is how the Cosa Nostra or Mafia in Italy and America work. There were rankings, from the head – The Boss (Sir Jason) with a *consigliere*, a lawyer. Strider seems unlikely, but you see where I am going with this. *Capos*, or captains and soldiers like Krupp and this Jaffery fellow."

"Who are the captains?" Theodora asked.

"Well," said Bing-Wallace enthusiastically, placing his hand on a file, "this Brunhilda Baumgartner woman, I suggest."

"Does it say so somewhere, Philip?" Alec asked.

"It sort of does. Her name comes up. She was mentioned in the WASP file as one of the 'associates'. This is, or was, a huge network. We must hand this all over to the authorities as soon as we can, Alec."

"Well, let us just finish our research first … and get it copied." Alec was worried. He saw a big story slipping out of their hands. "We only have Ferdi's word about all this. There seems to be no other people alive to corroborate that Sir Jason is involved, other than those implicated as WASP associates."

There was a silence as they digested everything that had been said so far.

Bing-Wallace carried on. "Jaffery lives on a farm that produces reeds for thatching in Newhaven. Why the baron knows so much about him is because not only did he bring the baron over with these very files just before the end of the war, he also brought over the Barrett Collection from Portugal to Falmouth with Father Dent or whoever he is."

"Really?" said Alec. "In what? Does it say what kind of boat?"

"Apparently, an old German E-boat disguised as a leisure cruiser, would you believe."

"How on earth do you disguise an E-boat? They're huge," Alec said. He wondered why his friend Dan James had not mentioned that the boat was a German motor torpedo boat.

"Anyway, this is the man who probably brought Krupp over," Bing-Wallace surmised.

"We need to find this man and question him," Charlotte said, walking in with a tray of tea things. "We should get to him before the police do."

"Why, Charlotte?" Alec asked.

"I want to know where Krupp is. And my uncle, come to that. Does the file say where this farm is?"

"Yes," Philip said cautiously. "You are not thinking of going there now, are you?" he asked as Charlotte went to the cupboard beside the front door and took out her coat.

"No, I am going home first." She was planning something. She stood at the door, everybody looking at her as she waited. She sighed when nobody said anything, and said abruptly, "Alec, would you be kind enough to drive me to Victoria Station? Theodora, I think you should join me."

"Oh … right, darling. On my way."

"But don't you want to hear about Father Dent, your father?" Bing-Wallace asked.

"No, she doesn't," Alec said quietly, sensing Charlotte's mood. "I think she wants to go home. I will take the ladies to Sussex. You stay here, Philip, and read through these files thoroughly. We need names of the people involved, preferably alive. I will call you here tonight."

"Alec," Charlotte started to protest, "you do not need to drive us all the way."

"Yes, I do, and I will be delighted. We need to talk about things anyway."

"Must we?" she said jadedly. "I think I know what I want to do."

She opened the door with purpose, giving Alec hardly any time to get his coat on. She grabbed her bag and walked to the lift. Theodora hurriedly gathered her things. "Wait, darling, not so fast, for the love of God!"

"This will be nice. We can see the New Year in tomorrow together, in Sussex," Alec said to Theodora quietly.

"Well, I hope the New Year brings some peace for Charlotte, Alec. She needs peace."

31

The night was drawing in early on New Year's Eve. Sir Jason waited in the cold parlour in the dark farmhouse. There was no light, other than a pale amber glow from a hurricane lamp on the coffee table, lighting up his face. He read a newspaper whilst smoking a cigar, a pistol lying beside his right hand on the table. He wore a thick black cashmere and wool coat to keep out the cold.

Outside, hidden in one of the tractor sheds was his huge maroon Bristol motor car, and leaning against it was the thin, angular shape of John Alderson, smoking a cigarette, gazing at the near-full moon. He wore a sheepskin coat, the collar pulled up around his neck, a tweed cap on his head.

He pushed himself off the Bristol when he heard the faint throb of diesel engines coming up the creek to the boathouse hidden in the reeds. Alderson tapped on the window of the parlour to alert Sir Jason. The light in the parlour was doused low.

The night to the east was black and tranquil; the colourless reeds stood out in the moonlight against the matt-black night sky. There was a constant hiss of breeze through the reeds that grew from the edge of the farmyard all the way down to the dunes beside the sea, a quarter of a mile away. Every sound made could be heard by Alderson back in the farmyard, from when the engines of the E-boat were cut, to the staggering through the reeds of a man, the grunts of pain when he fell, to the curses when he had lost his way. As Krupp lurched closer to the edge of the reeds, Alderson could see his torch beam panning back and forth, trying to keep to the path.

The front door of the farmhouse opened, and Sir Jason appeared, holding a hurricane lamp.

"John?"

"Yes, sir." Alderson flashed his torch and moved to where he calculated Jaffery and Krupp were going to emerge. As Krupp staggered out of the reeds, he did not see Alderson standing behind him. He stopped, breathing heavily, his attention taken by Sir Jason standing there on the front doorstep of the farmhouse.

"Sir Jason? Is that you?" Krupp said incredulously.

"Yes, Major Krupp. What have you done with our friend Jaffery?"

"He was driving me crazy. I killed him."

All the time Krupp was talking he kept the torch on Jason. He was desperately trying to find something in his pocket.

"Mr Alderson," Jason said calmly, "would you be kind enough to ask Major Krupp to surrender his weapon?"

"Certainly, sir." John Alderson crept up behind Krupp and stuck the barrel of his pistol into Krupp's ribs. Krupp gasped in shock and dropped his Luger. "Thank you, Major Krupp, sir," he said politely and picked up the Luger.

"*Himmeldonnerwetter!*" Krupp yelled at the thin grinning man who slid around to the front of Krupp like a snake, his torch shining in his face. "You got me by surprise, boy! Jason, what is going on? Why are you here?" Krupp demanded.

"There's been some rather unfortunate developments, thanks to you." Jason strolled over to where Krupp and John Alderson were standing.

"What do you mean?" Krupp said defensively.

"Not only did you fail to kill the person you were meant to kill, but you killed the one person that I specifically told you *not* to kill. The only person who would get us the files."

"Well I—"

"Then you leave a trail of bodies from Sussex to London, and to top it all, you shot at me and hit me!"

"That was a mistake, I didn't know you were the boss! Hilde told me who you were. I tried to miss … Sorry, but at least I did not wound you badly. And it took away any suspicion that—"

"There has never been any suspicion directed at me. I was a respected and much valued English businessman – a Member of Parliament, a cabinet minister – until you started messing things up for me." Jason scowled at Krupp. He turned and started to walk back to the farmhouse. Krupp picked up his bag and limped after him with Alderson coming up at the rear.

In the farmhouse kitchen, Alderson lit three more hurricane lamps. Krupp and Sir Jason sat opposite each other, either side of a grubby wooden table that had not been cleaned in many years. Sir Jason had spread out a newspaper as though it were a tablecloth. Krupp looked up at the unlit central light.

"There is no electricity here as you can see, Krupp," Jason said leaning back in his chair, a pistol held limply in his hand. "And it seems you have also, amongst others, killed one of the very few people who can get us out of the country in a hurry."

"Why do you need to leave?" Krupp looked around at Alderson, who was sitting quietly beside the doorway holding Krupp's Luger, pointed down.

"Again, thanks to you, the files have been recovered."

"Good news. Do you have my file?"

"As I was saying, recovered and being held by Freya Jorgensen, or Baroness Saumures, in her rather large friend's flat in Battersea."

"The art man?"

"No, he is not an art man," Jason said with some impatience, "he is a war correspondent – a journalist." Krupp sat back, confusion over his face.

"So why did you send me a telegram?"

"Because I need you to do your job properly. I want you to go and get the files and kill anybody who has been near them or has read them, which includes any policemen. You are good at killing people. The trouble is you seem to kill the wrong people."

"Don't treat me like some kind of a … a *Dumm ignorant narr*!" Krupp flared up and slammed his hand on the table. "Why don't you or your boy here do the job? I was OK being Günther Wolff until you found me."

"I got you out of Plötzensee Prison early, didn't I?" Jason snarled back. "I think that deserves some gratitude. You would be serving another eleven years at least if it was not for me."

There was a pause. Krupp glanced back at Alderson and saw he was now standing, the Luger slightly readier to be used.

"And what is this about the police?" Krupp began to calm down.

"As far as I know, the police have not yet been given these files. Strider tried to get them, but he is an idiot. He must have told them where the files were to be found."

"But he didn't know," Krupp blasted. "I asked him before I went down to the house in the country. He thought they would be there. The queer wouldn't tell me, and Deller swore he had no knowledge of the files – any files."

"Strider did not mention that to me this afternoon," Jason said after a while. There was a long silence. Then Jason asked, "Tell me, why did you threaten my niece at my house? It served no purpose."

"You wanted me to."

"Only to find out where the files were! You were meant to kill her."

Another silence. Krupp looked decidedly uncomfortable. Probably because he had an armed person sitting behind him in silence. Alderson was enjoying Krupp's discomfort.

"I could do with a drink if I am going to sit here being threatened and ridiculed," Krupp said sulkily. Alderson caught Jason's eye, who gave Alderson a slight nod. Alderson went to a briefcase that lay beside the sink, opened it and produced a bottle of Haig Dimple whisky. He was being watched by Krupp.

"No schnapps?"

"Not exactly a drink of choice for us English, due to the war," Sir Jason said, holding out his hand to take a silver tumbler from Alderson.

Krupp made a quick movement. Jason showed no alarm, whereas Alderson dropped the tumbler and jumped quickly back, crouching down with the pistol levelled at Krupp's head.

Krupp laughed. He picked up another silver tumbler from the table. He then picked up the bottle of whiskey, took the cork out with his teeth and poured a half tumbler. He did the same for Sir Jason.

"You are going to have to trust me, Barrett," Krupp said after slugging the whole half tumbler of whisky down.

"You will call me Sir Jason, if you don't mind."

"It's not going to be 'Sir' for very much longer, after they find out about you," Krupp said with a small, dry laugh.

"Well, let us hope that does not happen. I need you to get these files and eliminate all involved. We will then take Jaffery's boat to Spain and then on to Argentina via Florida. The money I have paid you is more than enough for you to live handsomely."

"Huh! You think so? I haven't seen much money from you yet."

"Well, do your job, Major Krupp. You have to work hard to get payment from me. And at the moment you are not exactly doing a good job."

There was another silence.

"Why Florida?" Krupp asked.

"My yacht is there, in the port of Key West." Jason drained his glass.

"Is the boy coming with us?" Jason took no notice of Krupp's question.

"Major Krupp." Sir Jason stood. "I am not going to help you escape the British police, or pay you, if you do not get those files on me and WASP, and kill my niece, the journalist Ballentine, the Turkish woman, Deller, and all involved. Do you understand me?"

Krupp scowled up at Jason.

"Why didn't you tell me Freya was your niece? And what is this about Deller being her father?"

"That is my business. Deller was our gardener in Paris before the war. He killed Charlotte's mother when Charlotte was small. Are you going to get these files or not?"

"I am going. Got a car?"

"There is one in the barn next to my Bristol."

"That is a police car," Krupp protested.

"All the better to get to where you are going in a hurry then."

"Good point."

"I would start at Alec Ballentine's flat in London," Jason said, eyeing Krupp. "That is where our operative says they went after collecting the files from Saumures's strongbox. Here is the address. My operative is keeping an eye on the flat."

"What operative?" Krupp was indignant. "Why can't he get the files and kill everybody?"

"Because, Krupp, not everybody has your indiscriminate skills. You have twenty-four hours and then I go, you don't get paid, and you will have to swim back to Germany."

Krupp stood. He held out his hand towards Alderson for his pistol. Alderson looked for approval from Jason, who nodded his consent. Alderson ejected the magazine and the round in the chamber, placed the pistol in Krupp's hand and ejected the bullet into his other hand. Alderson took out his own pistol and held it to his side and indicated to Krupp to go through the kitchen door first. Krupp picked up his small leather bag.

Alderson and Krupp found the old police car. Krupp got in to find that the car battery was low.

"You do the handle, boy," he said. Alderson gave Krupp a double glance, not showing any anger, which, gratifyingly, annoyed Krupp. Alderson went to the front of the car and wound the starter handle until the old black Wolseley spluttered to a start.

"There is hardly any petrol in the tank," Krupp protested.

"There is a garage in Newhaven," Alderson said flatly. "Buy some." He walked away as Krupp backed out of the garage and drove off. The small black sign on the roof of the car glowed faintly, the word "Police" visible. The blue flashing light that should have been on top of the sign had been removed by Jaffery.

32

"There is a small turning to the left along here somewhere."

"There are a lot of reeds down there."

"I'll drive very slowly just in case the— Christ, look out, you bastard!" Alec blurted, just as a police car, with no lights on, turned out of the reeds from a hidden driveway, and started towards them on the same side of the road. It swerved to the other side with only feet to spare.

"That was a police car, I think. I could see the little police sign on the roof," exclaimed Alec incredulously.

"Yes," said Theodora from the back seat in a voice that wobbled, "and did you see who was driving it?"

"No?" Alec and Charlotte said together.

"Jost Krupp!"

After the initial shock of hearing Krupp's name, Alec flung the car into a quick three-point-turn, slightly incongruous in a heavy Bentley, and chased after the police car.

"Are you sure, Theodora?" Charlotte asked.

"Yes."

"What shall we do, Alec?" Charlotte said.

"I think we follow him, see where he is going," Alec said, trying desperately to see where the police car had gone.

"There he is!" Theodora said, and they all saw the car parked up ahead, a good hundred yards away. The car lights were switched on and it sped away. It turned onto the road to Newhaven and joined other traffic.

"We are going to lose it," Charlotte cried.

"No, we won't," said Alec. "Just keep an eye out for his number plate: 693 FPC."

"I can see it two cars up, and there is a police sign on the top of the car."

As they approached the outskirts of Newhaven, the police car went into a garage. Alec drew to the side of the road, well back from the garage and in shadow. They watched as a man sauntered out of the office and talked to someone in the police car. The man then filled the car with petrol. He collected some money and was talking to the man in the car when it sped off, the garage man gesticulating after him.

"Don't we think we should tell the police?" Alec said to the women.

"We will lose him if we stop. Come on, Alec, we must keep up. I am not prepared to allow Krupp to surprise me again. Where is he going? To London or the Petworth road?" Charlotte wondered. "I think he is going to Petworth, to our house." Sure enough, Krupp headed along the Brighton Road, on to Worthing, then Shoreham.

"Why does he keep stopping?" Charlotte asked.

"I imagine he's looking at a map," Alec said.

There were plenty of cars on the road, people off to parties to celebrate the arrival of New Year.

As they came over the brow of the hill at the little hamlet of Crossbush, the lights of the historical town of Arundel and the castle twinkled over the flat plain of the River Arun. Distracted by the view of Arundel's lights as they drove over a railway bridge, Alec realised Krupp's car had vanished.

"Where's he gone?"

"He's gone into the station," Charlotte said. Krupp must have suddenly turned off left into Arundel station car park at the bottom of the hill. The Bentley went straight on, the women straining to see if they could see Krupp in the driving seat, but he had parked facing away from the road.

"I am going to park up here by the field gate and wait for him to drive past," Alec said.

"What is he up to?" Theodora asked, not expecting an answer. They could see the Wolseley parked outside the station. "Do you think he has spotted us?"

"Is he getting a train?" Charlotte asked.

"Does the train go to London from here?" asked Alec.

"Yes," said Charlotte, "it's the main line to London. The station is for the Duke of Norfolk."

"Are they running this evening?" Alec was a little concerned. The last thing he wanted was to let Krupp out of his sight.

"They would not be running on New Year's Eve, surely?" Theodora said.

They sat in the silent Bentley for what seemed hours, Theodora and Alec keeping an eye on the motionless police car, with Krupp still sitting in it, parked just beside the station steps. The station seemed closed, just a single light over a noticeboard.

Charlotte was looking at Alec. She reached out and stroked his thigh. He turned with a start to look at her.

"You OK?" he asked.

"I'm all right, thanks, Alec." She took his left hand in hers, his hand far bigger than her cold hands. She said quietly, "Thank you for doing all this." Seeing a question in her eyes, Alec smiled ingenuously, but she didn't ask him anything. Even in the low light, she glowed with beauty. Alec felt vitalised. He could see how the bravery of a man was emboldened before a joust when a lovely maiden tied her favour on his arm or his lance. "I will always be grateful to you, you know, no matter what becomes of us."

"What do you mean, whatever becomes of us? Is something going to happen to us?"

"I hope not. It is just that no one has ever been so kind to me, other than Theodora, of course."

"Of course," said Theodora, still looking out the small oval rear window.

"And, Alec, I think, or rather hope, you are doing this out of respect for me, for altruistic reasons." Alec frowned.

"I am doing this for you ... and Theodora – not for a story, if that is what you mean."

"No, no, I know that."

"I may have in the beginning helped you for the story, but not now." Alec looked out the back of the car again at Krupp's car.

It occurred to Alec that Krupp might have slipped out of the car without them seeing. He was about to turn around and drive down to the station when he saw the Wolseley lights come on and drive slowly out of the station again. Krupp drove towards them, driving towards Arundel. Alec decided to pull out and drive on ahead of him so that he did not suspect he was being followed. Alec pulled out as the Wolseley was a hundred yards behind and sped off as fast as possible.

They drove over the bridge that spanned the River Arun, and the Bentley slipped into a little road on the right, on the other side of the bridge, out of sight of the Wolseley. They looked out the rear window, waiting for Krupp to drive past.

"We will wait here for Krupp and then follow him at a good distance behind. I cannot think of another main road he would take other than the road over the Downs to Petworth. The other road goes to Ford, going south to the coast … going nowhere. Or Chichester – but why would he want to go to Chichester?"

The Wolseley slipped passed them and drove through Arundel, up the hill to the castle, where they lost sight of him as he turned the corner.

"Come on, Alec," Theodora encouraged, "or we will lose him."

"No, we will not. I don't want him to spot us. We are not exactly inconspicuous in this car and there isn't much traffic, so we cannot hide."

They waited another couple of minutes and then Alec started the engine and moved off up the hill to the castle walls, past the huge Catholic cathedral, and onto the road out of Arundel and over the Sussex Downs. At each brow of the hill, they tried to see the lights of Krupp's police car in the distance. On a long, straight section of road they could see a car in the distance, but they could not tell if it was the Wolseley.

The Bentley raced on over the hills and Downs. As they came out of the tree-lined straight road, a low full moon lit up the Downs in a blue-grey light. At the summit, they came to crossroads: straight on to Petworth, or right to Amberley, deep in the Arundel valley, or left to Chichester.

"Do you know where we are, Alec?" Theodora sounded concerned and slightly scathing, which Alec thought was unnecessary.

"I grew up around here. I had a friend who lived in Amberley, just down that road, and I was raised in Chichester, down that road. The Fontwell racecourse is just down there too."

"Which way would Krupp go for Petworth?"

"Straight on, I imagine, unless he has got lost – or he is thinking of getting a good seat at the races." Alec thought he would lighten the mood but it didn't work.

The crossroads was in a wide shallow dip. As they drove up over the crest of the hill, the road disappeared down a long, very steep hill.

As they descended the steep hill, Alec saw the shadow of a car in the moonlight, on the bank to the side of the road, with no lights on.

"Hang on, I think it's Krupp," Alec said in alarm.

"Where?" Charlotte asked.

"Parked up on the bank there. I am not going to be able to stop in time. I will have to speed up."

There was no time to take prevention. Alec knew that Krupp planned to ram them as they descended the hill, or he was hiding somewhere on the side of the road, ready to shoot at the driver. "Get down low in the car in case he shoots," he shouted. The women crouched down, not uttering a word.

As they drew nearly level with the Wolseley police car, Alec could just see a puff of smoke come out of the exhaust pipe.

"He's going to ram us. Hold onto something."

Alec calculated that if he left it to the last second, he could break heavily and go behind the Wolseley. He saw the lights of another car slowly ascending the steep hill, on the other side of the road.

Alec was now only feet away from the Wolseley; it had not moved.

"He aims to follow us, I think."

But no. Krupp gunned the motor and sped down the grass bank to intercept the Bentley. Alec braked hard, the tyres howled.

He turned the Bentley to the left to go around the back of the Wolseley, which was now travelling at speed. He hit the back of Krupp's car with the right wing of the Bentley and at the same time mounted the bank at the side of the road. The back end of the Wolseley was pushed downhill, but Krupp had anticipated this and put on a hard-left lock. When the Wolseley escaped the hit from the Bentley, it sped across the road, turning hard downhill, straight towards the ascending little car. The car could not see the Wolseley, being blinded by the Wolseley's lights as it sped towards it, and jinked away to its right only to see the lights of the Bentley coming straight for it. Alec quickly turned back up the bank to avoid the little car. He could not see where the Wolseley was. The little car came to an abrupt halt on the wrong side of the road. The Bentley hurtled on downhill, Alec frantically looking in all his mirrors for the Wolseley.

As the Bentley came to the bottom of the hill, Alec saw he was going at seventy miles an hour. He put on his brakes.

"I can't see Krupp," he said in a panic. "I think he is behind us, but I can't see his lights."

"Nothing out the back window," Theodora said.

"As soon as you see him, duck down. He may have a pot-shot at us."

"I can't see him … Yes, I can! He's halfway up the hill. He's stopped," Theodora shouted.

"I'll draw in here." Alec pulled over, and Charlotte took a pair of binoculars out of the glove compartment and handed them to him. "Charlotte, you will find a seat belt somewhere there. Strap it over your lap – I think we are in for a bit of fast driving."

"Oh God!" said Theodora.

Alec opened his door and put the binoculars to his eyes. He scanned the left-hand side of the road. Halfway up the hill, he could just see the Wolseley in the glow of the little car's lights. It had hit a tree on the side of the road, steam coming up from the engine bonnet. Alec then heard a shot. He swung the binoculars round and saw Krupp pull a body out of the little car, then take a second shot at the driver's head. Krupp got in the car, started the engine and turned the little car around to descend the hill towards them.

"Christ, he has shot the driver and is after us."

"My God, he never stops," Charlotte said in a high-pitched voice as Alec quickly got into the Bentley and put on his seat belt.

"He will never catch us in that little Austin, so I think we should get to your house before he does, inform the police, and prepare for his arrival."

"Good idea," Theodora said. "Except, would he go to Burton Park? I wish I had brought a gun with me." She sat back and looked out the back window at the dark road behind the Bentley. The road twisted and turned with no other cars around.

"I don't know," said Alec, "but I think we have got to call the police as soon as we get to the house."

"God, this is chaos," Theodora said.

Charlotte sat silently, rubbing her hands together as though she was washing them. Alec saw how her mouth was set in a grimace. He couldn't imagine how she was feeling.

33

The little black Austin England slewed up the muddy track to the farmhouse. The house was dark, save for a light in the parlour, which went out when the lights of the car came around the reeds. Two torches then shone onto Krupp from the front door.

"Krupp, what are you doing back here so soon?" Sir Jason sounded unusually angry.

"They were waiting for me as I drove out of here." Krupp got out of the Austin and limped towards the torchlights. "I need a cane. Mine broke in the car when I crashed it."

"I will see what I can find, sir," Alderson said, more to Sir Jason than Krupp.

"Well? What happened? You say 'they' were waiting. Who was waiting?"

"That man who was with Freya at your house, and Freya. I came out of the farm track here and a big Bentley was coming straight at me, blinding me with its lights. I saw it again as I drove over a bridge. It was parked, hoping not to be seen."

"Ballentine," Sir Jason said thoughtfully. As Krupp got close to the farmhouse door, John Alderson appeared with a walking stick. Krupp grabbed the stick from him and barged inside the house, and sat at the parlour table in the darkness. Alderson turned up the hurricane lamp. Krupp sat at the table, his hands cradling his head, sweat droplets on his brow.

"I presume this car was forced into your ownership under duress, Krupp?"

"*Ach was?* – what are you talking about?" Krupp looked at Jason in contempt. He felt Jason was talking down at him, using long English words he did not understand.

"Did you steal that car?"

"Yes!" Krupp yelled and threw his hand out irritably, as though he was flinging a stone.

"Why?" Sir Jason sat opposite him.

"Because I crashed the other one when I tried to ram the Bentley. I hit the road kerb and then a tree, and the front wheels were badly … Anyway, I got this one. I think we should go now."

"Go where, precisely? I don't see the incriminating files – the WASP file, at any rate."

"Well I haven't got mine either, but I bet the police will be here soon. That man will phone for the police as soon as he gets to a telephone. He knows this place; he knows about the car, and I bet he saw me kill the driver."

"Again, Krupp, you astonish me." Sir Jason was sitting very close to Krupp. He talked in a calm, low voice, which annoyed Krupp intensely. "How many people – innocent people – are you going to slay before you kill the one I have paid you for?"

"You have not paid me yet, you old …" Krupp shouted. Jason put his index finger to his lips to quieten Krupp's eruption.

"Major Krupp, I got you released early from prison, you have lovely *temporary* lodgings in my castle overlooking Lake Constance, and a stipend …"

"A stipend? What is this stipend?"

"A wage or salary. I gave you this wage so that you could do me a service, namely find and return these files that Baron Saumures has kept for me. You were meant to threaten the baron, not kill him, to obtain the whereabouts of these files. You were then given the location of Baroness Saumures—"

"Who is your niece! You never told me this."

"I do not think it's any of your business whether she is my niece or—"

"*And* Deller's daughter! I mean, what is this?" Krupp looked around at his audience with a forced laugh, to see if Alderson was also laughing. He was not.

"If you must know, she chose to disappear. So I chose to then take her house in Paris."

"What do you mean? Le Palais is her house? How can that be?"

"My mother – her grandmother – foolishly left it to her. But that is not the point here; she must be dispatched. What I did not know until our first meeting two months ago was that it was she who killed my business partner, Jean de Tournet."

"Which makes your stupid sister a very rich widow," Krupp said with glee.

"Sir Jason, I really think we have to go," Alderson quietly interjected.

222

"Yes, yes, John, you are right. Now then, Major Krupp, how far to London did you get?"

"I was going to Burton Park Place," Krupp said with an element of defensive pride. Jason sighed and dramatically hung his head as though in despair.

"You will go to London and see if the files are there. I don't think Ballentine would have taken them with him to come here," Jason said, half to himself.

*

Rupert the butler was rushing about with drinks. He was wearing a cardigan over his smart white shirt, striped grey trousers and slippers. He was plainly not expecting his mistress, Theodora and a guest two hours before the New Year was about to be celebrated. The Tanner brothers and their mother, the cook, were all in the huge kitchen, the radio on, a bottle of red wine from the cellar on the table with four glasses. When the doorbell rang, Rupert cautiously opened the front door only to see his mistress standing there, looking exhausted.

As soon as they got through the door, Theodora said, "Rupert, light the fire in the small drawing room and bring some drinks."

Charlotte stooped down to Bonzo, who came racing up to them when he heard their voices.

"Yes, madam. Milady—"

"Get on with it, please, Rupert, and call up the Tanners," Charlotte said as they walked towards the study door.

"They are here, milady. We are celebrating."

"Send them to me, Rupert." Charlotte then looked contrite. "I am sorry, Rupert, but I have just seen a man murdered by that German, Krupp!"

"Oh! I see, milady. I will attend to everything immediately." Rupert felt the blood drain from his face. He relocked the front door. The memory of the carnage in the study two months ago still affected his sleep, and ever since, he felt slightly sick every time he entered the study.

*

"Detective Inspector Jack McMillan, please." Alec was on the phone as soon as he got to the study. "This is Alec Ballentine. He will know what this is about. Thank you."

"McMillan here, Mr Ballentine. Everything all right? I was just off home to see in the New Year." The inspector sounded a little fed up.

"I am sorry, Mr McMillan, but we have just seen Jost Krupp. He was driving, would you believe, a police car."

"Good God! Where was this?" McMillan covered the mouthpiece and Alec could hear him yell instructions.

"We nearly hit his car as he came out of a farm track in Newhaven."

"Where are you now, sir?"

"Burton Park Place in Petworth, Sussex."

"When did you see Krupp?"

"We first saw him around seven this evening."

"Why have you left it so long to report this, sir?"

"We wanted to follow him to see where he was going. I did not want him disappearing."

"Commendable, sir, but I still think—"

"I am sorry, Inspector, but please allow me to finish." There was a silence on the phone, which Alec took as the inspector waiting for his report. "We followed Krupp to Arundel, where he stopped in the railway station car park for quite a long time. We thought he may be catching a train to London."

"We, sir?"

"Lady Saumures, Madam Theodora Smith and I."

"I see, sir. Sorry, carry on."

"He then carried on through Arundel onto the Petworth Road. As we came down a long hill – Bury Hill—"

"I know Bury Hill, sir."

"As we came down the hill, I saw that he, Krupp, was parked up the bank on the side of the road, ready to ram us. I could not stop in time and tried to accelerate so that he would miss us. He came at us at great speed. I swerved behind him, and he went over the road and nearly smashed into an Austin England – it was a black, or a very dark small car – ascending the hill. When I got to the bottom of the hill, about a quarter of a mile from where we nearly crashed, I could see that Krupp had collided into a tree and the front wheels were badly damaged on the kerb of the road."

"Is that the last time you saw him, on Bury Hill?"

"I am afraid the tale is not quite over, Inspector. He then shot the driver of the Austin England ... twice. I could see he was dead. Krupp shot him in the head. I witnessed it through my binoculars."

"I see, sir," said the inspector through gritted teeth, and then Alec heard him shout instructions to phone Petworth police and get someone to Bury Hill.

"We raced on to the manor to report to you, Inspector. I regret we do not know where he went in the Austin England. Its number plate was XBN 554." Alec heard McMillan bark out more instructions and the number plate details.

"What happens in Newhaven, Mr Ballentine?"

"It is where a man called Jaffery lives. He has a farm there that grows reeds or something. Apparently, Jaffery worked for the Nazis during the war. Not a nice chap." Alec was not going to go into WASP, it was too complex.

"I see, sir. How have you come across this knowledge?" McMillan's manner changed slightly to one of suspicion, which made Alec cautious.

"Well, it's a little complicated. There is a set of files that was compiled on Nazi sympathisers, also on the SS and Gestapo, mostly in Paris—"

"Is this going to take long, sir? As I'd better get going."

"You must let me finish, Inspector. These files, called the Wasp Trap files, were compiled by Ferdi Saumures. He brought these files over from France, just after Paris was liberated, and they were used for war crimes trials."

Alec could hear the inspector sighing on the other end of the phone.

"I wonder if you could send me these details?"

"There is one thing you should know, Inspector: Baron Saumures kept back six of these files."

"Did he now," the inspector said, clearly more interested.

"Yes, he has a file on a group or organisation called WASP."

"Why was that, sir? Why did he keep back these files, and what is … wasp?"

"The life of his wife was being threatened if he did not. So he hid the files."

"And you found them?"

"Yes, recently. The other files were on Jost Krupp, this man Jaffery, the baroness's stepfather, Jean de Tournet, her father, Franz-Joseph Deller – Father Joe Dent – and" – Alec paused for effect – "Sir Jason Barrett. Who is, or was, head of this movement called WASP."

"I see," the inspector said, now sounding cautious. "And we are talking about *the* Sir Jason Barrett MP, minister, owner of *The Sentinel*, friend of Churchill and the ex-king, et cetera, et cetera?"

"The same," Alec said. "I think he is at this farm in Newhaven, aware that his file has been discovered."

"Have you read the file?" McMillan sounded incredulous.

"I have leafed through it. But my colleague Philip Bing-Wallace is at my flat reading through the files in detail now." Alec suddenly thought of something with alarm. "Inspector, could you send round a police car as soon as you can and get Philip and the files out for safety? I hope I am not too late."

"Address?" McMillan barked.

"Flat Five B, Overstrand Mansions, Prince of Wales Drive, Battersea Park. Top floor."

Charlotte and Theodora were looking at Alec with concern. They passed a tumbler of whisky and water over to him and he took a long drink.

Alec could hear McMillan growl out orders to get over to Alec's flat, apprehend anybody who was there and gather any files they could find.

"It is going to take at least two hours for anybody to drive up to Battersea Park from Sussex," said the inspector.

"Yes, but Sir Jason will have people working for him in London. He has people who work for him at his paper, and his house in Wimbledon. They may also be part of this group," Alec pointed out.

"I will call you there when we have picked up your friend, Mr Ballentine. In the meantime, I would like the details of the farm in Newhaven." Alec opened his mouth to tell him when McMillan said, "I would advise you, Mr Ballentine, *not* to mention any of these accusations … assertions, should I say, about Sir Jason to anybody else. You may be prosecuted for—"

"Mr McMillan! I am an experienced journalist. I know exactly what I can or cannot legally write and publish. I would be grateful if you could gather up my colleague Mr Bing-Wallace before any harm befalls him."

*

"We really must go now, Sir Jason." Alderson was getting twitchy. "I think the police will be on the doorstep quite soon."

"All right, John." Sir Jason stood stiffly, so did Krupp.

"I think we could all get into your car, Sir Jason," Krupp started to say, but Jason came up close to him.

"Shut up, Krupp, and listen." Jason stood in front of him, eye to eye, angry – something Krupp was unprepared for. "You will take my Bristol up to London, to Ballentine's flat, and if the files are there, pick them up. Do *not* kill anybody. Your friend Baumgartner will be there to meet you." Jason held out his hand. "In fact, give me your pistol."

"I will not give you my gun," Krupp said.

226

"John, if he does not give you his pistol, shoot him in the stomach in ten seconds."

"Yes, Sir Jason," Alderson said as though he was taking dictation.

"Who is going to kill Freya ... or Charlotte then?"

"It is too late for that. You have killed the only bargaining tool. Give me your weapon. You are not going to kill anybody else. I am running out of patience."

Krupp knew he had spent the last bullet in the magazine of his Luger on the driver of the little car. He reluctantly handed over his pistol.

"Thank you. Now the bullets," Jason said, dropping the magazine out of the handle with expertise. Krupp handed over a flat white waxed cardboard box, empty of bullets. "Do you have any of those syringes you enjoy using about you?"

Krupp scowled at Jason. "How do you know about that? No, I don't. The chemist I get the stuff from died from using too much of his own product."

Jason took a deep look into Krupp's eyes and squinted. He abruptly stood back, turned and walked towards the door.

"Where are you going? How are you getting to London? In that little car?" Krupp laughed.

"No, by boat," Jason said as he walked out of the parlour, followed by John Alderson. Over his shoulder he shouted at Krupp, "When you have the files, meet us on the Chelsea side of Albert Bridge. We will be moored there in two days, on Tuesday the second of January. We will be there at about ten in the morning and we will be there for three hours only. If you are not there, we'll go on without you."

Krupp looked in astonishment at Jason's back as he walked out the front door. Alderson followed his master, then suddenly stopped and walked back to Krupp, who was at the front door, unsure what to say or do.

Alderson dangled some keys. "Keys to the Bristol. If you have time, you can sell it. All the papers are in the glove compartment."

"But my money. Where is my money?" Krupp asked in bewilderment.

"If you join us at Albert Bridge in two days' time, then you will be remunerated after you hand over Sir Jason's files, all six files, including, most importantly, the WASP file."

"But what if I cannot get the files?" Krupp whined.

"Then, Major Krupp, you do not get paid. But for the work you have done to date, you have the Bristol."

"But … *das ist schrecklich!*" Krupp spluttered in fury.

"Good evening, Major Krupp. Do not hang around here if I were you. I should think your actions have alerted the authorities. Happy New Year." Alderson turned to catch up to Sir Jason who was striding through the reeds towards the boathouse.

Krupp tried to walk after Alderson, but he had forgotten his temporary stick, and his back and leg were very painful. He watched the torches of the two men as they went through the reeds to the motorboat. He thought that he must have used most of the boat's diesel fuel. But then again, Jason or that Alderson would have thought of that. They could not be going to Miami in that boat.

Krupp went back to the farmhouse and found the walking stick in the kitchen. A thought occurred to him. He looked up the stairs and started to climb. He remembered going up the stairs before when he'd asked Jaffery for a gun.

He found the room they went in, a junk room with a portrait of an ugly, elderly woman who was Jaffery's mother. It was very dark. Krupp lit a hurricane lamp, pumped it up for more light, and opened the top drawer of a chest of drawers. No gun was there now. He went through the other drawers. The deep bottom drawer was heavy and whatever was inside moved and rumbled about. To his delight, when he eventually slid the drawer open, it was full of wartime German stick grenades, about thirty of them, all with deadly fragmentation sleeves on the top.

He found a canvas bag and put in twelve of the bombs and clambered down the stairs with them. He wondered if they were still working properly. Normally when you pulled the string ignition fuse at the base of the stick, you would have five seconds before the explosion. He needed to test one. He went back upstairs to the storeroom.

Just then, he heard the powerful diesel engines of the S-boat start up. He went to the window that looked out from the front of the house. Amongst the reeds, he could just see the roof of the boathouse and the channel down to the sea. He thought he could see a small light running along the tops of the reeds, and then the motors accelerated and gradually became quieter and quieter as the converted S-boat sailed away.

"Good luck finding fuel for that thing." He sniggered out loud, then wondered if it would have been safer to have gone with them.

"*Scheiße*, I don't care what happens to me, really. I have no money, I just have a lovely car." Krupp winced. He was in constant pain and feeling very morose. He sat in front of the chest of drawers. "I might as well just blow myself up." He had spent most of what Sir Jason had paid him on the high life in and around Friedrichshafen in Jason's castle over the past two months. He had bought a sleek white Mercedes 300 S sports car, which was parked at Emden, the port in Germany. Other than the remote possibility of seeing Freya again, there was not much to look forward to.

Krupp pulled out the drawer of grenades. It was stiff and jammed. He pulled harder and as he did so, the whole chest of drawers swung out. Krupp fell off the chair onto his bottom and a shaft of pain went up his back. He swore and tried to get up, levering himself on the chair, but the chair leg sank into a loose floorboard and the other end of the floorboard flew up. Krupp was on his bottom again and was about to curse when he saw, beneath the loose floorboard, lots of small dark-maroon canvas bags.

He picked one out of its hiding place and was thrilled to feel it was heavy and it chinked as he placed it on the floor. He untied the top and inside were six rectangle gold bars with "*Deutsche Reichsbank 500g Feingold 999.9*" embossed on each bar. It was Jaffery's miserly stash. Krupp knew he must have a hoard of cash somewhere. He opened two other similar bags; one had about two hundred small gold coins, the gold Krupp had paid Jaffery for his services.

Krupp stood up with renewed strength; if he could, he would have danced a jig. He pulled the four bags out of their hiding place into another canvas bag and heaved the bag down the stairs to the kitchen.

In the parlour, he set the bag down. He took out one of the bombs from the other bag, then unscrewed the porcelain explosive top, and gently took out the detonator and put the explosive safely away from the stick. He unscrewed the plug at the base of the stick, pulled the string, and the fuse immediately flared up and burned for about six seconds.

With a smile on his face, he went through all the drawers in the kitchen and the parlour until he found some baler twine. He went back upstairs to the drawer of remaining stick grenades and took one out, then unscrewed the plug at the bottom of the stick, rattled out the string fuse, tied the baler twine to the string, jammed the head of the stick grenade in the drawer and ran the twine down the stairs to the front door. He then went back up to the bedrooms and checked all the other floorboards to make sure there was no further gold.

In the kitchen, he picked up his bags of stick grenades and gold and limped as fast as he could to the Bristol. He placed the bags on the back seat, started it up and reversed the big, heavy car out of the shed. He drove it to the front of the house, parked and got out. At the open front door, he gathered up the twine, looped it around the lever of the parlour door handle, and then drew in the slack of the twine, closed the front door, and tied the twine to the front door handle as tightly as possible.

Krupp went to the back of the house, through the kitchen and out the scullery door, locking it and throwing away the key. He hobbled around to the front of the house, and just as he was getting to the Bristol, two police cars careered down the muddy farm drive and stopped in front of him.

34

"Where is Philip, Alec? Do you think he has been hurt or something?"

"I don't know." Alec wiped his hand over his forehead. He felt frustrated and tired.

"I think we should go to London," Charlotte said, nursing a glass of champagne that she had hardly touched and stroking Bonzo's nose. Bonzo had an amazing calming effect on both Charlotte and Theodora.

"Can we not wait for the morning, darling? It has just gone midnight and I am very tired." Theodora sank into the sofa in the small drawing room.

"I am just worried about Philip." Charlotte sounded fatigued. Alec had tried his own telephone number and Bing-Wallace's house in Chelsea, but he had not got an answer from either. *The Times* in Fleet Street only had some drunk cleaners, Alec assumed, answering the switchboard, and he was informed that there was nobody important in the building, followed by gales of merry laughter.

"I'll call Inspector McMillan again to see if anybody knows what has happened to him." Alec started to dial. The phone at the Battersea police station rang and rang until a harassed policeman answered.

"I would like to speak to Inspector McMillan," Alec said as calmly as possible.

"Your name, sir?"

"Alec Ballentine." There was a long silence at the other end of the line. "Hello, are you there?" Alec asked to confirm he had not been cut off.

"Sergeant Glass here, Mr Ballentine. We went to your flat as requested to find Mr, eh ... Bing-Wallace, was it?"

"Yes. Philip Bing-Wallace," Alec said, frustration in his voice.

"Well, there was no Mr Bing-Wallace there, sir, only a Miss Jane Gardener."

Alec could not place the name immediately but then it came to him. "The housekeeper?" he said incredulously.

"Whose housekeeper would that be, sir?"

"Sir Jason's, of course, in Wimbledon. Did they see anybody else in my flat?"

"No, sir, nobody. No files, nothing, just your stuff," said Sergeant Glass.

"Well, I don't know what to make of it," exclaimed Alec.

"We apprehended the woman, Gardener."

"Really? Why?"

"She had a concealed weapon, namely a small German Mauser pistol. She threatened Inspector McMillan with it."

"Good God. Thank you, Sergeant. We will be in London tomorrow."

"Today, you mean, sir?"

"Today, then, Sergeant. Goodnight – and happy New Year." Alec then put down the phone.

"What happened?" asked Theodora. "Philip is OK, isn't he?"

"I don't know. Nobody seems to know where he is. They found that housekeeper of Sir Jason's there, in my flat, would you believe. She seemed to be armed!" Alec held his hand to his forehead; he was getting a headache.

The phone rang, making everybody jump. Charlotte even stood up, looking distraught. "Answer it, please, Alec," she said, tension in her voice.

"Hello, Burton Park Place."

"Ah, there you are, Ballentine, dear thing. Happy New Year and all that."

"Bing-Wallace?" Alec yelled, a delighted smile over his face.

"Philip!" the women said in unison and in relief.

*

"This is the police. Get out of the car with your hands in the air."

Krupp was appalled. He switched off the engine of the Bristol and slowly opened the car door, his hands on top of the door for support. There was one police car with a single driver standing behind the open driver's door, pointing a rifle straight at him. The second police car, its lights cast over Krupp and the Bristol, had both doors open. The driver squatted behind the open door, holding a truncheon and looking quite absurd, Krupp thought. Blue lights flashing on the car roofs, the red brake lights and the bright headlight lit the night up like a carnival. Krupp could not quite see how many policemen were in the cars with the headlight glaring at him.

"What do you want?" he asked lamely.

"Are you Just Crap?" Krupp heard a slight snigger from the cars.

"No," he said, "my name is Günther Wolff."

"Do you know where Sir Jason Barrett is?"

"Yes, he and his driver are in the farmhouse, there." Krupp added, "There is a German in the house also."

"Is there anybody else in or around the farmhouse?"

"No."

"Constable Barry, you keep that weapon covering the suspect, we will go into the farmhouse." The policeman who asked all the questions and his colleague walked over to the farmhouse door and knocked.

"It is not locked," shouted Krupp. "Just go straight in. Give it a good push, it's stiff. The electric is off, use your torches."

They pushed the door open and went inside. Krupp got back into the Bristol quickly.

"Get out of the car!" the policeman with the rifle squealed. "Get out or I fire." Panic spread over the young policeman's face. Krupp reached over to the back seat and pulled out a stick grenade. The policeman was still shouting at him in a high pitch, not knowing what to do, looking over to the farmhouse, perhaps wondering if he should shout for help.

Krupp lay down over the front two seats. He undid the screw cap at the bottom of the wooden handle of the stick grenade, and rattled out the string fuse cord. He was wondering why his trap had not gone off. He saw the armed policeman, a dark young inexperienced-looking lad with big ears, pop his head over the windscreen to look inside the Bristol for Krupp. There was a small explosion from above the front door of the house, followed immediately by a thunderous eruption. A brick hurled through the rear window of the Bristol and crashed into the back of the driver's seat. At the same time, bricks skidded across the roof of the car and crashed into the young policeman, hurling him into the open door of the police car.

Krupp pulled the fuse string, quickly opened the driver's window, and hurled the stick grenade towards one of the cars. He started the Bristol and reversed rapidly. He turned, took out another stick grenade, primed it and hurled it at the second police car just as the first police car exploded.

He thrust the Bristol into gear and drove out past the second police car, and only just cleared the back end before that too was obliterated by the grenade. He drove quickly, sliding everywhere, to the end of the drive. He stopped, took out two more grenades, primed both and threw them into the reeds on either side of the muddy drive. The reeds exploded, and a rigorous fire started. By the time he was going over the brow of the hill on the London Road, he could see the fields of reeds ablaze.

"*Willkommen in 1956!*" Krupp sneered. He switched his headlights on and remembered to drive on the left-hand side of the road.

*

"For Christ's sake, where have you been, Bing-Wallace? I was phoning everybody."

"Well, just as you went this morning, I got a call from the local vicar."

"From Father Joe?"

"Yes. Nice chap. Bit of a lush, though," Bing-Wallace whispered into the mouthpiece of the phone.

"But where are you calling from, Philip?"

"What he calls the vicarage. It's a flat opposite his church. Not exactly what I would regard as a good living, if you see what I mean. No wonder he drinks."

"Is Philip at Franz-Joseph's house?" Charlotte asked with astonishment.

"It seems he is," Alec said, covering the mouthpiece.

"Are the girls there?" Bing-Wallace asked cheerily.

"Of course they are. Where else—" Alec broke off with concern. "Philip, where is Dent now?"

"In bed, comatose. He has been celebrating New Year rather vigorously."

"Well, thank God you're OK. Apparently, a woman, Sir Jason's housekeeper, broke into my flat to get the files."

"Good heavens. The files are safely with me. By the way, there was another file, hidden in the file on Krupp. Only two foolscap sheets."

"On who?"

"On Theodora."

"Theodora?" Alec said, looking at Theodora who was half asleep on the sofa. "Oh, she is fine," Alec said, adjusting his surprise so Theodora was not suspicious of being talked about.

"She's in earshot, is she?"

"Yup."

"There's nothing too bad. She was a member of the Nazi Party, but then so was her mother, apparently. It's all about her when she was quite young."

"We will talk later, Bing-Wallace. I am going to phone the police to tell them where you are and that you are safe."

"I am going to stay in your flat tonight and—"

"No don't, Philip," Alec shouted. "Stay where you are. God knows who else is out there. And Jost Krupp is at large."

"Krupp? Crikey. This *is* a to-do."

"Just stay there until I come and pick you and the files up. OK?"

"Very well, dear boy. Happy New Year."

"I hope so, Bing-Wallace, I really hope so. Bye."

"So, he is at Deller's house?" Charlotte looked very tired. "Is he OK? Does he still have the files?"

"Yes to both. Now, I suggest we all go to bed and go up to London early in the morning."

"It is already early in the morning, darling," Theodora said, standing uneasily. "I'm a little tipsy, I think," she said before walking towards the door. "I will be heavily armed, so don't surprise me too much when you wake me."

Charlotte and Alec both laughed.

Charlotte took Alec's hand. "Let's go to bed."

"I would love to," Alec said quietly, "but we should sleep." He was unsure why he said this, and he slightly regretted it when he saw a mock sullen expression on Charlotte's face.

After checking that the doors and windows were all firmly locked, Charlotte, Alec and Bonzo went to Charlotte's room. Rupert was asleep on the sofa in the staff pantry.

It was one o'clock in the morning on the first of January 1956.

35

The Bristol glided quietly into Wimbledon at around two o'clock in the morning. Krupp was drained, his leg was aching, his back felt like a shard of glass had been inserted between two vertebrae, and his right foot was swollen painfully inside his shoe. He drew up outside Alston House. He pushed on the gates to see if they would open. They were firmly locked and immovable. He rang the bell at the intercom repeatedly.

"'Ello?" A breathless voice of a lad crackled over the intercom.

"It is I, Günther Wolff, with Sir Jason's car."

"What did you say?"

"I have Sir Jason's car. Open up," Krupp shouted, and then as an afterthought, "Please, young man."

"One moment, please, sir."

Lights in the front of the house and at the gate lit up. The gate started opening with squeals of metal against metal, even louder it being a still night.

"I am sorry, sir, Sir Jason is not here. Miss Gardener is not here either. It's just me," a spotty youth said, his red-haired head looking round through a gap from behind the front door.

Krupp slapped his hand onto the front door, trying to push it open.

"I am not visiting, I am invited. Your master has gone anyway."

"Gone where?" The lad looked distressed. He held his dressing gown about him as though he was a virgin protecting his virtue.

"Show me Sir Jason's bedroom. I need to sleep," Krupp said as kindly as he could muster. "Come on, boy, I am tired. Let's go to Sir Jason's room. I need a drink, schnapps if you have it."

"Yes, sir …" Gareth looked troubled. "I don't know if I should. You see, there—"

"Look." Krupp was losing his patience. He gesticulated at the Bristol covered in mud, the back window smashed and scratches all over the roof. "I have his car. Alderson gave me the keys." He dangled the keys in the lad's face.

"Sorry, sir, I am a bit weary myself." He let Krupp in and then closed the front door and locked it again, looking at Krupp with undisguised trepidation. "Up the stairs, sir, the door straight ahead, please, sir. I will find you that drink."

"Thank you …?"

"Gareth, sir."

"Thank you, Herr Gareth. Is that the room of Sir Jason?"

"No, sir, that is the guest bedroom. Sir Jason would not like someone in his room."

"OK, Herr Gareth. I would like that drink, and some cigarettes."

"I will take your bags, sir."

"Be careful, that one is full of bombs." Krupp laughed, and Gareth forced a little laugh as he struggled with the bags. He looked surprised as one was disproportionately heavy.

Krupp lay on the guest bed, still fully clothed, nursing a tumbler of Geneva gin – it seemed the nearest to schnapps the boy could find. Krupp wondered what he was going to do for two days, and how he was going to get the files – or indeed whether he needed to get the files now that he was rich with Jaffery's money. He was a wanted man, however, everybody alerted of his presence. If he could get to Jaffery's boat without being spotted, he could get the gold out that way. Jason and Alderson would be no bother, an old man and a stringy young man. But would Sir Jason and the boat be there, or would he just disappear?

Scheiße, I don't care what happens to them now I have money, he thought. But how could he use it? It was all Nazi gold. He would have to find a fence – that was going to be difficult. Goddamn it all. What was he going to do?

He truly hoped he would see Freya again – lovely Freya. He could kidnap her, take her to Argentina. But that seemed unlikely. He would love to kill Franz-Joseph Deller, the drunk. He looked at the tumbler of the fiery clear spirit and took a sip. He took a long draw on the cigar that Gareth had found for him instead of cigarettes.

He waited for an hour before getting up. Gareth must be back to sleep by now. Krupp slid off the bed and opened the bedroom door. He walked down the dark empty landing to the first door. He opened it to find a large dark room. He drew the mahogany-red curtains and put on the bedside light. This was certainly Jason's bedroom. It was neat, masculine. Deep-red printed wallpaper covered two walls and the other two walls comprised the curtained double window looking out over the drive at the front of the house. A large double bed was pushed against the oak-panelled wall at the back.

He found a bathroom just off the bedroom, opulent in marble, with oak panels and mirrors. He looked at himself, startled by what he saw: dishevelled, dirty, with grey blotches on his forehead and under his eyes. The scar on his right cheek looked pronounced; his sparse black hair was greasy and untidy, his chin dark and unshaven. He ran a bath, got undressed and slid into the luxurious, steaming hot water. He lay back, still holding onto his drink and cigar, and emitted a huge sigh of pleasure.

After his bath, he felt clean and fresh. He had a shave. The hot water had eased the pain in his back, leg and foot. Swathed in towels and Jason's silk bathrobe, Krupp searched all the drawers and knocked on each panel around the bed. There must be a safe here somewhere, he thought.

Krupp noticed there was no art on the walls, just oblong ghosts where paintings once hung. He searched the cupboards and wardrobes. There was not much in the way of clothing; what clothes he could see were well worn. He tried on some trousers and shirts, replacing his soiled, rather damp clothes that he had been wearing for the past two days.

As he rummaged through the underwear drawer, he not only found some brand-new underpants but he also came across an old waxed pink paper box full of .445 bullets. After some more searching he discovered, wrapped up in a piece of towelling, a very old, large Webley Mark V service revolver with a fawn-coloured lanyard attached to the base of the grip. It looked in good order and all the moving parts were well oiled and clean. Krupp was delighted. He loaded it with five bullets and stuffed the weapon into the pocket of his newly acquired tweed jacket. As Jason was a little thinner, the clothes only just fitted.

He could hear Gareth pacing up and down the landing outside Sir Jason's bedroom.

"Are you all right, boy?" Krupp opened the bedroom door as Gareth went past.

"Sir," Gareth said anxiously, "I really have to ask you to leave Sir Jason's rooms and—" He stepped back from Krupp, astonished and aghast. "Are you wearing Sir Jason's clothes?" he said in horror.

"Listen, boy …"

"It's Gareth, sir. I don't like being called 'boy'."

"Listen, Gareth." Krupp sighed. "Your master has gone abroad for a long while. It would not surprise me if he decided to sell this place."

"He can't!" Gareth was appalled. "He can't just go. He is just redecorating; that's why there is hardly ..." Gareth paused, and thought, looking around the empty landing, the paintings gone, the sparse furniture downstairs. "What about the paper? What about me and Miss Gardener?"

"Yes, where is Miss Gardener anyway?" Krupp had wondered why this boy had been left to defend the house on his own.

"She has gone to pick up some files for Sir Jason from a journalist's flat in London."

"I see. When will she return?"

"She should have come back hours ago. She is not at the office and I do not know what to do."

"I see," Krupp said again. He looked at his watch: it was half past three in the morning. "We'll get some sleep now, and you and I will go and find Fräulein Gardener tomorrow. Sir Jason will be in London on Tuesday, so you can see him then."

"How do you know all this?"

"I told you. I have just seen him, with his servant."

"Mr Alderson, you mean?"

"I think he is called John."

"Yes, Mr Alderson. But Mr Alderson is not a servant."

"I am astonished, Herr Gareth. He seemed so incompetent." Gareth frowned. "Sorry, I meant competent. My English, you know." Krupp could see Gareth was becoming slightly more at ease with him. "Well, come on, Herr Gareth, off to bed with you, and wake me at seven in the morning. Sleep well."

Krupp slammed the door to Jason's bedroom before Gareth could protest. He heard Gareth wander off down the corridor to the back stairs and down to his quarters. Krupp released the hold on the pistol inside his jacket pocket that he had been pointing at Gareth's stomach all the time they'd been talking.

*

"My God, Ferdi's Bentley looks a little beaten up. Sorry," Alec said, rubbing his hand over a deep gash in the Bentley's right wing.

"Don't worry, Alec. It can be mended." Charlotte got into the car.

The Bentley purred away from Burton Park Place, Charlotte huddled in a substantial camel-hair coat, hoping the heater would kick into action soon.

"Why didn't Theodora want to come with us, do you think?" Alec asked as they drove off up to London.

"I have no idea. I wondered myself."

It was seven in the morning, on Monday the first of January, and there was nobody on the roads or out and about. It felt like the middle of the night. It was cold and dark, and the roads were a little icy.

"Philip found a small file on Theodora in Krupp's file, you know."

"My God. What did it say?"

"All Philip said was that she was a member of the Nazi Party."

"Oh, is that all? She was – she had to be." Charlotte hoped there were not going to be any other revelations that could risk Theodora staying in Britain, or worse, being her friend. "She has told me of quite a lot of things she had to do to keep alive." Charlotte tried to sound positive. "I suppose I was a member too. I have an *SS-Sonderpass* that I have kept. It's in a drawer somewhere."

"That does not make you a member of the Nazi Party, Charlotte."

"No, I suppose not. But Theodora went through a lot more to stay alive when she worked in Berlin. She was totally under the thumb of her disreputable mother, and then she basically became a prostitute, most of her clients being Nazis. Until Ferdi found her on one of his visits to Germany."

"Why did Ferdi go to Germany so much?"

"He was told to, I suppose. I never asked. He was so secretive, both personally and professionally. His only love was his art, I think. Why do you ask? Do you think Ferdi was working for the Germans after all?"

"No," Alec said firmly. "The files are proof that he intended to expose Sir Jason. He was protecting you. He must have loved you, Charlotte."

"Yes, I think he did, like a sister. I was his proof of masculinity – his *whiskers*. He hardly confided in anybody, or me, really. He was a very good judge of character. He saw Franz-Joseph for what he was. They were friends, you know, before the war."

"Were they ... How should I put it ..." Alec waved his hand around trying to work out how to ask.

"No, no, not that kind of friend. Deller isn't a homosexual; he sired me after all." As she said this, she gave a little inward shudder.

They were driving through Wandsworth, past the town hall and up the hill towards Clapham Junction, when Charlotte asked, "Will Philip write an article about what he has found in the files?"

"Only after I have edited it. He promised that we would share bylines."

"Bylines?"

"Written by ... *by* Alec Ballentine or even *by* Baroness Charlotte Saumures." He caught Charlotte smiling at him.

"I like your name, Alec Ballentine. It's romantic."

"Thank you, but a 'ballotine' is a bit of boiled, rolled-up stuffed chicken, not as romantic as 'Baroness Charlotte Saumures'. I wonder why you didn't end up living in Luxembourg with Ferdi?"

"He's never lived there as an adult. He spent his early years at school – well, a tutor – in Luxembourg with his cousins. His mother was English, and they moved here, to Burton Park Place, all except his father who stayed and worked for the Germans in the occupation."

"So his home was here?"

"Yes, basically. That is why he worked for the secret service in France. It was a perfect cover." Charlotte leant over and rested her head on Alec's left shoulder. It took him slightly by surprise. "I wonder if, when this is all over, we can stay as friends?" she said under her breath and with a sigh, so that Alec could only just hear what she said. He was unable to answer. He really hoped they could become more than just lovers, if "lovers" was the right term for their relationship. He still could not work out what Charlotte wanted from him as a man. Perhaps at a better time he would ask. Or was he scared of what the answer might be?

*

"Mr Wolff?" Gareth said nervously from the door. Krupp was on his back, fully clothed with his overcoat spread over his legs, eyes closed, the remains of the extinguished cigar in his left hand, his right hand in the jacket pocket.

"Mr Wolff, sir," Gareth said, slightly louder.

"I can hear you, *junge*. Go and make a coffee," Krupp said without moving his head or opening his eyes.

Gareth had not slept a wink, his mind racing as to what was best to do. He even considered running off and seeing if he could find his master at the newspaper office. He was shocked to see the telephone cables had been ripped out of the wall. Both downstairs phones were disabled, the only functioning phone being in his master's bedroom.

*

"Where is that coffee, Gareth?" Krupp remembered the boy's name as he limped into the kitchen. The small kitchen smelt of delicious coffee, real coffee from Jamaica or Colombia, not powdered chicory.

241

"Coming up, sir." Gareth had a tray of coffee, a jug of hot milk, sugar, and an ornate Wedgwood cup and saucer. "Sir? I am very worried about Miss Gardener. I wonder if I should not remain here in case she returns."

"I think I know where she is." Krupp poured a cup of black coffee and sat at the kitchen table. He took a deep inhale of the coffee aroma. "When do the rest of the servants come to work?"

"It's only me and Miss Gardener, sir. Mrs Chapel, the cook, only comes on special occasions and weekends."

"Well, you make a good cup of coffee. Where does Sir Jason keep all his files?"

"In his office in Fleet Street."

"None here?"

"No, he seldom does any work here; in fact, he is seldom here." Gareth looked at Krupp questionably.

"Don't worry, *junge*, I am not here to steal the silver," he said with a small smile, "but we might have to sell the car."

"You can't sell the Bristol." Gareth was appalled. "It's not yours." His West Country accent was getting stronger.

"Sir Jason gave it to me. I have all the papers."

"Oh." Bewilderment showed on the young man's face.

"Do you drive, Gareth?"

"Yes, I drive Sir Jason when his chauffeur is off."

"Where is the chauffeur now?"

"He will be at the office, I suppose. He never comes down here. That Mr Alderson drives Sir Jason home sometimes."

"Who is Mr Alderson?"

"What do you mean, sir?"

"What does he do for Sir Jason?"

"He's his friend, not a secretary. He is part of Special Branch." Gareth must have seen some confusion in Krupp's face. "Special Branch are special police."

"Useful man to have around. Sir Jason treats him like a servant."

"He is not a servant." Gareth thought for a while. "Miss Gardener is. Miss Gardener's my boss. Sir Jason never normally tells us what to do, only her."

"Well, Mr Alderson has gone away with Sir Jason. He was the one who gave me the Bristol."

"I see, sir."

"Are you a Nazi, Gareth? Do you work for WASP?" Krupp asked as he took a sip of coffee. Gareth's mouth dropped open. He stood back, shaking his head, his mouth opening and closing, astonished by the question.

"No! I work for Sir Jason. I am bloody well not a Nazi! How dare you—" He broke off abruptly as he saw Krupp's face tighten.

"Well, I am," said Krupp, unsmilingly, "and so is your master, Sir Jason."

"He is not a Nazi!"

"Is there a locked cupboard or a safe somewhere in the house?" Krupp asked after a moment's silence.

"Yes, there is one in the drawing room. I don't have a key – he keeps it locked all the time." Krupp heaved himself up with the walking stick and marched off towards the drawing room. "You will not be able to get into it," Gareth yelled as he followed Krupp out of the kitchen.

In the drawing room, Krupp found the locked cupboard. He looked around for something to break into the cupboard and grabbed a fire poker from a rack of fire tools. He drove the poker through the door, levering off the panel. Gareth winced from the doorway as Krupp unceremoniously dismantled the cupboard door and pulled it off in pieces.

"What have we here?" Krupp said dramatically and stepped aside. Gareth was surprised to see a radio transmitter. Krupp pulled out some books. "Code books," he said with authority, pointing at the titles in German. "And look what else." From the bottom of the cupboard he dragged out a light wooden box that opened to reveal a kind of typewriter machine. It had no carriage for paper, instead a row of gaps where coded wheels could be inserted. "This, Gareth, is a German encryption communications machine."

"A what?" Gareth craned his head, looking at the typewriter-style machine.

"A decoder, for decoding German messages during the war. This machine is missing the vital three discs that go in the back here."

"German?" Gareth was disbelieving. "Sir Jason worked for the Germans?"

"Yes, and I am also working for the Germans, and I need you to drive me to a place called Battersea."

"But you are a Nazi!"

"So is Sir Jason."

"Nazis don't run anything … they are all dead." Gareth was getting more agitated. "I am not going anywhere until I see Miss Gardener or Sir Jason. You planted that machine there so it looks like Sir Jason is a Nazi."

"You saw me break down the door. And when would I have had time to plant this" – Krupp was losing patience, waving his hand at the Enigma machine and the radio transmitter – "this thing, and all the books?"

Gareth sat on the chair in the middle of the room and looked pensive. "OK, Mr Wolff, I'll take you to Battersea. I will go and get dressed."

Gareth did not know what was going on. First, he'd had to collect all the files he could find on Sir Jason in Mr Strider's office whilst Mr Strider was at a meeting with Sir Jason. Then, this terrifying man, Günther Wolff, shot his employer, but now says he is a Nazi and friend of Sir Jason's. Gareth had no idea his employer was a Nazi spy during the war, but then he hardly remembered the war. The Nazis had killed his father and older brother. He would not know what to do if he saw Sir Jason. Would he knock Jason down? Take him to the police? There had to be a plausible explanation … there had to. Wolff must be lying, somehow.

36

"My dear old things, how lovely to see you both." Philip Bing-Wallace welcomed Charlotte and Alec to Deller's vicarage flat as though it was his own flat in Chelsea.

"How are you doing, Philip?" Alec said, looking around the dingy but neat sitting room, which smelt of whisky and body odour. "We had better get you and Deller out of here. Krupp is around and out for blood. Where is Deller?"

"In bed, sleeping like the dead," Bing-Wallace said. "No Theodora?"

"She stayed behind. I think she has had enough of London," Charlotte said as she went through the sitting room looking for the bedroom. "Is he in here?" She pointed to a closed door. Bing-Wallace nodded.

Charlotte knocked gently on the door and opened it cautiously.

"Charlotte, do you want me to … shouldn't I?" Alec looked concerned, Charlotte presumed about what she may see. However, she was probably beyond shocking.

The bedroom was lit by a single bedside light with an emerald-green shade with gold tassels around the edge, standing on a dark-brown chest of drawers. The room was surprisingly tidy, but dusty and a little malodorous. There was a clothes rack with a black suit, a cassock and a black tie, two grey and one white shirt on hangers, and discarded folded clothing on a cheap bent-cane chair. A small single bed contained the rumpled body of Franz-Joseph Deller, snoring under a tangle of sheets and blankets.

Charlotte was about to cough loudly when she spotted a framed black-and-white photograph on the chest of drawers. It was of a young, attractive woman. She picked it up to take a closer look. She had never seen this informal image before. Alice Barrett, her mother, stood wearing a dark dress with two rows of large light-coloured buttons, a contrasting belt around a very slim waist, her pale gloved hands on her hips, her head thrown back, laughing. She looked so happy, pretty, her hair loose and flying in the breeze. Charlotte would have loved to have known her.

"I stole that from your house, must be thirty years ago," Deller said groggily. Charlotte nearly dropped the frame in shock.

"I … I'm sorry, I …" Charlotte collected herself. She placed the frame back onto the chest of drawers. "I have never seen that portrait before."

"No, I suppose not." Deller drew himself up in his bed. He tried to neaten the blankets and wrapped them around himself up to his chest. He wore a vest. He brushed his sparse hair with his hands and smoothed down his beard.

"What was she like?" Charlotte asked.

"That is a very big question, Freya." Deller's eyes widened as he realised his mistake. "Charlotte," he quickly corrected. "I loved her very much."

"That was not my question."

"Oh." He looked down at his hands, clutching the blankets in thought. "She was shy … a dry sense of humour, always happy …" He sighed and corrected himself. "Mostly happy, and very beautiful, like you, Charlotte."

"Ferdi said she was selfish and quite sad," Charlotte said.

"Ferdi didn't know her as well as I did. She was selfish, but I forgave her selfishness. I would forgive her anything."

"But you killed her!"

"I didn't, Charlotte, I really didn't," Deller protested, his voice hoarse. His eyes started to glisten. "It was a terrible accident. She lost her footing … it was very windy and …" He stopped. A tear rolled down his cheek into his beard. "I ran away in misery. I was very confused."

"Drunk, more like," Charlotte said, not giving way to any kind of compassion.

"Yes, I had been drinking. She had told me that she had never loved me and just wanted me to go. She wanted you to herself."

"But you were my father. Why didn't you take care of me?"

Deller dropped his head. He wiped his nose on the sheet. He tried to control himself.

"Charlotte, I am not your father. Your father, I think, is a man called Luke."

Charlotte cast her eyes to the ceiling in disbelief.

"What is this?" she cried angrily. "I don't want anything from you. I have plenty of money."

"No, no, it is nothing like that. I cannot have children, was never able to. I had a medical thing, called an X-ray—"

"I know what an X-ray is," she blurted angrily, like a spoilt child.

"… on my hips when I was a boy – one of the first X-rays. I was checked in Austria. My damned parents wanted grandchildren, Aryan grandchildren, so I was tested. I am infertile, Charlotte." Charlotte sat heavily on the end of the bed. "Just look at me! How could I father something so beautiful? Your hair would be a different colour. Luke was blond, as far as I remember."

"Why are you telling me this now?" Charlotte asked, less heatedly.

Deller said nothing. He pulled his legs up so she did not sit on his feet.

"I am sorry, Charlotte. Nobody other than me knew about this."

"Who is Luke? Luke what?"

"Luke Jarret – I looked him up just after the war. He is dead now. He was killed during the war, fighting in Paris with the Free French. Your mother told me about the time she went to a woman, Madame Belle, who helped young ladies in Paris in the nineteen twenties – rich young ladies who were about to get married. She taught them about married life and how to please their husbands. Luke was her son and showed them the …" Deller reddened. He had plainly not thought he would have to talk about this to anybody, let alone Charlotte.

"Well? What did he show them … these women like my mother?"

"The technique of making love. Alice teased me that Luke Jarret had a thing for her," he whispered.

Charlotte saw in his face that he was telling the truth. This would have been her only parent, she thought, her only remaining family – other than her traitorous uncle and insane aunt. She felt a mixture of guilt and regret that she had not been a bit nicer to Deller. He was just a sad, wretched man who had stolen her paintings.

"Charlotte, the last thing I told your mother was that I could not have been your father. She swung at me with a rock in her hand. I ducked, and she went over the handrail."

"My God."

"I loved Alice, but she did not love me. She used me."

"That's enough now. I don't think I can take much more of this. Jost Krupp is on the loose. He is looking for the files on Jason."

"Most of those were put together by me and Ulrich Fuhrman," Deller said, "for Ferdi's files. We had to keep the files from publication because Jason threatened to kill you and Theodora and everybody you loved if it was not kept secret. He was part of a group, a powerful group that could do terrible things …" He stopped and closed his eyes. "He was also going to expose Ferdi as a homosexual, that your marriage was a sham. He would take over your estate … Paris … including Ferdi's estate, and all of your stepfather's business – the steel company. He was going to have so much power, so much money. Now he is going to go to jail, and possibly be executed for treason and murder." He coughed nervously. "And I can now die at peace, knowing you are safe."

"I see." Charlotte mellowed. "So that is what all this is about: power and money. Jason was not concerned for his long-lost niece." She sat on the bed again and eyed Deller with a little more compassion. "Why did Ferdi have to die?"

"He got in the way of Krupp. He was saying terrible things to Ferdi, saying he was unnatural. Krupp was threatening me, and you, that he would find you and slice you …" He swallowed hard. "Did you know Ferdi was a …?"

"Yes, from when we first met, I think," Charlotte said.

"I had no idea until that night, when Krupp called him all those horrid names. How did Krupp know?" Deller was incensed. "I never considered it, that he was a homosexual. How did I not see? He was handsome, all the girls wanted to know *him*, not me." He sighed. "He never had girlfriends, I suppose." He looked reflectively into space and then suddenly hit his drawn-up knee with his fist. "Krupp called him terrible names. I went to hit Krupp – I hated him. Ferdi stepped in between Krupp and me, just as Krupp swung his dagger. It ended up in Ferdi's neck." Deller looked up to the ceiling, blinking back tears. "Ferdi turned to me and fell on me, his hand on the dagger, trying to get it out. I fell backwards onto the floor. Ferdi sank to his knees and fell on my legs. I tried to take out the dagger" – a tear ran down his cheek – "but he died." He looked back at Charlotte, wiping away the tear. "Krupp said you were next if I told anyone he was there. I had to admit to killing Ferdi or …" He hid his face in his hands. Charlotte felt she should feel more sympathy for her former father, but she could not.

"I cannot believe you did not know Ferdi was a homosexual," she said. "And we do not know each other that well. Why should you worry about Krupp killing me for the files?"

There was a long silence, broken every now and then by Deller sniffing. Charlotte pulled out a handkerchief from her sleeve and threw it at him with an irritated tut.

"Your nice friend, Philip Bing-Wallace, has written a piece for the newspapers," Deller said, "about Jason and his Nazi contacts, and WASP. My work mostly. I found out about these people. My parents were captains of WASP and helped Jason run it from Germany." He swung his legs off the bed, dragging the blankets and sheets off too. "I am going to get up now. Wait for me in the sitting room with Theodora."

"I have come with Alec Ballentine. Theodora is back home."

"I hope she is safe," Deller said with some alarm.

"We have a couple of guards and she is armed. As am I," she said proudly and pulled out a small handgun with a silencer on it.

"Were you going to use that on me?"

"No." Charlotte strode over to her mother's photograph. "By the way, where are all my fake paintings?"

"Jason has them in his Thames warehouse on King Henry's Wharf. He had me locked up there until last night. I got out and went round to Mr Ballentine's flat and found Mr Bing-Wallace."

"You've been incarcerated all this time in a warehouse?"

"More hiding than imprisoned, to be honest."

"I want them returned, my paintings. They are mine and I want to hang them back on the walls of Nineteen Avenue Foch." Deller's face was ashen against his dark beard. He looked ill. "I am happy that you are not my father," she said. "Do you remember trying to make love to me in the shed at Le Palais?"

Deller seemed confused. He studied Charlotte's face, clearly trying to remember. Then realisation struck. "I made love to Alice, not you." Confusion came back over his face. "I would have remembered if it was you."

"You are an ill man, Franz-Joseph. You have addled your brain with drink. How did you ever get this job as a vicar?" Charlotte said, trying to look sympathetic.

"Your uncle, Sir Jason. Who else? He wanted to make sure he knew where I was at all times."

"When did Ferdi know you were here, in London?" she asked with slightly more force.

"When I contacted him two days before he died."

"Why did you contact him?"

"I was worried about something Sir Jason said to me when I was caught selling the painting," Joseph said quietly, not meeting Charlotte's eyes.

"What did he say?" Charlotte raised her voice.

"That he would get Jost Krupp to …"

"What?"

"That either Krupp would get these files off Ferdi or I should. And if it was down to Krupp, he would just … well …" He left the rest of the sentence in the air.

"Well Krupp did, didn't he?" Charlotte said. "Did you ever believe in God? Or was this all a performance so you could get free wine? You're a …" Charlotte stopped, guiltily. Maybe this time she'd gone too far.

"I have always believed in God, Charlotte." He looked up at her like a dog that had been severely reprimanded. "If it were not for my belief, I would be dead by now. I hope you can forgive me."

"What for? Between you, my uncle and Krupp, I have lost my home, my inheritance, my family and friends, all of whom I have loved. You are mostly responsible."

"I have *never* deliberately killed a single person," Deller said with conviction. "Can you say the same thing, Charlotte?" Charlotte was shocked by the statement and was about to challenge what he said but found she could not. "I tried to warn you about Krupp."

"When?" Charlotte said incredulously.

"I can't remember. But I am sure I did. In Paris."

There was a long pause.

"It all stinks. You reek of deceit. I don't know what to believe any more." Charlotte felt anger rise up in her chest, and she walked out of the room, leaving Deller shaking his head in his hands.

"You OK?" Alec asked delicately as Charlotte emerged, looking contemplative, from Deller's bedroom. Bing-Wallace was reading something out loud and stopped, placed a finger on the page and looked up at Charlotte.

"Yes, thank you," she said. "Franz-Joseph says you have written a piece for the papers, Philip. May I read it?"

"Who? Oh, Father Joe, you mean? You all have so many names."

"Yes, we do," Charlotte said angrily, shocking Bing-Wallace and Alec. She saw their surprise and sighed. "I'm sorry, I'm a little confused at the moment. I don't quite know who I am or where I fit in with all" – she waved her hands at the files spread all over the dining table – "this."

She sat at the table with Bing-Wallace. She smiled sweetly at him. "Sorry, Philip, I would love to read the piece you and Franz-Joseph put together."

"Certainly, my dear old thing, um …" Bing-Wallace looked around for the piece of paper he had written on. "I will have to read it to you, as I have put it into shorthand."

"Fine," said Charlotte, trying to hide her impatience.

*

"There is a policeman standing outside the door as well, Mr Wolff," Gareth said nervously. He could not gauge Krupp's mood, or how he would react.

They were parked a couple of hundred feet away from the main entrance to Ballentine's apartment block in Prince of Wales Drive. Krupp was sitting in the back of the Bristol, silent and scowling.

"Go up to his flat and find out if the man is in – what was his name?"

"Ballentine, I think, sir. But what if they arrest me?"

"What the hell for? They don't know who you are. Just tell them, if they ask, that you work for Sir Jason and he wants to make an appointment with Mr Ballentine."

Krupp hissed at Gareth, who got out of the car again and turned before closing the door. "What do you mean, 'make an appointment'?"

"*Hirnlose ochse* – just go, see if anybody is there." Krupp tried not to shout and attract attention, but it did not work. An elderly pedestrian looked alarmed at the rear seat of the Bristol as they passed. The German language was still a little difficult to hear, even after ten years, for some older people.

"Get on with it, Gareth, there's a good fellow," Krupp said, trying to divert attention.

37

"*MP and former newspaper tycoon – a Nazi collaborator who may have helped Nazis invade Paris?*" Bing-Wallace opened dramatically.

"Maybe a bit too long for a headline, Philip. We will have to review it." Alec sat down to listen to the article they were sending to the London *Times*.

"It may be, Alec, but we have to be careful, legally. And you still cannot find Jason to answer these allegations?"

Alec shook his head, pensive. He wondered if this should go to the authorities first and be published the day after tomorrow, on the third of January.

"I recommence, dear things: *Sir Jason Barrett was the owner of the right-wing business paper,* The Sentinel, *in Fleet Street.*"

"*Was* the owner, Philip?" Alec interrupted.

"I found out last Friday that *The Sentinel* was sold just before Christmas, and—"

"Was it now," Alec said thoughtfully.

"And," continued Bing-Wallace, "that Alston Hall in Wimbledon was sold for vast amounts of money, and Jason has been renting it for the past five months."

"He has basically been planning this disappearance for quite a while, it seems," Alec pondered.

"How on earth did you find all this out, Philip?" Charlotte said, fascinated.

"Sleuthing, my dear," Bing-Wallace said proudly, tapping the side of his nose.

"I shall resume: *Sir Jason Barrett MP was the owner of the right-wing …* blah blah blah. *Now a junior minister in Mr Churchill's government, sources have revealed that he is, or was, head of an international espionage group called WASP.*

"*For most of his life before the war, Sir Jason was a high-ranking diplomat in France. His father, Sir Philip Barrett, was the British ambassador for Belgium* and then France. Barrett was re-elected as Member of Parliament for Tooting and Wimbledon in 1951. He sold The Sentinel *newspaper to the* Financial Express *last October, to concentrate, he said, on his political career.*

"Files recently discovered by the London Times *have revealed evidence that Sir Jason Barrett was allegedly in contact with the Nazi Party throughout the war. Allegations will be put to Sir Jason that he not only helped plan the German occupation of northern France and Paris, but he also advised the German High Command on the occupation, and the conditions of the Armistice with Marshal Petain in 1940, ensuring the Atlantic coast was not part of the French Free Zone.*

"Barrett was well known for his views on appeasement at the beginning of the war, and wanted Great Britain to join forces with Germany against the communists in Russia and France. It has transpired that he may have been, or still is, leader of WASP – War Against Socialist Parties. According to discovered secret files, WASP had some of the most powerful people in the world dedicated to fighting communism.*

"Barrett had lost the chance to become the French ambassador due to his political beliefs of appeasement, as the French were angered by his views. He resigned from his role in the diplomatic service and joined the British Secret Service. With his knowledge of French politics and the French people, he was thought to be one of the people who masterminded the SOE, the Special Operations Executive, for Sir Winston Churchill. Details of his operations with SOE cannot yet be confirmed without the permission of the British Secret Service.*

"I am going to confirm this story with a friend of mine," Philip said, "after I have had comments from *The Sentinel* and Special Branch. As soon as I finish here, I will phone for remarks whilst you copy the files. Anyway, I shall resume," Bing-Wallace said and swept his arm over his head like a ballet dancer introducing himself onto the stage.

"Hold on, Philip," Alec interrupted. "I don't think we can name Sir Jason yet."

"Why on earth not?" cried Charlotte.

"Because it is sub judice," Alec said emphatically.

"I had a feeling that may be the case, dear boy," said Bing-Wallace. "I just thought that as it has not gone to trial, or under judgement, we could use his name as an accusation."

"We will have to run it past the lawyers anyway, so we will keep him in," Alec said. "But in the event we can't use his name, there is nothing to stop us insinuating who it is, pretty heavily."

Charlotte was confused as the discussion went back and forth. Alec wanted to phone the legal department at *The Times* but remembered it was a Bank Holiday. In the end, Philip conceded that Jason's actual name could not be used. Alec agreed that they could leave in everything else, including "newspaper proprietor", but not perhaps which newspaper.

"Very well," Philip said somewhat curtly, "I shall resume: *According to the statements in these files, Barrett – sorry – the former newspaper proprietor, throughout the war, was purportedly good friends and secretly in contact with Admiral Canaris, and latterly, Martin Bormann, Hitler's right-hand-man, when Canaris fell out of Hitler's favour.*

"*According to the evidence provided by these files, the Fleet Street newspaper proprietor was introduced to, among other prominent Nazis, Hitler's architect, Albert Speer, in 1934. Speer was also Hitler's closest military adviser just before the war. Evidence from a letter – allegedly from Speer – to the Fleet Street newspaper proprietor, thanking him for information about the Paris defences and the Free French army. A photograph of a letter allegedly from the Fleet Street proprietor, also included in these discovered files, advises Force Yellow – the German invading army – to avoid the Maginot line entirely and invade through neutral Belgium and the other Low Countries. There is no evidence that totally confirms these letters are genuine, or, indeed, from Speer or the Fleet Street newspaper proprietor.*

"*In June 1940, when the Nazis occupied Paris, the Fleet Street newspaper proprietor was back in London and became liaison officer between the secret services in Britain and agents in France. It is possibly no coincidence that the invading Nazi forces occupied a house in Avenue Foch, Paris, owned by the newspaper proprietor's family. The house was then used for the entertainment of senior Nazi officers. The files document that the Fleet Street newspaper proprietor had allegedly been credited with over thirty British agents and Free French operatives being captured, tortured and killed.*

"*The Fleet Street newspaper proprietor's operative—*"

"Oh, Alec, this is ridiculous," Charlotte cried. "We all know it's Jason. Why do you have to keep referring to him as the Fleet Street newspaper proprietor?"

"It is because we only have one source, Ferdi, who is dead – the only person who has accused Jason of being head of WASP. This piece in the newspaper may bring out someone else who recognises that it is Jason."

"I see." Charlotte looked dubious. "Do go on, Philip."

"Don't worry, my dear, we'll get the bugger. I shall resume: *The Fleet Street newspaper proprietor employed the services of a paid assassin – a Nazi, ex-SS Major Jost Krupp, who is thought to be going under the name of Günther Wolff. Krupp, who is still at large, was witnessed shooting dead Mr Jeremy Bates, a milkman and father of two, on Bury Hill, near Arundel in West Sussex. Krupp then stole Mr Bates's car when he crashed his own vehicle, a stolen police car. Krupp, who is also alleged to have killed three other people in England last year, was captured but then escaped officers of Scotland Yard in October last year. He is presently known to be in London or the south-east of England. He is believed to be armed and highly dangerous. Should anybody see Krupp, please dial 999 immediately. Jost Krupp is wanted by the police for murder, vehicular theft, and assaulting police officers. He is five foot eleven inches tall, with a dark complexion, thinning black hair and a thick scar under his right eye, running down his right cheek. He speaks with a thick German accent and walks with a heavy limp.*

"*The Fleet Street newspaper proprietor has disappeared and has not made any comment about these allegations. The editor of the Fleet Street newspaper said of his employer's whereabouts …*"

"I still need to get Jack Flowers to comment, but this is going off to the police and the Foreign Office now," said Alec with a pleased look. "I am going to my flat. I need to make a copy of these documents before we hand them over."

Bing-Wallace saw Deller enter the room looking pale. "Ah, there you are, old chap. Feeling better? I wonder if we could get your comments on—"

"Are you considering going to your flat, Mr Ballentine?" Deller interrupted Bing-Wallace.

"Yes, to copy the files."

"I think you will find it easier and safer if you went to your flat via the back entrance," Deller said seriously.

"I don't know if I have a back entrance to my flat."

"There are fire escapes to all the floors and the roof at the back of the building. If Krupp is going to be anywhere, he will be somewhere near, even in your flat."

"The police have officers at the front door and inside," Alec said. "They apparently found Jason's housekeeper there: Jane something."

"She is called Brunhilda Baumgartner," said Deller flatly, "and is very dangerous. She is Jason's home bodyguard. She is a high-ranking member of WASP."

"I gather you were the one who found out about WASP for Ferdi Saumures," Alec said, approaching Deller. Deller shrunk away from him as he got closer, like a dog that knows it is about to be beaten.

"You will have to ask someone else about that."

"But how did you know where to look? What alerted you to—"

Deller shouted, "As I said, you will have to find out from someone else. I don't want to talk about any of this ever again!"

Alec walked away and sat at the table with the files. Bing-Wallace was gathering the files together and whispered, "We are going to have to get him to talk about WASP and what it was about somehow, Alec."

"I know, but I think he's feeling a little raw at the moment."

There was an uncomfortable silence.

"I simply do not understand," Charlotte said from the corner of the room where she had been sitting, silently listening to the newspaper story. "Krupp storms into Jason's house, shoots Jason, terrorises us all, and all this time Jason, who is injured on the floor, is Krupp's employer. Brunhilda Whatsit is also a Nazi spy, and probably the boy Gareth, and, it seems, Strider. They are all like Jason ... Nazis!"

"Yes, it seems so," Alec said, wondering where this was going.

"What about the staff at *The Sentinel*?" Charlotte asked.

"Possibly Flowers is an ex-Nazi sympathiser, and Jason's secretary, Alderson," Alec surmised.

"Alderson is not Sir Jason's secretary," Deller said quietly, still standing at his bedroom door, leaning against the door frame.

"Yes, he is," Alec said. "I was introduced to him as—"

"He is Jason's pet Special Branch detective."

"But that is incredible, dear thing!" Bing-Wallace said and started shuffling through the files.

"Should we not get all these people first before that article is published? Or they will all vanish, like Jason," Charlotte said.

"We don't 'get' them, Charlotte. That is the job of the police," Alec said forcefully.

"But they lost Krupp once and they are not armed. Krupp will kill them if they get near."

Alec was feeling uneasy. Charlotte had that defiant look, her chin jutting forward, gritting her teeth, eyes sharp, her cheekbones rouged and pronounced.

"Charlotte, old girl, we must, and we will, tell the authorities." Bing-Wallace went over to her. "We must get Jason to answer these allegations. What do you think, Franz-Joseph?" Bing-Wallace turned to see that Deller was no longer at his bedroom door. "Anyway, the best people to deal with Krupp are the police."

"Well, come on," Alec said. "It will take ages to knock out this piece on the typewriter and get these files copied and photostatted, so we must get started. I think Deller is right: we should go the back way, in case Krupp is around the front waiting for us."

"Where's he gone?" Bing-Wallace asked on discovering Deller must have left the flat.

"To his church, I imagine," Alec said. "Come on, we must get going or we'll miss the deadline for tomorrow's press."

*

"You are like the stench of a dead rodent, Krupp. You don't know where it is coming from, or when it will turn up."

Krupp whirled around when he heard his native language to see Franz-Joseph Deller leaning through the broken back window of the Bristol, a small pistol levelled at his head.

"Deller, you drunk shithead, how nice to see you," Krupp said in mock joviality. "Come and join me on the back seat. We will talk of old times." All the while Krupp was trying to get the large British Army pistol out of his coat pocket. Deller came quickly around to the driver's door and slid onto the driver's seat on his knees, still with his small pistol trained onto Krupp's head.

"What have you got there?" Deller saw Krupp struggling with something in his coat pocket. "Put your hands behind your head, Krupp," Deller snarled. He leant over the seat and jabbed the pistol into Krupp's forehead; Krupp put his hands behind his head. Deller felt the handle of a pistol and took it out of Krupp's coat pocket.

"This is a magnificent beast," Deller said, holding the larger pistol up to Krupp's head and putting the small pistol into his trouser pocket.

The two men stared at each other, eye to eye. Deller felt unadulterated rage; the anticipation of revenge was exciting him. Krupp's expression was a mixture of sullen defiance and a small amount of trepidation.

"You could never kill a man, Deller. You are a weak drunk who worships a non-existent god and a goddess who is a whore."

"Shut up, Krupp, I am going to kill you. I am." Deller nearly screamed with anger. "You are a murdering dog, you are slime, you are not worthy to speak her name!"

"At least I fucked her, Deller. You haven't. Oh, isn't she meant to be your daughter?" Krupp put on a sneering smile.

Deller cocked the pistol and pushed the muzzle hard against Krupp's head. "Go to hell, Krupp!"

He pulled the trigger. Krupp gasped loudly.

38

Charlotte looked up at the mottled red metal staircase winding steeply up the building. She could not remember what she was like with heights – she was about to find out.

"I would be on the top bloody floor," Alec muttered and started up the fire escape steps. "Bing-Wallace, you bring up the rear so if Charlotte falls, she's got something soft to land on." Charlotte and Bing-Wallace's eyes met with raised eyebrows.

"After you, my dear. And, Charlotte, make sure you hold onto something."

Each carried two files in a canvas shopping bag and steadily ascended the fire escape, the flights of steps zigzagging up the tall building. As they got to the top, to everybody's surprise – including Alec's – there was a roof garden. Wooden chairs with green mould were scattered about, some tipped up on their side, plainly thrown about during the winter winds. Two long planters with dead brown plants in them sat against an ornate metal fence on the edge of the flat roof that had been recently painted in red-oxide paint.

"This door is locked, unsurprisingly," Alex said. An idea came to him. He reached into his trouser pocket and brought out a bunch of keys. One of the keys easily unlocked the door. Alec turned to Charlotte and Bing-Wallace with a proud smile, as though waiting for applause.

*

There was a loud click as the hammer hit, but no bullet was discharged from the large pistol. Deller looked at the revolver with horror and pulled the trigger again. Krupp could see the bullets in the revolving barrel and when he saw the trigger go back, he realised the firing pin was missing. Jason's weapon had been decommissioned. He grabbed the pistol barrel and pulled the Webley out of Deller's hand. Deller desperately fumbled for the little pistol in his trouser pocket. Krupp smashed the butt of the heavy Webley onto the side of Deller's head, instantly knocking him out. He went limp. A large gash spread across the side of his head and blood coursed down his ashen face into his beard.

Krupp reached across the driver's seat and whipped out the small pistol from Deller's pocket. He checked to see if there were bullets in the magazine; there were only two and a cartridge in the chamber. He opened the door and got out, jarring his bad leg at the same time. He shouted an oath in German, then realising his outburst, looked around to see if anybody had heard. It was a cold, cloudy morning, and nobody was around. The policeman was still at the front door of the journalist's building, a hundred metres up the road. He could just see his helmet on the other side of a hedge.

Krupp went to the boot of the Bristol and took out one of his two canvas bags. It was reassuringly heavy. He kept a constant eye out for the journalist and Freya. He did not want them to see him before he saw them. He pulled a stick grenade out of the canvas bag, leaving about six grenades.

*

Charlotte, Alec and Philip arrived at Alec's apartment door. A surprised policeman put up his hand as they approached. "I am sorry. Nobody may come up here, sir, it is restricted," he said officiously, his face grim.

"This is the owner of the flat," Charlotte said sweetly. "Surely we can go in?"

The policeman's severe expression instantly melted when he saw her.

"I will have to check with the inspector, madam," he said, looking unsure. "Please wait here. I will just go down to the office to—"

"Use our phone," Charlotte cooed. Alec watched as she steered the young police constable to her bidding.

"Yes … well … thank you, madam." He flushed as she lightly touched his forearm. He then turned serious and said in an official voice, "Would you please all remain on the landing until I have checked with the guv … the station." A thought came to him. "How did you get up here, sir?"

"The fire escape at the back of the building. My main door key works in the fire-door lock." Alec proudly held up his house keys. "Then up to the roof and in through the roof access. Again, using this key. There is an old roof garden just through that door." Alec pointed at a door at the end of the corridor.

"I see," the constable said with a little worried scratch of his chin. "Can I take your names, please?" He took down Alec and Charlotte's details in his notebook, licking his pencil. He then went into Alec's flat.

Alec turned to Charlotte and raised an eyebrow. "Really?"

After a moment's hesitation, Charlotte smiled in understanding. "I find that it is useful to be charming and slightly flirtatious towards men."

"Lady Saumures?" a voice said from behind the wire mesh of the central lift shaft.

"Yes? Who is it?" Charlotte sounded wary.

"It's me, Gareth Mackintosh. Sir Jason's assistant. At the house in Wimbledon."

"Hello, Gareth," said Alec kindly. "Come up, we are trying to find Sir Jason. What brings you here?" Gareth walked up the final flight of stairs, the spots on his face looking pronounced against his pale skin. He looked around to see where the policeman was. He was slightly out of breath. He then looked down the lift tower to check the lift was still on the ground floor.

"That man, Mr Wolff, made me drive him up here." Charlotte gasped. Gareth looked at her with concern and carried on. "He's in Sir Jason's Bristol, parked down the road."

"What are you doing here?" Charlotte asked, agitated. "Are you working for that man?"

"No," Gareth wailed. "He threatened to kill me if I didn't do what he said!"

"Don't worry, Gareth." Alec patted the boy on his shoulder. "We will get the police to collar him. He is wanted for murder, anyway. Where is he? In the car waiting for you?"

"I think so," Gareth said miserably, looking down the lift shaft again.

"And who do we have here then?" the policeman said as he came out of the flat. Gareth seemed to shrink behind Alec.

"This is Mr Mackintosh. He assists us," Charlotte said grandly.

"How did he get past John ... Constable Gage?"

"He let me in when I said that I was Lady Saumures's assistant."

"I see. You can go in, sir, milady, but please do not move anything. Are these the files that woman was looking for?" The policeman pointed at Bing-Wallace's battered satchel and the shopping bags. "The inspector asked me to ask you."

"They are," Alec said. Philip held the satchel closer to him.

"Apparently, there has been a request from Sir Jason Barrett for these files to go to him."

"I bet there has," Charlotte snorted. "Who told you this?"

"The inspector will tell you when he gets here within the next half hour," the constable said authoritatively.

"You'd better get back on the phone straight away, Constable, as Jost Krupp, who is wanted for murder, is—"

Just then, an enormous, rattling explosion erupted from outside the building. Everything shook, glass could be heard shattering.

"What the hell was that?" the policeman shouted and tore down the stairs. Charlotte, Gareth and Alec went quickly into Alec's flat and straight to the window that overlooked the park. There was nothing to see on Prince of Wales Drive as far as Alec could see, so he opened the window and leant out. "Was it Krupp?" Charlotte asked urgently.

"I can just see up the road," Alec shouted back, half his body out of the window. "Christ, what a mess. Yes, there is Krupp, limping away with a bag. Call the police."

"Gareth, would you dial 999 and ask for the police?" Charlotte asked the boy, nicely but firmly. "The phone is over there. Tell them that the fugitive Jost Krupp, or Günther Wolff, is walking beside Battersea Park. Which way is he walking, Alec?"

"Towards Queenstown Road," Alec said, coming back into the flat. "He is not going very fast."

"No, he has something wrong with his leg," Gareth said and went over to the telephone.

"I'm going after him," said Charlotte. She pulled a small pistol out of her handbag.

"What are you doing, Charlotte?" Alec blocked her way as she strode towards the door.

"Let me pass. I do not want him disappearing again."

"No, the police will get him." He took the pistol out of Charlotte's hand. "Where did you get this?"

"If he gets away, Alec ..." Charlotte scowled at him.

"He will not get away." Alec went over to a cupboard and rolled out a large square machine on little wheels. "He is not going to get far with that leg. He is bound to be armed and I am nervous of any of us getting too close to him." He plugged in the photostat machine and it began to whirr. "I will get copies of the files first, and I need to type up the article," Alec said, watching Gareth phoning the police on the other side of the room. "I could get Gareth to do them whilst Philip and I type."

"The police are on their way to the scene," said Gareth with a worried look.

"Did you tell them about Krupp?" Charlotte asked.

"Yep, and they seemed very interested as to how we knew it was Krupp, so one of them is coming here." He paused and looked in wonder at Alec's machine. "What is that?"

"It's a photostat machine, warming up. I need you to copy all these files and bits of paper, if you don't mind, whilst we do some important typing. Lady Saumures can help you."

"Yep, that's fine, except I don't know what to do with a photostat machine. What does it do?"

"It copies documents very fast – it takes a kind of photo of them."

"Gosh," Gareth said in wonderment.

"Gareth?" Charlotte sat down on the sofa and arranged all the files on a coffee table. "Why were you with Krupp in Jason's car?"

"He suddenly turned up last night, or rather this morning – it was very late." Gareth looked worried again. "He said something about Sir Jason giving him his big car and that Sir Jason was a Nazi during the war."

"Did he?" Charlotte looked dutifully intrigued.

"Yes, and he said he needed to get to London to meet up with Sir Jason."

"So, you got the impression that Krupp was working for Sir Jason?" Alec asked.

"Yep, and Miss Gardener has disappeared."

"I am afraid we think she is a Nazi spy as well, Gareth. Her name is Brunhilda Baumgartner," Alec said airily.

"Really? Miss Gardener?"

"Yes, I am afraid so." He beckoned Gareth to come over to the machine to get instruction. "You slide in a document here and press this green button; the document is photographed in the machine, and a copy flops out here after two minutes. You don't have to wait two minutes each time, just when you hear a bell and then you put in the next bit of paper. Keep them in order."

"Gosh, this is a great machine," Gareth said excitedly. "I never liked Miss Gardener anyway, she was always scolding me."

"How on earth did you get a job with Sir Jason, Gareth?" Charlotte asked.

"My mum was his cleaner for years. She asked if I could have a job. Sir Jason said I could if I learned German."

"You speak German?" Charlotte and Alec said in unison.

"Yes, fluently. Sir Jason did a lot of work in Germany for the …" Gareth went quiet; he must have realised that he may have been helping Jason work for the Nazis and not the War Crimes Commission, or whatever post-war good works he thought Jason was doing.

"Come on, Gareth, we must get these files copied."

"Yes, sir," Gareth said quietly and then turned to Charlotte. "But Sir Jason is your uncle, Lady Saumures, isn't he?"

"Yes, he is, Gareth. I have only recently met him again after more than fifteen years."

Gareth was silent. He went to the photostat machine and started duplicating the files. He read some of them as he waited for the copies. He turned as the door opened and a man in a raincoat walked in.

"Inspector McMillan." Alec welcomed the inspector. He looked very serious. Charlotte quickly stuffed the little pistol fully into her handbag, as some of it was poking out.

"I have Assistant Commissioner Jeremy Adams with me, sir," said the inspector.

"The car that exploded was Sir Jason Barrett's, Inspector," Alec said. A dapper, thin man in a fur-collared fawn coat walked in. "Mr Ballentine, Lady Saumures, I don't think we have met. My name is Adams."

"Delighted, Commissioner, and this is Mr Gareth Mackintosh." Alec introduced Gareth, who went very pale again.

"I have just been informed that the vehicle that exploded in Prince of Wales Drive belongs to Sir Jason Barrett, sir," McMillan said to Adams.

"Ah," said Adams, holding his chin in concentration.

McMillan carried on. "I hope not to distress you, Lady Saumures, but there are the remains of a body, maybe two, in the vehicle."

"Must be Krupp," shouted Gareth joyously.

"No," said Alec, perturbed. "I saw Krupp, or a person answering to the description of Krupp, walking towards Queenstown Road. I hope the police will have picked him up by now."

"Are you sure there was a body in the car, Inspector?" Charlotte asked. "What did he look like?"

"I regret," McMillan answered slowly, "the body was too …" He was clearly struggling to think of a delicate way to put it.

Charlotte just said, "Oh, I see."

"We can't really tell if it was a man or a woman."

Charlotte looked anxiously at Alec. She must be thinking of Theodora, and how Krupp had kidnapped her the last time. "Where was the body, Mr McMillan?" she asked abruptly.

"In the driver's seat, Lady Saumures. The bomb must have been in the boot." Charlotte sighed with relief.

"Well, if it isn't Krupp, sir, who could it be?" Gareth threw up his hands. "I only drove Krupp up from Wimbledon, only him."

"Tell me, Mr Mackintosh, how is it you drove Mr Krupp up from Wimbledon in Sir Jason's car?" asked Inspector McMillan as he walked over to Gareth, who looked up nervously at the policeman.

39

"A lady on the phone for Lady Saumures, madam. What shall I say?"

"Give me the phone, Rupert." Theodora took it from him. "Can I help you?"

"Good morning, please may I speak to Lady Saumures?" asked the clipped voice of Jane Gardener.

"I am afraid she is not here at the moment," Theodora said cautiously. "Who may I say is calling, for when she returns?"

"Oh, this is Jane Gardener, Sir Jason's housekeeper."

"Good God!" Theodora was surprised but quickly composed herself. "Lady Saumures is attempting to trace her uncle and is in London trying to establish his whereabouts."

"I see," Jane said ponderously.

"Can I help at all, Miss Gardener? This is Madam Theodora Smith, Lady Saumures's companion."

"No, thank you, Madam Smith." Jane was still hesitant. "Well, perhaps. I have been arrested and I am at Battersea police station."

"Good God," Theodora said again. "What have you done, may I ask?"

"Well, I was in Mr Alec Ballentine's flat."

"What do you mean, in his flat?"

"Sir Jason asked if I could go and see Mr Ballentine. When I arrived at his flat yesterday, I knocked and the door was open, so I went in. There was nobody there, so I waited for Mr Ballentine to return. The police arrived instead and arrested me, I presume for trespass."

"I see, and you need Sir Jason to vouch for you, or even Mr Ballentine, I assume?" Theodora was puzzled.

"Correct," Jane said simply. The conversation went dead.

"Do you have a telephone number I can call you back on?"

"Well, yes, Battersea police station, I suppose." It sounded like she was asking someone else in front of her. "Yes, you can call me here apparently – I don't know the number."

"Don't worry, I will find it. I will ring round and see if I can find Sir Jason or someone else that can help you."

"Thank you, Madam Smith, I am obliged. Goodbye for now." The phone went dead.

Theodora went through the phone book for Alec's phone number.

*

On the other side of the roundabout, at the bottom of Queenstown Road, Krupp found two bombed-out terraced houses, standing against a viaduct on which a railway line ran. The wrecked buildings had no windows or a front door, just a sheet of corrugated metal roughly nailed to the door frame. Krupp looked around to see if anybody was watching him. The road was filled with black smoke from the burning Bristol motor car being blown down Prince of Wales Drive by a north-westerly breeze. The smoke had completely covered his escape.

He pulled the corrugated metal sheet aside and squeezed into the house. It smelt of rats, dank moss and damp wood. There were black, dead and rotting stinging nettles in what was the front room of the house. The roof was gone and droplets of rain were splattering through. None of the three floors above remained.

He cautiously looked out of the window, through the holes in the corrugated iron, back up Prince of Wales Drive. Smoke was billowing everywhere from the Bristol, which was well alight. There was a distant ringing of a bell from the fast-approaching fire engines coming up from Battersea Park Road and the King's Road. He then saw policemen running along Prince of Wales Drive towards the roundabout. He ducked down. He looked around the abandoned building to find an alternative escape route. There was only a very small gap through to the back of the house. He eased himself through and pulled down some rubble behind him to disguise the gap. He took out the small pistol, hoping he would not need it.

Krupp would just lie up here until the dust had settled. He looked at the map he had found in the Bristol and worked out where he was.

He sat in the only dry spot of the ground floor, in what must have been a cupboard or a larder, at the back of the house. The place shook every now and then when a train rumbled past. How could people live so close to a train track?

he wondered. He hauled his collar up around his head and pulled his legs up painfully. He stacked bricks all around him, like a mini castle, and placed rusty sheets of corrugated iron over his head and shoulders so he had a thin opening to see anybody who came through the gap in the wall.

What to do now? He would not be able to get to the flat now; that boy had probably gone to the police. And he had just blown up his only transport. He consoled himself with the thought that he had lots of gold. He folded his arms in deep satisfaction, the rucksack of gold between his legs. The top of the bag was open and the gold inside glowed. A feeling of contentment ran through him at the sight of his riches. It was like sitting beside a small fire, warming, glowing, glistening.

He heard shouting outside the wrecked house. Someone knocked at the corrugated iron door to see if it would budge – which it did not as Krupp had put a large roof truss up against it. He took hold of the pistol and held it ready for anybody who might come too close. He took out one of the two remaining stick grenades and primed it ready to pull cord and detonate.

I could try and get to the boat tomorrow, he thought. I have gold, I could bribe Jason's man. He turned over in his mind the many problems he would have to face. Would Jason take him without the files? He decided he could not be bothered with Jason, he could go to hell. Krupp would simply kill him and steal the boat. Anger flared up, then, almost as quickly, he descended into misery. "I would love to have seen her one last time, though," he said aloud, hopelessly, as though in prayer. It was late afternoon, already getting dark outside. An owl called way above his head. He heard another owl in the park across the roundabout call back. He lowered his pistol and cursed the owls.

*

"Yes, Sergeant, Miss Jane Gardener is Sir Jason's housekeeper," Alec told Sergeant Glass after Theodora called him. He stood looking out at the wisps of smoke from the burning car, which was being put out by the fire brigade. Charlotte was beside him, trying to listen to the phone call.

"And did she have your permission to be in your flat?"

"Well, she was looking for me and Lady Saumures and apparently saw that the door was open. I believe my friend Bing-Wallace may have forgotten to close it." Alec wanted to get Jane Gardener released so that he could find out more about Sir Jason.

"Then we have the pistol she was carrying," Sergeant Glass argued. Alec gaped.

"Are you OK?" Charlotte said with concern.

"I don't know about that, Sergeant," Alec said, gesticulating with his hand, hoping for some inspiration. "She may have a legitimate reason for carrying a weapon. Jason was part of the secret services, you know. She may be one of his operatives."

Sergeant Glass thought for a while. "I will talk to the guv and see. She will not be out until tomorrow anyway. Good evening, sir."

*

"Theodora, that woman will be released tomorrow morning." Charlotte phoned Burton Park Place with the news. "Give her a call. Alec and I will meet her." Charlotte felt exhausted.

"Are you all right, darling?"

"Not really. I fear Deller was blown up by Krupp, just outside of Alec's flat. We can't find him anywhere, not in his flat or in the church. It must be him."

"My God. Your father?"

"Well, it transpires that he was not my father after all."

"I am coming up, darling. You need me," Theodora soothed.

"You don't have to. I think I will be back tomorrow if we cannot find Jason. Alec has sent the article he and Philip wrote on Jason and Jost Krupp to the papers." She suddenly felt annoyed. "That bastard Krupp has got someone else killed. And of course, the damned police cannot find him. There he was, limping up the pavement one minute, and he disappears the next!"

"My God, did you go after him?"

"No, Alec would not let me. I am not at all happy with him at the moment."

"He must have been thinking of you," Theodora said.

"No, he was not," Charlotte said indignantly. "He was just worried I would get in trouble with the police."

There was a long, angry pause.

"Jane Gardener is also a Nazi spy, apparently," Charlotte said bitterly. "Got some kind of German name. She will certainly get hurt if she does not tell us about Jason tomorrow – I will make sure of that!"

Charlotte was breathing heavily.

"Where are you staying, darling?"

"Here at Alec's. It's too late to go anywhere else."

"OK. I will see you tomorrow morning, darling. We will find them together – you and I – and we will kill them. If we are arrested, we will escape. It's easy with these police. Then we'll move back to Paris."

40

After a fitful night in the bombed-out house, Krupp clambered out into the misty, dank winter's dawn. It was not cold, but he felt shivery and damp. He was sick with hunger, sweaty, and his leg was painful and numb. Getting his leg to carry his weight – and the weight of the gold – took some time and lots of oaths. It was about seven thirty, the second of January. It was still dark, and the roads were damp and shiny. There were a few cars and lorries going around the roundabout, heading up and over Chelsea Bridge, going back to work after the New Year celebrations.

He stopped at the roundabout to gather his bearings. He stood under a lamp post, took out the John Bartholomew map of London and worked out where he was going. He adjusted the reassuringly heavy bag slung over his shoulder. He saw that he was quite close to the river and Chelsea Bridge.

Krupp stood looking at the charred remains of the Bristol, fifty yards up Prince of Wales Drive and surrounded by bright red-and-white warning planks of wood and red oil lanterns. He looked from behind the lamp post just in case the policeman guarding the wreck saw him. It was too far away to see any detail, and it was dark. He started to walk up the road towards the river.

A car came very close to the kerb where Krupp was. It went through a puddle and splashed water over his shoes. Krupp stepped back, looking down at his wet shoes, and was about to berate the driver when he saw something in the gutter glittering in the car lights. Three half-crowns and a florin – nine shillings and sixpence! Krupp scooped the coins up, not really knowing their value, and put them in his pocket. "Even richer," he chortled. "This is going to be a good day."

He walked like a drunk with a hangover slowly up the road towards the bridge, the park on his left. The walking stick was beginning to feel weakened; it must have a split in it. He kept close to the metal railings under the overhanging trees to keep as hidden as possible. Only a few street lights were still burning.

As he approached the bridge, he saw on the other side of the road a catering caravan with a serving hatch. A man in his vest and a grey-white apron was working inside, lit by a paraffin light. He had no customers, so Krupp limped over, drawing his new riches out of his pocket.

"Yes, mate," the man said, cigarette dangling in the corner of his mouth. He had one eye half-closed to stop the smoke getting into it.

"I would like some tea, please," Krupp said in his best English. The man's expression changed. He shoved out a cupped hand and growled, "That's a tanner." Jost put up his hand with the coins in his palm. The man sighed and took the two-shilling piece, and carelessly dropped one-and-sixpence back into Krupp's hand with a snort. He poured hot, steaming deep-brown milky tea into a white enamelled metal mug, from an oversized teapot. Krupp saw a blackboard listing "Bacon Roll 1/6". As the man put the mug of tea onto the serving counter with a sugar pourer, he picked up a teaspoon attached to a chain and dropped it into Krupp's mug of tea.

"'Ere y'are, mate." He was about to say something else when Krupp drew himself up, mustering every ounce of self-control. The man froze when he saw Krupp's black eyes glare out from under his angry eyebrows. He snarled through gritted teeth and sneering lips.

"Give me two rolls with bacon … mate."

The man looked hesitant. He put out his hand. Krupp slammed down the rest of his money onto the counter.

Suddenly a van screeched to a halt behind him. Krupp had his hand gripped on the pistol butt, ready for someone to attack him. He did not quite draw out the gun. He saw a boy jump out of the back of the van with a pile of newspapers, which he threw at Krupp's feet, then he climbed back into the van and sped off to the next delivery.

The man suddenly appeared beside Krupp. He was surprisingly shorter than Krupp had imagined. He watched as the man got a knife, cut the twine around the stack, and started placing the papers into racks that hung either side of the serving hatch. Krupp drank his tea, watching the man at his task.

Krupp almost choked on his tea. He put the cup onto the counter and grabbed a copy of the London *Times*.

"Newspaper tycoon and British MP may have been a Nazi collaborator, by Philip Bing-Wallace and Alec Ballentine."

Krupp grabbed the paper out of the rack.

"That'll be—" the man started, and Krupp pointed to the money on the counter. The man muttered a thank you and said, "I'll sort out them rolls, mate."

Krupp walked over to the wall behind the caravan, spread the front page of the paper out under the street light and started to read. He opened the paper to page two for the rest of the story. He was startled to see not only a photo of Jason Barrett coming out of the *Sentinel* building with the caption: *"Sir Jason Barrett leaving the newspaper office that he sold a month ago to the National Financial Express"*, but also a picture of himself, in full SS uniform, taken twenty-five years ago, with the caption: *"Jost Krupp, aka Günther Wolff, in 1941"*.

"'Ere you go, guv," the man said to Krupp calmly, with some new respect. Krupp took the rolls, not even looking at the man, who was holding out his other hand with some change. Krupp brushed him away, and the man thanked him begrudgingly for the tip.

Krupp finished his tea, left the mug on the wall, picked up his bag and walked across the road. There were two taxi drivers standing at the caravan hatch now. "'Ere 'e goes, now," the man whispered to the taxi drivers. "Weird, 'e was. Left me a nice tip, though. Nice for a Kraut."

"You're not expecting a bleedin' tip from us, are ya?" cried the taxi drivers together.

*

"I am here to see Jane Gardener," Theodora said to the desk sergeant at Battersea police station.

"She's just coming now with the inspector."

"Thank you. Is she being released now?"

"Yes, she is," the sergeant said gruffly.

"Thank you, sir."

"Don't call me 'sir', madam. I work for a living. I'm a sergeant," he said, pointing to the chevrons on his sleeve. His prejudice irritated Theodora, but she was not going to make a fuss.

"Thank you, Sergeant," Theodora said, slightly confused by the difference between a sir and a sergeant. Men! she thought, always worried about their position in life, and how important they are in the eyes of other men.

She had not expected Jane Gardener to be released that morning. Theodora had come to see if she could help in any way, but it appeared she was

273

wise to have rushed up on the early train to Victoria after all. Jane Gardener appeared at the door with Inspector McMillan.

"Good morning, Madam Smith." Jane Gardener was clipped, precise, unsmiling, and looked incredibly sharp for a person who'd spent a day and a night in a police cell. She wore a plain black cashmere coat with a fashionable military-style collar. The coat must have been tailored as it fitted her short, slim figure precisely and came down to just below her knees. Her black hair was scraped back into a tight bun.

"Hello, Miss Gardener." Theodora mustered a smile.

"Miss Gardener is cleared to go," McMillan said, "but we may have more questions for her."

"Oh?" Jane turned on McMillan. "And why, may I ask, is that?"

"There is an arrest warrant for Sir Jason Barrett, and you may have some ideas about his whereabouts."

"An arrest warrant? What on earth for?" Jane was incredulous. Theodora detected some acting from her.

"Treason, miss."

"Come on, Miss Gardener." Theodora had promised to take her straight to the flat. "Let's go. I will tell you all."

Jane Gardener stood and eyed Theodora for a few seconds, clearly thinking about something. Theodora was getting impatient.

"Would you be so kind as to wait a minute longer, Madam Smith? I must go and wash my hands," Jane said, pointing to a ladies' lavatory.

"Yes, of course. I should have thought."

*

Jost Krupp walked into Battersea Park through the gate leading to the path that ran beside the river wall. He saw a bench to the side of the path and sat down to study the newspaper article. The light was not good and he had to strain his eyes to see the small print. He ate his bacon rolls. When he got to the part about him, he stopped chewing. He looked around guiltily. He was not, now, the only person here in the park. A few pedestrians were walking along the river pathway towards him, on their way to work. He decided he should be less exposed. He walked across the grass, away from the river towards a bandstand, and sat on the steps where there was a lot more light, looking all around for any danger.

He opened the newspaper and read.

*

"It's a bit cold and misty this morning, Miss Gardener. I will get a taxi," Theodora said.

"Where do you want to take me?" Miss Gardener asked.

"We are going to Alec Ballentine's flat, I thought, to—"

"Then we will not get a taxi. We should walk through to the next road, I think, to the park."

"Oh, OK." Theodora was suspicious. Jane Gardener seemed ingenuous, calculating.

They crossed Battersea Bridge Road and walked through to Albert Bridge Road and the park ahead. As they got to Albert Bridge Road, Jane suddenly stopped. Theodora, who was ahead of her, turned and said, "Everything all right, Miss Gardener?"

Jane undid her handbag and removed a paisley headscarf. As Theodora approached to see if she was OK, Jane took out a small pistol and pointed it at Theodora.

"Turn around, Madam Theodora. Please."

"What the hell are you up to? I am—"

"Be quiet or I will shoot you – not kill you, but wound you. Turn around. I want to secure your hands."

Theodora did as she was told. She kept a furious eye on Jane as she turned. There was no traffic in the small link road between the two bridge roads. Jane tied the paisley scarf expertly around Theodora's hands and behind her back, leaving one end of the scarf long, which she held in her right hand, which also held the pistol. "If you make any quick movements, the pistol will fire into your spine. Do you understand, Madam Theodora?"

"Yes," Theodora said sharply. "What is this for? What do you want us to do?"

"We are going to walk up to the river and into the park beside Albert Bridge."

"And what are we going to do then?" Theodora was becoming very uneasy.

"You will see." Jane prodded Theodora in the small of the back with her pistol.

The women crossed Albert Bridge Road, then went through the gates into the park.

"Do you know what you are doing, Miss Gardener? Where are we going?"

Jane Gardener said nothing. She looked around until she saw something in the distance. They walked through the park briskly, towards the bandstand.

When they were about twenty yards from the bandstand, Jane Gardener pulled on the headscarf binding Theodora's hands. Theodora thought it was because of the few commuters walking towards them. But it was not.

"Do you see the man sitting on the steps, Madam Theodora?"

"Yes, I do. What of—? My God, it can't be."

"Do not say a thing or I will shoot you in a place where you will never walk again." Jane shoved Theodora to speed up.

"You are good with your threats. Anybody would think you were German!"

Jane said nothing. A commuter hurried past, his face wrapped up in a scarf, his head down, his bowler hat covering his eyebrows. He took no notice of the women.

*

Krupp looked up from his newspaper to see two sets of legs, one in slacks, the other in stockings and a black coat, both standing close to each other. His hand went to the pistol. He did not look up into their faces until one said, "Jost?"

It was Hilde who spoke. He saw Hilde behind Theodora. She was smiling widely, whereas Theodora looked at him like thunder.

"Hilde!" he shouted, a huge smile on his face. It stretched the scar to a hideous shape on his cheek. Then he turned to Theodora again and the smile disappeared. "I see you have found the empress. Hello, Theodora."

"Who is 'Hilde'?" Theodora asked sardonically. "I thought she was called Jane."

"She is my everything, my saviour," he said, smiling down at the small frame of the woman beside Theodora.

"Jost, we must get to the bridge. They will be waiting for us," Hilde said urgently.

"What ... Barrett? They don't arrive until ten this morning."

"No. They are there now, since six this morning."

Krupp looked up towards the river and Albert Bridge. He felt there was some treachery going on. Barrett had said ten in the morning to him. He took Theodora by the arm. He looked at her hands bound behind her and smiled mischievously. He walked painfully on one side of their captive, and Hilde the other, towards the river wall. "That is the third bit of luck," Krupp seethed. "First, dispatching that idiot Deller—"

"You are a murdering bastard!" Theodora shouted.

"Keep your voice down." Hilde jabbed the handgun into Theodora's ribs painfully.

"What use was he? He was getting in the way and he never fulfilled our bargain."

"And the other two bits of luck?" Theodora asked more quietly. She looked upset; if Krupp did not know her better, he would have said she was close to tears.

"I eluded the police and made good my escape."

"That is not difficult, is it?" Theodora scoffed.

"That is enough from you, Madam Smith," Hilde said. "We must hurry, Jost. Kill her if she holds us back."

"I couldn't do that, Hilde. She was the one to get you out of jail and bring you to me." Krupp had a sudden realisation. "She is also a bargaining tool to keep Ballentine and Freya off our backs!"

As they got to the river wall, they could see the converted E-boat moored up on a pontoon on the other side of the river. It took them twenty minutes to cross the bridge to the steps down to the pontoon.

41

"I don't know what has happened to Theodora and I am worried." Charlotte was standing outside the police station with Alec, desperately looking for the women after being told that they walked out of the police station half an hour before.

"Well, let's drive round to the park and see if they are walking to the flat." Alec held the door of the Jaguar open for Charlotte to get in.

They drove through the park and could not see any women walking together. Alec turned right into Queenstown Road and headed away from the river towards Prince of Wales Drive and his flat. Still no women. There were very few taxis, and the ones they saw had men in the back seat reading newspapers.

They drove up Albert Bridge Road towards the bridge, and Alec stopped and parked just before it. "We should look in the park on foot, on the grass and in amongst the trees."

*

Krupp saw the boat as an old friend. Theodora saw it as a terrible threat to her life, and Jane, or Hilde, saw it as a dirty, rather smelly craft and dreaded having to get on it.

"Major Krupp, I trust you have the files?"

"No, Sir Jason, but we have Madam Theodora Smith instead," said Krupp.

"And this benefits us how?"

Krupp looked bewildered. Sir Jason spotted the newspaper under his arm.

"May I?" he said, holding out his hand for the paper. "And, Miss Baumgartner, any joy your end?" He scanned the newspaper and after reading the headlines, he growled, "I see not." He turned and stepped down into the cabin of the boat and shouted back at John Alderson, who was looking confused by all the new visitors, "We'd better get underway, John."

*

Alec heard the most horrible scream. He thought the scream was saying his name repeatedly, over and over again. He saw Charlotte running towards him, beckoning him to hurry to her.

"Alec, it's them!" she shouted hysterically, pointing at the river.

As Alec came up to Charlotte, she grabbed his hand and pulled him in the direction of the park gates.

"Charlotte, where are they?"

Charlotte was breathing heavily. "They are in a boat, a big boat on the far side of the river. I saw Jason and Krupp talking."

"Come on, then." Alec galloped towards the car and dragged Charlotte behind him. Charlotte then said with a slight sob, "Theodora was getting on the boat with that Gardener woman."

"What? Is Theodora working for—"

"No!" Charlotte shrieked at Alec. "How could you think a thing like that? She's being abducted!"

Alec's Jaguar fired over the bridge and as they turned right onto Chelsea Embankment, cars from both directions squealed to a halt as the Jaguar slewed into the road and parked facing the wrong way.

Charlotte and Alec leapt out of the Jaguar and raced down to Cadogan Pier. But where the boat had been moored was now an empty gap. Charlotte let out a huge sob and fell onto the decking in a heap. Alec looked downriver and saw a boat going very fast for the Thames, passing under Chelsea Bridge.

Alec looked at Charlotte. She was sobbing loudly and uncontrollably. He went over and picked her up off the deck of the pontoon. She shook him off and looked at him, her face red with fury. Alec was taken aback. He was confused. He did not know what was happening to Charlotte other than sheer misery.

"This is all down to you, Alec," she yelled. She straightened up, rolled back her shoulders, strode up to him and slapped his face with such force that he staggered back and almost fell over the edge of the pontoon into the river.

"What do you mean, Charlotte? What can you mean? This is not down to me." He started to lose his temper. "You cannot blame me for what your uncle and Krupp have done."

Charlotte was rooting around in her handbag. To Alec's horror, he realised she was looking for her pistol that was still in his flat. "Charlotte, what are you thinking?"

"I could have killed Krupp. I could have gone to get the Gardener woman and killed her. We could have done more to stop that bastard taking Theodora!

Those files, Ferdi's bloody files, we could have just handed them over to Jason and all this would be—"

She stopped, eyeing Alec with contempt. Alec was full of bewilderment. How could she blame him for all this?

"Come on, Charlotte, we must get the police to stop them."

"They have gone, Alec." She gestured towards Chelsea Bridge.

"Yes, but the police!"

"You bloody stupid man. They will disappear. You will not find them. The damned police will certainly not find them." She looked at Alec. "I am going to find them! And I do not need you to help any more."

Alec was stunned by her anger towards him. He felt pain in his stomach at the thought that she may hate him. "Come on, Charlotte, the car's up there. We can follow them."

Charlotte glared at him. "It is too late, Alec. I do not want your help. I do not want to see you ever again. If they kill Theodora, you'd better hide from me!"

She stormed off the pontoon. Alec stood still, his mouth open in shock, rubbing his left cheek where Charlotte had slapped him. He was deeply hurt. He sat down on the wooden pontoon and looked downriver towards Chelsea Bridge. He spread his legs out and propped himself up by his arms as if he was sunbathing, except there was a cold wind and a threat of snow in the air. He then looked up at the steps up to the road, to where Charlotte had stormed off. His mind was spinning. What was he going to do now?

It was the last time Alec would see Charlotte for many years.

Part Three

42

The Times
16 July 1974, San Carlos de Bariloche, Argentina.

Murdered man in Argentina could be alleged traitor Sir Jason Barrett.
By Philip Bing-Wallace

The body of a man thought to be Sir Jason Barrett was found at a burnt-out lakeside mansion in the Argentinian town of San Carlos de Bariloche, nearly a thousand miles west of Buenos Aires. Sir Jason was 83 and went under the name of Johann Cuartel. Papers discovered by Interpol show compelling evidence that Cuartel was indeed Jason Barrett.

Barrett had been living in the infamous town of San Carlos de Bariloche, known for harbouring notorious Nazis, and enjoying a luxurious lifestyle since his escape from British justice in January 1956. Barrett was wanted for treason and conspiracy to murder.

According to Argentinian police, he was murdered by poison. His body was discovered along with the bodies of his assistant, alleged to be former British Special Branch officer John Alderson, and housekeeper, Brunhilda Baumgartner. Both had been shot in the head. Alderson and Baumgartner were also wanted by British police.

Sir Jason Barrett was a senior figure in the Foreign Office during the war, a Member of Parliament and a junior minister after the war. Controversial files were discovered by The Times that allege Barrett was head of the WASP organisation (War Against Socialist Parties). Using his knowledge of French politics, he had advised the Nazis on the invasion of France and the occupation of Paris in 1940. He had been serving as a senior official in the British embassy in Paris for many years prior to the war. The files also allege that, through his accomplice, Jost Krupp, aka Günther Wolff (an ex-SS major), he was responsible for the deaths of many secret service operatives during the war, and had people killed to keep his identity safe.

Barrett owned *The Sentinel* business newspaper. The right-wing journal was bought by an Australian newspaper magnate in 1955. Barrett was involved with trade in steel to Germany after the war; however, the economy was close to total collapse until the economist Wilhelm Röpke advised the British to stop trading in steel with Barrett and some other industrialists, who were not helping the recovery of Germany's economy. Röpke went on to salvage the German financial rescue.

There is no clue as to who might be responsible for Barrett's death. Suggestions of Mossad or past members of the Forces Françaises de l'Intérieur (FFI – the French underground army, disbanded after the war) have been vehemently refuted. A search for Jost Krupp is under way. He is wanted for questioning in connection with previous murders in Argentina and Great Britain, including the murder of Baron Ferdinand Saumures, a man and a woman at the Saumures's house, and two policemen in Sussex in 1955. Krupp is still at large and is believed to be living in Germany.

The Wiesenthal Trust are helping with the search for Krupp, cooperating with Interpol, and are also looking for Dr Aribert Ferdinand Heim, who was part of the German secret service, the Abwehr, under Admiral Canaris. He is presently at large after evading capture in 1952. Dr Heim conducted medical experiments on Jewish people, mainly women, at Nazi-run concentration camps. According to the evidence obtained by The Times, Dr Heim introduced Barrett to Albert Speer, who was Hitler's closest military adviser just before the war. Some letters, allegedly from Speer to Barrett, have been discovered, thanking Barrett for providing information about the Paris defences and French army positions. There is no evidence that these letters are genuine or indeed from Speer.

We were unable to get any comment about the murder from Barrett's only living relative, Baroness Charlotte Saumures. Krupp was suspected of murdering Lady Saumures's husband, Baron Ferdinand Saumures of Luxembourg, in revenge for supplying evidence against Barrett and Krupp. The baroness gave evidence against Barrett at the Barrett enquiry in 1957.

A Red Notice for the arrest of Heim was issued by Interpol and is still open for both Krupp and Barrett. Barrett's body will be flown back to Britain for formal identification.

43

December 1976, Argentina

In another life, he was called Jost Krupp, then Günther Wolff, but he needed to hide from his Nazi past. For the past eighteen years he had lived in Argentina, as Boris Adalwolff, a German philanthropist.

He was excited. The day before he'd received a letter from an old friend – a girlfriend during the war – who wanted to meet up with him. Where better but at the Alvear Hotel in Buenos Aires, and to see in 1977, the New Year, with her beside him?

He checked himself in the mirror. He looked good in his white tuxedo jacket, black silk bow tie and well-pressed trousers with a satin stripe down the side. He wore a new shirt his sons had bought him, with rather ornate fashionable frills running down either side of the mother-of-pearl buttons, accentuating his corpulent belly.

He had not seen Freya for maybe twenty years. He longed to see her beautiful face, her violet-blue eyes, wonderful body and long golden hair again. His heart quickened. Hopefully she would not have lost her beauty. He, as he looked at his image in the mirror, was not nearly as handsome as he once was. The scar below his left eye was still pretty evident, but it was Freya, after all, who gave it to him. His right leg was not at all good and prevented him being the elegant young man he was during the war. He remembered that it was, again, Freya, who plunged his *SS Schutzstaffel* ceremonial dagger into his leg in 1943 and then shot him with his own pistol, clipping one of his vertebra. His mobility was slow and painful. He was in his sixties and feeling his age. Freya must be late forties or even fifty, Krupp thought. He no longer held any malice for her. He was excited to be close to her again.

"*¿Está bien,* señor Boris?" a lady's voice asked gently from behind him.

"Fine, thank you, Agustina. I am going to meet a very old friend."

Agustina was busy picking up clothes from the floor of the large bedroom. Krupp was speaking German and Agustina only spoke Spanish. "*Sí*, señor Boris," she said automatically and carried on clearing up his mess.

Agustina was middle-aged, with a round pretty face and alluring dark-brown eyes that always seemed to smile. She was one of the few Argentinian servants who was not afraid of her employer. In fact, she was slightly in love with him, and Krupp knew it. He enjoyed flirting with her and being able to grasp various parts of her ample body or drag her onto his lap and bury his head in her bounteous bosom whilst she shrieked with glee, pretending to beat him off. She would giggle shyly and say that she would tell her husband, Louis, who was Krupp's gardener and driver.

"*¿Louis está listo para llevarme a* Buenos Aires?" Krupp asked if Louis was ready to drive him into Buenos Aires, in his poor Spanish, which always made Agustina giggle. "*Sí*, señor," she said.

"*¿Dónde están mis hijos?*" Krupp asked where his twin eighteen-year-old sons were. Erik and Cord Adalwolff were constantly out, when back from their school in America. They were both dark and handsome and could only be told apart by their hair: Erik had lustrous, wavy hair and Cord had thin, straight hair, each preferring the other brother's locks. They had not returned to Argentina from school in California for two years. Both boys had become very American.

"*En la cocina esperando,* señor."

"Waiting in the kitchen for me, are they?" Krupp muttered. "Waiting for their old father to hand out the cash, I suppose."

"*Sí*, señor."

He tweaked his bow tie to perfection.

*

Jost Krupp had arrived in Argentina with a fortune in stolen Nazi gold. He changed the name he was using at the time, Günther Wolff, to Boris Adalwolff, and obtained matching papers, an Argentinian passport and driving licence.

His escape from England in 1955 with his employer, Sir Jason Barrett, was a close thing. He believed he was going to die, which would have been a pity as he would not have been able to spend the vast amount of gold he had stolen. Thank God for the fortuitous meeting with Hilde and Theodora in Battersea Park.

They left London in Jaffery's motorboat. It cost Krupp ten per cent of his gold. The journey to France was fraught with tension. Theodora – now not a useful bargaining tool – was in the way and Barrett was going to put her over the side of the boat. Krupp wanted her to go with him to South America. Hilde Baumgartner wanted her dead. Theodora was kept tied up in the cabin.

As they got into Le Havre in the late afternoon, it was still just light. Theodora was allowed to come up on deck for some fresh air. Her hands were untied, and she was told to sit on the cabin roof. Alderson was at the capstan, steering the boat down the narrow estuary. As the estuary narrowed into the river Seine, Theodora saw, cruising towards them, a large coastguard launch. Nobody else had noticed, as they were all discussing what was to become of her. Theodora stepped out of her shoes and quickly went up to the bows of the boat. Alderson saw her and pointed a pistol at her.

"Stop right there, Madam Theodora!" he shouted. Jason Barrett looked up from a chart, Krupp scampered up from the cabin with Hilde.

"Don't shoot her, John," shouted Barrett. "Coastguard ahead."

"I will bear away and lose them, sir," said Alderson.

As he turned the wheel, Theodora emitted a terrifying scream, and sprang off the bow into the water as it turned. The coastguard launch was only fifty metres away and saw Theodora go over. "What shall I do, Sir Jason?" Alderson said with alarm.

"You fools!" said Krupp. He took Alderson's pistol out of his hand, smashed his left elbow into Alderson's face and mounted the capstan block. The boat was still turning. He fired all remaining eight bullets in Theodora's direction.

"Will you desist, Krupp?" Barrett yelled over the shots. He picked up Alderson and pulled Krupp off the capstan block with surprising strength. "Mr Alderson, get this craft turned about. We'd better find fuel in Cherbourg or Roscoff. We must be in La Coruña by tomorrow evening."

Theodora swam to a sandbank and was picked up by the coastguard launch. The E-boat went back out to sea at great speed.

*

The group of fugitives went over to Florida on a steamer from the Spanish port of La Coruña, then to South America in Barrett's yacht. Krupp landed up first in Santiago Vázquez, near Montevideo in Uruguay, and then, after a feeling that he had been spotted, Krupp moved to La Plata near Buenos Aires, Argentina.

He met Idoya when he was surveying her house in La Plata in view of buying it. She was a tall, elegant Argentinian woman who spoke fluent German and had many sympathies with the Nazis. She was a devout Protestant Christian in a mainly Catholic country.

She saw Jost Krupp, an ex-major in the SS, as a romantic figure, injured in the war doing heroic deeds. He had exaggerated his injuries to the extent that she admired and loved him even more. He was more interested in her lavish house overlooking Plaza Moreno and the La Plata cathedral, in a suburb of Buenos Aires. There was a good view of everything from the front of the house and a small service road and car parking at the back for easy escape.

Idoya satisfied Krupp's carnal appetites that had been starved for many years. Hilde Baumgartner had decided to remain with Barrett rather than go with Krupp. In fact, Krupp was convinced Barrett, Alderson and Baumgartner had informed the authorities of his whereabouts in Uruguay.

Idoya gave Krupp twin sons in 1958 and they were his pride and joy – as they were for Idoya. However, when they were ten years of age, it was apparent their father was training them into ways that upset and troubled Idoya. Krupp was educating them in the world of murder and selling arms. He had a lucrative business of killing people for money – lots of money. His charismatic sons would charm themselves into a target household, by offering to do work or as charity workers, like boy scouts, and allow Krupp to enter the house or office and murder whoever his client desired dead. There was plenty of work in Argentina and Uruguay, plenty of people the Nazis, and the arms dealers, wanted dead, and the charming, unthreatening, fat old cripple with very little hair and an amiable smile was easy not to notice.

In 1960, Adolph Eichman was kidnapped from his Buenos Aires home by the Israelis and transported back to Israel for trial. This sparked alarm within the clandestine German Nazi community. Krupp knew, however, he was not that important in the search for Nazis by the Israelis. He was technically still dead, despite his brief recorded appearance in England in the nineteen fifties. As far as he knew, the British authorities were still looking for Günther Wolff.

*

In 1974, Krupp received a letter posted to him care of the Alvear Hotel, Buenos Aires. The envelope was addressed to Señor Boris Adalwolff and had a red wax seal of the Argentinian ex-president Juan Perón. It was handed to him with reverential ceremony in the privacy of the hotel manager's private meeting room.

Krupp cracked the seal, and with trepidation, opened it to find a second envelope. The second envelope contained a letter, signed by a man Krupp had never heard of, Damian von Crump. The letterhead bore the emblem of the WASP organisation. The letter was accompanied by a banker's draft for ten thousand US dollars. To Krupp's consternation, the inner envelope was addressed to SS Major Jost Krupp:

Dear Major Krupp,

We would appreciate your services to eliminate the former Director General of WASP, Jason Barrett.

You will find, attached, all details of his present whereabouts, as well as details of the security and other members of the household at his residence. There are two other people associated with Barrett that need to be silenced: John Alderson and Brunhilda Baumgartner. Barrett's house is to be thoroughly searched for any and all documentation associated with WASP. These documents must be sent to us. Please use the postage-paid addressed envelopes enclosed. You can take any compensatory valuables you may consider due to you from Mr Barrett's house.

Mr Barrett has become a liability and we have recently understood that he is willing to talk to the authorities about the role he played in WASP, before and during the last war. He is also willing to name his colleagues in the organisation, which includes you. This cannot be tolerated. No trace of WASP should be left to be found by other parties.

You must not leave any evidence of your involvement, or who commissioned your services. Please leave the enclosed newspaper articles on Jason Barrett's body.

I am sure we can rely on your total discretion and secrecy. I trust the enclosed banker's order will cover any inconveniences. The money will be released to you after you have succeeded in your task.

Please destroy this document at your nearest opportunity.

Yours sincerely,

Damian von Crump
Assistant to the Director General, WASP

44

Erik and Cord Adalwolff's practical education started in 1974. Krupp had managed to inveigle his twin sons into the household of Jason Barrett, now known as Señor Cuartel. Krupp's sons had charmed their way into redecorating Barrett's mansion. They offered not only their skills in design, but also they would paint and redesign the guest wing of the house.

"Gentlemen … *caballeros*," Señora Baumgartner said jauntily. She appeared beside Erik's stepladder and smiled up at him. "Señor Cuartel would like to meet you."

Erik looked at his brother, who was sanding down a window frame.

"For what reason, señora?" Cord asked.

"He enjoys meeting people."

"He enjoys meeting his workmen?" Erik said.

"Yes," she said plainly. "Come now to the library for some coffee."

"We must wash up first," Erik said, climbing down the stepladder, showing the señora his hands covered in paint.

"Very well, but be quick. Meet me at the library door."

"Why does he want to see us, brother?" Cord asked as he washed his hands.

"I don't know, but this may give us the opportunity to finish him off. Get the poison."

Erik went to his bag. He removed two syringes and put one into a special holder in his boot. Cord took the other and did the same.

The brothers found the library door, but no señora. Erik knocked. "Enter," came a gruff reply. Cord opened the door to see an elderly white-haired gentleman sitting at his desk, his eyes cast down onto his writing. Cord flashed a look at his brother. Erik went back to the office door and closed and bolted it. At the sound of the bolt being closed, Señor Cuartel looked up. He opened his mouth to say something when Erik went swiftly round the back of his chair and clamped his hand over the old man's mouth, holding his head against his chest. Cord took out the syringe from his boot, went over to the now struggling old man, and plunged the needle into his thigh. The man stopped moving momentarily, and then carried on more frantically, his muted cries getting louder. Erik regarded his watch – this should only take thirty seconds to work.

Señor Cuartel's cries and his struggles gradually subsided. Cord released his grasp of the señor's mouth. He looked at the old man's face; it had turned white and his eyes had nearly completely rolled up into his head. Foam started to form around his lips.

"Get the señora, Cord, Señor Cuartel seems to be ill." Erik felt a huge sense of achievement and had to stifle a guffaw, as did Cord as he went to the door, unbolted it quietly and opened it to find Señora Baumgartner just outside. She swung round when the door opened. She looked furious. Cord adjusted his expression to one of distress. "Señora! Quick, something has happened to the old man."

"John!" the señora yelled in a near scream as she rushed to her employer. "What did you do to him?"

"Nothing, señora." Erik was acting as though close to tears. Cord was most impressed. "We knocked, he said to enter, we went in, he told us to close the door, and he then stood up, held his stomach—"

"And his head," interrupted Cord, remembering the symptoms they had prepared.

"And his head, and fell back in his chair."

"What's happened?" The man who'd interviewed the brothers entered the room. He spoke in English. The señora then told the man something in English – the word "ambulance" was used. Erik looked at his brother with a fleeting expression of delight.

"You two will go back to your work," the man shouted at the brothers. "I will deal with you once we have treated Señor Cuartel."

"Is he going to be all right, señor?" Cord asked with great concern.

"He'd better be, for your sakes!"

Erik pulled his brother away before Cord could say any more. They sauntered back to the other end of the house, into the room they were preparing to decorate. Within twenty minutes, they heard an ambulance siren draw up to the front of the house. The brothers went to the front door to greet their father. The man came out of the library, cast an annoyed eye at the brothers and went to their father, who was dressed in a white coat carrying a bag. The man recognised their father and was about to say something when Krupp took out a silenced pistol from the bag and shot the man in the head.

"Where is Baumgartner, boy?" he hissed at Erik.

Erik jerked a thumb at the library door. "In there, Father."

"Good boys!" He glanced at Cord and gave them both silenced pistols. "Go and finish off any servants. I will deal with Hilde."

Krupp limped into the library. Jason Barrett was on the floor, foaming at the mouth, a small amount of movement in his arms. Hilde was kneeling beside him. She looked back but must have only glanced at the white coat. "Quickly, doctor, he is only just alive. I don't know—" Krupp fired a bullet into Barrett's skull. Hilde screamed as blood splattered her face. She turned to look at the assailant. "Jost!"

"Hello, Hilde. Had you hoped to think me dead?" Hilde gaped. Her eyes went from Krupp's face to the pistol and back again. She was now sitting on the floor. "I know it was you who informed on me to the Uruguayan authorities. Did our moments together in Bordeaux mean nothing to you?"

Her expression changed from astonishment to resignation in moments. She was, after all, a highly skilled spy for the Nazi secret service – the SD. "I am not on my own here, Jost, there are guards everywhere. And there are two men in the house who—"

"My handsome sons, you mean, Cord and Erik?" Her shoulders dropped. "Your guards know that your master is ill – that is why I am here with the ambulance."

"What are you going to do with me, Jost?" She began to stand up but Krupp took a step back and waved her down with the barrel of the pistol.

"With regret, my dear, I am going to have to shoot you. Orders."

"Whose orders?"

"It came from the new director general of WASP."

"WASP does not exist any more, Jost. You know that. You were recruited by Sir Jason, released from prison early, solely to ensure all references to WASP were extinguished. Which you failed at. So, who are you working for?"

Krupp's temper was gradually rising. "We had a good time together, Hilde. I will remember you as you were back then. Goodbye." He raised the pistol. "Don't look at me!"

"No wait, wait, wait—" The silenced pistol fired twice to the heart and when she fell back onto the floor, Krupp put a bullet into her head. He looked down at her pretty face. She was not quite as beautiful as Freya, but she was great fun.

It took thirty minutes to go through the whole house, inch by inch. They filled the ambulance with everything of value. Krupp could not find anything about WASP in the library or in Jason Barrett's bedroom. He discovered a photograph of John Alderson embracing Hilde fondly, taken in a garden somewhere. A brief rush of jealousy unreasonably surged within him. He stamped on the picture and placed the broken bits on an incendiary bomb, setting the time for thirty minutes, as he had done with five other bombs scattered about the house.

"Father, one of the guards is approaching the front door. What should I do?"

"Let him in, Cord. I will get rid of him. We must go now anyway. The house is set to go up in twenty-eight minutes."

The guard was let in. When he saw Alderson dead on the floor, he reached for his sidearm, but it was too late. He was silenced instantly with a bullet to the head.

The ambulance, lights and siren blazing, sped through the gates, hastily opened by the remaining guards.

From the contents of the safe – which included some of the gold Krupp had paid Barrett for helping him escape from London – and the valuables in the house, Krupp had amassed a sizeable amount of money – money used to send the boys to America, where both were enrolled in the University of California.

Idoya was distraught at what had happened to her sons, and that she would only see them once a year, at Christmas. She pleaded with Krupp to allow her to leave him and stay with her sister in California, so she could see them. When he refused, Krupp told Erik and Cord their mother had committed suicide by gassing herself in the oven. He did not tell them that he encouraged her suicide with force.

Krupp took the banker's order to his bank. He saw, to his extreme annoyance, the cheque was payable to "Herr Jost Krupp", not to "cash". How had he not seen this before? He was not, after all, able to take his fee, but he felt somewhat compensated by the booty he had gathered from Jason Barrett's house.

*

"Where are you going tonight, Father?" the twins asked, trying to conceal their amusement at his preening in front of the mirror.

"I am going to meet a lady," he said with undisguised pride.

"You know Agustina does not speak any German?" Erik said, and both boys howled with laughter.

"I am going to meet a girl, or should I say a lady: a baroness, in fact. She was once my girlfriend."

"You mean Freya?" They both looked astonished. "But we thought you wanted to kill her."

Krupp gazed thoughtfully and proudly at his handsome sons. Both brothers had square jaws, high foreheads, and both stood well over their father at one point nine metres. The twins had bodies of sportsmen, broad shoulders and thin hips, with muscular arms.

He wanted to change the subject.

"And what are you boys doing tonight to see the year in?"

"We are going into town later, to find some women. Bet you would like to join us rather than catch up with some old girlfriend," Erik said.

"Well I am going to meet a goddess!" Krupp said proudly.

"Surely she will be old and wrinkled, like you, Father," Cord teased. Krupp thought for a moment. He must not expect Freya to be the vision she was twenty years ago. But he was sure she would not be fat and ugly like him. His heart ached. He imagined the disappointment on her face when she saw him.

"No," Krupp said quietly, thinking that he probably did not want to meet her after all. "No, she will still be a goddess, I reckon." He felt a tug in his stomach of worry about his inadequacy – something he had seldom, if ever, sensed.

He turned away from his boys and limped down the hallway into the large drawing room, went over to the drinks tray, and poured himself a drink. As he drained the schnapps, he glimpsed himself in the large fireplace mirror.

"Curse it," he said angrily. "It is not as if I am going to marry the bitch." He stroked the scar under his right eye. "*She* did this, after all."

"But will you be safe, Father?" The boys followed him into the drawing room. "What if she is Mossad or British Secret Service, or even the Policía Federal?"

"That is why I am meeting her in a public place – lots of people. Louis will be out back if there is trouble. And I will be armed." He patted a small shoulder holster under his white tuxedo.

"Louis will be out back *where*, Father?" Cord asked with an element of anger. "We worry about you, and this is the first time we've known you to be reckless."

"Don't worry, boy. We have been pretty quiet lately, and the hotel knows me. I'll be OK." Nothing was going to prevent him seeing the only woman he truly loved, and possibly the most beautiful woman he had ever seen. Even though she tried to kill him, he still felt she loved him.

Louis coughed at the door to the drawing room. "*¿Está listo*, señor?"

"Yes, ready, Louis." He picked a silver-topped ebony stick out of the umbrella stand, replacing it for the plain brown cane he used every day. He put on his dark glasses. He wore dark glasses all the time when he was out of the house, a kind of disguise, he supposed, but it also gave him an air of menace – plus they were quite big and covered up most of the scar below his eye.

He went out into the dark, damp, humid evening and into the waiting black Mercedes, still thinking of Freya and what she would look like, what she would be wearing. Would Theodora be with her? Theodora was the same age as him, so could even be dead. The authoritarian Turkish whore did, after all, introduce Krupp to Freya in 1940 when he first arrived in Paris during the occupation. Theodora was an old friend from Berlin, so it would be nice to see her, but not now.

However, Theodora might still be angry about being abducted by him and Hilde in London twenty years previously – a long time ago.

*

It was ten o'clock when he arrived at the Alvear Hotel, in Recoleta, the elegant part of Buenos Aires, full of opulent restaurants and the best hotels. Krupp loved the hotel and he spent a lot of money there, using it as a kind of meeting room and for entertaining clients.

Krupp climbed the sweep of steps, challenging his leg and back, up to the gold and glass doors that were whisked open by a cheery liveried doorman with a huge black moustache.

"*Wir kommen, Herr Adalwolff*," he said in his best German. Krupp was always impressed by the memory of doormen. He tipped the doorman well, and then realised why they memorise names of their regular customers.

He limped into the Champagne Bar, a room of lavish gold and marble walls and a white marble floor with dark-green and gold patterned rugs. The garish reproduction Louis Quinze ornate scarlet and gold chairs and sofas clustered around low glass-topped tables. The lights were dim; cigarette smoke hovered in the air and swirled away when a waiter scampered past with a tray at high port, expertly balanced on his fingertips.

"Where is everybody?" Krupp asked the waiter. "There are not many people in the bar."

"They are mostly in the ballroom, Señor Adalwolff, listening to the new opera singer, Raúl Giménez. Many people there, all celebrating the arrival of another new year. Big party!"

Krupp sat on an opulent Louis Quinze sofa at the far end of the room, the furthest point from the bar entrance, so he could see Freya's arrival. It would give him time to compose himself. He refused a drink but ordered a cigar. He selected a thick cigar from a silver cigar case lined in cedar wood, and lit it from the taper the waiter produced. He sat in anticipation. He suddenly thought that she may be here already, and waved the waiter impatiently away, standing to look more closely around the room. He felt a bolt of pain in his back and his damaged leg after getting up so quickly. She was not there. He sat again, took a deep draw on his cigar, and closed his eyes until the pain in his back subsided.

He wondered if he should pop a nitro-glycerine heart tablet under his tongue just in case his heart should race and he felt faint. But he decided his heart would have to cope.

Whilst waiting, he began to feel agitated. He changed his mind and ordered a Martini to settle his nerves. How *did* Freya find him? he wondered. He took security very seriously. Now his sons spent most of the year at the University of California he went out more. He may have been spotted by one of Freya's friends, but that seemed unlikely. Krupp was becoming uneasy. Was this a trap? The invitation had been left at the hotel, just like the letter from the director general of WASP. Perhaps she was part of WASP; her uncle was head of WASP, after all. Why, he wondered, was he not more worried about being discovered? It was the thought of seeing her again, he supposed. He could see why his sons were concerned. He stroked his tuxedo, feeling the reassuring lump of his pistol.

It was now eleven thirty, the time he had arranged to meet Freya. He sat up straight on the sofa and took off his dark glasses. He fiddled with his tie and brushed down the ruffles on the front of his shirt, regretting putting on such a ridiculous garment. It was meant to be "modern", his boys assured him. He swiped back his thin grey and black hair, flattening it over his head, and did up the middle button of his tuxedo, ensuring the pistol holster did not show.

*

"Are you going to be OK about doing this?" the older woman whispered.

"We have practised enough. Are you sure that is him? He seems so old and fat – harmless." The younger woman sounded calm and collected.

The man who the older woman had pointed out through the bevelled glass in the door was rotund in his white evening tuxedo and black bow tie. He had a smear of dark hair on top of his head and a band of greasy dark hair above his ears. A scar from his right eye ran down to a thin moustache.

"He is only a few years older than I. And, believe me, he is certainly not harmless." She stroked the younger woman on the cheek, looking into her large smoky-blue eyes. Then she stood back from her to check her shimmering gold halterneck evening gown and long white kid gloves that covered her arms to well over her elbows. The dress fitted well and was producing the effect she desired. She felt a surge of pride. "Your mother wore a dress just like that twenty-five years ago, to great effect. You look lovely." The older woman kissed the younger on the cheek with deep affection.

"I am going into the bar now," the younger woman said. "I will meet you outside afterwards."

"You don't want me to stay here?" The older woman was anxious.

"He may see you. Anyway, it will make me nervous. I don't want you to watch me." She gave the older woman a kiss on the cheek, turned slowly and went into the bar.

45

The door to the bar opened. Krupp momentarily held his breath as he saw a woman walk slowly in. It was not Freya. He exhaled. However, the young woman was, incredibly, even more beautiful than Freya. She could not be older than twenty. Disappointed, he relaxed and watched this vision go up to the bar and ask a question of the barman.

She turned and walked towards Krupp. She moved like smoke from the end of a cigarette in a still room, languorous, smooth. Her beauty stopped the conversation of the few people she walked past. Eyes of envy, lust, admiration, longing, followed her every move as she glided through the sumptuously furnished, dimly lit Champagne Bar. Krupp realised she was moving through the room deliberately towards him. He held his breath again as she approached him. His heart thumped against his lungs, making it hard to breathe out. Krupp sat up and he gulped when she saw him and looked straight into his eyes. He felt a tingle up his spine as she seemed to float, slowly, like a ghostly spirit between the tables. He wondered if she was real or a spectre. This could not possibly be Freya, he thought, and yet there was something …

She arrived at the table. She relaxed a knee. Their eyes met, a small smile on her lips. Krupp suddenly remembered his manners and stood, hauling himself up with the aid of his stick and the arm of the sofa. It could not have been an elegant move, he thought with annoyance. He should have remained seated.

"May I join you?" she said in perfect German.

"Yes, of course," Krupp whispered, surprised his voice was not quite working.

Her long gold dress shimmered like the sinking evening sun over a tranquil lake, hugging the shape of her slender body. It took Krupp back to a superb time at Le Palais in Paris during the war. The skin of her naked back and shoulders as she turned to sit down seemed to glow, smooth and soft, a cascade of auburn hair falling down to her shoulder-blades. The only jewellery she wore was an ugly silver cross with a long, thin shaft and a short cross-piece, dangling on a delicate silver chain. Krupp thought he had seen this cross before. It hung in the V of her plunging neckline.

They sat on the plush red-and-gold French-style sofa, and to Krupp's amazement and delight, she sat close to him, only her patent leather black handbag between them. A breath of scent, lily of the valley, swept over his senses, again taking him back to Paris in 1941. He tried desperately not to let out a long, contented sigh. The piano player took his seat and started to play.

"Champagne?" he asked, snapping his fingers at a waiter.

"Very dry Martini," she said, keeping her eyes on his, a charming smile for a "please". He hardly looked away at the waiter to give his order for two dry Martinis.

They said nothing to each other until the cocktails arrived. She looked around the virtually empty bar, allowing him to cast a lingering gaze at her, from her beautiful open face and lustrous hair down to the outline of her long thighs beneath her gold dress.

The cocktails were set down on the low glass-top table, on paper coasters, in front of them. Her dress tantalisingly revealed a lot more of her cleavage as she leant towards the table to pick up the drinks. She handed one to him. She clinked the glasses together and then drained the Martini, including the lemon twist. She placed her empty glass on the table and, looking deep into his transfixed eyes, pulled out the lemon twist from between her lips, pursing her lips seductively together. He gulped his Martini down. He felt a small film of sweat start to form on his brow. He set down his glass onto the table.

He could not take his eyes off this vision beside him. He opened his mouth to speak. She placed her handbag to the other side of her and slid even closer to him. She leant towards him, her cheek only inches from his lips. She raised an elegant, gloved forefinger and placed it softly on his lips. He was lost in her eyes as she moved closer to him, pressing her body against his, relaxing him, beguiling him. He could feel her breasts against the side of his chest. The excitement of her closeness made him take a long intake of breath. He smiled under her light touch on his lips, a feeling of elation flowing through his body.

She came up very close to him. He thought she was going to kiss his cheek, but instead she whispered in his ear; a tingle went all over him as he could feel her breath. "You are about to die, Jost, a painful, but swift death.

Something you don't deserve." He was struck with horror. He looked at the woman, his eyes blinking rapidly. She had a lascivious smile.

His back suddenly arched in a spasm of pain. She seemed to be nearly on top of him, holding him down, her hand gripping harder across his face. He struggled to breathe. A burning sensation rose from his stomach to his throat. He stared into her eyes as a veil of darkness descended.

After she closed his vacant eyes, Alice took a slow look around the room. They had not been noticed. The waiting staff were hovering around the bar at the other end of the room, waiting for the chimes of the New Year to sound. She put his cocktail glass into her handbag and took out a thick vermillion envelope and placed it into the dead man's hands. She kissed him on his cheek, leaving a red lipstick print. She stood and walked slowly out of the bar.

*

Alice got into the back of the large limousine. The streets were full of people celebrating the New Year. "Is he dead?" Alice was asked in an excited whisper.

"Yes, Mama. Theodora pointed him out to me. There is no doubt."

It was the first of January 1977 and Charlotte sat proudly in the back of the Chrysler Imperial limousine. She put her arms around her daughter and squeezed her. She winked at Theodora, who had a large grin. "At last. We are rid of him. Rid of all of them."

Theodora turned, slid open the partition window and spoke to the driver. "Back to Fray Bentos, please, driver."

It had taken over four hours to drive from Fray Bentos docks, in Uruguay, to the Alvear Hotel in central Buenos Aires. Because it was New Year's Eve, the guards on the Argentinian side of the Puente Libertador General San Martín bridge were just waving the very small number of cars through. Coming back there was no traffic or border guards on the bridge – as they'd suspected. The streets of Fray Bentos were still alive with drunk people at four o'clock in the morning.

On the yacht, *The Baroness*, they – Charlotte, Theodora and Charlotte's daughter, Alice – all sat in the top lounge; it was a bit drizzly to sit out on the deck.

The Baroness was an elegant, ocean-going yacht belonging to Charlotte's yacht charter company, acquired from her uncle's estate when he disappeared. The yacht had a royal-blue seventy-metre hull. There were six en-suite staterooms and a dining room that could cater for twenty-six guests. A staff of eight, including Captain Auguste and chef Jonathan, looked after them. This was the first time Charlotte had used the yacht; it was normally chartered out.

"How are you doing, darling?" Theodora asked Alice, with as much concern as she could muster. Alice was sitting close to her mother, both Alice's hands in Charlotte's cold hands, Charlotte's thumb stroking the top of her daughter's fingers.

"Fine, thanks," Alice said softly. "I have never seen a person die. All the anger I had for Krupp, and what he did to our family, has evaporated, it seems."

Theodora stood, steadying herself as the yacht hit a wave. "Well it is done now, and nobody will be the wiser," she said, going to the drinks cabinet. "Why could we not fly to Buenos Aires, for heaven's sake?" Theodora was not a natural sailor.

"You know why, Theodora. We did not want to have any evidence of us being in Buenos Aires," said Charlotte. "That is why we docked in Fray Bentos in Uruguay and went over the bridge down to Buenos Aires—" Charlotte started to cough. Alice sat up and held her mother in her arms until the coughing subsided. "May I have a brandy, Theodora?"

"Yes, darling," Theodora said with an anxious look. She was the only one who knew Charlotte was dying. Charlotte did not want Alice to know. Alice thought her illness was temporary.

Alice had volunteered to poison Krupp instead of her mother, so as not to make Charlotte's condition worse. They trained for every possible scenario – if they were at a restaurant, the back of a car with a driver, or if there were a third person in the Champagne Bar with Krupp. Krupp on his own in a near-deserted bar was what they'd all hoped for, and got.

Captain Auguste had paid a docking fee in US dollars cash, which the junior harbour master pocketed, taking no mooring details of *The Baroness*. They slipped out of the port unnoticed. A lively Atlantic crossing to Le Havre followed, via a stop for two days in Madeira.

*

It was not until the following early morning, once the New Year had been ushered in and people were wandering off to bed, that the Champagne Bar manager tried to awake Herr Adalwolff. It appeared this elderly customer had too much to drink and was out cold, with the evidence of a female encounter on his cheek and a strange smile on his face. So, they covered him with a blanket and informed the concierge that Herr Adalwolff would be sleeping it off in the Champagne Bar and not to bother him.

*

Once back home at Nineteen Avenue Foch in Paris, the whole incident was not spoken of again, until Thomas Henkel arrived to collect his fee.

Thomas Henkel was short, fair-haired, with a face that looked younger than his forty-three years. He was, apart from his five-foot-eight stature, nondescript, which was an advantage for a private investigator. He had been hired by Theodora to track down Jason Barrett and Jost Krupp. He had located both.

"I think you should know that Günther Wolff, aka Boris Adalwolff, married soon after he arrived in Argentina." Henkel stood stiffly at attention before Theodora in the study, raising his eyes from the file to see if there was any reaction from her. Theodora kept an enigmatic look of mild interest on her face. "His wife, Idoya, committed suicide in 1973—"

"Tch – I should think he stuffed her in the oven himself or pulled the trigger," Theodora scorned.

Henkel resumed. "... leaving twin sons, Cord and Erik Adalwolff. They are eighteen years old and live in California."

This time there was a reaction from Theodora. "That makes it a bit worrying," she said. "Do we know anything about these boys?"

"No, ma'am, not much. They did not seem very close to their father," said the ex-Pinkerton detective.

Theodora sat back in her desk chair, concerned. Henkel was from New York; he was abrupt and to the point – precisely what Theodora liked about him.

"I would be grateful, Mr Henkel, if you would find out all about these Krupp or Adalwolff brothers."

"Very good, ma'am, I will get on to it immediately."

"Thank you, Mr Henkel. Are those the documents Krupp sent you about WASP?"

"Yes, ma'am, from Barrett's house. Here is the uncashed money order."

"Very good, Henkel. You said he would probably not immediately spot that the money order was put in his Nazi name. That was a good plan."

"Thank you, Madam Theodora. I note that news of Krupp's death has been in the papers only recently, two weeks after his ... demise."

"I know. At least the world will know of all his offences and his war crimes, thanks to the file left beside his body. I wonder who killed Krupp?" Theodora said with a smirk hidden from Henkel as she lowered her eyes.

"Indeed, ma'am."

"Then thank you, Mr Henkel. I will enjoy reading your report."

Henkel hesitated. "Yes, ma'am, but would you like me to read about my findings on—?"

"No, thank you, Mr Henkel. I must attend to the baroness now. Thank you again." Henkel looked disappointed. Theodora stood, ending the meeting.

Henkel left the thick file on the desk, in front of Theodora.

"I will keep you informed, ma'am. I'll get back to you as soon as possible. My fee note receipt is in the file for your records."

Theodora handed Henkel an envelope. He took it and placed it into the inside pocket of his plain grey suit. "Thank you, ma'am." He turned and walked out of the study.

46

News of Jason Barrett's murder in 1974 came as no surprise to Alec Ballentine. He and Philip Bing-Wallace had written a book about Jason Barrett and the WASP conspiracy after his death was reported, using information from files sent anonymously to Alec. The book was called *The Wasp Trap*. It was a huge success and had two reprints. However, there was controversy over whether there was such an organisation called WASP, and the people named, who were still living, contested the book's authenticity, pointing out it was the views of just one man. As a result, it became one of the biggest sellers of the year.

After writing two other books about the SOE and MI6 during the war, Alec became a very successful writer of historical drama – real historical drama. He retired from journalism and wrote several successful novels, one of which was made into a film starring his brother, Adam Ballentine.

His good friend and compatriot, Philip Bing-Wallace, retired. He enjoyed ill health – he frequently went to the doctor complaining of something and was upset when the doctors said he was perfectly fit. Alec and Bing-Wallace met up once a month in El Vino in Fleet Street. Bing-Wallace had always wanted to paint and was now concentrating on his art.

But success for Alec came at a huge cost. He thought Charlotte must have been convinced he was responsible for the death of Franz-Joseph Deller and the abduction of Theodora, that it was his fault that Sir Jason got away. Moreover, he had, yet again, allowed Jost Krupp to vanish without answering for the murders of Ferdi, Christina and Bernard.

Krupp was never caught or prosecuted for his awful war crimes, or the murder of Christina's husband, Bo, and all the people he tortured and executed during the war in Avenue Foch, Drancy prison and in South-West France. And, as it transpired, the atrocities at Oradour-sur-Glane. Krupp was identified as one of the officers on that fateful day by one of the very few survivors of the massacre, eight-year-old Roger Godfrin.

Alec was bewildered and devastated when Charlotte walked off, leaving him on the Cadogan Pier in Chelsea, never to see or contact him again – until June 1977, over twenty years later.

Alec stood on the driveway to Nineteen Avenue Foch, looking at the restored house. There was a large brass plaque on the high gate pillar, saying *"Musée des Contrefaçons et Falsifications"* – the Museum of Fakes and Forgeries. A sliding sign was in the *Fermé* position. It was a breathless, warm, sunny June day, and Paris could not be prettier.

He had never seen the original building at Nineteen Avenue Foch, but he was sure it would have been a lot more sophisticated. The house had been badly and unsympathetically rebuilt after the bombing during the war. The centre of the house was not the same style or quality as the two wings either side of the front porch. Alec was surprised.

He stood at the tall ornate iron gates. They were open to a light gravel driveway. The drive went up to a modern porch, with three large blank windows either side of the new glass double doors of the porch. The porch had a plain slate roof. There were no pillars, no ornate stonework. There was a vast multi-paned arched window above the new porch that dominated the front of the new section of the house.

Alec strode up to the porch doors. He checked his reflection – pink-and-white striped shirt with a plain blue tie beneath his dark-blue double-breasted blazer, cavalry twill trousers with sharp creases, and shiny chestnut-coloured brogues. He worried about the military bearing he was portraying; perhaps he should have dressed less formally. He quickly removed the tie and undid his top button. He still, he considered, could cut a dash, even in his sixties. What was left of his hair was cut very short.

The invitation from Charlotte's secretary in his breast pocket was for one thirty – it was one twenty-eight. He pulled the bell pull and a clanging ring could be heard inside. He felt a pang of déjà vu from twenty years ago, when he stood outside Burton Park Place.

A butler in full morning clothes and white gloves came to the door.

"Oui, monsieur?" he said as he opened the door. His mouth smiled, but his eyes showed something resembling contempt.

"I am Alec Ballentine. I have an appointment to see Lady Saumures."

"Thank you, Mr Ballentine," the butler said in heavily accented English – surprisingly, not French but a German accent. "You are expected. Please, would you like to wait in the library? This way, please." The butler allowed Alec to step through into a huge hallway, not only lit by the window over the porch but also a domed skylight.

Paintings hung on magnolia walls. Every painting had a two-inch mustard-yellow *C* painted in the bottom right-hand corner.

The butler opened the library door and Alec went into a grand panelled room with floor-to-ceiling bookcases on two of the walls. The three newly installed windows to the front of the house allowed plenty of light to flood in. The floor was scattered with Persian rugs and dark-brown leather sofas and chairs. The room smelt of age, a mixture of cedar wood and cigar smoke.

Alec examined some of the books on the shelves. He heard one of the doors, disguised as a bookcase, open, and Charlotte walked in. Alec inhaled shakily on seeing her.

Theodora walked quickly up to Alec with a warm smile, her arms open in greeting. She had hardly aged, although once she was up close, he could see she was heavily made up.

"Alec, darling, it has been far too long." Theodora pecked him on each cheek, then stood aside and said, "And here is Charlotte for you."

Charlotte was older, her hair shorter, cut just above her shoulders, lighter in colour and less lustrous. She was still a beautiful woman and Alec's heart ached when he saw her. It was unfair that after all these years she could possibly look even more beautiful. There were wrinkles at the corners of her eyes and around her lips, and she looked a little tired. She was thin, but still elegantly balletic.

"Hello, Alec." She was demure, possibly shy? Alec could not work out what it was. She couldn't still be holding a grudge, could she?

"Hello, Charlotte, are you well?"

She offered a small smile, hesitated and said, "Yes, I suppose so, thank you." An odd response, Alec thought.

There was an awkward silence. Charlotte kept her eyes on a spot on the carpet.

Alec turned to Theodora. "How did you escape Barrett and Krupp?" Alec wondered if he should have raised the subject so soon after his arrival.

"You must have known, Alec."

"Not in detail."

"It was in Le Havre. I was not well in the boat – I got very seasick and Krupp undid my hands so I could drink water." Theodora coughed slightly, giving a nervous glance at Charlotte. "As we entered Le Havre, I asked to go up on the deck for fresh air. I saw a coastguard patrol boat going past, so I threw myself overboard. I was rescued by the coastguard off a sandbank."

"What happened to the rest of them?" Alec asked.

"They just shot off, back out to sea. By the time I was rescued, they had long gone. Don't know where, but I believe just down the coast."

"We found out a few years later that they were in Argentina," Charlotte said. She was unemotional. "I had hired people to keep an eye on them. Jason died, you know."

"Yes, I did know; we wrote a book …"

"Yes, well." Charlotte crossed to the windows looking out onto Avenue Foch. She wore a silk powder-blue dress and a dark-blue cashmere cardigan over her shoulders. "You will also know that Krupp was … died in Buenos Aires," she said.

"Yes, I read about that – quite a comprehensive file about him was found on his body."

Charlotte said, "I don't know what happened to the others, Jane Gardener and John Alderson. Probably raising children and alpacas somewhere."

Alec said a little nervously, "They died along with Jason."

Charlotte dropped her head. She was trying to say something, Alec thought. He was about to ask what it was. "Yes, they are all dead," she said emphatically, watching the birds through the window. "We made sure of that." Alec wondered what she could possibly mean by that. He wanted to ask but did not have the courage.

Charlotte was plainly uncomfortable about Alec being there. He was anxious about her. She looked ill.

"Come on, darlings, let's join the others," Theodora said happily. She took Alec by the arm and guided him into the hall, past the stairs under the gallery landing and into the drawing room – the *salle de séjour*. The windows, all new with modern metal frames, were open to the great gardens beyond. The summer flowers were doing very well. A soft warm breeze kept the large room cool and scented with flowers and mown grass.

As they entered the room, two people stood and looked at Alec with curiosity.

"Alec." Charlotte walked over to a thin, handsome young man with lots of dark wavy hair. He looked smilingly at Alec, his head tilted to one side. "This is Monsieur Albert Russe, our lawyer. And this …" Charlotte took a deep breath. "Alec, this is who I really want you to meet. This is Alice Saumures, my daughter."

A girl of astounding beauty, in simple tight dark-blue cotton slacks and a white silk blouse with billowing pirate sleeves, stood and looked pensively at Alec. She had long, wavy auburn hair, and smoky-blue eyes, which were large and mesmerising. She gave Alec a smile that shone. She was tall and seemed faintly familiar to Alec.

"Your daughter, Charlotte? How can this be?" Alec was feeling a little light-headed.

"I am also *your* daughter," Alice said in nearly a whisper, smiling widely, her eyes glistening. She took Alec's hand and kissed him on both cheeks.

Alec sat heavily onto a chair. His eyes stung, as though salt had been thrown into them. He wiped away a tear hurriedly when his vision blurred looking up at Alice. She knelt in front of him. "I am your daughter, and I am twenty-one today. I was only told of your existence last week."

"When I got this invitation." Alec patted the letter in his inside pocket.

"Well, sort of." Alice pressed on. "Maman told me about my father being a journalist, three years ago, but she said" – she paused and cast her eyes towards Charlotte with an uncomfortable look – "she thought you were dead. That is all anybody said about you." She stood and went to her mother. "You were pretty vague about my father, weren't you, Maman?"

Charlotte looked sad and meditative, her arms crossed over her tummy as though she had stomach ache.

There was a small burn of fury in Alec's throat. He felt like bursting into a rage at what he thought was a betrayal. Then his eyes rested on his daughter as she sat beside him on the sofa, and the flames of his anger were snuffed out.

"Well," he said as though he was about to talk to a child, but then realised that she was an adult. "Well, you are a sight." He felt it was rather a feeble thing to say. "What do you do? Are you at school, or ..."

"I am at the Paris American Academy, studying film, fashion and design."

"Just like ..." Alec started but remembered that she was just like nobody she would know – she would not have heard of his actor brother, Adam. He had hardly done anything of note for ages. "Are you enjoying yourself?" he continued.

"Alice is also a very successful fashion model and actress," Theodora said proudly.

Alec turned and saw Charlotte standing at the window, still with an air of uneasiness about her. He rose from his chair, stroking Alice on her shoulder and giving her a proud smile. He went over to Charlotte, passing the young man, confused as to why he was here. He drew up close to Charlotte. Looking at her, he felt the same love he had always had for her. Her eyes met his, apologetically.

"I am so sorry, Alec. Every June, I pluck up the courage to phone you or write, but I never have. As the years went on, I lost more and more of my nerve."

"You are not a coward, are you?" He kept his voice steady. His emotions were in turmoil, to say the least.

"Alec, there is little excuse. I must have had some kind of emotional breakdown that day so long ago beside the Thames. Believe it or not, I have not been a very happy person since," Charlotte said, taking his hand in hers. Her hands were cold. She was not looking into his face but at their linked hands. "I know that you loved me, and I loved you, but I am a terrible person."

"Why are you a terrible person? Charlotte, why have you brought me here now?"

"Now you two," Theodora interrupted. "We have Monsieur Russe here, and we need to get this business sorted out."

"What business?" Alec said as the young man walked towards them. "Isn't he part of Gautier, Russe and Strider?"

"Eric Strider was prosecuted by his partners and it is just Gautier and Russe now, monsieur," Russe said charmingly in English. "Monsieur Strider died in 1974 – took his own life, we think."

Alec had known about Strider. He had been involved in his trial for treason in 1956. Strider was sentenced to twenty-two years, but was released early, in 1974, from Ford Open Prison. There was a distinct possibility that he may have been killed by WASP, but nothing could be proved. He was found hanging off Blackfriars Bridge with a note in his pocket saying he was not able to live with himself, written in German.

Alec went back to Alice and sat down as requested.

"Alice?" Charlotte encouraged Alice to start some prearranged speech.

"Papa," she said self-consciously, and then, "Do you mind if I call you Papa?"

"That's fine," Alec croaked, uncomfortable being a father let alone being called "Papa".

"Papa, I wanted you to be here for my eighteenth birthday. We tried to ask you here three years ago, but you were fighting in Vietnam."

"I was not exactly 'fighting' in Vietnam, I was one of the reporters, witnessing the US withdrawal."

"Well, we tried to anyway." She dropped her head.

Alec said, "But you said you did not know of me until last week!"

"Maman told me you were a great friend in London when I wanted to go and see The Mamas and the Papas at the London Palladium with some friends at school."

"The what?" Alec looked at Charlotte.

"An American pop group they all love here," Charlotte said.

"I tried to get Maman or Theodora to take me, but they both said they would not. I asked if they knew anybody in London and you came up ... but you were in Vietnam, or away."

"And we gathered Philip Bing-Wallace was very ill, after a fall," Theodora said.

"Yes, he's OK now but a bit doddery," Alec said. "He's nearly eighty. He certainly would not go to a pop concert."

"Alec." Charlotte came over to where he and Alice sat together. "I want to bequeath most of my estate to Alice, but I need someone to look after her estate until she is twenty-five, and to help manage it after my death."

"What is going on, Charlotte? Why—?"

"Now Alice is twenty-one, I just need to get things sorted out. Will you help?"

"A trustee, you mean? But surely Theodora ..."

"Theodora as well as you, and Monsieur Russe." Charlotte seemed anxious.

Alec's heart stopped. Why was she asking this now? Alice was eyeing him expectantly with a happy grin. Theodora seemed apprehensive, serious, her hands together as though in prayer, her forefinger tips on her pursed lips.

"Mr Ballentine," Russe said softly, like a French funeral director, "the estate is considerable and it needs management. We are administrating three large estates: the late Baron Saumures, the late Mrs Stella de Tournet, and her husband, Jean de Tournet's estate. And there is some residue from Jason Barrett, assets seized by the state after he fled England. Lady Saumures's estate includes three substantial properties in Paris, one in Brittany, Petworth and various smaller properties, including some in Lewes, Sussex, an apartment in

Paris and a house in Concord in the United States. There is also a considerable amount, we think, in private Swiss bank accounts that we are investigating. A total estate worth" – Charlotte nodded her approval – "a little over thirty million francs – about four million pounds, possibly up to six million."

There was a stunned silence. "And, of course," he carried on, "there is this house and grounds from Baroness Saumures's grandmother, and other bequests." He waited for a reaction from those gathered, and when nobody spoke, said, "Madam Theodora Smith has been promised this house and—"

"OK, thank you, Monsieur Russe," Charlotte interrupted. "I think I need to talk to Mr Ballentine alone. We will go into the study." She stroked Alice's cheek tenderly when Alice stared at her mother curiously. "We will be back soon, my love. I just need to go through some paperwork with Alec."

47

Alec looked around the light and airy study. A grand piano stood in the corner beneath a large window, covered in framed photographs, including one of Alec and Philip Bing-Wallace after winning a literary prize. It was an original press image. There were lots of Alice on fashion runways, and more poignant for Alec, of her growing up, from a baby.

Alec took a long time to look at all the photos, mentally selecting one he would like to keep for himself. Charlotte sat down on a leather sofa and patted the seat for Alec to sit beside her.

"Can I have copies of these, the ones of Alice growing up?"

"Yes, of course," Charlotte said gently.

"And one of you and Theodora …?" Alec suddenly stopped short. With horror, his attention was drawn to a portrait of Hitler, hanging in a shadowy corner. Part of the bottom of the portrait was ripped. "Why on earth have you got a portrait of that man up in the study?"

"Ferdi painted it. It was part of our escape plan from here … you will have to get the full story from Theodora." She patted the sofa seat beside her again. "Come and sit. I need to say something."

She watched him sit down beside her. She edged closer to him, her eyes, glistening, met his. She placed her cold hands on his. "Alec, I am going to die soon." He felt the blood drain out of his face, a lump formed in his throat. He felt a mixture of desolation and rage. "I have cancer and there is very little they can do about it. I have about six weeks to three months."

"Oh, my good God! … And, I presume," Alec choked, "Alice does not know, or even suspect, it would seem?"

"No, but she may do now. Theodora is the only person who knows. Russe suspects, I think, hence his indiscreet ramble about my assets. I have spent a lot of money on the best doctors. Alice knows I am ill but believes it is curable."

Alec sat on the edge of the sofa looking into her sad deep violet-blue eyes, now with wrinkles at the edges. Her eyes shimmered with unresolved tears, her once flawless skin now covered in powder concealing the blemishes of age and illness. She smiled, a smile that did not quite reach her eyes; they just fluttered. "I am so sorry, Alec. I wish I had the courage to have called you earlier."

"I have not been able to love again, you know," Alec said. "Sophie Younghusband – or Sophie Clark as she is now – married an art dealer. She tried to rekindle something a year after you left."

"Did she?" Charlotte sounded indifferent. "She helped get the collection back here. I suppose that is why she tried to renew her relationship with you – when I was out of the picture, as it were."

"Possibly, yes, possibly," Alec said meekly.

"But, Alec," she carried on in earnest, "I have this huge estate. It must be managed for Alice. I don't want her to marry someone that will end up ... I need you to make sure she is kept away from gold diggers."

Alec nodded whilst searching Charlotte's face. Was she being honest with him? Or was this some kind of strange apology? "Why did you not tell me as soon as Alice was born?"

Charlotte blinked back tears. "I am my mother's daughter, I suppose. I wanted Alice to myself. I did not want to share her with a man or a husband. It sounds cruel, I know, but that is the truth."

"And I was not trustworthy to you?"

"I have difficulty in trusting men, Alec. I am sorry, but I have never really loved a man – except, perhaps, you." She put her hand gently on his cheek and looked at him fondly.

Alec said, "There's been an empty gap in my life ever since you left me and ran from the pontoon beside Albert Bridge, twenty years ago. It occurs to me you must have been carrying Alice even then."

Charlotte closed her eyes, tears silently coursing down her cheeks. He kissed her on her lips lightly and stood. She stood and put her arms around him. He completed the embrace – it felt the same as it had all that time ago. They stood holding each other for at least two minutes, possibly longer.

He saw on the wall behind the sofa the portrait of Charlotte's mother, Alice Barrett. "Was that painted by Ferdi?"

"Yes. I saw it in Ferdi's gallery by chance during the war. That is how we met."

"Her face is so happy, pretty and bright. Reminds me of you that Christmas. You were so joyful."

"We only knew each other a few months, and yet what an impact on our lives those few months had." She tilted her face up to Alec's. "Thank you for those few months, Alec. Thank you for your love, for your comfort. I wish I could have loved you more, but I have a stone heart with just a corner still flesh for Alice."

48

Charlotte died three weeks later in Theodora's arms and holding her daughter's hand. Her final, painful breath was taken in her bed in Nineteen Avenue Foch. She refused to go to hospital, and Alice and Theodora respected her decision.

Alec did not think he could ever feel more miserable. He remained in Paris and visited Avenue Foch nearly every day. He took Alice out to the theatre, to restaurants, and they got to know each other. He would spend at least half an hour each day talking to Charlotte and Theodora before Charlotte said she was getting weary.

He arrived from the little hotel he was staying at, half an hour after she died. Theodora had phoned him with the dreadful news. He went to the side of her bed, a white sheet neatly folded down below her chin, her hair brushed, a merest suggestion of make-up on her beautiful pale face. Alice and Theodora were at the foot of the bed.

"Kiss her goodbye, Alec," Theodora said. He bent over Charlotte and gently kissed her forehead and turned to leave the room. He saw, above the fireplace, the painting by Klimt, *Girl on a Golden Pillow*. He remembered the Christmas of 1955, the first time he had made love to Charlotte and fallen in love with her. He sighed deeply and left the room without looking back at Charlotte's bed.

He sat on his own in the *salle de séjour* gazing vacantly out to the garden. It felt like something had clamped around his heart, painfully squeezing it – he had to keep swallowing to stop from weeping. He could not remember the last time he cried; it might even have been when he was a child. Not even when his mother died had he felt like he did now.

Alice walked into the *salle de séjour*, unaware that Alec was sitting there. She went to the window, her willowy figure slightly hunched, her arms hugging her stomach. She was not crying. The garden was bathed in hot July sun.

"Alice," Alec called quietly. She did not hear him. "Alice, come and sit by me. Tell me about your mother."

Alice turned. Alec stood and walked slowly over to her and proffered a hand for Alice to hold. Alice broke into tears and raced over to him. She fell into his arms, her head on his shoulder, buried into his jacket. He hoped he could comfort her as much as she comforted him.

"Oh why did she not tell me sooner?" she sobbed.

"That she was ill?" Alec asked.

"About you ... that she is ... she was ill ... why was she so secretive about being ill?" She looked up at him. "We did so many things together. She came with me when I went on modelling shoots, she would be there, sometimes with Theodora – who would frighten off men hovering around me. We were great companions, we had fun. We travelled everywhere, we ..." She stalled, looking a little guilty. "We did things together."

"What kind of things?" Alec asked cautiously.

There was a question in her eyes, but Alec could not work out if she was assessing his trustworthiness or working out how to ask the question.

She cast her eyes down and said, "We spent a lot of the last two years travelling together ... with Theodora."

"That was nice," Alec said carefully. "Where did you go?"

"I had fashion shoots all over Europe. Maman and Theodora would be with me – I think as chaperones more than anything else. As I said, Theodora's primary function was to frighten off men."

"I am not surprised. Did you go to America?"

There was a long silence.

"We had private investigators working for us, trying to find ... you know. We were in South America mostly."

Alice turned away from Alec and went back to the window. She did not say any more.

Alec was worried. He had heard how Krupp had been murdered, and things were alarmingly falling into place. He thought he knew that Krupp killed Jason Barrett, but he also thought it could have been arranged by Charlotte or Theodora. He was now concerned that Alice could also be involved. Any foreboding about her role in Krupp's death was mostly dispelled with pride. She turned back to him and put her arms around him.

"Thank you for being here, Papa. I do not think I would be able to deal with this without you."

"Yes, you would have. You have Theodora."

"Yes," Alice said hesitantly. There was a long period of silence. They held onto each other, Alec in rapture. A daughter who he could quite easily love and look after was now in his life. Someone who could take the place of the gulf of emptiness that had been inside him for the past twenty-odd years.

"There is something you should know about me," Alice said, her head against Alec's shoulder.

"Can it wait?" Alec was anxious about what she was going to say.

"No," she said bluntly. She took in a long breath. "Because my mother was so ill, I killed Jost Krupp in Buenos Aires."

Alec's heart sank. "Why have you told me this?"

"You needed to know. Theodora is tracking down Krupp's twin sons."

Alec pushed her away from him. "Oh my God, why? She cannot put you into this kind of danger."

Alice was calm, like her mother used to be in the face of danger. "That is what my mother said just before she died. She made Theodora promise to leave everything alone."

Alec kissed Alice tenderly on the forehead, relief seeping back.

He said, "I will take care of you. You should be enjoying yourself. Come and stay with me in London, we can have a ball! I will introduce you to lots of handsome—"

"I would love to come back with you, just for a bit. Don't want to do much."

Alec hated the thought that Alice may have had a similar upbringing to her mother. That perhaps she would have seen the ugly side of life, rather than be brought up like an ordinary young woman. It would, he decided, be his obligation to ensure that Alice's life from now on was as normal as possible.

Alec heard the doorbell chime. He assumed it was an ambulance or a doctor. Moments later Theodora entered the room, an expression of alarm on her face.

"What is it, Aunt Theodora?" Alice asked. "What can have possibly happened?"

Theodora's eyes were red-rimmed. She hissed, "It's the police, *chérie*."

"My God!" Alec said, looking at Alice with horror and then back at Theodora, his mind racing. "This cannot be happening!"

Theodora held out a visiting card. "He is the *Commissaire Général de Police* Henri Jarret!"

There was a gentle knock on the door and a handsome face popped his head around the door. "I am sorry to intrude on this terrible day. Your man has just informed me … I will leave now and return after the funeral, or at a later date."

"What is this about, monsieur?" Alec asked angrily.

The man came fully into the *salle de séjour*.

"I am so sorry, I had hoped to meet Lady Saumures in person. I had no idea she was ill."

"Why?" Theodora asked abruptly. "What has the police got to do with Charlotte?"

"Oh!" Jarret put up his hands. "Nothing to do with the police. I am here in a personal capacity."

"Did you know Charlotte?" Theodora asked, less stridently. Alice and Alec were still holding onto each other, both distressed, both wondering who this man was.

"My name is Henri Jacques Jarret. My father was Luke Jarret. When my mother died last month, a letter from my father was passed on to me."

"What has this to do with Charlotte, for heaven's sake? Get on with it!" Theodora shouted, tears rolling down her cheeks in anger. Henri Jarret lowered his head. He had wavy golden-blond hair. He drew out a piece of paper from the inside pocket of his well-cut grey suit. He sombrely unfolded the paper and walked over to Alice.

"Mademoiselle, I believe I am your half-uncle."

There was a silence. Alice looked at the man in disbelief. Alec wondered what he should do. He felt like bundling the man out the door and giving him a kick in the pants to send him on his way. But instead, he went over to Theodora. He took the card out of Theodora's hand and studied it closely. The man was not a crank. He seemed perfectly sane and sincere … and a very senior policeman, according to his card.

"How have you come to that conclusion, monsieur?" Alice asked quietly and unemotionally.

Jarret opened up the letter in his hand. "*My dear Henri,*" he read. "*In 1944, a priest called Franz-Joseph Deller—*"

"What!" exclaimed Alec and Theodora together.

Henri Jarret carried on without looking up from the page. "… *appeared at my door in Paris. He was looking for Madame Belle Jarret and her son Luke. I said that I was Luke but that my mother – your grandmother – had died. He then told me an extraordinary story.*"

"But this is …!" Theodora could not finish the sentence. She sat heavily onto a chair.

"Do you know what this is about, Theodora?" Alice asked.

"I am not sure, darling." She looked worried but did not attempt to stop Jarret. Alec just wanted him to go and leave his daughter alone.

"Shall I carry on, mademoiselle?"

"Carry on, please. But get to the point, could you?" Alice said.

"Very well. *The priest claimed to be the lover of Alice Barrett. He also said that Alice had a daughter called Charlotte, and named him, the priest, as her father. He claimed that he could not be the father, due to having X-rays on his hips as a young man, which had rendered him infertile.*"

"For Christ's sake, where are you going with this?" Alec shouted. "You know that Alice's mother, Charlotte, has only just died? Today! Could this not wait?"

"No, we need to know, Papa." Alice stroked her father's arm to calm him down. "Was my grandmother, also called Alice, your father's lover as well?"

"I believe that was what he was saying."

"Deller did say to Charlotte, just before he died," Alec reflected, "that he was not Charlotte's father. He was then murdered by Jost Krupp." He turned to Alice. "Charlotte had said he claimed that another man was her father."

Alice walked up to Henri Jarret and smiled sweetly. "I am so pleased to meet you. I am only sorry you were too late to meet my mother. I bid you good day, Uncle." Alice turned her back on her new uncle and faced Alec and Theodora. She had a sad smile on her face and opened her arms to be hugged.

Alec and Theodora took Alice into their arms. All three wept for Charlotte. Henri Jarret put the letter and his card on a side table and left.